Harry Bowling was born in [Bermondsey, Lon]don, and left school at fourteen to supplement the family income as an office boy in a riverside provisions' merchant. He was called up for National Service in the 1950s. Before becoming a writer, he was variously employed as a lorry driver, milkman, meat cutter, carpenter and decorator, and community worker. He lived with his wife and family, dividing his time between Lancashire and Deptford before his death in 1999.

HARRY
BOWLING
Ironmonger's
Daughter

First published in 1989
by HEADLINE BOOK PUBLISHING PLC

This edition published in paperback in 2015 by
HEADLINE PUBLISHING GROUP

1

Cataloguing in Publication Data is available from the British Library

ISBN 978 0 7553 4040 8

Typeset in Times by Avon DataSet Ltd,
Bidford-on-Avon, Warwickshire

Printed and bound in Great Britain by
Clays Ltd, St Ives plc

HEADLINE PUBLISHING GROUP
An Hachette UK Company
Carmelite House
50 Victoria Embankment
London EC4Y 0DZ

www.headline.co.uk
www.hachette.co.uk

To Val Chapman, with fond memories.

With thanks to my agent Jennifer Kavanagh,
and to my editor Jane Morpeth.

Part One

Part One

Prologue

The year of 1920 had spawned a good summer but, when the winter took grip and nightly fogs drifted in from the river, tired workers left the factories, offices and wharves to hurry home as quickly as possible. Belching smoke from the factory furnaces and from the lop-sided chimneys of the shabby houses and tenement blocks merged with the wet fog and made it sulphurous. The fog rolled into the Bermondsey backstreets, a yellow soot-blanket that snuffed out the night light from the hissing gaslamps and made the cobblestones wet and slippery. Inside the ramshackle houses coke fires were banked up and draughty doors and windows were plugged with old coats and yesterday's newspapers. There was no inclination to chat on the front doorsteps, nor to stop off for a pint of ale as the November fogs thickened.

On a Friday in mid November the weather turned bitter cold. The cold red sun was shut out as the Thames fog swirled through the cobbled riverside lanes and out into Bermondsey. It thickened during the early afternoon and the dismal sound of fog-horns carried from London's river as tugs struggled to place their trailing barges into safe anchorage before night fell. Traffic slowed and trains crawled out to suburbia through the yellow, poisonous blanket, and homeward-bound workers held scarves and handkerchiefs to their mouths as they moved wearily home.

The fog blotted out the view for old Fran Collins but she gazed out from a fourth-floor window in Jubilee Dwellings anyway. She had done all she could for the moment and everything was at hand. Kate Morgan was resting comfortably and Fran knew that it would be some time yet. The room was warm and clean and the dampened coke was piled high in the grate. The warmth radiated around the shabby room and Fran Collins tucked her hands into her crisp white apron. 'What yer 'opin' for, luv?' she asked.

Kate shifted her position in the kitchen chair. 'I don't care. So long as it's all right.'

Fran looked closely at the woman. All the tales she had heard about Kate Morgan's love life, the men she had supposedly been with and the identity of the lover who had made her pregnant were of little interest to her at the moment. She had been summoned to deliver the child and she could sense that the woman facing her in the chair was not disposed to discussing the whys and wherefores of her condition. Fran straightened the front of her apron and walked through into the tiny bedroom that led off from the front room. Everything looked ready. A small fire burned in the grate and the bedclothes had been turned back. A rubber underlay had been placed beneath the freshly laundered white bed sheet, and on the chair beside the bed was the maternity bundle. Fran checked once again through the napkins which had been cut from thick towelling and found the clean nightdress and a pack of muslin. She took the tin of vaseline and the thin scissors from the washstand and placed them on top of the bundle beside the bed before going out of the room.

The kettle had boiled for the second time and when Fran Collins returned from the scullery she glanced at the fidgeting Kate. There was something about the woman that puzzled the street's midwife. Almost without exception, all the confinements she had attended over the years were happy events. Happiness always seemed to shine out from her clients' eyes, which were bright and clear, even when the pregnancy was unwanted or when the latest birth would bring more hardship to the family. There was a short time when, just before the pain took over, that special light in the woman's eyes expressed the satisfaction at reaching her time. Kate Morgan's gaze did not reflect any satisfaction, Fran thought. The woman's large blue eyes were dull and lustreless: a deep hurt reflected in her empty stare.

In the street below Jubilee Dwellings the fog covered the ugliness of the place. It blanketed off the dilapidated tenement block and the row of tumbledown houses opposite, and it shut out the drab metal factory which stood astride the end of the turning. The swirling fog shrouded the rusting iron gates of the factory and laid its cold fingers on the cobblestones and on the grey slates of the roofs. It wrapped itself suffocatingly around the one streetlamp and squeezed out the cold light. In the full light of day, after the fog had cleared, the grey ugliness of Ironmonger Street would reappear, one of the most unsightly turnings in Bermondsey. It stood some way behind the Tower Bridge Road and it boasted two corner shops at the entrance: one, a rag shop that was hardly ever opened; and the other, an oil shop. Next to the oil shop was a pair of large wooden gates that led into a yard which was used to store the Tower Bridge Road market barrows and stalls. From the yard the four-storeyed tenement block carried on and ended short of the factory wall. A narrow alley led around to the back of the dwellings and it was there that the tenants placed their refuse in a large bottomless bin. As the rubbish built up the bin disappeared beneath the stinking pile and every Friday it was recovered by the Council dustmen, who carried the rubbish out from the alley in large wicker baskets.

On that fog-bound night in mid November, Kate Morgan gave birth to a baby girl. It was nearing eight o'clock when her waters broke and the reliable Fran Collins calmly took control. Fran was a sixty-six-year-old grandmother whose husband Tom was a docker at the Surrey. Their four children had all flown the nest, were married, and had broods of their own. Many of the local kids had been delivered by Fran, who was often called upon when there was no money to pay for the doctor. She usually got paid, eventually, but she never refused the summons to a birth, whatever the time of night or the state of the weather. Her grey hair was tied up in a bun on the top of her head and her large dark eyes shone out from a moon-face. She was a buxom lady, and her calm manner helped her charges through even the most difficult of labours. Fran Collins had had no formal training; the whole business seemed to come naturally to her, and she had gained invaluable experience over the years.

The birth of Connie Morgan was a straightforward affair and it was over very quickly. When both mother and daughter had been made comfortable Fran took her leave. As she edged her way out into the pea-souper she could not help but puzzle over the moment she had placed the tiny bundle into Kate's arms. The 'look' was missing, she felt sure. It was a certain look that made her glow inside every time she placed a new-born baby into its mother's arms and watched her gaze upon her child for the very first time. Tonight there had been no gaze of wonder and love, only a look of resignation. Maybe she was wrong, maybe it was her own tiredness and fatigue that made her miss the glance. She hoped so. But, as Fran Collins inched along to her front door, she was convinced that all was not well with Kate Morgan.

Chapter One

As the wind carried large snowflakes against the windows of the tenement block early on Christmas morning Kate's sister Helen also gave birth to a daughter. The confinement was a long and difficult one and Doctor Morrison was in attendance. He looked serious as he snapped his black bag shut; he had seen the signs all too often before. He glanced at the white-faced woman who lay back against the pillow, her arm cradling the child, and he smiled sadly. 'I'll pop in again tomorrow,' he said. 'You try and get some sleep now.'

Matthew Bartlett hovered by the bedroom door and, as the doctor turned from the bed, he stood back and glanced anxiously into the man's serious face. Doctor Morrison put a finger to his lips and motioned with his eyes to the front door. Matthew followed him across the living room and waited while the doctor buttoned up his overcoat. 'What is it, doctor?' he asked finally.

'I'm not sure yet. I need to see the child tomorrow. In the meantime make sure your wife gets some sleep. She's exhausted.'

Matthew felt his heart miss a beat. His mouth went dry and he struggled to form the words. 'Is anyfing wrong wiv the baby, doctor?'

Dr Morrison looked hard at the man. 'I suspect there might

be a deformity of the spine,' he said gravely.

Down in the street below the sound of happy children carried up to the quiet flat in Jubilee Dwellings. The snow was falling heavily now, and already the cobblestones were hidden beneath a white carpet. Kate came down from her flat on the floor above to see her sister's baby and to offer to cook the Christmas meal. Matthew politely refused. Helen and the baby were sleeping and he wanted to be alone. The doctor's words had stunned him. How could such a thing happen, he wondered, and on Christmas Day? Wasn't it meant to be the holiest of days? How could God let a baby be born deformed on Christmas Day? Maybe the doctor was wrong. They weren't always right. He bit on his bottom lip. How could this thing happen to us?

Down in the street someone hailed their neighbour. 'A merry Christmas to yer, Bert.'

'Merry Christmas,' Matthew whispered aloud to himself as he buried his head in his hands.

On the last Sunday in January Connie Morgan and her cousin Molly Bartlett were christened together at the tiny church in Bermondsey Street. The christening service was attended by very few of the Ironmonger Street folk. Mrs Walker, Kate's next-door neighbour was there, resplendent in the new hat she had bought for the occasion. As the party walked through the arched portal and into the white stone-walled vestibule they were greeted by Fran Collins, who bent over each tiny bundle in turn, gently easing the shawl back. She looked up at Kate Morgan with concern showing in her eyes. ''Ow is the little mite? Is she sleepin' well?' she asked.

Kate nodded briefly and a ghost of a smile creased her lips. 'She's no trouble,' she said. And as an afterthought she added, 'Thanks for comin', Fran.'

The midwife smiled back. It was her custom to attend the christenings of all 'her babies'.

When Molly was held over the font she cried loudly, but when the blessed water was splashed over Connie's forehead she screwed up her tiny face and then went back to sleep. Mrs Walker nudged Fran urgently. 'I thought all babies cried at the christenin's.'

Fran Collins shook her head. 'Most do, although some sleep right frew the service.'

Mrs Walker leaned towards her. 'She's gonna be a placid one, you mark my words. I ain't 'ardly 'eard the little mite cry at all, an' I would 'ave 'eard 'er. You can 'ear every bloody sound in our buildin's.'

Fran winced as the vicar gave the old lady a cold glance. 'Shh! Yer not s'posed ter swear in church,' she admonished her.

Mrs Walker looked abashed. 'I wasn't swearin'. Anyway, most of them vicars swear. You ought ter 'ear ole Farvver Kerrigan swear when 'e's got a drop o' terps down 'im. 'E'd make the devil 'imself blush.'

Fran winced again and took hold of the old lady's arm. 'C'mon, luv, it's all over now.'

When the group was outside in the cold morning air Matthew Bartlett took his baby daughter from Helen and held her close against the cold wind.

Kate turned to Fran and said, 'Wanna carry the baby back ter the street?' Fran smiled and took the tiny bundle in her arms. She accepted that Kate was paying her a compliment by the suggestion, but something deep down inside her told her that her earlier hunch was correct. All was not well with Kate Morgan. The street midwife almost detected a sigh of relief as Kate handed over the child.

The party walked back along the Tower Bridge Road, past the shuttered shops and the shrimp and winkle stall before turning off into the backstreets. When they reached the corner of Ironmonger Street, Mrs Walker caught sight of Jerry Martin the oil shop owner as he swept the pavement outside his premises and she nudged Fran Collins. 'Look at that miserable ole sod. 'E'd crack 'is face if 'e smiled.'

Fran, benign as ever, merely smiled. She had always felt a little sorry for the wizened-looking character with the spiky hair and the metal-rimmed glasses, although she had occasionally been the victim of his sharp tongue.

Jerry Martin was known by everyone in the street as 'Misery Martin' but, as far as Jerry was concerned, he felt he had very little to smile about anyway, and he certainly professed no loyalty to the little turning. When someone once walked into his dismal-looking shop and asked him why he didn't take down all his shutters his reply was, 'Leave orf! The bleedin' kids round 'ere would fink nufink of lobbin' an 'ouse brick frew the winder'.

Jerry had been trying to sell his business for some time, but no one seemed to be interested in the corner shop. In fact most strangers would pass the little turning with a casual glance and hurry away with no regrets for not having entered the cul-de-sac named Ironmonger Street. The local folk had no desire to enter the turning either. No one ever did, unless they lived in the street or worked at Armitage and Sons, Sheet Metal Workers. Ironmonger Street had got a bad name over the years though one or two of the more notorious families had since moved on. The stigma remained and, when one particular tallyman walked into the lamp-post while consulting his account book and then walked dazed out of the little backstreet with a large bump on his forehead, the story got around that he had been caught in a compromising situation and thrown out of the house by an angry husband whose wife had spent the weekly payment and had offered her services in lieu. Folk in the infamous backstreet ignored the slanderous asides and were proud of their ugly turning. Some even boasted of the fact that there were some 'right 'ard nuts' living there. Folk spun stories and the goings-on in the street had become almost mythical.

Matthew Bartlett was troubled as he climbed the stairs of the tenement block on that Sunday morning. He knew that 1921 was going to be a bleak year for his family. He was on short time at the furniture factory and he had read in the daily newspapers that over two million people were unemployed and many more were, like himself, on short-time working. Helen had said that the Armitage factory was putting workers off, according to old George Baker, who lived in one of the houses, and whose daughter Mary worked as a metal stamper at the factory. Matthew had also heard of the unrest in the local docks and wharves; there was talk of a strike and he was well aware of the effect it would have in the area. He sighed deeply as he clutched the warm bundle in his arms tighter and he felt suddenly guilt-ridden. What right did he have to bring a child into this world when he was struggling to earn enough to survive? What sort of burden had he placed on Helen? He had fathered a child who was malformed and sickly, and who would need constant care and attention. There would be hospital visits and doctor's bills. He would have to find the money somehow, and always there would be the constant threat of being put out of work. Behind him on the stairs he heard Helen's laughter at something Kate had said and he could feel a movement in his arms as Molly started to whimper. He looked down at his tiny, defenceless daughter and hoped he would be able to do all right by her.

Chapter Two

The Horseshoe Public House stood on the corner of John Street, a small turning between Ironmonger Street and the Tower Bridge Road. The pub was popular with the local folk, and it was here that they gathered to discuss the state of affairs. Most vociferous of all was the domino team, who would often pause between games to expound on current events and anything else that took their fancy.

'An' I'm tellin' yer, Knocker, that Lloyd George is gonna 'ave ter do somefink,' said Harold Simpson, a grizzled old man in his seventies who lived two doors away from the pub. 'The country's goin' ter the bloody dogs. Look at yer unemployed. Two bleedin' million out o' graft. They should 'ang the bleedin' Kaiser!'

Harold's next door neighbour Knocker Johnson moved his glass of beer out of the reach of Harold's flailing arms and rubbed his grey stubble. 'What's 'angin' the Kaiser gotta do wiv the state o' the country?'

Harold took a quick sip from his beer and wiped a grubby hand across his full moustache. 'I tell yer what it's gotta do wiv it. That there war we've jus' bin frew 'as milked this country dry. Bloody millions o' pounds it's cost us, an' look at the way fings are now. Two bleedin' million out o' collar an' now there's the miners on strike an' talk of the transport workers joinin' 'em. Most o' those what's workin' are on short-time. The only people earnin' money are the bloody pawnbrokers. My suit's 'angin' up in Harris's more often than in me poxy wardrobe. I tell yer straight, Knocker. That there Kaiser Bill is larfin' at us. You mark my words. We ain't 'eard the last of that bleedin' stiff-legged bastard!'

George Baker sipped his beer and pushed his metal-framed glasses up on to the bridge of his nose with a forefinger. 'I dunno about 'angin' the Kaiser. I reckon they should 'ang ole Armitage.'

'Why?' Harold piped up.

'Don't yer know what 'e's gorn an' done?'

'No,' replied Harold. 'Any danger o' you tellin' us?'

'Well 'e's put all 'is workers on short time, ain't 'e? Me eldest daughter works there. She said it's quite bleedin' likely they'll all get their cards if fings don't pick up very soon.'

'I don't see what else 'e can do if there's no work,' Knocker butted in.

George banged a domino piece down hard on the table top. 'I'll tell yer what else 'e could do. 'E could show a bit o' loyalty to 'is workers, that's what. 'E could keep 'em all on full time an' let 'em clean the place up or somefink. You take them there winders. Bloody well filfy they are. An' what about them gates? There's as much rust on them as on ole Widow Pacey's pram she uses fer the bagwash. Ole Armitage could get 'em ter paint the gates. Matter o' fact 'e could get 'em ter give the ole place a lick o' paint.'

'It's all very well you sayin' that,' Knocker replied, 'but it all costs money.'

George's cue had been delivered. 'Money?! That ole goat Armitage is werf a packet. The bleedin' wages 'e pays 'is workers is disgraceful. My Mary only brings 'ome twenty-seven bob after stoppages. She works bleedin' 'ard fer that, I can tell yer.'

Harold looked dolefully at his diminishing pint. 'I still say they should 'ang the Kaiser.'

George brooded as he shuffled the domino pieces. 'I've seen ole Armitage drive in our turnin' in that posh motor car wiv those two dopey-lookin' sons of 'is in the back, an' I've said ter meself, George, there ain't no justice. There just ain't no justice. There's 'im ridin' about in that jalopy, an' there's me wivout two pennies ter rub tergevver.'

The fourth man in the group leaned back in his chair and folded his arms over his corpulent stomach. 'Yer right, George. I fink it's what yer lotted out for. Some 'ave the luck, an' some get kicked in the kybosh. You take them Bartletts in our turnin'. My Fran was tellin' me that their kid was born wiv a curvature o' the spine. On Christmas Day, too. 'Parently there's nufink can be done about it. The poor little mite ain't got the best o' starts, 'as she?'

The year wore on and an overcast summer gave way to chill autumn winds. There had been little to rejoice about as short-time working continued, and only the pawnshops were doing good business. The relief officers called round to the homes of those unfortunates who had to seek assistance, and any item of furniture or chattles deemed a luxury had to be sold before any help was given.

Mrs Clara Cosgrove was waiting for a visit from the relief officer after her husband lost his job at the local tannery. And as she walked back from the market she had a worried look on her face. The small loaf and the two pound of potatoes she carried in her bag had used up the last of the housekeeping money and there was still a doctor's bill to be paid. At the corner of Ironmonger Street she almost collided with Helen Bartlett.

''Ello, girl. Where's the babies?' Clara asked.

Helen grinned and jerked her thumb in the direction of the tenement buildings. 'Matt's mindin' 'em while I pop down the market. 'E's on short time.'

Clara shook her head sadly. 'Gawd knows what's ter become of us all. I'm waitin' fer the RO ter call. I tell yer, 'Elen, it's made me ill 'avin' ter call 'em in, but there was no ovver way. First me ole man got put orf, an' now 'e's laid up wiv that there bronchitis. I dunno which way ter turn.'

Helen squeezed the old lady's arm and fished into her purse. ''Ere, Clara, there's a couple o' bob till fings look up. It's all right, Kate gave me a bit extra fer lookin' after Connie.'

Clara looked down at the florin and then into Helen's eyes. 'Gawd bless yer, luv. I'll pay yer back soon as I can.'

When the relief officer called on Mrs Cosgrove he cast his covetous eyes over the tidy parlour as the small woman glared at him, her arms folded over her aproned bosom. 'How long have you lived in the street, Mrs Cosgrove?' he asked in a thin voice.

''Bout firty years or more. Me an' my Fred moved 'ere when we got spliced.'

'Hmm. Now what about that piano?'

'What about me pianer?'

'Well, I'm afraid you'll have to sell it, Mrs Cosgrove.'

'Do what?'

'That's right. I'm afraid it will have to go before we are in a position to offer you any assistance.'

Until that moment Mrs Cosgrove had controlled her anger but the thought of being parted from her beloved piano proved too much. 'Now listen 'ere, yer long skinny git,' she said, her face reddening, 'it's lucky fer you me ole man's upstairs in bed wiv bronchitis. 'E'd 'ave given yer the back of 'is 'and. Now piss orf out! Yer can keep yer palsy few bob! We'll manage wivout yer 'elp.'

15

'But, but . . .'

'No buts. Jus' piss orf out.'

The white-faced official hurriedly left Ironmonger Street and one more bad mark was chalked up against the little turning.

As the foggy December days followed the windy autumn things looked up a bit and a few seasonal jobs became available as the dockers were enjoying a busy time unloading cargoes of fruit for the Christmas markets. Mr Cosgrove got a job stamping out biscuit tin lids at the Armitage factory, and Mrs Cosgrove was able to keep her beloved piano. Matthew Bartlett's flagging spirits were cheered by the news that normal hours were to be restored at the furniture factory where he worked, and he whistled to himself as he left for work on Monday morning. Now, with Christmas drawing near, there were presents to buy for Helen and the baby, and there was also a loan from the moneylender that had to be cleared up.

It was late on Christmas Eve when the two sisters met in the Bartletts' flat in Jubilee Dwellings. The gaslit room was cosy, with a tarry-log burning brightly in the grate. Helen had hung up some coloured paper-chains and spread a clean tablecloth over the rickety table. A few greetings cards were arranged on the high mantelshelf, and in one corner a tiny Christmas tree stood in a bucket, garlanded with silver strands and tiny bonbons. The smoke-streaked ceiling and grimy papered walls were brightened by the colourful decorations and the traditional bowl of nuts placed in the middle of the crisp white tablecloth.

Helen sighed as she took a bottle of port down from the dresser. 'Has Connie settled in okay?'

Kate nodded. 'Yeah, she's fast asleep.'

Helen poured some port into two small glasses and handed

one glass to her sister. Kate took a sip, enjoying the sweetness. Helen sat down heavily and toyed with her glass. 'This time last Christmas I was gettin' the first twinges.'

The sound of a baby coughing came from the bedroom and it was Helen who got up quickly to check on the two babies in the bedroom. When she returned she filled Kate's empty glass and sat down facing her. For a short while there was silence.

'What time are yer expectin' Matt?' Kate asked.

Helen shrugged her shoulders. ''E's 'avin' a drink wiv 'is workmates, an' the pubs are open till twelve. 'E won't be in much before.'

The two women faced each other across the table. Since Helen married they had drifted apart. Kate's numerous relationships with men had been surrounded by rumours and Helen had been critical of her sister's lifestyle, so there had been rows. Now, the birth of their babies seemed to draw them together again, though the strain in their relationship still simmered below the surface. At twenty-eight, Helen was two years younger than her sister, although she looked the elder of the two. Her figure had filled out and her face had become slightly bloated. Her dark hair was pulled tightly into a bun at the nape of her neck and there was some puffiness beneath her small brown eyes. Kate had her father's complexion. Her eyes were pale blue and her hair was fair and inclined to be wavy. Her figure was still firm and slightly padded around the hips and her full breasts stood out against her tight dress. She had a high forehead and small nose, and her lips were thin, which could sometimes make her appearance seem rather stern.

A stone shot out from the tarry-log and Helen got up and turned the log over with a poker. ''Ave yer thought about gettin' yerself married, Kate?' she said, still staring into the flames.

Kate laughed mirthlessly. 'Men! I've given 'em up. Who needs 'em?'

Helen turned and looked into her sister's pale face. 'I was finkin' about Connie. Every child should 'ave a farvver.'

Kate felt the old animosity towards her sister rising within her. 'My baby's got a farvver, but she'll never know 'im.'

'Won't yer ever tell 'er about 'er farvver – when she's older I mean?' Helen asked, sitting down again.

Kate shook her head slowly. 'No. What's the good? She'll know soon enough 'er muvver wasn't married. What do they say about kids like Connie? Born the wrong side of the blanket? That'll be enough for 'er ter go on wiv.'

Helen winced at Kate's bitter tone. She clasped her hands together and arched them under her chin with her elbows resting on the table. 'You know best, Kate. But if it was me . . .'

'Look, 'Elen. I've made me mind up, an' that's the way it's gonna be. I don't want 'er ter know about 'er farvver, an' you're the only ovver person that knows who 'e is. I want yer ter promise me you'll keep it from Connie when she's old enough ter start asking questions.'

Helen nodded. 'If that's the way yer want it.'

'That's the way I want it,' Kate said with emphasis.

Helen reached for the bottle of port. 'Come on, Sis. It is Christmas. Let's 'ave anuvver drink.'

Kate let her shoulders sag and smiled. She felt sorry for the way she was behaving, but she was always aware of her sister's disapproval of her lifestyle. Helen had been the plodder. The first man, the only man, she had known was Matthew. Helen was the strong one in their marriage, but then Helen was like their mother. She had been strong, too. She had handled their father's weakness for drink with quiet resolve, and when he had finally walked out on the family when the children were still very young she had cried briefly, then took over the role of provider. It was the struggle of making sure there was always enough bread on the table, always enough money to pay the rent man and the tallyman that finally killed her. The early morning cleaning and taking in washing and sewing had worn her out until there was no life left in her. And Beatrice Morgan had been one of the first to succumb to the epidemic of influenza that swept the area in 1919.

Kate's thoughts were interrupted by Helen getting up quickly and going once more into the bedroom. When she returned and sat down at the table she sighed deeply. 'Connie's as quiet as a lamb. But Molly's restless. It's 'er chest. I fink it's the croup.'

Kate looked hard at her sister. She could see the concern and fear in her eyes and she felt a wave of pity rise up inside her. 'Don't worry. She'll be all right. She's a fighter.'

Helen laughed mirthlessly. 'She's gotta be, Kate. It's gonna be 'ard fer 'er. The 'ospital said 'er growth will be stunted an' 'er lungs might be affected later on.'

Kate saw the tears well up in Helen's eyes and she reached out and clasped her sister's hands in her own. 'Try not ter worry too much, sis. There'll be lots of 'elp when yer need it. I know you an' me ain't always seen eye to eye, but we've gotta ferget the past. We're family, ain't we?'

Helen smiled and dabbed at her eyes. 'I'd like that, Kate. I 'ope our two kids grow up close. They'll be family to each ovver too, won't they?'

'You betcha. They'll be inseparable those two, you mark my words.'

A cold moon looked down on the ramshackle backstreet and lit the ugly prison-like factory that straddled the turning. Shadows of the rusted iron gates fell across the empty and deserted yard, and a rising wind rattled the glass case of the street gaslamp. The turning was empty, except for one drunken reveller who staggered along the pavement, his face obscured by the turned-up collar of his overcoat. A cloth cap was set askew his dipping head and he carried a quart bottle of brown ale under one arm. The drunk reeled two paces past Mrs Cosgrove's house then staggered back and almost fell against the street door as he grasped the iron knocker. When the door opened, a patch of light lit up the cobblestones and the sounds of a ragtime piano carried out into the street. Someone was trying hard to imitate Sophie Tucker with a rendering of 'Some of These Days', above raucous laughter and, as the door slammed shut, the sounds died.

In Jubilee Dwellings everything was silent.

The Bermondsey folk toasted their neighbours that Christmas, and then they toasted in the New Year. The Great War was still fresh in their minds and now they were fearful for their jobs. Everyone hoped for a peaceful future, and an end of being poor, although for most folk it seemed that the days to come would be very bleak.

Up in the tenement block in Ironmonger Street as the distant chimes rang out the old year Helen and Matthew clinked glasses and drank a toast to the two young babies who were sleeping unconcernedly in their cots. Next to each other before a brightly burning fire, they sat talking into the early hours of the new year and, as Matthew began to broach a sensitive subject, Helen was immediately on her guard.

'Won't she even try ter get some maintenance money? I mean, it's only right.'

Helen looked into Matthew's pale grey eyes and saw his concern. 'You know 'ow she is. Kate's a proud woman. She won't ask fer nufink.'

'But she wouldn't be askin' fer 'erself. It'd be fer the baby.'

Helen shrugged her shoulders, hating Matthew probing. She had never let on to him that she knew the identity of

Connie's father. She had told him more than once that she had not been taken into Kate's confidence but she was sure he did not believe her.

'I can understand 'er bein' reluctant, 'specially if the bloke's married, but surely she could sort it out wiv 'im some'ow?' Matthew persisted.

Helen felt her temper rising. 'Look, Matt. I don't know if the baby's farvver is married or not. I've told yer umpteen times, Kate ain't told me anyfink. She don't take me into 'er confidence, she never 'as. It's only since the children were born she's started comin' in ter see me.'

Matthew sipped his beer and thought for a while. 'I wonder if it's somebody round 'ere? From the street I mean?'

'I'm not interested,' Helen said sharply. 'It's none of our business. Kate's bin out wiv a lot o' fellers. She's never bin interested in settlin' down wiv one man. Mum always said she takes after our dad. 'E was always footloose, even after they was married. I honestly don't fink Kate could settle down.'

'It's different now though,' Matthew said, sitting up in his chair. 'She's got a kid ter look after. Every kid should 'ave a farvver. It's gonna be 'ard wivout a man ter provide fer 'em.'

Helen stared into the flickering coals. 'My sister's a determined woman, Matt. They'll get by. It'll be 'ard, but as I said, she won't take charity. Anyway, there's not many fellers who'd take on somebody else's kid. The pair of 'em will get by. As fer young Connie, she'll grow up wiv 'er muvver's stubbornness, I'm sure.'

The clock on the mantelshelf chimed the half hour. The wind rattled the windows and a down-draught sent smoke billowing into the room. Matthew waved his arms to clear the air and Helen poked at the ash with the poker, her face sad. As long as she could remember, she had looked forward to Christmas with great excitement. She had loved helping her mother to make paper-chains and put up the decorations, she had loved the visits to the late market in Tower Bridge Road. She remembered when she was a child and had gone on those trips to the market along with her parents and Kate. She recalled the wide-eyed excitement just looking at the stalls displaying piles of fruit and nuts. She remembered the hissing Tilley lamps that bathed the stalls and barrows with a bright white light, and the special treat after the shopping was done when her parents went to the pub and she and Kate sat on the step sipping gassy lemonade that made her nose twitch, and nibbled on huge Arrowroot biscuits. The memories of those childhood Christmas times had made the festive season special – until last Christmas.

Her joy at having a baby at the most happy time of the year for her had been snatched away the following morning, when the doctor told her that Molly would have to go to the Evelina Children's Hospital to see a specialist. The knowledge that her baby would grow up deformed had been hard to bear. Matthew had been reduced to tears and she, too, had felt hollow and cheated. She had had to be strong for both of them. For a short time she had been terrified that her husband would reject the child, but he had, thankfully, become totally devoted to Molly once he had grown used to the idea of her deformity. For herself, the knowledge that her child would have a cross to bear for as long as she lived made her even more determined that at least Molly would have all the love it was possible for her to give. She hoped that she and Kate could become closer. It would be really nice if Molly and Connie grew up as friends as well as cousins.

Chapter Three

Just after Connie's second birthday Kate got a seasonal job at the Armitage factory. Her sister looked after Connie during the day, which was an arrangement that suited Helen's needs. It gave the two children the whole day to play together, and let the closeness they had felt very early on develop into a strong bond of friendship. Helen could already see the physical differences between the two as they played happily together. Connie was a sturdy-limbed child who toddled around confidently; Molly was inclined to fall about as she tried to copy her playmate. Helen noticed that Connie was already an inch or two the taller and she felt a lump in her throat as she watched Molly smiling and laughing at Kate's fair-haired daughter, wondering if Molly's evident difficulties had already started to give her pain. Connie seemed to be a very placid child, and she never become angry or annoyed at Molly's awkward shows of affection. Helen felt a great comfort in seeing Connie accept her daughter, and yet it only made her think of the problems her daughter would probably have to face as she grew older. How many times would Molly be rejected, pushed away, and perhaps even laughed at? She hoped with all her heart that Connie would always be a friend and would protect Molly from others' cruelty.

* * *

Early in 1923, trade at Armitage picked up and Kate got a permanent job there. She worked a stamping machine and although the work was hard and repetitive she was happy in the knowledge that at last she was bringing in a steady wage, even if it was barely a pittance. Overall the wages paid to the Armitage workers were very poor. There was some unrest amongst the factory hands and talk of joining a trade union, but no one wanted to be labelled as a troublemaker and so the griping was normally aired at the street corner and the doorsteps after working hours.

George Armitage, the owner of the factory, had an intuitive feeling that his workers' discontent could become dangerous. He stood at the window of his large comfortable office looking down at the yard, a smart, upright man despite his advancing years. The factory that he had built up from practically nothing had been his whole life, but now that his wife had died he was beginning to feel very weary, and he realised that perhaps it was time for his two sons to take over the running of the business. His elder son Peter would assume general control, and Gerald would take responsibility for organising the production. He sighed as he thought of the problems that would arise. There was too much tension between the two brothers. Peter was competent and serious-minded, and happily married with a young son, whereas Gerald was overconfident and brash, and his marriage was breaking down badly. George knew that his boastful younger son would try to dominate Peter, and he realised that discontent among the workers would be aggravated if Gerald went ahead and sacked Joe Cooper, the well-liked young foreman, and some of the older hands on the factory floor. George Armitage gazed out over the yard as the wind disturbed scraps of paper wrapping and torn pieces of cardboard. I wonder what all this will come to, he thought.

His thoughts were disturbed as Gerald opened the door and walked confidently in.

'Hello, Gerald,' George said. 'Sit down for a minute, can you? I've just been thinking about a few things.'

As Gerald made himself comfortable in an easy chair he noticed the worry and concern on his father's face. He always felt irritable when his father called him in to discuss business, for he believed that the matters which often caused his father so much concern could be summarily resolved quite simply, without so much fuss. His lack of real power in the company irked him, and he was impatient for his father to hand over control to him and Peter.

George Armitage looked over at his son with stern eyes. 'Are you having any trouble with the workers wanting to join trade unions, Gerald?' he asked shortly.

Gerald shrugged dismissively and a ghost of a grin appeared on his chiselled features. 'Well, I've heard rumours about rumours, Father,' he said. 'But it's not worth paying any attention to them. If they are true, it's only one or two idiots getting above themselves. Most of the hands are no problem at all.'

'Mmm.' For some time George seemed to study a piece of paper on his desk and then suddenly he looked up. 'Gerald, I want you to organise an outing,' he said.

'An outing!' his son said, hardly able to disguise the incredulity in his voice.

'That's right. I think it'll take their minds off trade unions and pay rises and God knows what else. A nice summer trip to Southend. Lay on a barrel of ale and some sandwiches, and a meal at the other end.' George smiled to himself as he felt in the pocket of his waistcoat for his pipe. 'Yes,' he continued, 'we'll reap the benefits in the long run, I feel sure. By the way, Gerald, order the charabancs from Thomas Tilling. I know one of their directors and we should get a nice discount.'

Gerald tried not to show his scorn. Outings for workers, he thought, trying to come to terms with the idea. Beer and a meal as well. We might as well put their wages up and give them the bloody afternoons off!

'I think it would be good if one of us put in an appearance on the day, Gerald,' George continued. 'Would you be prepared to do that? You know, do a short speech before they sit down to eat and keep an eye on things. Well? Will you do it?'

'If you insist, Father,' Gerald said curtly. He was cross with his father's stupidity and he rose quickly to leave. 'I have to go. We were having a problem with one of the machines downstairs.'

'Of course, son,' his father said, leaning back in his chair. 'I'll see you later to finalise the details.'

Gerald closed the door behind him. George Armitage leaned forward on his desk and breathed heavily as he gazed around his large office. Now the initial excitement of the idea of an outing had worn off the long hours of the day seemed to pass very slowly and the room in which he spent so much time seemed to have become more and more empty.

A few days later the news spread around the Armitage factory that there was to be an outing in the summer, and for a time the grumbles about the low wages diminished. One or two workers were sceptical though.

'I'll believe it when we're on that charabanc,' Mary Baker remarked to her friend as they walked out through the factory gates one Friday evening.

Joyce Spinks giggled. 'Won't it be luvverly. I 'ope that Johnny Sandford goes. 'E's really nice.'

Mary grinned. 'You'd better be careful. Johnny Sandford's got a reputation.'

'I don't care,' her friend replied. ''E could put 'is shoes under my bed any night!'

Just outside the factory they saw Kate Morgan talking to one of the young lads. Mary nudged her friend. 'Look at 'er chattin' 'im up. She's old enough ter be 'is muvver.'

Joyce pulled a face. 'She'd 'ave anyfing in trousers. If we do 'ave a day out she better keep 'er eyes orf o' Johnny. I'm bookin' 'im.'

'Are yer linin' 'im up fer the outin', Kate?' Mary called out.

Kate Morgan walked over smiling. 'What outin'? I'll believe it when it 'appens.'

'That's just what I was sayin' ter Joyce,' Mary said, nodding. 'If they do row the boat out are you gonna go?'

''Course I will,' Kate replied. 'All that free beer an' all those fellas. I might find meself a chap.'

'What about yer baby?' Joyce asked, a touch of hostility creeping into her voice.

'Connie's no trouble,' Kate answered, quickly. 'She's good as gold wiv me sister. Anyway, I'm not lettin' a kid tie me down. I've seen enough of it round 'ere. I'm gonna enjoy myself while I can.'

The two friends started off along the street and Kate veered off towards the tenement block. 'If yer can't be good be careful,' she called out, smiling.

'An' if yer can't be careful remember the date,' Mary countered, when Kate was out of earshot.

They reached Mary's house and stopped by the front door. 'What shall we do ternight?' Joyce said.

'We could go up the Tanner'op, Joyce. I 'eard there's a new band there. We could practise the foxtrot an' the quickstep.'

'I don't fancy dancin', Mary. That fella shoutin' down the megaphone gives me an 'eadache, especially after all that noise in the factory.'

Mary thought for a while. 'I know. Let's go up the South London. Marie Lloyd's up there. It'll be a good show. We'll 'ave ter line up fer tickets though.'

Joyce looked up at the evening sky. 'It's a nice evenin'. Let's jus' go fer a long walk.'

Mary squeezed her friend's arm. 'We could take a tram ter the Embankment, an' walk along the Strand,' she said excitedly.

Joyce turned up her nose. 'What d'yer wanna go over there for?'

Mary shook her head in disbelief. 'Ain't yer never bin up the Strand? There's all those posh ladies in their fur coats an' latest dresses, an' there's lots o' really 'andsome men in top 'ats and smart suits all goin' in ter see the shows. It's really excitin', Joyce.'

'Okay, I'll come round soon as I finish me tea. I've gotta be in by eleven o'clock though. If I'm late me ole man'll skin me alive.'

Mary laughed aloud. 'Your dad'll be too pissed ter know whether you're in or not. 'E always goes up the Horseshoe on Friday nights, don't 'e?'

'Not any more, Mary. 'E's on short time again.'

As the summer days lengthened, excitement grew at the Armitage factory. A notice had gone up in the canteen stating that the firm's outing to Southend would take place on the first Saturday in July. The workers' rumblings about becoming unionised ceased for the time being, and Gerald Armitage had to concede that perhaps the old boy was right after all.

The day of the outing was warm and sunny, and the street folk watched from their doorways as the Thomas Tilling charabancs drove slowly out of the turning. The women sat upright on the open vehicles, showing off their new summer hats and their crisp cotton dresses, while the men, grinning widely, had their hair slicked down and some even wore silk scarves, knotted at the neck and twirled around their braces. George Baker watched as the Armitage workers left the street, then he turned to Toby Toomey.

'Gawd 'elp Soufend when that lot gets down there.'

Toby looked on enviously and wished that the totters could have an outing to Southend.

The long summer day had turned to night and a full moon was rising over the rooftops when the charabancs returned, drawing up at the end of the turning. Helen Bartlett heard loud voices and then Kate's footsteps on the wooden stairs and when she opened the door she saw her sister coming along the landing, a surly look on her face. Kate's fair hair was hanging loosely and raggedly about her drooping shoulders and her knee-length, mustard-coloured coat was unbuttoned.

'Did yer 'ave a nice day?' Helen asked.

Kate glared at her sister and nodded without comment, her mouth tight.

'Connie dropped off ter sleep,' Helen said, eyeing her sister intently. 'She'll be okay wiv us till mornin'. Are yer all right?'

Kate moved on to the next stairway. 'Yeah, I'm jus' tired. It's bin a long day,' she said turning and wearily climbed the stairs.

Helen sighed and shook her head slowly as she went inside and closed the door. Matthew looked up from the armchair and ran his fingers through his wiry hair. 'She's pissed I s'pose?' he said quickly.

Helen sat down facing him with a sigh. 'I wonder about that girl sometimes. I dunno about Soufend. She looks like she's bin to a funeral. She didn't even ask about young Connie.'

Matthew's face showed his disgust as he got up and walked into the bedroom.

* * *

During the days of short-time working and ragtime music, amid the gas-lit tenements and ramshackle houses of the tumbledown backstreets, the daughters of Kate Morgan and Helen and Matthew Bartlett slept peacefully, while all around the signs of industrial strife were growing. The humiliation of accepting starvation wages, the desperate scramble for a day's work in the local docks and wharves, accidents in the saw mills and in the factories inspired the activists to organise their fellow workers into trade unions. Industrial diseases in the tanneries, lead mills and skin factories outraged the health workers, and questions were raised in Parliament. There were calls for proper hygiene and safeguards in workplaces, and when little was done the atmosphere of resentment and anger grew stronger.

In the backstreets of Bermondsey very little changed. Women sat in the corner-street pubs drinking 'Lizzie Wine' while they shelled their peas into containers resting on their aproned laps. The men drank pints of porter and slipped out of the pub to place their dog bets with the street bookmaker – keeping one eye open for the local bobbie. Children played in the gutters and paddled in the muddy River Thames, and the more daring climbed the barges and dived into murky water beside the huge iron buoys, or scrambled down into the empty holds and scooped up nut kernels and coconut husks. In Ironmonger Street the children spoke in whispers about a strange old lady who pushed a pram covered with washing to the local laundry every Monday morning. Legends had grown up around Widow Pacey and, as she slowly walked along pushing her contraption, some of the younger children would hide in doorways, unable to take their eyes from the long white hairs on the end of her chin. The older children said she was a witch who cooked babies for her supper and carried the bones down to the river hidden in her pram. When their parents heard the stories and smacked them for talking nonsense, they knew that the legends must be true.

Connie and her cousin Molly were too young to have understood such stories, but Molly cowed whenever the bagwash lady passed by, frightened by the mere presence of the woman. Connie reacted in a different way, however; her large eyes stared out solemnly at Widow Pacey's bristling chin and at the laden, squeaking pram, and her small round face remained impassive. A contest of wills developed. The widow would smile or wink at the inseparable young children, but she got little response, except for Molly's frightened look and Connie's wide-eyed glance. When looks, smiles and gesticulations failed, the Widow Pacey tried to win the children over with toffee bars as she left for the laundry one morning. On her return trip the bagwash lady saw that the two children were halfway through the toffee sticks, faces smudged and hands stuck to the sweets. But still there was no smile forthcoming, and Widow Pacey gave up trying. One or two of the older lads who had seen the toffee bars being handed out spread the word that Widow Pacey had taken to poisoning children.

One person in the street was sure he had found a way to keep the local children in order. And one dismal morning he took delivery of a large brown paper parcel. Misery Martin's normally dead-pan features changed into an expression of pleasure as he quickly secreted the parcel under the counter for the time being. At the end of the day, after he had put up the only shutter he had bothered to take down that morning, he slipped the bolts on the front door and went back behind the counter. He placed the large parcel on the linoleum-covered surface, slit the string with a sharp knife and opened the bundle. There in front of him were two dozen thin canes. Misery picked up one by its curved handle and brought it down on the counter sharply. The swish and smack sounded loudly in the quiet shop and a wide grin creased the shop owner's face. That's just what the little brats around here need! he thought, considering how to display the canes in the most threatening manner. The parents in the street are always going on about giving their kids a good hiding. Let them buy these canes, they should do the trick. One good thrashing with one of these little beauties should be enough, he ventured to himself.

The expression on the oilshop owner's face as he thought about his new merchandise would have shocked the street-folk. No one had ever seen him smile – except for Mrs Walker. When she walked into his dingy shop one day for some nails.

Misery adopted his usual weary tone. 'What size?'

'Two inch,' Mrs Walker said, changing her weight from one foot to the other.

Misery shook his head. 'I ain't got two inch. I've got inch an' 'alfs, an' I've got two an' 'alfs, but no two inch.'

Mrs Walker puffed out her cheeks and bit on her bottom lip in consternation. 'My ole man will be pleased,' she groaned.

'What's 'e want the nails for?' Misery asked.

''E's puttin' a shelf up in me scullery. I bin askin' 'im fer weeks ter put me one up but . . .'

'What size is the wood?' Misery cut in, not wishing to hear Mrs Walker's matrimonial problems.

''Bout this size,' the lady said, spreading her thumb and forefinger.

'Inch an' 'alfs will do. 'Ow many d'yer want?'

'I dunno. Enough ter put a shelf up I s'pose.'

Misery reached down below the counter and scooped up a handful of nails and threw them into the scale pan with a vengeance. 'That'll be tuppence,' he said, glaring at his customer out of his narrow-set brown eyes.

Mrs Walker thought for a moment, frowning. Misery scratched his wiry grey hair as he stared at the lady. 'D'yer wan 'em or not, muvver?' he rasped.

'I'd better see me ole man first. If I get it wrong 'e'll be in a right ole mood.'

'Please yerself,' Misery muttered as he tipped the nails back into the box under the counter.

Mrs Walker turned on her heel and started for the door. She caught her foot in the doormat on the threshold, slipped down the step and stumbled out into the street. When she had straightened her hat and regained her composure she looked around into the open doorway. She was about to give Misery Martin a piece of her mind about the maintenance of his shop when she saw his face. A huge grin had spread over his features. He reminded her of one of those evil-looking door knockers down Tanner's Alley that she had always hurried past. Mrs Walker turned smartly without making any comment and walked back to the Dwellings.

'Bloody ole goat,' she grumbled aloud with a shiver. ''E should be struck like that! Larffin' at people's mis'aps. It's the only time 'e's 'appy.'

The long summer times were balmy and days of blue skies were followed by starlit nights. The winters were severe, with poisonous fogs and winds that chilled the bones. In the dockland slums, beyond the whitened front doorsteps and crisp lace curtains, the houses were infested with bugs. Wax tapers were lit and applied to the bedsprings and soft green soap was packed between woodwork and plaster in the constant battle against infestation. The local people frantically kept themselves clean with carbolic soap and Lysol and, as money was short, they would use homemade medicines and applications for their ailments: bread poultices, soap and sugar applications for boils and abscesses, and vinegar-soaked towels for septic throats. Steam kettles were used to ease bronchitis in children and horse hairs were tied around warts.

During the 'twenties, as Connie Morgan and Molly Bartlett grew up in the little backstreet behind the Tower Bridge Road, the street became used to the sight of the two cousins toddling around together, inseparable. Connie was becoming tall and leggy whilst Molly's growth was slow and painful. Her flat round face was set upon a short neck, but her large dark eyes shone out like defiant beacons, and her laugh was infectious. She waddled along, swaying from side to side beside the pretty fair-haired girl whose pale blue eyes were set in a finely moulded face. Connie's placid character contrasted sharply with her playmate's changing moods. Molly's alert and agile mind was trapped inside her retarded body and it often made her frustrated and angry. Connie quietly bore the brunt of her anger and changing moods with gentle patience. When the street children chased a ball or followed coloured glass marbles in a scurry, Connie would stay close to Molly. It was as though she had made herself responsible for her cousin's safety and wellbeing and, whenever Helen watched the two together, it tugged at her heart. She had cared and tended her sister's child since Kate first took the job at Armitage's. When she had suddenly left the factory after the outing in twenty-three, Kate had got a job as a barmaid and young Connie was left more and more in Helen's care. Helen had grown to love the girl as though she were her own and she was aware of the deep bond between the children. It helped to quell the grinding bitterness and heartache at seeing her own child's malformed body struggling to develop and mature.

Chapter Four

During the early 'twenties the Government changed hands with almost monotonous regularity until, in 1924, a Conservative government under the leadership of Stanley Baldwin took office and remained in power for five years. Then, in 1926, a general strike paralysed the industrial areas, and in Bermondsey the trams stopped running and the docks and wharves closed. Some local factories shut, and in the Armitage factory some of the younger members of the workforce attempted to organise their own support for the strike by walking out and standing at the gates. The main section of the workforce was confronted with hastily prepared leaflets when they reported for work one Monday morning and many workers joined the protesters at the gates. Joe Cooper was standing amongst them. Joe had earned the respect of nearly every worker at the factory. He had been instrumental in helping to improve relations between the workers and management and in the process he had made an enemy of Gerald Armitage. Gerald saw that Joe could coax and cajole the best out of the factory hands and he was jealous of Joe's influence. He was convinced that the foreman was the troublemaker behind the growing demands for the factory to become unionised. But Joe had also earned the respect and trust of Peter Armitage, the factory's new managing director, and he was not afraid to take the shop floor grievances directly to Peter and bypass his more inflexible brother. Although this was a blatant infringement of normal procedures it was an arrangement which persisted, and it caused a few eyebrows to be raised.

Peter Armitage stood at the window of his office, looking down at the yard. His father had recently handed over control of the business to him, and the realities of running the factory weighed heavily upon him . . .

With a deep sigh he left the window and slumped down at his desk. His forefinger twirled the paper knife as he thought about the conversation he had had with his wife Claudette the previous evening. They had been sitting beside the log fire and Claudette was industriously working on a piece of embroidery. Suddenly she had looked up. 'Will the factory have to close, Peter?' she asked.

'I think it's more than likely, my dear,' he replied. 'The strike seems to be spreading everywhere.'

Claudette clicked her tongue. 'But you can't allow yourself to be dictated to. You'll have to stand up to them. Gerald was saying that it's only a few troublemakers leading the rest and he thinks it's about time you showed them just who's running the factory.'

Peter had given his wife a withering glance. 'Exactly. I think Gerald should bear that in mind, too,' he growled and flicked open the evening paper. And, just as he had turned to read it, he had caught a strange smile on Claudette's face as she worked the needle through the tapestry . . .

The sound of loud voices coming from the yard jerked Peter out of his reverie and he got up and went back to the window. He watched with growing anxiety as some of the workers defied the call for solidarity and marched defiantly through the pickets. Scuffles broke out and the situation became tense.

Some of the strikers were holding up banners calling for support for the miners and, as other workers tried to pull them down, the fighting got worse; banners were broken and the sticks used as clubs. As he watched the disturbance by the gates Peter was shocked and sickened. His trusted foreman Joe Cooper was fighting on the side of the strikers, and Peter saw him punching out at a couple of strangers who were trying to snatch a banner from one of the female workers. Peter was convinced that the two ruffians did not work at the factory.

The door opened and Gerald strode in. 'Miss Jones has already called the police, Peter,' he said quickly. 'They'll sort out this bloody mess.'

Peter looked hard at his younger brother and pointed in the direction of the yard. 'Who are they? Those two thugs don't work here.'

Gerald looked down towards the gates. His brother noticed the ghost of a wry smile cross his face. 'I don't know them,' he said. 'They look to me like strike breakers.'

'They look to me like strike breakers, too,' Peter said pointedly. 'Are they the strike breakers you were telling me about who were involved round at the Matthew's factory last week?'

Gerald glared coldly at his brother but didn't speak.

Peter looked down into the street and saw Joe Cooper lying on the ground, several boots raining kicks into his curled-up body. Other workers started to drag the attackers off as police rushed up to the gates and pulled the fighters apart. With its bell ringing, a Black Maria roared into the turning and screeched to a halt. Peter watched people being bundled unceremoniously into the back of the van, and he saw the half-conscious figure of Joe Cooper dragged along the cobbles and thrown in with the others. He turned away from the window and looked at his younger brother, his face contorted with anger. 'I suppose you think this is the way to deal with this sort of thing?' he said loudly.

Gerald's face darkened. 'What are you accusing me for?' he said with a nonchalant shrug.

'You must think I'm stupid,' Peter said, his voice quiet and scornful. 'A friend of yours gets strike breakers in to deal with his troubles and you think it serves his workers right, and now you don't know what's been going on down there?' He shook his head. 'Bring in the toughs and let them beat up the workers. If the old man gets to hear of this it'll kill him. Christ Almighty, Gerald, you're a fool.'

His younger brother's face reddened with anger. 'This business belongs to the family. I've got as much right as you to look after its best interests. What gives you the right to preach to me?'

Peter breathed in deeply. He knew that if he continued he would be opening a black chapter in Gerald's past that they had agreed to bury. He walked around behind his desk and sat down heavily. Gerald watched his progress, a look of distaste on his handsome features. Peter said nothing. He clasped his hands on the desk top and pressed the tips of his fingers together until the nails went white. After some time he looked up into his brother's eyes and said quietly, 'They'll be needing you on the factory floor if we're to get the machines running, Gerald.'

Gerald turned and stalked to the door. He paused before turning again to face his elder brother. Peter's head was bent forward and he appeared to be inspecting a document. Gerald eyed him warily; he knew that his past misdemeanour would always be held against him, and would be used to make sure he behaved. He was trapped. 'I'll come up later when I've sorted things out,' he said coldly, and stepped out into the passageway, shutting the door behind him.

* * *

The General Strike lasted just nine days, and the factory strike less than one week. Joe Cooper appeared at the Tower Bridge Magistrates Court and was fined ten shillings for disorderly conduct. His bruised and battered head remained unbowed as he paid the fine and walked out of the court to back-slapping and cheers from his workmates. The next Monday morning an apprehensive group of workers walked through the gates of the factory and clocked in. There were no cases of victimisation, but the following week the management declared that working hours were to be increased by one hour and the early Friday finish would now be a thing of the past. Though they could do nothing about it, it angered the subdued workers and made Joe Cooper all the more determined to bring trade union membership into the Armitage factory.

Another confrontation which took place during the strike was the subject of discussion at the next domino group get-together.

'We was all outside the pie shop in Tower Bridge Road,' George Baker began. 'I was standin' there mindin' me own business an' eatin' me 'ot pie, when along comes this tram. Yer could 'ave knocked me over wiv a feavver. I says ter young Bernie Cornbloom, " 'Ere, Bernie, the trams are s'posed ter be on strike ain't they?" " 'S'right," 'e says. So I looks up the road an' there's this dirty great tram wiv a geezer drivin' it who wasn't yer regular tram driver. 'E 'ad this posh coat on wiv a fur collar, an there was a copper standin' on the platform next to 'im. The tram was packed wiv them bleedin' office workers from Tooley Street. This copper 'ad 'is arms folded over 'is truncheon an' there was anuvver copper on an 'orse trottin' be'ind. Before yer could say Jack Robinson, young Bernie grabs me pie an' runs out in front o' this tram. 'E aims me dinner at this geezer who's drivin' the tram an' it 'its the copper instead. Right in the dial it caught 'im. Everybody starts cheerin' an' clappin', an' young Bernie's orf like the clappers wiv this copper chasin' 'im. Some o' the lads jumped on the tram an' tried ter pull this driver geezer orf. Now, the copper on the 'orse don't know whevver ter chase Bernie Cornbloom, or 'elp the scab volunteer. 'E yanks the poor 'orse's neck round an' it slips on the tramlines. Over it goes an' this Tom Mix copper can't get up. 'E's got 'is leg trapped under the animal. Ole Clara Cosgrove is standin' watchin' the fun an' suddenly she grabs an 'andful of eggs orf of Teddy Oldham's stall an' starts peltin' the copper wiv 'em. Talk about a laugh. I ain't laughed so much since ole Knocker 'ere got pissed that night an' mistook ole Clara's 'ouse fer the urinal.'

'I don't remember doin' that,' Knocker said, stroking his thick stubble.

''Course yer don't. You was legless. Yer made a right mess of 'er passage wallpaper, I can tell yer.'

'Did they catch Bernie?' Harold Simpson asked.

'No fear,' George said emphatically. 'Bernie runs across the road, roun' the corner, an' straight frew ole fat Sara's front door.'

'Blimey! I bet she was pleased,' laughed Knocker.

'Not 'alf. She grabs young Bernie an' tries ter pull 'im in 'er bedroom. Bernie told me 'e didn't know whevver ter give 'imself up an' take 'is medicine, or take some of 'ers.'

'What did 'e do, George?' Knocker asked.

'Gawd knows. 'E never told me what 'e did.'

'What would you 'ave done, George?' Harold asked.

'I'd 'ave give meself up. I ain't too keen ter get a dose o' the clap. Ole Sara's 'ad 'alf o' Tower Bridge Road in 'er place.'

'Yer right there,' Harold agreed. 'I've even seen ole Ferris the chimney sweep divin' in an' out o' there.'

'Fat Sara ain't got a coal fire. She's on gas,' Knocker chipped in.

''Ow the bloody 'ell d'you know?' Harold piped in, amid roars of laughter.

As the 'twenties drew to a close the young cousins became settled into their lessons at the local Webb Street School. Every morning they walked to school together, and every afternoon they strolled home, lazily laughing at the peculiar teacher who took them for lessons. It was already apparent that Connie would develop into a very pretty adult: her deep-set blue eyes were very striking, their colour vividly shaded. Her long blond hair reached down almost to her waist, and was usually tied carelessly at the back of her neck with a black lace, revealing her rounded forehead. She moved with childlike grace and her posture was straight and proud. By contrast Molly did not appear to be growing very fast, her pathetic young body looked thick and squat with her back becoming more and more rounded. She managed to walk at a steady pace, although she tended to sway from side to side when she tried to hurry, and her breathing was quick and shallow. Her flat face was constantly changing in expression; it was as though all her suffering, all her struggles to accomplish the day-to-day tasks were written in her round face and reflected in her large dark-brown eyes. The constant awareness of her condition had made her look older than her tender years. She already seemed to have lost the carelessness of childhood and behind her simple appearance there was a maturing mind that was fast outstripping the growth of her tragic body. Already, as a nine-year-old, Molly was beginning to interpret the looks and the remarks of people on the streets. Their attitudes were often well meant and sympathetic, but their careless and unthinking pity pierced the child's heart.

One day Connie and Molly were later than usual coming home from school. Helen Bartlett put on her coat and scarf and went to look for the youngsters. As she reached the bottom of the stairs she found Connie with her arm around Molly's shoulders. Her daughter seemed to be crying.

'Molly, what's wrong?' she called out, rushing up to them. She leant down and gently touched the side of Molly's face, but her daughter would not look up. She stared at the ground, tears running down her cheeks and falling from her chin.

'Connie, what's the matter?' Helen asked, looking over at her niece. Connie looked away, and Helen could see that she did not want to tell her. 'Come on luv, what's bin 'appenin'?' she asked her quietly.

Connie frowned. 'It's those Flynn kids,' she said. 'They kept on sayin' "umptybacked" and callin' Molly names. So I bashed 'em.'

'Oh, Molly darlin', come 'ere,' Helen said as she went to cuddle her daughter. But Molly burst out sobbing and pushed past her to hurry away up the stairs.

Although Helen and Matthew were devoted and adoring towards their only child, whose disabilities made them pander to her every need, they sensed that Molly found it very difficult to believe she could be loved. Connie, however, received no such lavish affection from her mother, although she was kept clean and well clothed. For the most part Kate never seemed to be around. Her job as a barmaid took her out every evening, and at weekends there always seemed to be parties and appointments which left Connie either alone in the flat or in Helen's care. More and more Connie turned to Helen for her needs, and the gap between Kate and her daughter widened. There were also times when, for reasons that the young child did not understand, she was suddenly taken from her own flat and foisted upon Helen, even though it was clear that Kate remained at home. This usually took place at the weekends, and the two children became quite used to sharing the same bedroom. Over the years it became more and more difficult for Connie to approach her mother. Conversations between them were very rare, and whenever Connie asked about her father she was told quite coldly that her father was dead and she should not keep asking those sorts of questions.

Connie was chatting to her cousin on their way home from school one day when Molly suddenly asked, 'Why ain't yer got a dad, Connie?'

'Me dad's dead,' she said.

''Ow did 'e die?'

'I dunno.'

'When did 'e die?'

'I dunno, Molly. Me mum didn't say.'

'What did 'e look like?'

'I dunno.'

Molly turned her dark eyes towards Connie and said, 'It mus' be 'orrible not to 'ave a dad.'

'Oh it's all right, I s'pose.'

'We could share my dad,' Molly said suddenly, her eyes sparkling.

'We share 'im now, silly, I'm always stayin' in your flat.'

Molly thought for a time and then said, 'I know. Why don't you ask my mum about your dad? My mum knows everyfink.'

That same evening when the two girls were sitting in front of the coal fire in the Bartlett's flat, Molly looked up as her mother came into the room and nudged her cousin. 'Go on. Ask me mum.'

'Ask me what, Molly?'

Connie put down her colouring book and looked up at

Helen. 'I asked me mum about dad, Auntie 'Elen. Mum said 'e's dead. Did you know 'im?'

Helen sat down in her fireside chair and stared down into the enquiring eyes of her niece. She wanted to tell the truth. She knew that it was not right to keep such a thing from the child. She had a right to know, but Kate was still adamant that Connie was not to be told anything about her father, and Helen realised that she would have to go along with her wishes. 'I'm sorry, Connie. I didn't know your dad. 'E died when you was a baby.'

'Didn't mum ever bring 'im round ter see yer, Auntie?' she asked.

'No, she never did,' Helen said truthfully.

In 1929 the Wall Street crash made headline news. Shares tumbled everywhere and there was talk of a world-wide depression. Unemployment rose to three million. A blight quickly struck all the large industrial areas and thousands of factories closed; almost everywhere workers were put once again on the dreaded short-time working. In Bermondsey, folk realised that the times were going to get even harder as more and more workers received their notices and the docks and wharves ground almost to a standstill. Over the next few years the effects of the economic slump bit deeply everywhere and a grey, depressing gloom overhung the whole of the docklands. During 1931 Ironmonger Street lost one of its most loved characters. Fran Collins died two months after her husband Tom, and the whole street turned out to pay their last respects. Many of the families who stood at their front doors sobbing quietly into handkerchiefs had good reason to be grateful to old Fran. She had slapped the breath of life into many of the street's kids, and right up until the end she had retained her cheerfulness and good-natured attitude to everyone. One middle-aged lady stood sobbing loudly. Fran had delivered all of her seven children and for the last birth the payment was still owing.

In that same year the Armitage Factory closed for a whole day in mourning for George Armitage who had died in his sleep. In his will he had stipulated that all his workers were to be given a day off with full pay on the day of his funeral. But, in these times, the closing of the factory for a day seemed almost ominous to the workforce rather than a special boon.

'I dunno. It's bin a bad year, what wiv one fing an' anuvver,' Joe Cooper said one day to old George Baker. 'There was ole Fran goin', an' ole Armitage. It seems 'alf the characters round 'ere are leavin' us ter get on wiv it.'

George sucked on his pipe and looked up the street. A slow smile spread over his grizzled face as he watched the antics of the man who had just pushed a battered old pram into the turning. The contraption was laden down with bits of old iron and, as the man struggled to keep it on a straight course, pieces of scrap fell from the load and bounced over the cobblestones. 'There's a few characters still knockin' about this turnin',' George grinned. 'Just look at that clown Toomey.'

The Toomeys were looked upon as a strange crowd by the street folk. Toby Toomey was a frail, harmless-looking individual who struggled to earn a living by pushing an ancient pram through the streets to collect scrap iron and old newspapers. He invariably wore a battered trilby hat and an overcoat that almost reached his down-at-heel boots. Toby was fearful of his domineering wife Marie, and very much aware that nothing he did was right in her eyes. Marie was a large woman with straight black hair which hung down her back. Her face was always powder-streaked and her eyes dark and brooding. The Toomeys had a daughter Lillian, who was fast gaining a reputation for being a 'loose woman'. Lillian was in her twenties, and her way of dressing was a constant talking point amongst the street folk. She wore very high-heeled shoes and dresses which were either too short or too tight. She used heavy make-up and outrageous hats and, like her mother, she had raven hair and very dark eyes. Lillian and her mother were a formidable pair and Toby had realised early on that it was useless to argue with them. Nevertheless, he harboured murderous thoughts as he struggled to manoeuvre the pram into his passageway, against a tirade of abuse from Marie.

The decade moved on slowly, and there was no respite from the suffering and deprivation of the poverty-stricken back-street folk. Pawnshop owners were the only people who could afford to walk around with satisfied smiles on their faces. The pawnbroker shop in the Tower Bridge Road was particularly busy, and it was now a weekly meeting place for many of the women of the area. It had become the usual ritual for the matriarchs of the family to parcel up their husband's suit or overcoat or maybe a pair of linen sheets and hurry over to Uncles with the bale. They would join the line of patient customers, stretching out from the back room, along the dark passageway, and sometimes out into the street. If the pawnbroker was in a good mood they might get their bale pledged for seven shillings and sixpence if it contained a decent suit or overcoat, and five shillings for a pair of sheets. The articles would be exchanged for a pawn ticket on Monday mornings and redeemed that Friday or Saturday when the few shillings earnings came into the home. It had become a way of life for many, and some pawnbrokers began to take advantage of their customers' desperate need.

It was a cold autumn Monday morning when Mrs Cosgrove parcelled up her Fred's best suit. Now in her late sixties, Mrs Cosgrove had been caring for her invalid husband for the past year, and she knew that he would not miss his best blue serge in his condition. It troubled her to have to make the visit, but she could see no alternative. When she reached the pawnshop the queue stretched almost to the door. Waiting in front of her in the line was Mrs Halliday who was carrying a large bundle under her arm.

''Ello, girl. What you doin' 'ere? Buyin' a bit o' jew'llery?' she said.

Mrs Cosgrove gave her a toothless grin. 'Same as you, Ada. I'm tryin' ter work the oricle.'

'Gawd 'elp us, Clara.'

'I fink 'E'd better. Nobody else seems ter be.'

The queue moved forward and Ada Halliday whispered into Mrs Cosgrove's ear. 'I 'ope the old bastard ain't bein' too fussy terday. If 'e is I'm in the shit.'

'Why's that, Ada?'

Ada looked around to make sure they were not being overheard, then she gave Clara a huge wink. 'Me mate's borrered me best coat ter go to a funeral, so I wrapped up me old ironin' blanket an' the pissy ole coat the moggie sleeps on an' I took a chance. If ole ugly's in a good mood 'e won't bovver ter open me bundle. Blimey, 'e's seen enough o' me this last few months, an' it's always bin me best coat I've brought over.'

Clara hid a grin behind her raised hand. ''Ere, Ada. I 'ope ole ugly ain't got a sensitive snozzle. I can smell that pissy ole coat from 'ere.'

'That ain't me bundle yer can smell,' Ada whispered. 'It's ole muvver Adams up front. She takes in all the stray mogs. 'Er place smells like a public urinal in Pennyfields.'

The line of customers moved slowly forward, and at last it was Ada's turn to present her bundle. ''Ere we are, same again,' she said with bluster.

The wizened figure who stood on a raised dais behind the high counter slapped the bundle down hard on the polished surface and sighed deeply. It had been a heavy morning and he was feeling nauseous. Every bundle he had opened smelled of moth balls or lavender water. Then there was the moggie lady with her smelly blankets. It was all getting too much, he groaned to himself as he threw the bundle through the hatch behind him and proceeded to write out the pawn ticket. 'There we are,' he said, slapping down a handful of coins on the table. 'Seven an' six less fourpence, an' there's yer ticket.'

Ada grinned at Clara as she turned to go. 'See yer later, girl. I'm orf 'ome ter do me ironin'!'

Chapter Five

In 1933 a name began to appear regularly in the daily newspapers which soon became more and more well known to anyone who followed the international news. Political cartoonists were fascinated by the new figure and some of their drawings began to worry those who were old enough to see something all too real and familiar in the caricatures; an ominous reminder of the past. Old George Baker was sitting with Joe Cooper in the public bar of the Horseshoe and he prodded the newspaper which was spread out on the table in front of him. 'Yer Kaiser was one fing, Joe, but this Adolf 'Itler's a sight more dangerous. See what it ses in 'ere. 'E's took the country out o' the League o' Nations an' got forty million votes fer rearmament. It's bloody frightenin' when yer fink of it. If somebody don't stop 'im it'll be anuvver bloody world war, mark my words.'

Joe's mind was on other things and he grabbed the two empty glasses. 'Pop, you're givin' me the bloody 'ump! Let's get a refill.'

The events that were shaping the destiny of the world were of little interest to Connie Morgan and her cousin Molly. In 1934 they were both fourteen and feeling very grown-up as, during the year, they discussed the prospect of trying to get a job together when they left school at Christmas. Although work was generally hard to find, many firms were taking on children straight from school to learn machine work of all types. It was seen by many employers as prudent to use what was little more than child labour to keep their costs to a minimum. Kate wanted Connie to get a job in an office, though, and Helen was afraid that her daughter would find it hard to get any type of job at all. The cousins' school-leaving certificates did not paint inspiring pictures of their capabilities. They were identical, as were those of all the school-leavers that term: 'Good at needle-work and housecraft. Punctual and trustworthy'.

Kate was still working as a barmaid and most of her free time was taken up with an endless round of parties and so the two friends spent most of the time together during the holidays. Helen and Matthew had gone to the pub on Christmas Eve and the two youngsters were sitting in Helen's front room listening to the wireless that Matthew had bought only a couple of days before. The fire burned brightly in the grate, and paper chains were hung around the walls. A sprig of holly was pinned over the fireplace and Christmas cards lined the high mantelshelf. Outside, the night was cold and windy, with a pale moon peeping through moving clouds. Connie crossed her legs under her and rested her arms on her lap as she sat on the hearth rug. Molly was sprawled out on her side facing her, her chin supported on her cupped hand. The room was warm and cosy and, after listening to the wireless for a while and chatting about trivial things, Molly brought up the subject of work.

'I wonder what jobs the labour exchange will offer us, Con?'

Connie shrugged her shoulders. 'I bet they won't send us after office jobs. Me mum keeps on at me ter get a job in an office. She reckons I should learn ter type an' do short'and. I don't wanna work in offices, Molly. Most o' them office workers are real posh. I couldn't talk posh, could you?'

Molly laughed and sat up. 'Fancy us bein' all posh. The kids round 'ere wouldn't talk to us. Anyway, those office fellas 'ave got funny names, like Clarence and Rodney. There's a fella who works in the office at Armitage's called Bertrum. Fancy 'avin' a name like Bertrum. I couldn't go around all day sayin' names like that. I'd burst out laughin'.'

Connie grinned and leaned forward. 'I reckon they'll send us ter Shuttleworths, or Peek Frean's. Most o' the girls who left last term work at Shut's.'

'Cor! Fancy 'avin' a job packin' choc'lates. We could eat 'em all day, Con.'

'What about workin' at Peek's, Molly? Cream biscuits, jam rolls, and luvverly choc'late digestives.'

Molly pulled her knees up. 'I bet yer don't get a chance ter touch a fing. I bet they've got some ole witch of a forelady standin' over yer all day. Someone like Widow Pacey.'

'P'raps they'll send us ter one o' those bottlin' stores,' Connie said, as she picked up the poker and stabbed at the glowing coals.

'What would we 'ave ter do there, Con?'

'Well, accordin' ter that Rita Arnold, yer label wine bottles an' do packin'. She's worked there fer ages.'

Molly stretched her legs and rubbed the side of her back. 'I 'ope we do get ter work tergevver, Con. The labour exchange might send us ter different places. Can't we say we wanna work tergevver?'

'I s'pose we could do,' Connie replied.

Molly's face became serious and for a time she stared into the fire. Presently she looked at Connie. 'S'posin' they won't give me a job?'

'What d'yer mean, Molly. 'Course they'll offer yer a job. You could do any job I could do.'

'I dunno. Lots o' firms won't take people like me on. Bella Richards couldn't get any jobs at all. I don't fink she's ever 'ad a job since she left school.'

Connie looked into her friend's large sad eyes and felt a familiar wave of pity flowing through her. 'Don't be so silly, Molly. Bella Richards is not like you. She's got somefing wrong wiv 'er brain. She keeps 'avin' fits. That's why she can't get a job. There's nufink wrong wiv yer brain. You was always better than me at classes. You'll get a job anywhere.'

Molly stared back into the fire, her eyes fixed on the flickering flames. 'Will yer get married one day, Con?' she asked suddenly.

Connie laughed, and a slight flush tinged her pretty face. 'Oh, I dunno. I might, one day.'

'Will yer 'ave lots o' babies?'

'I might. What about you?'

Molly's eyes had remained fixed to the flames. 'Yer need boys ter make babies, Con. Boys won't wanna go out wiv somebody like me.'

Connie leaned forward and squeezed Molly's arm gently. 'Yes they will. You jus' wait. Now let's ferget boys. Let's talk about Christmas presents, an' mince pies, an' 'ot chestnuts.'

Laughter rang out in the cosy room, while across the gaslit landing, in the flat opposite, old Mrs Walker wrapped her thick shawl around her frail shoulders and dreamed of Christmas long ago. The laughter that carried into her drab, draughty flat was the laughter of the street in more tranquil times, when the ragtime piano blared out, and when the banging coming from the scullery was music to her ears. The shelf was now hanging off the wall, although she did not notice. The fire was dying in the grate, but she did not take heed. She pulled the shawl tighter and closed her eyes.

* * *

Throughout the whole of the depression years West End restaurants and clubs still took deliveries of clarets and Madeiras, French Sauternes and vintage ports. The bottling stores and wholesale wine merchants around the Tooley Street area remained on full-time working to meet the demand, and it was there that the two young school-leavers found their first jobs together at John Priday and Sons. Connie was put to work labelling French wine, while Molly was placed on a different work bench, a couple of folded sacks on her stool to give her height, pasting out year labels for the bottle necks. With some trepidation, the two began their working lives.

The hours seemed long, and the work was dull. The only relief came when the daily tot of wine was handed out. The women labellers chuckled as Molly took her first sip of wine and pulled a face. It tasted like vinegar and she had difficulty in swallowing it. Connie, too, found the taste strange, but it was not long before both girls got used to it and in fact even began to look forward to the wine break. The ribald jokes, and the raucous laughter which often brought the foreman out of his office to see what was going on, were at first frightening to the cousins. But the women, mostly old hands, took the two young girls under their wings, and though life in the bottling stores was tedious and hard, in no time at all the young girls felt that they were part of the group. They soon began to understand the logic of the bawdy jokes which were, more often than not, directed towards the men workers.

Liaisons were established, and the banter and repartee often resulted in little favours being done by the men to ease the workload. Women could take a break in the toilets to have a smoke or take a swig from a bottle of wine that had been secreted behind the cistern while one of the men took over the labelling. Other little favours helped everyone through the day and, when someone had a birthday, one of the men would run over to the bakers across the road from the stores and fetch cakes. The most important reason for befriending the men, however, was the fact that the bottling stores worked on a bonus system. To have an ally amongst the men meant that the full boxes of labelled bottles would be more quickly removed and another empty box made ready; it could also ensure that a speedier supply of labels and paste kept production going and the bonus figure being reached.

At five o'clock every evening the two friends left the dank, gas-lit railway arches where the bottling stores were situated and walked home arm in arm to Ironmonger Street. As they walked through the warren of little backstreets to reach their homes they usually talked about their funny workmates and the young lads who were employed to load and unload the vans and horsecarts. One of the lads, a scruffily-dressed individual with an impish look, had seemed to have taken a shine to Molly and it was the subject of much talk amongst the older women. Molly was finding his attentions embarrassing, and she always blushed when the lad came through the arch and gave her a huge wink. Connie though was grateful for his friendship and she decided to find out a little about him.

The opportunity presented itself when the bottling machine broke down one morning. While the broken glass was being extracted from the cogs the labellers took a well-earned rest, and some of the lads came in to the bottling arch for a chat. The impish character sidled up to Connie and leaned on the work bench. ''Ello. What's your name then?' he asked, his eyes gently mocking her.

'Connie Morgan. What's yours then?' she countered.

'Michael Donovan. I live in Tower Bridge Road,' he said quickly, flicking a tuft of hair from his eyes with a quick move of his head.

'I live in Ironmonger Street,' Connie said.

Michael's eyes lit up and he broke into a grin, showing a row of wide even teeth. 'Ironmonger Street. Cor! That's a right ole street ter live in.'

Connie gave him a hard stare. 'What d'yer mean? Our street's okay. I've lived there all me life. Molly lives there too. We're cousins.'

'I know you're cousins. They told me,' he said, nodding to the group of women who had produced a pack of cards and were beginning a game of pontoon. 'Why don't yer cousin talk ter me when I wink at 'er? Is she shy?'

'She is a bit, I s'pose,' Connie conceded.

'I used ter go out wiv one o' the girls 'ere,' Michael said, standing up straight and puffing out his pigeon chest. 'She left though. Got anuvver job in an office.'

'Oh, an' is that why yer packed 'er up?'

'I didn't pack 'er up. She packed me up,' he admitted as he toyed with a pasting brush.

Connie studied the tall, slim lad and felt suddenly sorry for him. His demeanour was innocent enough, although she sensed a fierce pride simmering below the surface. His face was open and friendly and his unruly mop of fair hair almost covered his ears. His clothes seemed to be hanging on him, and his boots were tied up with string. He had a pleasant smile and his full lips were constantly moving. He seemed somehow to be different from the rest of the lads in that he took every opportunity to chat to everyone within reach.

''Ow old are yer?' Connie asked suddenly, flushing at her own impudence.

'I'm nearly seventeen. 'Ow old are you?'

'I'll be fifteen in November,' Connie replied.

'Yer just a kid, Connie. Don't worry though. I'll keep me eye on yer. Some o' those women are crafty,' he whispered,

55

nodding in the direction of the card players. 'They'll give yer all the worse jobs, you bein' new an' everyfing.'

'I'm not a kid,' Connie retorted sharply. 'I'm only a little bit younger than you. Anyway, yer not a kid once yer start work,' she added pointedly.

'What's up wiv yer cousin, Con?' Michael said, in an effort to change the subject.

'What d'yer mean what's up wiv 'er?'

'Well, she looks sort o' different. Like she's a dwarf or somefink.'

Connie was furious at his impudence, and wanted to lash out with her tongue, but something stopped her. He seemed genuinely interested in Molly's condition, and she saw the look of sympathy and concern on his elfin face.

'Molly's got a spine defect. She was born wiv it. That's why she gets shy when boys talk to 'er,' she said quietly. Michael's look of puzzlement made her go on. 'Yer see, Molly finks people pity 'er. She gets mad when people pity 'er.'

'Can't the 'ospital do anyfink – ter make 'er walk better I mean?' Michael asked.

Connie shook her head. 'No. 'Er mum told me she might 'ave ter wear irons on 'er legs soon. Don't you tell 'er that, will yer?' she said, her eyes widening.

''Course I won't. What d'yer take me for?' Michael said indignantly.

Connie glanced over to where her friend was working and saw that the group on that particular bench was huddled around one of the women who seemed to be pointing out something from a catalogue. Molly appeared to be interested in what was being shown and did not seem to have noticed the conversation she was having. Connie looked back at Michael who was leaning against the work table, his arms folded across his chest. 'I've not seen yer in Tower Bridge

Road,' she said. 'I'm always there, doin' shoppin' fer me aunt.'

'I live in Albion Buildin's, near the bridge. I live wiv me gran,' he said, looking down at his scruffy boots.

'Ain't yer got no mum an' dad then?' Connie asked.

'They split up when I was a little kid. I can't remember much about 'em. I remember a little bit about me dad. 'E was very big. All I can remember about me mum is the scenty smell. She always smelt really nice. I can't even remember what she looked like.'

Connie looked down at her fingernails. 'My dad's dead. At least that's what me mum tells me. I don't know really. 'E might still be alive.'

'D'yer live wiv yer mum, Con?'

'Yeah. Why d'yer ask?'

'Well yer said yer go shoppin' fer yer aunt.'

'That's right, I do. I stay wiv 'er an' Molly a lot. Me mum works in a pub, an' she 'as ter go out a lot.'

The belt was now clear of broken glass and it looked as though work would start again very soon.

Michael stood up straight. 'Fanks fer the chat, Con. I'd better get outside, or that ole goat Bradley'll start shoutin'.'

Connie smiled at him. 'Somebody mentioned you was tryin' ter get in the navy,' she said. 'Is that right?'

Michael's eyes lit up. 'Yeah. I'm waitin' till I'm seventeen next month an' I'm gonna sign on fer seven an' five.'

'What's seven an' five mean?'

'Seven in the service, an' five years in the reserve. It's what yer gotta do if yer wanna join up,' he said as he moved away from the work bench.

'See yer later,' Connie called out.

'See yer, Con,' he smiled.

* * *

1935 was Jubilee year, and in May lots of backstreets in dockland held parties for the children. In Ironmonger Street some of the folk gathered together in George Baker's house to make arrangements for a street party. George was now in his early seventies and still sprightly. His daughter Mary was there, too. She had married Frank Brown, a docker from the next street, and they had two young children. Joe Cooper sat at the table with a note pad in front of him holding court.

'Now listen,' he said. 'We've gotta go roun' wiv the collectin' boxes. People ain't got much, we know, but every penny'll count. We've also gotta scrounge some fruit an' nuts from the stall-'olders, an' somebody's gotta pop in ter get a few bob from ole Misery.'

'I'll chat the stall-'olders up,' Mary said, wiping her baby's hands and moving the packet of margarine out of reach.

'I can make some jellies,' Clara Cosgrove piped in.

'I can bake a load o' fairy cakes if somebody can supply the stuff,' said Mrs Griffin.

'What about the clobber, Joe?' old man Baker said, knocking the bowl of his pipe on the fender.

'Well it all depends,' Joe answered. 'If we get enough money from the whip round we can get Union Jack pinafores fer the girls, an' paper 'ats fer the boys. There's also those Jubilee mugs on sale in the market. We might be able ter get some o' those an' fill 'em up wiv sweets.'

'What about tables an' chairs?' Mary said, dipping her baby's dummy in the jam pot and popping it in his mouth. 'I can't put any o' mine outside me front door, I'd be too ashamed. They're all rickety.'

'I know what. Let's go round an' see ole scatty Simmons,' Mary's husband said. ''E could let us 'ave some trestle tables an' benches from the school.'

''E wouldn't give yer the time o' day,' Mrs Cosgrove said

with venom. 'That ole goat's pissed 'alf 'is time.'

'That's all right,' Joe butted in. 'We'll talk to 'im when 'e's pissed. We'll get more sense out of 'im that way. If we play our cards right 'e might chip in a few cups an' plates.'

The group of organisers went about their various tasks, and soon the festivity supplies began to grow. Tony Armeda promised to donate a tub of his lemon ice-cream and the stall-holders gave generously. As one of them put it: 'We might as well do it wiv a good 'eart. Those bleeders from Ironmonger Street'll nick the bloody fruit anyway.'

Misery Martin proved to be a problem, however, and Joe Cooper decided to sort him out in his own way. 'Come 'ere you lot,' he shouted at a group of street kids who he found tying door knockers together and pulling on the string. 'I ain't gonna give yer a clout. Not if yer do as yer told. Now listen. This is what I want yer ter do.'

Misery Martin had been trying unsuccessfully to sell his business for years. No one seemed interested, and he blamed the street. 'Who'd wanna buy a shop in this bloody turnin',' he was grumbling to a commercial traveller he'd cornered in his shop. 'Them little urchins ain't civilised. Bloody savages, the lot of 'em. I'd give 'em a party! More like a good 'idin'. That's what they want. I 'ad one o' the farvvers in 'ere only yesterday. Wantin' a subscription fer the street party. I told 'im no, an' in no uncertain terms.'

The commercial traveller was backing out through the door with his head buzzing. 'I'll look in again next week Mr Martin.'

'That's what they need,' Misery called out to the disappearing figure. 'A bleedin' good 'idin'.'

Four grinning faces looked in the shop doorway and pointed to the canes that were hanging from the rafters.

'Go on, 'op it!' the disgruntled shop owner called out.

The four kids stood perfectly still, their mocking faces grinning evilly.

'You 'eard what I said. 'Op it!'

The kids remained perfectly still by the doorway. Misery hobbled around the counter and they disappeared. When he returned to the counter the kids were back. The aggravation went on all day. Next morning the kids came back and Misery spoke to PC Wilshaw, who promised to box a few ears if he came across the little ruffians. Little was gained from Misery's consultation with the law. As soon as the constable left the street back came the kids. By the end of the second day Misery had come to the end of his tether.

'What can I do ter put a stop to it?' he groaned to Joe Cooper, who had purposely gone in for a penn'orth of nails.

'Leave it ter me, Jerry. I'll sort 'em out. Yer won't be bovvered by 'em any more,' Joe said, pulling a serious face. 'Oh, by the way. Did I ask yer fer a contribution ter the street party?'

It's bloody little short of blackmail, groaned Misery to himself as he reluctantly handed over two one pound notes.

60

Chapter Six

The winter of 'thirty-five was very cold, with intermittent snow and ice and dense yellow fogs. The inclement weather affected trade, and transport was badly disrupted. Ships became marooned mid-stream, trains were cancelled, and the vehicles of cartage firms were abandoned throughout London, although the horse-carts usually got home. When the terrified animals were held by their halters and led along the road they usually calmed down, and when they somehow sensed that they were nearing familiar surroundings the car-men were able to jump up in the dicky seats and let the animals plod on without assistance. Another ploy of the car-men was to steer the iron-rimmed wheels into the tram tracks and glide home that way. It was not uncommon for car-men to miss the turn-off and find themselves in the tram depots, where they spent the night sleeping in one of the tramcars. The unfortunate horses had to bed down on the cold concrete surface, much to the chagrin of depot superintendents.

In October Kate Morgan lost her job as barmaid. She had been suffering with a bad cough which refused to get any better. Connie was worried; she could see the change. Her normally lively mother was pale and weak and had to spend some time in bed. Connie would take her tea and toast before she left for work, and Helen would look in during the day. But the cough only got worse and, when Kate was able to get up, the doctor sent her to the hospital for tests. She had contracted TB, and Connie was close to tears as she watched her mother leave in an ambulance to go to one of the new clinics that had just opened in Sussex. Helen had suggested that Connie stay with her, but the young girl was determined to look after herself. She knew that, as it was, Helen was hard pushed to care for her own family. Matthew was out of work again, and Molly had been ill twice that winter. Her chest was weak and the fogs made it hard for her to breathe. At work, Connie found some cheer in talking to the effervescent young Michael. His cheerful banter and infectious laugh made it easier for her to get through the day. Michael was so excited at the prospect of going into the Royal Navy, and he promised to keep in touch after he had joined up.

Connie was growing fast, her thin legs were becoming more shapely and her breasts were developing; her face was losing its childish appearance and her lips had become fuller and more expressive. Connie was a little confused at the changes she was experiencing, and felt the occasional tinge of excitement deep within her. She had also started to experience dreams that made her feel embarrassed and ashamed when she remembered them the next morning. The job at the bottling stores was becoming almost unbearable, and she had thought about looking for another one. Helen was urging Molly to leave the job, too. She had lost a lot of time lately because of ill-health and her mother blamed the damp environment of the railway arches for her daughter's illnesses, although she knew that it really only aggravated Molly's condition rather than caused it. The hospital had said long ago that she would always suffer because of her underdeveloped lungs.

Just before Christmas Connie went with Helen and Matthew to see Kate at the sanatorium near Hastings. The long wards were painted white and large windows let in the low winter light. The day was cold and dreary and a light rain had been falling since dawn. Kate was sitting in a comfortable chair beside her bed and when Connie saw her she was shocked. Kate was ashen-faced and her eyes had heavy dark circles around them. She showed little emotion as the small party assembled around her bed and Connie hugged her. The atmosphere was unbearably tense as the visitors tried to make conversation. Kate seemed preoccupied and bored with Helen's account of the current state of affairs in Ironmonger Street. Matthew was sitting on the edge of his uncomfortable chair without saying much, and Connie was silent and physically shaken at her mother's appearance. When finally she managed to tell Kate about her intention to change her job her mother merely nodded and looked away down the ward. Helen felt for her niece; Kate's attitude towards her daughter was one of indifference. Helen knew that there had never been any show of warmth or affection, nor any of the closeness that would be normal between a mother and her daughter and it rankled. She could make allowances for Kate's wayward behaviour and the numerous relationships she had had with men, but she could never forgive her for her coldness towards her own daughter. It was as though Connie was an unwelcome responsibility, and her presence was an intrusion into Kate Morgan's life.

At last, the two hours were up and the ward sister rang a small bell at the end of the ward. Kate looked relieved that the visit was over and she smiled mirthlessly as Helen said, 'You'll be 'ome soon, Kate.'

'I'm 'ere fer six months, sis,' Kate said slowly. 'Yer better get used to it – I 'ave.'

Helen's face was grim as she turned and walked down the long ward with Matthew and Connie following in her wake. At the door Connie turned to wave to her mother, but she was already talking to the patient next to her and she had her back to her daughter. Matthew noticed the look in Connie's eyes and with a rare show of emotion he put his arm around her shoulders as they walked out into the wide corridor.

Christmas was a sober affair. Connie spent most of the holiday period with the Bartletts and in Molly's company. Concern for her mother's health caused the young girl to be even more quiet and thoughtful. She knew enough about tuberculosis to realise that her mother would be in hospital for a very long time, and that often the disease proved to be fatal. Helen and Matthew watched the change taking place in their niece, but they could do little to alleviate her fears. They were also concerned that Connie insisted on staying alone in the flat.

'It's not right that she should be there all by 'erself, Matt,' Helen remarked. 'She'll only brood. She should stay wiv us.'

Matthew shrugged his shoulders. 'She's growin' up, 'Elen. She prob'ly wants ter spend some time on 'er own. There's nufink we can do, except keep an eye on 'er.'

Helen stroked the side of her face thoughtfully. 'It really upset me the way Kate was wiv young Connie. It was almost as though she didn't want ter see 'er. It's not right the way she treats the poor little mite.'

'It's what I've said all along,' Matthew answered. 'Connie's bin an inconvenience ter yer sister. She didn't want 'er, an' she's makin' a good show of lettin' the kid know – an' us if it comes to it.'

Helen did not answer. She did not want to get into an argument with Matt. He had been short tempered ever since he had lost his job, but she had to concede that he was right. Kate was ill, and so her attitude to her daughter at the hospital was, to some extent, excusable, but there had never been any show of love, only a tolerance and shallow affection. Helen worried about the long-term effects of Kate's attitude on her daughter. Connie was a sensible girl, but the mind was a funny thing, she mused. None of the love shown by the girl to her mother was reciprocated. And, as Connie was now growing up and beginning to understand things, she might soon start to judge her mother – and blame her.

The new year started cold and foggy. More factories closed, and the dole queues grew longer. In Germany the rantings of Adolf Hitler were sending shock waves across Europe. The German army marched back into the Rhineland and, when the Spanish Civil War broke out, the German air force interfered on the side of General Franco's forces. The majority of people in England, however, still espoused the cause of pacifism. Calls to re-arm were dismissed as scaremongering, and some cartoonists portrayed the pleadings of the 're-armers' as the insane ravings of evil factory bosses and avaricious arms dealers. General opinion held that another war was out of the question and few believed that Germany would ever dare to attempt another war against England.

Joe Cooper wandered slowly amongst the crowds at Speakers' Corner one Sunday in 1936. Occasionally there was a flicker of recognition as he passed a heavily built young man, but Joe would ignore him and walk on. Word had it that the Blackshirts were planning violence against one of the trade union speakers and the Bermondsey men were ready.

A loud-voiced orator was urging his audience to march on Parliament and demand a re-armament programme. ''Ave yer fergot 1914? Well I ain't,' he shouted.

'Nor 'ave I,' someone replied. 'I got gassed in France.'

An elderly man in a grubby mackintosh took a wet stub

from his mouth and called out, 'My ole granfarvver got gassed.'

'In the war?'

'No, in the kitchen. 'E done 'imself in.'

The laughter from the audience encouraged the heckler, and he rammed his hands into his coat pockets and rocked back on his heels. 'My ole granfarvver used ter come 'ere every Sunday, listenin' ter the likes o' you frightened the bleedin' life out of 'im. That's why 'e gassed 'imself.'

'I wish yer'd put a tanner in the meter an' do yerself a favour,' shouted the speaker, to more laughter.

'I ain't got a tanner. I'm on the bloody dole.'

'If this country 'ad the sense ter re-arm there wouldn't be any unemployment. We'd all 'ave a job ter go to,' the speaker continued, waving his finger at the heckler.

'Listen you,' his antagonist shouted as he stepped forward a pace or two. 'I ain't got no intention of workin' in a bleedin' arms factory.'

'By the look o' you, yer ain't got no intention o' workin' anywhere,' countered the orator, grinning at his own jibe.

'Why, yer saucy git. I was workin' when you was a dirty idea in yer farvver's 'ead. I can work wiv the best of 'em.'

'An' the worst of 'em,' a voice called out from the back of the crowd.

The orator struggled to regain the attention of his audience and he raised his hands skywards for order. 'Mark my words well, friends,' he began. 'If we let the Germans get away wiv it we're gonna be sorry. Before long they'll be marchin' up the Mall.'

The crowd erupted and one or two young men made for the speaker, their fists clenched.

'Order! Order!' shouted a heavily built man who was standing by the speaker.

The crowd held back as the big man faced them, his hands held out in front of his chest. 'Now listen, brothers,' he said in a broad Irish accent. 'As me darlin' ole mother used ter say, there are those who are for us, an' those who are agin us, an' my name's Maginnis.'

'Piss orf, Paddy. Go back ter yer own soap box,' someone called out.

The large Irishman smiled broadly. 'Sure 'tis an unsociable crowd ye are, so I'm away, my friends. But first I'll leave yerse with a blessin' ter be gettin' on with. When yer toime comes may yerse be in heaven a half an hour before the divil knows you're dead.'

The speaker turned his attention to his audience once more as the laughing Irishman walked away somewhat unsteadily. The heckler in the grubby mackintosh walked away, too, his eyes focused on another group who were shouting abuse at a speaker wearing a dog-collar and he walked over to direct a tirade of obscenities at the pacifist minister.

Soon the crowds began to drift away and Joe breathed easier. The Blackshirts were not going to put in an appearance today after all. I'm getting a little too old for all this, he told himself as he went to join his friends.

Connie Morgan heard it from Carrie Jones and she told Molly as they walked to work one Monday morning.

'There's jobs goin' at Peek's. Let's take the afternoon off an' go roun' there. They pay more than we're gettin'.'

Molly stopped in her tracks. 'Why wait? Let's go roun' there right now. I'm fed up wiv labellin', ain't you?'

Connie grinned. 'C'mon then, Molly. We might be lucky. The extra money'll come in 'andy.'

Molly nodded her agreement. 'My mum's worried. Dad got

'imself in debt wiv the moneylender again. If we get the job I can give up a bit more.'

'Me, too,' Connie replied. 'My mum's comin' 'ome soon an' she won't be able ter work fer some time yet.'

Molly took her cousin's arm as they crossed the Tower Bridge Road and walked purposefully towards Grange Road. The market stalls were already set up and the smell of fresh fruit carried on the slight breeze. Trams rattled by, and horse-carts made a crunching sound as the iron-rimmed wheels passed over the cobbles. When they neared the Trocette Picture House Connie squeezed her cousin's arm. 'Cor! Look Molly!'

The large poster over the entrance spelt out in bold red lettering: Frank Capra's, *It Happened One Night*, starring Clark Gable and Claudette Colbert.

'I fink Clark Gable's lovely, Con.'

'So do I, Molly.'

'We'll 'ave ter see that picture.'

'If we get the job let's celebrate an' go up there ternight.'

'Yeah, let's.'

Later that evening the two girls left the cinema and walked slowly back to Ironmonger Street. They had been silent for a while, each absorbed in their own thoughts. Suddenly Molly said, 'I didn't fink we'd get the job. I got scared when she asked me about bein' under the 'ospital.'

Connie laughed aloud. 'Wasn't she funny-lookin'. She reminded me of ole Miss Perkins at school. I nearly burst out laughin' when I saw them glasses on the end of 'er nose.'

Molly giggled. 'Jus' fancy. Twenty two an' sixpence a week, an' as many biscuits as we can eat.'

'Wasn't that smell nice,' said Connie as they turned into Ironmonger Street. 'I love the smell of biscuits, though I bet we won't be sayin' that after a few weeks there.'

They walked down the quiet, dark street and turned into the

block entrance. The gaslight flickered as they climbed the wooden staircase and tramped noisily along the landing. After bidding Molly good night Connie climbed the shadowy stairs to her fourth-floor flat and let herself in. The flat felt strangely cold, although the night was mild. She lit the gaslamp and drew the curtains and then she boiled the kettle and made herself a cup of cocoa. There were a few biscuits left in the tin and Connie smiled to herself. After a few weeks at Peek's I won't be able to look at these, she thought, as she nibbled on a stale digestive and sipped her drink. From outside the distant sound of a tug whistle and noises from the railway yard carried up into the room. A train whistle sounded faintly as she prepared herself for bed, and she was suddenly consumed by a feeling of loneliness. She missed her mother and hated to be in the flat alone.

Connie heard the clock on the mantelshelf strike eleven as she lay in bed staring up at the flaking ceiling. She and Molly would be starting their new jobs tomorrow and her mother would be home soon. She should be feeling happy, but instead she was aware of a strange feeling that seemed to be working away deep down inside of her. She sighed deeply and closed her eyes but sleep would not come. She twisted restlessly as her thoughts centred on her mother. Her illness was serious and she might not get better. Connie had overheard Helen talking to Matthew about how pulmonary tuberculosis had killed old Betty Flicker and Mr Brown. She had also commented that the way Kate had carried on hadn't helped. Connie wondered about those remarks. Her mother had been so secretive about her personal life. It was always, 'Somebody I've got to see' or 'I've been invited out'. She had never brought her friends back to the flat to meet Connie. Those nights she was sent to the Bartletts to stay might have meant that her mother was intending to bring someone back and didn't want her to know, Connie thought.

And why would no one ever let her know anything about her father? As much as she tried Connie knew she would not learn who her father was, or how he had died – at least not from her mother. Why should she be so secretive? What was she hiding? Maybe her father was still alive. Maybe that was why Kate didn't want her to know.

One day I'll find out the truth, Connie vowed, as she turned on her side and closed her eyes. Dreamy images formed into a tall dashing man with jet-black hair walking towards her. She sighed in her sleep, and pressed her cheek deeper into the pillow.

Chapter Seven

Solly Jacobs had a fishmonger's stall in the Tower Bridge Road market. Solly was a heavily built man in his forties, the eldest son of a Jewish immigrant from Poland. He was also a regular attender at the local synagogue and a leader of the Jewish community in Bermondsey. Solly had been growing concerned about the rise of the British fascists and he was determined that Oswald Mosley's crowd of Blackshirts would get a bloody nose if they attempted to go ahead with their intended march along the Old Kent Road.

Solly's cousin Hymie had been present when Oswald Mosley marched down the Mile End Road at the head of his black-uniformed followers and the following week he paid his relative a visit.

'I tell yer, Solly, it was sheer bloody murder. The swine were chantin' and jeerin', and when our lads tried to break up the march the police on 'orseback lashed out with their truncheons. There were a few cracked 'eads and one or two of the boys got trampled by the horses, but that was only the start. Outside the synagogue some young lads rushed the column. My God, it was terrible! Young Bernie Meyer got pushed through a shop window and another young boy got a bottle in 'is face. The fightin' spilled into the side streets an' the swine were kickin' out at everyone. They've got to be stopped, Solly.

71

We've got to get more organised or we're done fer.'

The big fishmonger's face darkened with anger and he laid his hand on Hymie's shoulder. 'Listen my friend,' he said softly. 'We all know about the sufferin' of our people in Germany, an' we all know we mustn't let it 'appen 'ere. I've already called a meetin'. Rest easy, I'll keep yer informed.'

Two days later Solly gathered his group together in the backroom of his local pub, The Swan and, to enthusiastic applause, he vowed that the Blackshirt swine would live to regret it if they ever set foot in Bermondsey. Solly held his hands up for silence and when the cheering and clapping died down he introduced the guest speaker.

Joe Cooper stood up and hooked his thumbs through his wide braces. 'Yer might ask, brothers, what's a gentile doin' at a Jewish gatherin',' he began in a loud voice. 'Well I make no excuses fer bein' 'ere ternight. I'm a trade unionist, an' your fight is our fight. If we allow this fascist scum ter ride roughshod over us ordinary people, then we deserve the consequences.'

Loud applause greeted his statement and Joe leaned forward, his clenched fists resting on the bare wooden table. 'Let me ask yer somefink, bruvvers. Is there anyfink in yer teachin' that ferbids yer from bein' trade unionists? Is there anyfink that ses yer can't vote, or can't be as equal as yer gentile bruvvers? 'Course there ain't. But I tell yer. There's a lot in the manifesto of the British Union of Fascists that ses jus' that. The Blackshirts are comin' fer you lot terday. They'll be comin' fer us termorrer, an' they'll be comin' fer Gawd knows who the next day.'

The clapping and cheering went on as Solly slapped Joe Cooper on the back and clasped his hand in a show of gratitude. Joe waited for the noise to die down then he hooked his thumbs through his braces once more. 'I only wanna say one more fing, bruvvers. When yer face the Blackshirts my lads'll be there wiv yer.'

The meeting had broken up and Solly stood beside Joe in the public bar. Jack Rabin, the landlord, had been talking to a small group of men and when he came over he leaned over the counter. 'There's some more wanna sign up, Solly. If this keeps up we'll 'ave a bloody army by next week.'

Joe sipped his beer. 'I'll muster a good crowd, Solly. A lot o' the lads remember the Armitage trouble way back. They ain't fergot what 'appened to us when we was out on the cobbles. The firm got the 'ard men in. It's them sort o' gits that's marchin' wiv Mosley, yer can bet on it.'

Solly nodded his agreement. 'We gotta be careful, Joe. We ain't gonna be dealin' wiv know-nufinks. Them Blackshirts know the score. They got right nasty in Mile End. A few of our boys got a pastin'. One got aimed through a plate-glass winder. It got ugly, I can tell yer. The law's gonna be out in force on this march. We've gotta be shrewd or we won't get anywhere near the fascist bastards.'

Joe finished his drink and put his hand up when Solly offered to buy another. 'I've gotta get goin', Solly. My Sadie ain't too well. She don't like me bein' out fer long.'

The Jewish fishmonger watched as Joe Cooper walked out through the door, then he turned to Jack Rabin. ''E's a good man, Jack. We need the likes of 'im ter stand wiv us,' he said.

The landlord looked thoughtful. 'I dunno, Solly. I'm always a bit cautious about that sort. I don't want us ter be used as fodder fer their battles.'

Solly laughed aloud. 'Jack, yer gettin' suspicious in yer old age. Let me tell yer about Joe Cooper. I've known 'im fer ages. Joe's a foreman at the tin bashers in Ironmonger Street. 'E's bin campaignin' fer years ter get a union in there. Back in twenty-six 'e was up front in a strike at the factory. The owners brought in a team ter break up the strike an' Joe Cooper ended up on the floor wiv boots goin' in all round 'im. 'E got took away in a Black Maria an' ended up in front of the beak. I tell yer, that man's got principles. I'll tell yer somefink else as well. Joe's wife is stuck in a wheelchair wiv polio. She's bin that way fer years. If Joe ain't out at meetin's 'e's lookin' after 'er. Yer don't 'ave ter worry about 'im.'

The pub landlord stroked his chin. 'If 'e's after startin' up a union at the factory, 'ow comes they ain't sacked 'im?'

'They're not that stupid,' Solly laughed. 'Joe knows 'is job. They don't come no better. All the workers likes 'im and 'e gets the best out of 'em. The guv'nors know that. No, Jack. They ain't that stupid.'

Connie and Molly were settled in their new jobs at Peek Frean's biscuit factory. The Bartletts were on relief, as Molly's was the only money coming into the household. Kate had come home from the sanatorium and she spent most of her time sitting by the window, looking down on the street. Her body was constantly wracked by a dry, rasping cough and Connie became increasingly worried as she watched the life slowly draining from her mother. Every morning, before she set out for work, Connie helped her mother into the armchair and brought her tea and thin toast, then she made the bed and tidied up. When the weather was cold Connie would light the fire and bring in a supply of coal which she piled up in the scuttle beside the hearth. In the evening there was the usual round of chores to do before she settled her mother for the night. During the time Connie was at work Helen came in with a meal. Kate rarely ever ventured out and, on the one or two occasions that she managed to get down the stairs and out into the street, she was immediately seized with a spasm of coughing. Her face became drained of colour and she had to lean against the wall until she recovered enough to move. During the first few months her party friends had called around often to see her, but slowly the number of visitors diminished until there were no callers or enquirers – except for the people from the street. Connie's life settled into a dull, monotonous routine, she rarely ever went out in the evenings or at weekends, and her only chance to get away from the depressing flat was when she slipped downstairs to chat to the Bartletts. Helen and Matthew were becoming increasingly worried about the girl.

'It ain't natural fer a kid that age ter be nursemaid an' drudge. She should 'ave a life of 'er own,' Matthew remarked.

Helen had to agree with her husband. 'I'm worried sick about 'er, Matt, but what can we do? There's nufink we can do. All I wish is that Kate would show a little more affection to 'er. That kid would get more appreciation from an outsider. I feel really sorry fer the poor little cow.'

The long, repetitious hours spent working on the factory belt and the mundane, thankless chores were slowly taking their toll. Connie was growing into a woman without experiencing the normal carefree life of a teenager. She was not yet sixteen and already she had the responsibilities and cares of a mature adult. At the factory, those who knew of Connie's circumstances understood her refusal to socialise outside of working hours, but others saw her as aloof and hard to get on with. She would have loved to join them on their nights out, but always there was her sick mother waiting impatiently for her to put the key in the lock each evening. Kate was becoming very miserable, and if Connie stopped to chat on the street corner or outside the factory gate for a few minutes longer than usual she would accuse her daughter of not caring, and of spending too much time away from the flat. Connie could only grit her teeth and ignore the unreasonable outbursts. Only at night in her small bedroom when she sat reading or merely resting on the bed, could Connie allow herself to unwind. Then she would sometimes break down and cry in her misery and pain.

Once or twice Kate seemed to rally, and it was on those rare occasions she would sit upright in her high-backed chair beside the window and chat vivaciously about some of the jobs she had had. Connie listened intently, hoping her mother might let slip something about her father, but it was not to be. Once Kate mentioned her time at the Armitage factory, and that she had left the firm the week following a factory outing. When Connie prompted her mother to go on, Kate had replied that there was a bit of an upset and it was of no consequence. She had then lapsed into a moody silence and stared thoughtfully down into the quiet evening street.

On the last Friday evening of November, as the young girl hurried home from the factory, she had a strange feeling of unease. Molly was off sick with her chest and Kate had been racked with a particularly bad coughing spell that morning. The weather was cold and damp, with a fog settling in. Connie stopped off at the Tower Bridge Road for some bread and fresh milk, and when she finally arrived home she was met by a worried-looking Helen.

'It's yer mum, luv,' she said. 'She's 'ad a bad turn. The doctor's bin. 'E said she's gotta go away.'

Connie hurried past her aunt into the drab interior of the flat. Kate was sitting up in bed with a blanket pulled around her shoulders. She was drained of colour, and her eyes were black-rimmed and sunken. Connie sat on the edge of the bed and took her mother's clammy hands in hers. A sickening rush of fear and dread made her tremble as she asked, 'What is it, Mum?'

'I'm dyin', child. I can't get me breath. The pain's terrible.'

For a moment or two Connie felt panic. She tried to control her emotions and force a smile. 'You'll be all right, Mum,' she said. 'It's the cold and fog. When yer get ter the 'ospital they'll give yer somefink fer the pain. You'll feel better then.'

Kate squeezed her daughter's hands in a weak grip. 'You're a good child, Con. I know I've not bin one ter say much, but I know what yer've give up all these months ter look after me. I'm only sorry I won't be able ter make it up ter yer.'

Connie felt the tears rising. 'Don't talk like that, Mum. You'll be okay. You see if yer don't.'

Kate withdrew her hands from Connie's grasp and pulled the blanket tighter around her sagging shoulders. 'Listen, Con. I don't fink I'm gonna see this place again, so I want yer ter pay attention ter what I'm gonna say. I've not bin a family woman like me sister. I've gone me own way an' enjoyed me life, 'cos that's the way I wanted it. I never wanted ter settle down wiv a man, until I met yer farvver. I didn't want ter fall fer a kid eivver, but I did. When you come along I was feelin' sorry fer meself, but I 'ad ter accept me lot. You know what they say, if yer makes yer bed, yer gotta lie in it. I've gotta say this, though, yer never brought me any trouble. Yer've . . .' Kate's words were interrupted with a spasm of coughing and Connie handed her mother a handkerchief. When she finally ceased and wiped the cold sweat from her forehead, she smiled weakly at Connie. 'Yer've always bin a lovin' child,' she said, 'an' I know I ain't appreciated yer the way I should 'ave. I know 'ow yer've give up yer nights out ter look after me.'

Connie's eyes misted and she stared down at the bedclothes. 'I'm not worried about goin' out nights, Mum. I'd sooner be 'ome lookin' after you.'

Kate reached out and squeezed her daughter's hands. 'Yer a very pretty girl, Con. One day soon the boys are gonna start knockin' fer yer. Jus' promise me somefink.'

Connie nodded as she kept her eyes averted from her mother's face.

'Promise me you'll find a nice lad an' settle down. Don't play the field like I did, girl. It'll only bring yer un'appiness.'

'I promise, Mum,' Connie said tearfully.

Kate forced a weak smile. 'That's my girl. Now go an' make me a cup o' tea before the amb'lance comes.'

November had brought some extra orders to the Armitage factory and the workers were put on full time until Christmas. Mary Brown and her friend Joyce Spinks both got work there again and during their first lunch break they sat together in the canteen and gossiped.

'I don't like that foreman, Joyce.'

''E ain't a patch on Joe Cooper,' Mary said.

'Yer tellin' me,' Joyce replied, as she wiped her plate with a piece of dry bread. 'The silly bleeder's bin up an' down that gangway all mornin'. Every time I looked round there 'e was, starin' at me.'

Mary grinned. 'I reckon e' fancies yer, Joyce. 'E ain't married, yer know.'

'Well I am, an' in any case, I don't fancy old age creepin' all over me.'

Mary pushed her empty plate away and lit up a cigarette.

'I didn't know yer started smokin',' Joyce said in surprise.

'Yeah, I started when our Maggie was born. Couldn't get no sleep fer the first few months wiv 'er cryin' an' I found it settled me nerves.'

'My Arfur can't stand me smokin',' Joyce said. ''E reckons women who smoke look like prossers.'

Mary snorted. ''Ow many prossers does your Arfur know?'

Joyce dismissed her friend's remark with a limp-wristed wave. ''Ere Mary. They tell me Joe Cooper ended up gettin' six months.'

'Yeah, that's right. 'E should get a couple o' months off fer good be'aviour.'

Joyce took out a small mirror from her handbag and studied herself for a few seconds. 'I bet Joe's wife's cut up, 'er bein' the way she is.'

Mary puffed on her cigarette and blew a jet of smoke ceiling-wards. 'I dunno about that. They don't get on, yer know. Poor ole Joe 'as ter do everyfink fer 'er. 'E pushes 'er everywhere in that wheelchair, an' I've seen 'im up the market gettin' the shoppin'. Poor sod was like an errand boy.'

'Who's lookin' after 'is missus while 'e's away then, Mary?'

'Why, that relation of 'ers. Miserable ole cow she is. I fink she was the one who poisoned 'er mind. Every time I saw Joe an' 'is missus out tergevver she was always moanin' at 'im. Mind you though, 'e was always 'avin' ter rush off ter meetin's. 'E'll never change.'

'I dunno, Mary. 'E might be different now. 'E's got time ter fink about fings. It mus' be 'ard goin' away fer bashin' up a couple o' Blackshirts.'

Mary laughed. ''E didn't get six months fer bashin' up Blackshirts. Joe got nicked fer punchin' a copper.'

'Did 'e? I didn't know that.'

Mary nodded knowingly. 'My Frank was up the Old Kent Road when it 'appened.'

'July wasn't it, Mary?'

'No, it was in June. Joe an' a load of 'is union mates was standin' wiv the Jew boys when Mosley's marchers come up. Somebody slung a brick at 'em an' the police on 'orses galloped up wiv their big sticks slashin' out. Accordin' ter my Frank there was a lot o' Mosley's supporters waitin' in the crowd. The fists were flyin' everywhere an' Joe caught this copper in the jaw so they took 'im away. That last affair outside the factory went against 'im. Most o' the ovvers got bound over. Bloody shame really. Trust poor ole Joe ter get roped in.'

'Yeah, it's a shame,' Joyce said feelingly. ''E's such a nice bloke really.'

Mary outed her cigarette in a saucer. 'What about that time 'e got the Jubilee party up fer the kids. 'E even got ole Misery Martin ter chip in, though Gawd knows 'ow 'e managed that. Ole Martin wouldn't give yer the drippin's from 'is nose!'

''As 'e still got that shop, Mary?'

'Yeah. Misery's bin there fer over twenty years. 'E's breakin' up now though.'

Joyce scratched the back of her head and watched the progress of a young lad who was trying to reach the table without spilling any of his soup. 'It ain't changed much round 'ere, 'as it, Mary? D'yer remember when we was kids?'

Mary nodded her head slowly. 'What about after work on Fridays, when we used ter go up West. We used ter dream about findin' ourselves a couple o' toffs, an' what did we both end up wiv? Two lads from Tower Bridge Road.'

Joyce sniffed. 'I wouldn't give my Arfur up fer no bloody toff.'

'No, nor would I,' Mary said. 'My Frank's as good as gold. It makes yer fink, though, don't it?'

The hooter sounded and there was a noisy scraping of chairs as the workforce started to leave the canteen. Mary gathered up her handbag and waited while Joyce looked at her reflection in the small mirror once more.

'You mind yer don't wipe an 'ole in that plate, Pete,' Mary said with mock seriousness to the young lad who was busy mopping up the last of his soup with a hunk of bread.

Pete ignored the jibe and burped loudly as he pushed the plate to one side.

'C'mon, Joyce. It's like feedin' time at the zoo round 'ere,' Mary groaned.

Chapter Eight

Connie spent another quiet Christmas with the Bartletts. Kate was settled in the sanatorium and her condition had improved slightly, although her cough was still giving her trouble. Helen was now going out early each morning to do office cleaning, and Matthew was supplementing his dole money by selling bits and pieces of haberdashery from a suitcase in the East End markets. Every Monday morning Helen Bartlett would take her best pair of sheets to the pawnbroker's and accept the seven and sixpence in exchange so that her husband could buy his wares. The business had to be done 'over the water', away from the snoops and busybodies at the Relief Office. The wholesalers in Brick Lane sold off the remnants of their stock to people like Matthew, but he had to wait until the bulk buyers had been accommodated. On a good week Matthew recouped his original seven and sixpence by Thursday, with just enough bits and pieces left over to make a tiny profit by the end of the week. Some of the Eastenders who frequented the markets made a show of interest, picking up the thimbles, collar studs and coloured cottons as if they had been looking everywhere for them.

''Ere look, Sal. 'E's got collar studs. Me ole man's right out o' collar studs.'

''E's got packets o' needles an' all, Queenie. I gotta lot o' sewin' ter do. I fink I'll get a packet.'

Matthew was not fooled. Nearly every week Queenie needed collar studs, although he was sure that her husband now possessed more studs than shirts. As for Sally, she must have mislaid dozens of needles – she had bought a packet every Friday for the past two months. But Matthew was eternally grateful to Eastenders like Queenie and Sally whose patronage allowed him to retain some of his dignity, which he had felt he was gradually losing in the endless dole queues.

The year of 1936 ended with a major topic being discussed in every pub and on every doorstep in dockland Bermondsey. In the Horseshoe the old domino group would have had much to say about the abdication, but the only survivor, George Baker, rarely ventured as far as the pub. A new generation was holding court. Terry Hicks and Bill Mullins were dockers, and conveniently lived a few doors down from the pub.

Terry, the new spokesman, was adamant. 'I tell yer, Bill. 'E's the King of England. 'E's not the same as the likes o' you an' me.'

'The likes o' you an' me wouldn't marry a foreigner who's already wore out two ole men, Terry.'

'Well I reckon 'e should put the country first. Yer can't go against the church an' the country when yer a king. I mean, there's yer coronation an' yer pomp an' splender. It's yer 'eritage, Bill.'

'Sod yer pomp an' splender. 'E could get married in a regist'ry office like anybody else.'

'C'mon, Bill. Yer can't do fings like that when yer a king o' yer country. Just imagine Edward walkin' down the town 'all steps wiv that there Mrs Simpson on 'is arm an' some soppy bleeder runnin' down the steps after 'im, shoutin' out, "don't forget yer crown, Ted".'

When the laughter subsided Terry went on. 'All right, I grant yer that 'e's in love wiv 'er, but what's ter stop 'im gettin' spliced ter lady so-an'-so an' givin' 'er one every once in a while fer the sake o' the Royal line. 'E's got ole Mrs Simpson on the quiet an' everybody's 'appy.'

'P'raps 'e don't want ter marry some ugly ole aristocrat, jus' ter please the likes o' you, an' I don't s'pose that there Mrs Simpson would be very 'appy wiv that arrangement, Tel.'

'It ain't a question o' what makes Mrs Simpson 'appy. 'E's got the country ter fink about, Bill, an' in any case, 'e don't 'ave ter marry an ugly aristocrat. There mus' be a few good-lookin' ones amongst 'em, surely ter Gawd.'

Bill refused to be shaken. 'I don't care what yer say. 'E's got the right ter pick an' choose, jus' like anybody else. I say good luck to 'im. At least 'e's got the guts ter come out wiv it.'

The argument was suspended while fresh pints were brought from the crowded bar and then the discussion went on until closing time.

The young couple had met by chance, and at first she had almost walked past without looking at the upright figure in a naval uniform. It was he who stopped and hailed the pretty blond-haired girl.

''Ello, Con. Remember me?' he said brightly.

Connie flushed as she looked up at the grinning Michael Donovan. 'Yer did it then,' she exclaimed, her eyes travelling from his polished shoes up to his cap, which was perched at a jaunty angle. 'I didn't reco'nise yer, Michael. Yer do look smart. 'Ow long yer bin in the navy?'

'Six months. I'm stationed down in Portsmouth, but I'm off ter sea next week.'

Connie put her shopping bag down on the pavement and rubbed her stiff fingers together. 'When d'yer go back off leave?'

'Sunday night. We're sailin' on Tuesday. We're goin' ter Gib,' Michael said proudly.

'Gib?'

'Gibraltar. Well, that's our first port o' call. We're goin' on ter the Med.'

'Lucky you,' Connie said, smiling as she looked into his fresh-cut features. 'I'll be finkin' about yer when I'm sittin' there packin' 'orrible biscuits.'

Michael took off his cap and ran his fingers through a mop of fair hair. ''Ow's yer friend Molly?'

'She's okay. We're still workin' tergevver, but at Peek Frean's now. She's bin off work a lot lately. She was pretty rough over Christmas.'

Michael reached down and picked up Connie's shopping bag. 'C'mon, I'll carry it back fer yer.'

The two young people threaded their way in and out of the Saturday morning shoppers and turned off into a side street. Michael walked with a slight swagger and Connie felt strangely elated as she walked by his side. She could not help but notice the change in the lad. His gaunt face had filled out and it had a healthy glow about it. He seemed to have grown taller and put on some weight. Connie had to concede that he looked quite dashing in his uniform and she gave him a few shy glances as they walked towards Ironmonger Street.

'I was finkin',' Michael said suddenly. 'Would yer like ter come up the Globe ternight? There's a good film up there.'

Connie almost blurted out yes, but she checked herself and appeared to consider the offer for a few moments. 'Okay. What's on?'

'It's a musical. "Swing Time", wiv Ginger Rogers an' Fred Astaire.'

Connie did not confess to the lad that she had already seen

the film; instead she pretended surprise. 'We'll 'ave ter get up there early. It'll be packed,' she said.

The red February sun gave little heat and the coppery cloud foreboded more bad weather. Smoke drifted upwards from red chimney pots, and moisture clung to the hard cobbles and grey-slated roofs as the two strolled into Ironmonger Street. Ahead, the ugly factory loomed up in the dull morning light and, halfway down the small turning, they could see the knife-grinder bent over a spinning stone, his foot working away at the treadle. One or two children were playing in the street, and Misery Martin, now a grizzled, bent figure, was sweeping the pavement outside his shop, his lips moving as he muttered to himself. To the left, the tall tenement block looked drab and forbidding, and to the right the row of rundown terraced houses were nearly all sporting clean lace curtains and whitened doorsteps. The two stopped at the block entrance and Connie took the bag from her escort.

'Fanks, Michael,' she said. 'What time yer comin' round?'

'I'll be 'ere sharp on seven. Shall I wait 'ere fer yer, Con?'

'All right. See yer then, Michael,' she said.

'By the way, call me Mick, all me pals do.'

Connie stood by the entrance and watched the swaggering figure walking away along the turning. When Michael had disappeared from her view she hurried up the stairs and handed Helen her shopping. Later, as she pottered about the drab flat, Connie felt pangs of excitement in the pit of her stomach. Michael had altered since the last time she had seen him, and he certainly looked handsome in his uniform. She hummed happily to herself as she brushed the threadbare carpet and dusted the china ornaments. Tonight would be exciting, and tomorrow she would be able to tell Molly all about it. With the thought came a sudden feeling of guilt and she sat down at the table. How would Molly react? she wondered. Would she be happy for her, or would she feel she was taking second place in her affection? Connie felt suddenly confused. She was aware how dependent Molly had become lately. As her health deteriorated Molly seemed to have lost her eager interest in things, and her world had grown narrow and confined. Connie was the only real friend Molly had, and now she began to feel it as a burden. It seemed that through her love for Molly, she was being held back from her natural instincts and inclinations and forced to continue a childhood she was quickly outgrowing. As Connie sat alone in the quiet flat the sad, misshapen figure of her cousin would not leave her thoughts. Connie felt an anger welling up inside her. She wanted her first date to be a happy, exciting evening, but feelings of guilt were already tormenting her. Why did Molly have to make so many demands upon her? For a moment, sitting thinking at the table, Connie could hardly recognise herself. She quickly dismissed her ugly thoughts as she clenched her hands tightly and bit on her lip. She was being so silly, she told herself. She loved Molly and here she was creating a big problem out of such a trivial little affair. Her shame made her flush and she tried to calm her feelings. It was just going to be a night out – her first night out with a boy. Perhaps in her nervousness and anticipation she was just making problems for herself. Connie realised that if she allowed herself to carry on thinking about things she would only become more unhappy. With a deep sigh she rested her head on the table and pressed her tightly closed eyes against her arm.

It was seven o'clock exactly when Michael Donovan walked into Ironmonger Street. The turning was quiet and a rising wind rustled dirty bits of paper and toffee wrappers and carried them along the gutter. At the entrance to the tenement block the young sailor halted and thrust his hands deep into the pockets of his service raincoat. He waited patiently for a few minutes, then he turned and walked slowly along the length of the street. Ten minutes later his elation was turning to disappointment. There was no sign of Connie. Maybe there was something wrong? Perhaps her mother had forbidden her to go out? Michael decided to give it another ten minutes and then go home. As he turned he saw her coming towards him, her shapely figure clearly outlined beneath the tight-fitting coat she wore. Connie's hair was pulled back behind her head and tied with a black bow, and he noticed that her face seemed flushed. Michael smiled as she reached him and he could see a slight puffiness around her eyes. Her full lips were parted in a self-conscious smile and her even white teeth shone in the darkness of the evening.

'I'm sorry I'm late,' she said breathlessly. 'I 'ad a lot ter do an' the time flew.'

Michael grinned as he held out his arm. 'I thought yer mum might 'ave stopped yer comin' out.'

Connie slipped her arm through his and felt a strange sensation as she set out beside him. 'Me mum's in 'ospital. She's bin there fer a long time now,' she said.

Michael looked at her. 'What's the matter wiv 'er, Con?'

'She's got TB.'

'I'm sorry. Is she gettin' better?'

'No. She's gettin' worse. Mum ses she's never gonna get out o' there.'

Michael lapsed into silence as they walked towards the Tower Bridge Road. Connie shivered against the wind and gripped his arm tighter as they reached the deserted market and turned in the direction of the Old Kent Road. At the Bricklayers Arms they turned left into the main thoroughfare and saw the queue forming outside the little picture house. The tired-looking commissionaire was standing at the head of the queue, his hands behind his bowed back and his ill-fitting, braided uniform coat almost touching the pavement. Connie and Michael joined the queue just as the ticket office opened up. Soon the couple was climbing the winding staircase and entering the small balcony above the main auditorium. The air was scented and warm, and soft interval music was playing. Michael steered Connie into the back row and helped her off with her coat which she laid over her knees. After a while the lights dimmed and the show began. At first Connie sat upright, very aware of the lad's presence and feeling slightly ill at ease. She strived to relax and enjoy the evening, although her new high-heeled shoes were beginning to pinch. Michael was silent during the whole of the first film but when the lights went up at the interval he turned and smiled at her. 'Would yer like an ice-cream or somefink?' he asked her.

Connie shook her head. She felt too embarrassed to say yes and she held her hands tightly in her lap. Michael fished into his pocket and produced a paper bag which he opened noisily. 'Fancy a boiled sweet?' he asked, leaning towards her.

Connie took a sweet and felt his arm pressing against hers. He screwed up the paper bag and put it in his pocket and a woman in the seat in front turned around and glared at him. The young couple's eyes met and Michael winced comically. The sudden look and the silent communication between them seemed to break down the first barrier for Connie and she relaxed slightly.

The lights had dimmed and the stars of the film were now dancing lightly across a wide stage. Connie watched their movements closely, fascinated by the way in which their bodies moved together. Suddenly she became aware of Michael's arm slipping around the back of her seat. Soon his hand was resting on her shoulder and she felt her cheeks grow hot. Without moving her head she looked at him out of the corner of her eye and saw that he appeared to be as engrossed in the film as she was. The dancing ceased and the stars embraced. Michael was now leaning against her and she felt a strange new emotion welling up inside her. It was nice sitting in the darkness of the cinema with Michael. She could smell brilliantine and the faint aroma from his uniform. At that moment Connie felt very grown up. Her escort had now slipped his hand under the top of her arm and she found herself leaning towards him. His fingertips were gently stroking the side of her breast and she stiffened her arm. The film was reaching its climax and Fred Astaire was serenading Ginger Rogers. As the stars kissed Connie felt Michael's breath on her cheek and, as she turned her head slightly, he kissed her quickly on the side of her face. She looked quietly into his eyes and his lips touched hers lightly and then pressed hard. The kiss was short and awkward, but Connie was breathless with excitement. She knew that it was something she would treasure. Her first romantic kiss was just as she imagined it would be, and it felt wonderful.

The audience stood until the national anthem had finished then quickly made their way to the exits. Connie and Michael walked down the staircase and out into the cold night. They were both silent and absorbed in their own thoughts. Michael was feeling pleased with himself. The girl by his side was pretty and desirable and he could still sense the kiss. Connie was feeling dreamy and warm, although the wind was cold against her hot cheeks. She had wanted the kiss to go on for ever and there was a stirring deep down inside her which was new and exciting. She could feel his warm body against hers as they walked along the deserted Tower Bridge Road and her arm resting on his instilled a feeling of intimacy that made her shiver with pleasure.

They had reached Ironmonger Street and the block entrance when Michael turned and looked at her. 'Can I see yer again before I go back off leave?'

Connie smiled shyly. 'If yer want to.'

Michael took her by the arm and led her into the darkness of the stairway. His arms reached out and pulled her to him. Connie did not resist. Her eyes closed as he bent his head. His lips were slightly open and she opened hers to meet his searching mouth. The kiss was lingering and intense and when they finally parted Connie was gasping for breath.

Michael pulled up the collar of his topcoat and smiled sheepishly. 'I've gotta catch the seven-fifteen from Waterloo. We could go fer a walk in the afternoon if yer like?'

Connie nodded. 'All right. What time d'yer wanna call round?'

'Is 'alf past two okay?'

'Yeah, that'll be fine. Good night, Mick.'

'Good night, Con,' he said huskily as he pulled her close once more and kissed her quickly on the lips. Connie watched him turn and walk away and before he looked back she was hurrying up the shadowy stairs. Her heart was pounding and she felt strangely light-headed as she put the key in the lock. Once in the solitude of her flat she put the kettle on and slumped down in the armchair. The fire was out and the room felt chilly, although inside Connie was glowing. She could think of nothing but the handsome sailor lad who had been responsible for her first romantic kiss. She smiled to herself in the darkness and stared into the ashes of the fire. She could still feel his arm around her and his fingers searching for her breast. She remembered how her initial feeling of shock had quickly disappeared and had been taken over by a sense of abandonment. She had wanted to be kissed and held close for a long time. Suddenly she frowned. Would he think her too forward? she wondered. The girls at work were always talking about what men were like. 'Give 'em an' inch an' they'll soon 'ave yer drawers off,' Kathy Greenwood had said. 'Don't let 'em 'ave a feel on yer first date, they'll fink you're easy,' was another bit of advice Kathy gave to all the girls. Connie wondered what Michael was thinking on his walk home. Maybe he thought she was easy? Would he come round tomorrow? The kettle was popping and Connie roused herself. Tonight her fantasies would weave around him and she would hold him in her dreams. Tomorrow was another day.

Chapter Nine

Joe Cooper had slipped quietly back into Ironmonger Street and he lost no time in looking up an old friend. He and Solly Jacobs sat in the Horseshoe on a cold February evening discussing the growing crisis.

'I tell yer, it's gotta come, Solly. Mark my words, 1937's gonna be a dodgy ole year.'

The big fishmonger sipped his beer thoughtfully. 'Yeah I fink yer right, Joe,' he answered, wiping a large hand across his lips. 'I was listenin' ter the wireless last night. They was goin' on about that bastard 'Itler, an' 'ow 'e's whippin' up the feelin' against the Jews and Communists. Trouble is, there's a lot o' sympathisers in this country too. Those Blackshirt swine 'ave bin on the march again while you was inside. We 'ad another set-to wiv 'em a few weeks ago. A few 'eads got cracked an' some shop winders got smashed as well.'

Joe grinned mirthlessly. 'I know, Solly. We did get the papers in nick.'

Solly shrugged his massive shoulders and looked hard at Joe. ''Ere, 'ow yer gettin' on at the factory?' he asked suddenly. 'I bet there was a few raised eyebrows, when yer walked back in there?'

Joe smiled. 'Most of 'em seemed pleased ter see me, but I don't fink the management was too happy, 'spesh'ly now it looks like we're goin' union.'

* * *

Earlier that same day a heated discussion had taken place at the Armitage factory. Gerald Armitage had been sitting in his brother's office, nervously toying with his fountain pen. 'It's a bloody nuisance that Joe Cooper's back, Peter,' he said, avoiding his brother's gaze. 'Some of the workers think nothing of talking openly about forming some kind of workers' union now.'

Peter sighed. 'There's nothing to be done about that, Gerald,' he said with deliberation. 'You know the agreement's still binding. There's no going back on it, for all our sakes, and especially for yours.'

Gerald continued to stare at the carpet. 'You never let me forget, do you Peter?' he said with controlled anger.

Peter looked across at his brother. 'I know you don't need me to remind you, Gerald,' he said, a note of pity creeping into his voice. He got up from his desk and walked across to an armchair.

'Straight out of prison and back to his old job with a "hello, how are you? and welcome back",' Gerald said with cold derision. He shook his head. 'No, there's nothing we can do. I know that, Peter. That man's going to turn us into a laughing stock.'

Peter leaned back heavily in his large leather armchair. 'Look Gerald, of course I'd do anything for the best interests of this company. I've already been in touch by letter about the agreement.'

Gerald looked up quickly. 'You have?'

'Yes, but it wasn't well received, to say the least. The answer was terse and specific. The arrangement stays the same.'

Gerald dropped his gaze. 'You know Cooper's going to foment trouble,' he said slowly. 'It won't be long before we have another strike on our hands.'

'It may be that we have to start some kind of talks,' Peter said with resignation. 'But let's face it, Gerald. Joe Cooper gives us a fair day's work, the workforce respect him and he manages to get the best out of them. The way things are going, the government could be initiating a re-armament programme any day now, and we may well be looking forward to a healthy contract.'

'But that's the point I'm trying to make, Peter. If we allow a union inside our factory we'll be plagued with silly stoppages and walkouts. It's happened to every firm that's allowed them in.'

Peter took off his glasses and pinched the bridge of his nose. 'Times are changing, Gerald. The main complaints most unions have are over conditions of work. We've provided a works canteen, we've improved safety, and we've even gone so far as to promise a review of working hours. Most of our workers have been with us a long time. They know the hardships of short-time working and they're terrified of being put off again. Besides, for every worker who remains faithful to the union there's another who doesn't give a damn about it, so long as he or she can get a week's work and have some money to take home. And Joe Cooper knows that, he's no fool.'

Gerald said nothing. As Peter watched him gazing down glumly at his hands he thought of how much his brother had changed in recent years. Much of the brashness and fire had left him, and he seemed almost to be a mere shadow of his old self, lost and defeated.

There was a knock on the door and Miss Jones entered the large office. Alice Jones had been with the company for more than twenty years, during which time she had served two generations of the Armitage family. There was not much that Alice did not know about the company intrigues. As secretary she handled all the correspondence, as well as being on hand at meetings. Even the most confidential information somehow reached her ears. The office partitions were not all that thick and she had been surprised just how much could be heard by leaning back in her chair and pressing her good ear to the wall. She was a quiet, unobtrusive character, and it stood her in good stead. She had a knack of becoming almost invisible when it suited her purpose, and many a dropped word or opinion was inadvertently expressed in her presence. She was well aware of the nature of the current discussion between the two brothers and she put on her most detached look as she placed a sheaf of documents in front of Peter and silently departed to resume her vigil at the office wall.

Peter had been waiting for the Ministry applications for tender and when he saw the papers his eyes lit up. 'Gerald, I've got these forms to work on. I'll need your help on the output figures for the last quarter,' he said with a sudden smile.

Gerald nodded slowly. 'I'll get them sent up by this evening,' he said. 'By the way, when is young Robert starting? I could certainly do with some help. Things are begining to pile up.'

Peter stroked his chin thoughtfully. His son had just finished college and had shown some reluctance to enter the family business. He had informed his father that he wanted to go into the pharmaceutical industry, and the elder Armitage had explained his reasons for wanting his son to join the family concern. Peter was convinced that before long there would be another war and he wanted his only son to be holding down a vital position within the company and so be protected from the inevitable call-up.

'I'm hoping Robert will be starting here within the next month or two, Gerald. He's going on a walking holiday with some of his college chums before then. So I hope you can hang on for a while,' Peter said kindly.

'Well, I'd better get working on those figures, Peter,' his

brother said as he stood up and made for the door. Outside Miss Jones eased her chair away from the wall and lowered her head over her battered Remington.

On a Sunday afternoon in mid February two young people strolled arm in arm along the tree-lined Tower Gardens. The day had been cold and bright, and already the watery sun was starting to dip down behind London Bridge. It was quiet, with just a few visitors wandering along the cobbled paths or resting against the huge cannons. Birds chattered overhead and down beyond the stone wall the gentle swish of the turning tide carried up the walkway. Across the River Thames the couple saw the idle cranes and the bolted warehouses and wharves of the Pool. Two ocean-going freighters were rocking gently in their berths, and in mid-stream a brace of laden barges strained against their moorings. Heavy clouds were gathering, and the slowly fading daylight made the massive stone ramparts of the Tower of London appear forbidding. The couple walked slowly, the girl's long blond hair falling down almost to her waist, the lad, tall and upright, holding proudly on to her arm. They stopped as the lad pointed to a distant object on the far bank and, as they leaned on the wire fencing, his arm encircled her slim waist and she moved closer to him. A commotion behind them made the young people turn and they smiled as they listened to the two children talking.

'What's that place called?' asked the little girl who stood beneath a massive cannon.

'It's the Tower, soppy. Everybody knows that.'

'I don't.'

'Yes yer do, 'cos I jus' told yer.'

'What's them 'oles in the wall for, Tommy?'

'They're winders,' announced the boy who had just managed to scramble astride the cannon.

'Well they don't look like winders ter me. Winders 'ave curtains.'

'Not castle winders. Them winders is ter fire arrers from.'

The little girl sucked on a thin lollipop. 'Yer said it was the Tower.'

'Well it's still a castle. A fousand years ago soldiers used ter fire arrers out o' them winders.'

'What for?'

'Ter kill the enemy.'

'Who was the enemy, Tommy?'

'Pirates, I s' pose.'

'Tommy?'

'Yeah.'

'I wanna do a wee.'

'C' mon then, let's go 'ome. Yer can't wee 'ere.'

The couple chuckled at the children and then strolled on until they reached the arched gateway beneath Tower Bridge and then they started to climb up the wide stone stairs on to the roadway. It was quiet and devoid of traffic as they continued towards the centre span.

Down below, the swirling, muddy water lapped the stone bastions and eddied in small whirlpools. Michael looked into Connie's eyes and said quietly, 'Will yer come out wiv me when I get back from me trip?'

''Course I will,' she replied.

'I'll write ter yer soon as I can, Connie.'

'I bet you'll ferget. What do they say about sailors? A girl in every port!'

'I won't go out wiv anybody else till I get back, Con. We're goin' steady now, ain't we?'

'Yeah, I s'pose so. I won't go out on no dates neivver, Mick.'

Michael slipped his arm around her as they reached the end

of the bridge and looked into her pale blue eyes. "Ave yer got a photo of yerself?' he asked. 'I'd like ter take one wiv me.'

'No. I'll get one done soon an' send it on ter yer.'

'Fanks, Con. I'll keep it over me bunk an' I'll dream about yer every night.'

Connie giggled and pulled on Michael's arm. 'C'mon, Mick. It's gettin' late. If yer not careful yer'll miss yer train.'

They walked down to the Tower Bridge Road and slipped into the backstreets. The evening gloom was descending fast and the cold rising wind made Connie shiver. She held on to Michael's arm, happy in his company and vowing to remember these few days as the most exciting she had ever known. She felt like a grown woman and she knew there was so much more to discover. Michael seemed deep in thought and he did not say anything until they turned into Ironmonger Street. 'I've really enjoyed our times tergevver, Con,' he said at last. 'What about you?'

The young girl felt as though he had read her thoughts. 'It's bin luv'ly. I don't want yer ter go back off leave, Mick.'

They stopped at the buildings and stepped into the shadows. Michael pulled her to him and kissed her hard on the mouth. Connie felt herself trembling at the contact and she closed her eyes and let her lips mould into his. They parted, both breathing hard.

'I like yer a lot, Con. I'm gonna miss yer like mad.'

'Me, too, Mick. Come back soon.'

He turned and left her in the block entrance. Connie watched as he crossed the quiet street and saw him turn and give her a cheery wave. Her eyes misted as she waved back and then she turned quickly on her heels and hurried up the stairs.

The early months of 1937 saw a slight improvement as far as employment was concerned. Some of the Bermondsey factories went back to full-time working and more ships were coming in to berth at the docks and wharves. The Armitage factory had managed to obtain a government contract to produce ammunition cases and mess cans, as well as other less identifiable items for the services. The workforce were happy in the knowledge that, for the present at least, their jobs looked secure, although the items they were turning out gave rise to speculation. In the canteen, the women who worked the metal presses were discussing the implications of the new surge in orders.

'There was a bloke on the wireless last night,' Lizzie Conroy was saying. ''E was talkin' about us goin' ter war.'

Mary Brown took up her knitting and unravelled the four steel needles which she was using to produce a sock. 'If yer listen ter the wireless all the time yer'll go right round the twist. All yer get lately is about what's goin' on in Germany an' Spain. Only the ovver night I 'eard this bloke talkin' about us re-armin' ter stop a war. 'E said the Germans were buildin' up their troops an' ships an' fings, an' we're laggin' be'ind. If yer take too much notice o' the likes o' those people on the wireless yer'd put yerself in an early grave.'

Lizzie eased her bulk in the uncomfortable chair and patted her permed hair with the palm of her hand. 'What about all that stuff we're turnin' out? It's all army stuff. If it wasn't fer that work we'd be joinin' the dole queues. I fink it'll come to it sooner or later. My ole man reckons the Germans are itchin' ter 'ave anuvver go at us. 'E said we should 'ave stopped 'em when they put that 'Itler inter power. 'E's the cause of all the trouble.'

'That's easier said than done, Liz. People ain't prepared ter go ter war jus' like that. There's too many lives bin lost in the last war.'

Lizzie folded her arms and looked peeved. 'Well my ole

man studies the papers, an' 'e listens ter all the wireless talks, an' 'e said . . .'

'Look, Liz,' Mary cut in. 'You an' yer ole man can fink what yer like. As far as I'm concerned, there ain't gonna be anuvver war. All this stuff we're makin' is prob'ly ter replace the ole stuff. I know somebody who works in the Woolwich Arsenal, an' she told me all about the bullets an' shells they make there. She's bin workin' in the Arsenal since 'twenty-nine.'

'Well I 'ope you're right, Mary. I don't wanna see anuvver war,' Lizzie said.

'Gawd 'elp us if it ever starts again. My Uncle Bert got gassed in the last lot, an' 'is bruvver Maurice got invalided out as well.'

Joyce Spinks had been listening to the conversation and she puffed hard. ''Ere you two, can't yer change the subject? It's fair givin' me the creeps. Who yer knittin' them socks for, Mary?'

'They're fer me ole man's youngest bruvver. 'E's joined the territorial army an' 'e's asked me ter knit 'im a nice pair of thick socks 'e can wear wiv 'is army boots.'

'Gawd Almighty!' Joyce blurted out. 'I thought we was gonna change the subject'.

Lizzie laughed aloud. ''Ere. You seen that new bloke who come round inspectin' the place last week? 'E's a bit tasty.'

'That was Robert Armitage. 'E's the guv'nor's son,' Joyce said.

'Well 'e can ask me out if 'e likes,' Lizzie remarked, winking at Mary.

'I dunno. 'E only looks a kid.'

'Well kid or not, I bet 'e knows what 'e's got it for,' Lizzie said, pulling a face. 'I fink my ole man's sufferin' from loss o' memory. The only time 'e faces me in bed is on 'igh days an' 'olidays.'

'You wanna be careful, Liz. 'E might be supplyin' somebody else.'

'What! My ole man knows better than that. 'E knows very well that if I found out 'e was knockin' about wiv anuvver woman I'd cut 'is chopper off when 'e was asleep an' stick it in 'is ear.'

When the laughing had died down Joyce turned to Mary. ''Ere, talkin' about playin' around, you remember that turn out wiv Dirty Dora?'

'Who?' Lizzie asked.

'Tell 'er about it, Joyce,' Mary prompted.

Joyce looked around theatrically and leaned closer to the group. 'It was before you started 'ere, Liz. There was this woman who worked in the packin' shop. Dora Dillon 'er name was. Proper tart she was. She used ter come ter work like a Lisle Street whore. She wore tons o' make-up, an' lipstick, and bloody great 'igh 'eels. She did look eighteen carat. Anyway, she took a shine ter Jake Singer. Jake was the foreman in 'er shop. Married 'e was, wiv about five or six kids. This Dora kept pesterin' 'im. Every time 'e turned round, there she was makin' soppy eyes at 'im. 'Course, bein' like all the rest of 'em, open to a bit o' flattery an' silly as a box o' lights, 'e took the bait. Before long they was goin' be'ind the boxes fer a bit of "'ow's yer farvver". Everybody knew it was goin' on. It was the talk o' the factory. Dirty Dora used ter walk ter the factory wiv 'im an' wait fer 'im when they finished work. Brazen cow she was.

'Anyway, this was goin' on fer about six months or more, an' somebody shopped 'im ter Gladys, 'is wife. One day we was all workin' away when there was a right commotion. We looks round an' there's Gladys, wiv all 'er Gawd ferbids in tow, marchin' along the factory floor. "Where's the poxy knockin' shop?" she shouts out. Well, I tell yer, if you could 'ave seen

'er face. Scarlet wiv rage it was. There was the kids cryin', an'
'er pushin' 'er way down the aisle. Joe Cooper's tryin' ter keep
a straight face. 'E's twigged it right away. "Turn left at the
bottom an' go right in," 'e ses. Well, Gladys storms in, kids an'
all, an' she walks up ter Dora an' ses, "Yer got me meal ticket,
yer better feed 'em." Wiv that she smacks Dora round the
chops an' walks out, leavin' the kids standin' there. Dora was
snivellin' an' the kids was all bawlin' their 'eads off. Proper
turn out it was.'

'Tell 'er what 'appened next,' Mary prompted.

Joyce was enjoying her role as storyteller. 'Well, Gladys
marches up the gangway wiv 'er Jake followin' 'er. 'E 'ad the
little mites trailin' be'ind 'im an' 'e was pleadin' wiv 'er ter
take the kids back 'ome. We was all standin' there watchin'.
Suddenly she stops in 'er tracks an' ses to Jake, "On yer knees
then." True, Liz. She made 'im beg there an' then. 'Course, she
took 'im 'an the kids back but both Jake an' Dora got the sack.
Gladys an' Jake are like a couple o' lovebirds now, an' Dora
ended up marryin' a bloke a lot older than 'er. I see 'er only a
few weeks ago. Right scruffy cow she's turned out ter be. Jus'
goes ter show yer, don't it?'

Lizzie picked up her handbag as the factory whistle
sounded. 'I'll take the chance of a bit o' trouble if that young
Robert gives me the eye,' she grinned. 'My ole man would
prob'ly come up an shake 'im by the 'and fer 'elpin' 'im out!'

Chapter Ten

Bright spring days with lengthening hours of warm light helped to bring a little cheer to the backstreet folk. Even Ironmonger Street looked less ugly and off-putting when the sun lit up the terraced houses and penetrated the gloomy tenement block. The street dwellers were convinced that the factory owner had been affected by the sunshine when they saw the painters arrive and start work cleaning up the old rusting gates. Within a few days the iron entrance to the factory wore a bold green covering of paint and ladders were going up all around the red brick building. Even the factory sign was being scraped clean and the local wags made capital out of the renovations.

''E's gorn mad! Stark ravin' mad!' Bill Mullins said to his pal Terry. 'All that money 'e's earnin' 'as gorn to 'is 'ead. If those workers of 'is ain't careful they'll find themselves gettin' a rise.'

''E's sellin' the gaff,' Terry decided. 'Marie Lloyd's buyin' it off 'im. She's gonna turn it into a music 'all.'

'What, in Ironmonger Street? Yer wouldn't get those music 'all stars ter do a turn round 'ere. They'd be frightened o' the reception they'd get.'

'Not 'alf. All the kids would be standin' outside sellin' rotten fruit.'

The factory was looking much less forbidding in its new coat of paint and Peter Armitage was happy. The Ministry officials would be visiting the premises very soon to see how their contract was being implemented. I must remember to talk to Robert about new overalls for the machine-floor workers, he thought. We can't let the officials see the ones they're wearing at present, it wouldn't do. And they might ask to see the canteen. I must talk to the manageress. Maybe she could put a few more items on the menu. My office could do with a bit of a spruce-up too. I'd better have a word with Miss Jones. Perhaps she can get a few flowers or some pot plants.

Miss Jones was somewhat taken aback by the suggestion. 'Well I never did,' she remarked to her friend Mabel Southwick from the accounts office. 'I'm sure the man's verging on a nervous breakdown. If he's not pacing that office of his he's mumbling to himself. Now he wants me to get him flowers and pot plants, would you believe? I tell you, Mabel. If old Mr Armitage was alive he'd have a fit.'

Mabel giggled. 'You be careful. He might be thinking of doing some after-hours entertaining. It wouldn't be the first time a boss has made up to his secretary.'

Miss Jones straightened her blouse and snorted. 'Don't be silly, Mabel. Mr Peter is a respectable married man and, besides, I'm old enough to be his mother.'

'Well he must have some reason for doing what he's doing, Alice.'

Miss Jones pondered the mystery and came to the conclusion that it was probably his age. After all, men got those funny urges in middle life. She had recently read about the traumas of middle-aged men. She had discovered lots about the opposite sex in her life, mostly from books. In her younger days she had taken up with an older man who had tried desperately to lure her between the sheets. Miss Jones had found out in the nick of time that her romantic and persuasive companion was in fact a married man with two young children. Her world of romance was shattered and she decided that men were little more than animals with just one thought in their heads. She would not become anyone's chattel, and so Alice Jones remained celibate.

She had no regrets, except for the one time when old Armitage was alive. Her liking for George Armitage had clouded her usually clear judgement when, during a marital crisis, the factory owner had decided to seek the opinion of his loyal and trusted secretary. Alice Jones remembered the incident very well. He had been quiet and thoughtful for some time and one evening, just before the factory closed, he called her into his office and asked her to sit down. He had in fact wanted to know whether or not he should take home a bunch of flowers as a peace offering. He thought that maybe his wife might see the gesture as a sign of guilt and was seeking female advice about the problem. George Armitage broached the subject by saying first that it was very personal, and then he went on to ask if it would be correct to assume that a bunch of flowers was the right sort of gift to give to someone who was feeling neglected and not appreciated. Miss Jones was, of course, totally unaware of her boss's marital crisis and reacted by saying that flowers were unnecessary if there was true feeling between two people, secretly hoping he would ignore her advice. Armitage senior had grunted and was about to say something when he changed his mind and dismissed his secretary. Alice Jones was sure that he would overcome his lack of resolve, and she resigned herself to being patient. The aggrieved Mrs Armitage did not receive any flowers, and the loyal secretary to the factory owner waited in vain for her gift.

* * *

It was in the spring, too, that Molly Bartlett went into hospital for treatment to her spine. Her parents had already been told by the specialist that Molly's condition was a permanent one and that curvature of the spine was all too common amongst children in working-class areas; her natural growth and development would be impeded, and her breathing would become even more laboured. Both Helen and Matthew knew that there was little they could do except to make sure their daughter kept the six-monthly appointment at the hospital, and it was during the last visit that arrangements were made for Molly to be admitted for tests.

The doctors had said that she might benefit from a medical corset and that the support would make it easier for her to get about. Helen and Matthew were happy that there was a chance their daughter could be helped. Molly had been depressed and ill-tempered recently, which her parents put down to her worsening condition. She had almost stopped growing, and Connie was now head and shoulders taller than her ailing cousin. Even Connie was finding it difficult to communicate with Molly. When she had first told her, excitedly, about the date with Michael she had shown no interest and Connie felt it wiser not to talk any more about her boyfriend. When Michael's letter arrived from Gibraltar she decided not to say anything, but it troubled Connie that she had to keep part of herself from Molly. And it made her very sad to realise that, quite possibly, her cousin would never be fortunate enough to experience the same excitement.

When Molly went into hospital Helen informed her employers and requested that her cards be sent home. Molly's condition had become such that the journey to and from the factory was now getting to be too much of a strain. Helen realised that after the hospital Molly would have to find some other, less strenuous occupation. Connie herself was becoming bored with the dull routine of the factory and she, too, decided it was time to look around for some other type of work. It was Helen who suggested the Ironmonger Street factory.

'I was talkin' ter Mary Brown only yesterday,' she told her. 'She reckons there might be a job goin' in the Armitage canteen. She got it from one of the workers there. It might be worth yer while poppin' in an' askin', Con. At least yer wouldn't 'ave that walk every mornin'.'

Connie didn't feel very enthusiastic about serving meals in the factory canteen, but she was aware that there were not too many jobs available to her and it was very convenient, so she decided to give it a try. After all, what have I got to lose? she asked herself.

It was mid May when Connie went over to the factory and saw Dot Temple, the canteen manageress. The buxom Dot liked the look of the young girl and she decided to give her a chance.

'Yer'll 'ave ter be quick on the servin', me girl. That bleedin' load o' savages we've got workin' 'ere won't wait a minute. Don't take no ole truck from 'em though. If yer get any problems come ter me an' I'll give 'em what for.'

Connie felt ridiculous in her white apron and hat as she served up the sausage and mash, and meat and two veg. But quite a few of the factory workers knew her and their friendly welcomes helped her through the first awkward days. The management had their own private section and after one week Dot Temple felt her new worker was confident enough to begin serving there. It was strange at first, and the curious glances directed towards her made Connie feel uncomfortable. She was especially shy and nervous when it came to serving the young man in the smart blue suit who sat at the end of the long table. His mild curiosity made her feel clumsy and when he casually passed the time of day with her or just gave her a friendly smile Connie felt her face redden. The young man's continued show of interest slowly began to have a strange effect upon her and it was something that she did not quite understand. She took to glancing in the mirror and checking that her hair was tidy and her canteen uniform was properly adjusted before she began her duties. And, during the mornings when she had to help to prepare the food and lay the table in the management section, Connie found herself looking longingly at the clock. A feeling of excitement at the prospect of seeing the young man would grow as the morning went on. She was struggling to become more self-assured at serving times and found herself responding to his smile. On certain days, when the young man was absent, Connie felt disappointed, and when he appeared once more she perked up and felt contented for the rest of the day.

Connie quickly settled into the job and she soon became less nervous. The management were now calling her by her Christian name, and she liked the way the young man spoke it. She particularly liked his easy smile and casual manner. He was tall and fair-haired, with ice-blue eyes that seemed to bore into her. His face was lean, with an expressive mouth and a small straight nose. His voice was soft and cultured and had a humorous ring to it. Connie realised she was thinking more and more about him as the days went by and it worried her. She was getting regular letters from Michael and he had indicated in his last letter that he would be coming home on leave at the end of June. The excitement at the prospect of seeing her sailor lad once more was becoming tempered by her growing interest in Robert Armitage.

It was Dot who told Connie all about the new manager. 'That young Robert's a nice young man,' she gushed. ''E's really polite and friendly, not like the rest of 'em. 'E's bin ter college. Oxford, I fink it was. I 'eard 'e's trainin' ter take over from 'is ole man. 'E's only twenty-two but 'e's got it up there,' she said, pointing to her forehead. 'I mean, yer gotta be clever ter go to a place like Oxford ain't yer?'

Connie listened with guarded interest. She feigned indifference but secretly hung on to every word. Robert Armitage was invading her thoughts to such an extent that it frightened her. Nothing good would come of it, Connie told herself. He was educated, cultured and older than her. His interest in her was probably innocent and here she was weaving romantic dreams around him. He most likely had lots of girl friends, she mused. Why should he be bothered with a girl from Ironmonger Street whose Cockney accent would surely embarrass him if he ever introduced her to his friends? She was being foolish to allow her thoughts to wander so. She must keep some distance and not appear too eager to cultivate a friendship that would surely spell disaster.

The days had become routine, and she spent most evenings reading or listening to the wireless. When Molly came out of hospital towards the end of June she was in some discomfort with her new spinal corset, and Connie sat with her whenever she could in the Bartletts' flat and attempted to cheer her up. Every other weekend Connie visited her mother at the sanatorium and she noticed each time the increased deterioration in her condition. Most of the time the conversation was strained and forced, and there were times when the two of them sat in complete silence, Kate Morgan staring blankly and Connie biting her lip in anguish and sorrow. It hurt her to see her mother getting weaker, and it was always a relief when she was on the train heading back to London. The sanatorium depressed and frightened her. It was a place of stifled despair. Many of the patients were slowly wasting away, sitting around for long periods with blankets draped over their shoulders, staring dull-eyed into the distance, wrecked by the cruel pain of tuberculosis.

At the factory canteen Connie tried to ignore Robert's smiles and asides, and she avoided meeting his eyes as much as possible. But, try as she might not to encourage him, he became even more attentive.

Robert had sensed that something was troubling the pretty young server, and he was determined to find out what it was that had made her ignore him. Maybe he had inadvertently upset her, he pondered. If it was so, he would have to seek an opportunity to talk to her, and it would have to be done discreetly. It was management policy for the white-collar staff to avoid becoming too familiar with the workers. His father had warned him: 'If a good standard is to be adhered to, Robert, it is important to keep our distance. Remember, familiarity breeds contempt. The workers know their place, and it is for us to make sure we keep to the status quo. Any deviation might be seen as a form of weakness, and be sure, the workers would most certainly take advantage.'

It was the last Friday of June and after the lunch break most of the management had hurried away to finish their tasks for the week. Robert tarried until the last of the staff had departed from the table and then he sauntered over to the serving hatch and looked through. He could see the girl bending over the large sink, her uniform coatsleeves turned back to the elbows and her hands deep in the steaming water. For a few seconds he watched her, then he called her name. Connie turned with a startled look on her face.

Robert smiled disarmingly and beckoned her over to him. 'Have you got a few minutes, Connie? I'd like to talk with you,' he said.

'Is anyfink wrong?' she asked quickly.

'No. I just want a few minutes, if you can spare the time.'

Connie wiped her hands quickly on a roller towel and

dabbed at her hot forehead before following him through the door into the dining room. Robert was back at his place at the table and when she walked over he beckoned to a chair.

'Sit down a minute, Connie,' he said quietly.

She sat down quickly and looked at him with some trepidation.

'I hope you won't take this the wrong way, but I've had the feeling lately that I might have said or done something that has upset you.'

Connie took a deep breath. 'Of course not, sir. Why should yer fink that?'

He met her eyes and smiled. 'Call me Robert. It sounds a lot better than sir. Anyway, I just had that feeling. You seem to be a little distant lately. I've been missing that friendly smile of yours, if I may say so.'

Connie clasped her hands on the table and looked into his blue eyes. She could feel the exeitement rising from deep within her and she struggled to reply. 'I . . . I didn't realise I was actin' any different, sir . . . I mean Robert.'

He saw the flush in her cheeks and his eyes studied her carefully. He looked at a few wayward strands of her blond hair which had slipped down from under her cap, and at her blue eyes. He noticed her discomfort and he suddenly felt very sorry for her. He reached out and touched her clasped hands very briefly.

'I hope you like working here, Connie. I wouldn't like to see you leave us. You've brightened up the place. Old Mrs Kerrigan was all right, but I think the job was getting too much for her.'

Connie smiled shyly. 'I like the job, Robert. It's much better than the biscuit factory.'

'Oh, and what did you do there?'

'I was packin' biscuits all day long,' she replied.

Robert looked at her with some concern in his eyes. She was certainly very attractive. She must be around sixteen or so, he thought, and already factory fodder. She would probably end up married before long and have a brood of children to bring up in a grim, tumbledown backstreet. She would probably struggle on like the rest of the local folk and become old prematurely. She had obviously not had a very good education and yet she seemed very bright and intelligent. It was a shame, he thought, and something that he and his father had clashed over many times recently. The elder had maintained that there had to be a supply of uneducated people to work in the factories and shops and it was the way of things. Robert had disagreed strongly. Why should it have to be so? Why shouldn't working-class people have better chances of education and better housing? Why were there so many gas-lit streets when factories had electrical power? The houses in Ironmonger Street were lit by gas and yet there were electricity cables running down the turning. Peter had called his argument naive in the extreme. The cost of installing electricity was hardly going to be met by the tenants – and how could they be expected to pay more for improvements when they were hard pushed to pay the current rents? Robert's contention that local firms should seek to buy out the landlords and develop the houses for their workers angered his father. Robert knew that his ideas were considered to be dangerous and typical of university students. Peter had suggested that it was time for him to find out for himself how business worked, as a few months of practical experience might help to mellow his thinking. He would see then that running a factory needed a pragmatic approach. There was no time to dwell on the unfairness of life. Robert was sure that he would never share his father's views and he felt that he had made a mistake. He should never have allowed his father to persuade him to enter the family business. Now, as he sat with the poor, overworked young girl opposite him, the young man was troubled. Suddenly he realised he had been staring at her in silence. 'Is factory work the only type of work you've done?' he asked her quickly.

Connie nodded, and a slight smile crossed her face. 'It was the only sort of work goin'. I s'pose I could 'ave worked in a shop, but it's Saturday work an' the wages ain't all that good.'

Robert looked at her in silence for a moment. 'How old are you, Connie?' he asked suddenly.

'I'll be seventeen in November.'

'I suppose you've got a boyfriend?'

She felt he was becoming a little too inquisitive, but his face showed a genuine interest and so she nodded. ''E's a sailor. 'E's bin away at sea fer four months, but 'e's comin' 'ome on leave termorrer.'

Robert smiled. 'We are still friends, aren't we?'

Connie laughed with embarrassment and looked down at the tablecloth. When she lifted her eyes to meet his she saw a strange look there. ''Course we're friends,' she said. She glanced back in the direction of the serving hatch. 'I'd better get back ter work or Dot'll fink I'm slackin'.'

'We'll talk some again, Connie,' he said as he got up and buttoned up his jacket.

Connie went back to the sink, her mind in a whirl. There was something in the man's tone that had both excited and worried her. She wanted to think of Michael's homecoming and the pleasure of being with him and feeling his kisses once more, but instead she found herself dwelling on the conversation she had had with Robert Armitage. Her face was flushed and her hands were slightly shaking as she bent over the sink.

Chapter Eleven

Bright sunlight filtered through the drawn blinds and, as Connie opened her eyes, she heard the sound of the rag-and-bone man's barrow on the cobbles below. She looked at the alarm clock beside her bed and sat up quickly. It was nine-thirty on Saturday morning and she realised that she should have been up an hour ago. There was lots to do before she went to Waterloo Station to meet Michael. Connie jumped out of bed and hurried into the kitchen to light the gas under the kettle. While she was waiting for it to boil, she went back into her bedroom and poured cold water into a bowl from the matching blue china jug on the washstand beneath the window. As she looked through the curtains, Connie could see the old street vendor standing beside his barrow and he appeared to be arguing with Mrs Cosgrove. His hands were spread out in front of him in what Connie thought was a gesture of 'take it or leave it', and Clara Cosgrove seemed to be dubious, pinching her chin. It was a familiar scene, and she closed the curtains on it.

She slipped out of her nightgown and splashed the cold water over her face and upper body. As she dried herself on the rough towel, the girl studied herself in the dressing-table mirror. As if she was looking at a stranger she had never seen before, she followed the line of her hips as they curved up into her narrow waist. She was aware that she had put on a little weight around the shoulders, and around the tops of her arms and her thighs. Her small breasts were firm and rounded, and as she splashed the cold water on them her nipples grew hard. Connie smiled and then quickly dressed and went out into the tiny back kitchen.

As she sipped her tea and nibbled at the burnt toast Connie glanced at the shopping list that had been placed under her door by Helen as she went off to her early morning cleaning job. It was the usual procedure for Connie to go to the Tower Bridge Road market on Saturdays and she recalled how she had bumped into Michael there not so very long ago. After his months at sea he would probably looked tanned, she guessed, and he would no doubt have lots of stories to tell her of his travels. Would he take her in his arms at the station, or would he merely grin in that way of his and act as though he had only been gone for a few days? Connie swallowed the last of the toast and gulped down the now lukewarm tea. The flat was tidy and the curtains would not need changing for another week at least and the weather was so mild she didn't need to light the fire. She took down a china shoe from the mantelshelf and tipped it up on the table. It was there she kept the housekeeping money, and the money her mother gave her every other week to pay the rent. Connie had often wondered about where that money came from but Kate waved her questions away whenever she asked.

'It's a regular fing from when yer farvver died. While I'm alive the money'll be there, so don't let it concern yer, child,' she always said.

Connie thought that it must be some sort of insurance and, as her mother was not going to enlarge on what she said, she had to leave it at that.

The sun had risen high in the heavens by the time she left.

Children were playing in the street and, outside the Richards' front door, a few business-minded youngsters were busy chopping up apple boxes for firewood. For them, earning pennies on Saturday morning was all important. The money they got took them to the pie and mash shop and to the tuppenny rush at the Trocette cinema to see 'Flash Gordon' and 'Riders of the Purple Sage'. On a good day the pennies stretched to a bag of fruit and a toffee bar as well.

In the market the odour of fish and fresh fruit mingled with the smell of newly baked bread and rolls and at the cake shop a sweet aroma of hot apple pies and jam doughnuts drifted out on the morning air. The calls and the banter of the traders rang out and were drowned as the number sixty-eight tram clattered past. Lines of women queued patiently at the stalls, their pinned-up hair covered with nets and square cloth scarves. Their shopping baskets got heavier and their purses became lighter as the Saturday morning ritual took place. Connie's shopping basket was on her arm and she stopped to rest beside the Cheap-Jack stall. She cast her eye over the wares and saw amongst the profusion of bits and pieces a small bottle of Californian Poppy. Connie held it up and glanced at the dapper-looking stall-owner.

'Give us a shillin', luv. It's the real fing. No rubbish on this stall,' he said brightly.

Connie flushed slightly and put the bottle down on the pile.

'All right, make it tenpence. Yer gettin' a bargain. I'm givin' the stuff away terday. I mus' be mad, but anyfing fer a pretty gel.'

The young girl fished into her purse and took out some coppers. It might be a bit extravagant but, after all, Michael doesn't come home every day of the week, she thought to herself.

When she had finished the shopping, Connie joined the

Bartletts for the Saturday midday meal. Matthew brought back hot pies and mash and a basin of steaming parsley liquor. They all sat around the table in the front room and chatted about the week's events with the wireless switched on and tuned to a programme of medleys by the Harry Roy band. Connie always looked forward to the Saturday meal. It made a change from being alone. Molly was in a cheerful mood and the two girls laughed and chatted together. Matthew was still working the East End markets and he had managed to earn enough that week to buy a few badly needed groceries. Helen noticed that her husband seemed more relaxed than he had been for some time and she knew it was because he had heard that the furniture factory was opening up again and wanted its old skilled hands back. Matthew was a French polisher by trade and he felt optimistic about getting a regular job again. He joined in the light-hearted conversation and, when Molly asked him to tell Connie about the man in the Old Ford Road market, he looked at Helen and she raised her eyes to the ceiling and grinned at her niece.

'The times we've 'eard that story this week, Con.'

'Go on, Dad. Tell Connie,' Molly pleaded, her large round face beaming.

'Well, it was on Monday mornin',' Matthew began. 'I was in the market early, so I could get me pitch. Yer 'ave ter get there early or yer'll get squeezed out by the stalls.'

'Get ter the story, Matt,' Helen said. 'Connie ain't got all day.'

'Well, I was layin' me stuff out,' Matthew went on, 'when this ole man comes up. Funny-lookin' ole sod 'e was. 'E 'ad a row of medal ribbons pinned on 'is chest an' 'is boots were all worn out. There was no buttons on 'is coat. In fact it was tied up wiv string. The ole boy's face was black as Newgate's knocker an' 'e 'ad a dirty beard. It looked like 'e'd bin sittin' over a wood fire all night. Anyway, I started callin' out like I always do. "Come on, girls, get yer laces an' collar studs 'ere. Razor blades an' 'air-pins." Now this ole boy is jus' standin' there right in front o' me. I said to 'im, "Do me a favour, mate. Go an' stand in front o' somebody else. Yer blockin' me pitch." 'E didn't take a blind bit o' notice. 'E jus' stood there starin'. I was gettin' a bit anxious. I mean, yer can't expect people ter stop an' buy wiv this ole character standin' right in front o' yer. The bloke on the veg stall next ter me told me the only way ter get rid of 'im was ter give 'im a couple o' coppers fer a cup o' tea. Well, I tell yer, before I got me 'and out o' me pocket this ole tramp was 'oldin' 'is dirty mitt out. 'E grabs the tuppence an' off 'e trots. Ten minutes later 'e was back, large as life. Well I wasn't goin' ter give 'im any more money, so I tried ter ignore 'im. It was nearly eleven o'clock an' I 'ain't sold a fing. I was gettin' worried, I can tell yer. I 'ad ter do somefink quick. As it 'appened I 'ad a few safety razors in me case, so I picked up one an' took the wrappin' off. I waved it in front of the ole boy an' made an 'orrible face, then I called out, "Best razor blades yer can buy. Gavver round gels. See the demonstration." Yer should 'ave seen the ole boy move. Before yer could say Jack Robinson 'e was off like a shot out of a gun.'

Laughter filled the flat and then Helen got up and sighed in resignation. 'C'mon, let's get the table cleared. I've got me ironin' ter do.'

Back in her flat, Connie was getting ready to go to Waterloo. She continually glanced at the clock on the mantelshelf as she pottered about. Michael's train was due at four o'clock and it was now ten minutes to three. An hour would be plenty of time to get to the station, she calculated. The buses were frequent at that time of day. Connie looked in the mirror over the fireplace and ran her hand over her straight blond hair. She could smell the Californian Poppy and wondered if she had been too liberal with it. Her thoughts turned to what Helen had said just before she had left. 'You be careful, Con. You're only young yet. Don't get too serious. After all, you're not seventeen till November. There's plenty o' time ter date boys.'

Helen was becoming very protective toward her and Connie understood the reasons why. Helen had cared for her since she was a baby. She had always been there when Kate was out on the town, and it was natural for her aunt to feel as she did. Maybe Aunt Helen is trying to stop me behaving like my mother, Connie mused. But what did she do? I know Aunt Helen thinks Mum led a bad life, but did Mum really have a lot of men friends? She must have been lonely after Dad died. If he did. Perhaps that's the reason why Mum never talks about him. He might have just left. Maybe he has another girlfriend . . . Connie felt confused. She remembered the money that her mother had been giving her every other week and wondered if it was from her father himself? Perhaps her aunt was worried because she knew some horrible secret. Maybe she even knew where the money came from.

Connie's troubled thoughts would not leave and the clock was now showing ten minutes past three. She slipped on her coat and took her small handbag from the table. It seemed ages since she had seen Michael, and her heart pounded as she ran down the flights of stairs and out into the street. The afternoon was warm, and early summer clouds were drifting high in the blue sky as she hurried along the turning and made her way to Tower Bridge Road. A few people were waiting at the bus stop and Connie stopped behind them. Her stomach was full of butterflies and the sensation made her shiver in the warm sunlight. Feelings of excitement tempered with guilt ran through her. She had often thought about Michael in the dark hours and their kisses, and she had even seen him in her dreams, but he was never alone. As he came towards her she would see the misty figure of Molly standing behind him and her heart would become heavy. Connie knew that the feeling she had for Molly was one of love born out of pity. It could never change. Her new adult feelings were of a different kind and they were growing as her body matured. They were intense, physical, and very difficult to repress. They flowed over her when she touched her body and when she stood naked in front of her mirror. They were quite natural. So why should she feel guilty?

The bus had arrived and as Connie climbed aboard she noticed one of the girls from the biscuit factory sitting alone in a side seat. The two exchanged smiles and Connie sat down beside her. Brenda James was eighteen and involved in a passionate relationship with a married man. It had been common knowledge at the factory and Brenda was openly proud of herself. Her love life had been subject to much discussion on the belt and Connie remembered being a little overawed by the girl. Connie quickly fished into her purse for the fare.

''Ello, Con,' Brenda said. 'Where're yer workin' now?'

'I'm at the Armitage factory.'

'What yer doin' there?'

'I'm in the canteen,' Connie replied as she handed the conductor two pennies.

'I bet yer get ter meet all the nice fellers, don't yer?'

Connie smiled shyly and looked around to see if anyone was listening.

''Ow's yer cousin, Con? She went in the 'ospital, didn't she?'

She nodded. 'Molly's out now. They fitted 'er wiv a spinal belt. It 'elps wiv 'er walkin' but she said it's painful ter wear.'

'Poor cow,' Brenda said, shaking her head.

The bus squealed to a stop and a few passengers got off. Brenda eased sideways in her seat and turned to Connie. 'Where're yer off to?'

'I'm goin' ter meet me fella,' she answered proudly, feeling a little less overawed by the factory vamp.

Brenda patted her waved hair with the palm of her hand. 'I'm off ter meet my Frankie. We're goin' down ter Little'ampton fer the weekend. I told yer about Frankie, didn't I?'

Connie remembered at least two occasions when the saga of Brenda's liaison with Frankie had been related in great detail, and she nodded.

''E's married, yer know,' Brenda went on. ''E don't get on wiv 'is wife. She's a right misery by all accounts. Frankie said 'e'd leave 'er, but 'e's scared case she does some 'arm to 'erself.'

Connie was already wishing the bus journey would end. As Brenda carried on about Frankie, she looked out of the window, letting the words drift over her. Suddenly she was brought back to herself by Brenda's elbow digging into her side.

'You an' your bloke gettin' tergevver, are yer?' Brenda asked with a sly wink.

Connie flushed and looked around to see if anyone had overheard. 'We've only bin out a few times. I 'ardly know 'im.'

The bus jerked to a stop once more and a large man squeezed into the vacant seat beside the two. Brenda looked peeved as she was squashed between Connie and the puffing and snorting character. As the bus pulled away from the stop the man rolled against her and she gave him a wicked look. The next stop was Waterloo Station and in a short time the bus pulled up at the entrance. As Connie rose to alight from the bus she was dismayed to find that Brenda was getting off too.

The painted girl giggled. 'You meetin' your bloke on the station? That's funny, so am I.'

The two girls walked up the wide steps into the main

121

concourse when Brenda pulled on Connie's arm. 'I mus' go ter the ladies an' put me war-paint on,' she said rolling her eyes.

Connie was glad of the opportunity to be rid of her and she waved as she walked quickly away towards the platforms.

The station clock showed ten minutes to four. Connie read the arrivals board and saw that the train from Portsmouth was due on platform seven. She meandered along beside the platform barriers and watched the travellers coming and going. Noisy jets of steam hissed from the tenders and guards' whistles shrilled out. Hurrying families sweated and fussed as they made for the waiting trains and porters pushing large barrows of luggage called out for room as they followed well-dressed passengers out to the waiting taxis. Pigeons fluttered up and down from the iron girders and strutted between the feet of the crowds, and here and there people sat on wooden benches, killing time by browsing through newspapers and magazines.

The minute hand of the large clock clicked towards the twelve and the cloud of steam some way down the track made Connie's heart race. It was then that she saw Brenda walking arm in arm with a tall, heavily built man in his mid forties. He was dressed in a shabby suit and carried a mackintosh slung over his shoulder. The man had a ruddy complexion, and from the side of his shiny bald head ginger hair sprouted out over his ears. The man towered above his companion and Connie watched their progress from her concealed position behind a paper stand. Frankie was not at all as she had visualised. She had imagined him to be a dapper man with a clipped moustache and polished shoes, someone who smiled deceitfully from the corner of his mouth. The character with Brenda looked more like the sort of man who came into her street with a collecting book under his arm and a stub of pencil stuck behind his ear. Nevertheless Brenda looked happy in his company and seemed to be hanging on to his every word. They passed by and Connie breathed more easily as she moved along towards platform seven as the Portsmouth train shuddered to a halt before the station buffers and the carriage doors began to swing open. At last she saw him walking down the platform with that confident gait of his. He looks so smart in his uniform, she thought, waving to try and attract his attention.

Michael was carrying a duffel bag over one shoulder and a raincoat under the other. His cap was worn at a jaunty angle and his bell-bottoms flapped around his ankles as he approached. When he saw her a beaming smile creased his fresh face. At the barrier he reached out and held her forearm as he bent his head and kissed her gently on the lips. It was not as passionate as Connie had anticipated but his smile was warm and his eyes twinkled. They moved away through the station and out into the sunlight. She held his arm and walked proudly beside him, listening to his small talk and trying to look grown-up. She hoped he could smell the Californian Poppy, and that he liked her high-heeled shoes which brought her up to his height. There was the whole week ahead. A week when she could rediscover how his kisses felt and how nice it was to be with him. She could forget the loneliness and the waiting, and she could put all her fears and anxieties behind her now that Michael was home. She hoped desperately that his physical closeness would take away her night-time fantasies which wove themselves around a young man in a smart blue suit. She had forbidden herself to feel any desire for him but, unbidden, fantasies filled her dreams.

Chapter Twelve

The situation had got worse in Europe. In May the Prime Minister, Stanley Baldwin, had resigned and had been replaced by Neville Chamberlain. The Fascists had gained ground in Spain, and many international observers were concerned that Franco's forces would eventually line up with Germany and Italy in a European war. The call for faster rearmament was growing. The pacifists were beginning to lose ground in popular opinion, and it was now becoming clear in many people's minds that a war was more probable than possible.

In the summer twilight the two young people strolled through the park, savouring every moment of the time they had left together. It had been a wonderful week, with long evening walks and nights in the back row of a darkened picture house, whispering loving words to each other and stealing kisses as the time flew past. The little tendernesses and spoken secrets of the past week had already become special memories, and the knowledge that they would soon have to part lent a sharp poignancy to their last evening together. They could not hide the sadness that touched them both as they walked along the edge of the lake. Ducks dipped their heads beneath the water and then darted forward, leaving gentle ripples on the glassy surface. The trees overhead were in full leaf and from the rustling lawns the delicate scent of new-mown hay drifted down to the water's edge. Along the path they could see the bandstand and the departing musicians, colourful in their military uniforms. Above the lofty trees the evening sky was deepening from a golden hue to a grey shade of darkness and the shadows lengthened. The young couple left the lake and took the path which led out on to the paved promontory. The cold statue of General Wolfe rose above them and, far down below, the silver line of the river twisted and turned away into a distant blackness.

Michael broke the silence as he looked down on the quiet river. 'We'd better get down ter the bottom. They'll be closin' the gates soon, Con,' he said softly.

They followed the steep path that led down beside the observatory and reached the wide avenue. Ahead, the heavy gates were already shut and people were leaving by the side entrance. Connie looked at Michael and he gave her a brief smile. 'If we'd stayed much longer we'd 'ave bin locked in,' he said in mock fear.

Connie snuggled closer to him. 'I'm gonna miss yer, Mick,' she said sadly. 'It's bin really nice this week.'

Michael did not answer. His forthcoming trip was a hurriedly arranged affair. His naval squadron was leaving for the Far East within the next few days and his excitement was tempered by his growing feelings for the young girl on his arm. He had seen the disappointment on her face when he told her the news, and his imminent departure had made their brief time together all the more precious. They had learned much about each other during the past few days. At first Michael had thought it strange that Connie did not invite him up to her flat. They always met out in the street and at the end of each evening they had said goodnight in the darkened entrance to the buildings. It was after the first few nights that Connie had explained the reasons.

'I've got ter be careful, Mick,' she had explained. 'Me Aunt 'Elen is a bit worried. She finks I'm too young to 'ave a steady boyfriend. If I invited yer in she'd be bound ter find out an' she'd tell me mum. I don't want 'er worryin' while she's ill.'

Michael had accepted her reasons but he wished there was somewhere other than the block entrance they could go for their goodnight embraces.

They had boarded the tram and were now sitting side by side on the upper deck, their bodies moving together as the tram swayed and rocked over the rails. They held hands and looked into each other's eyes, oblivious to the casual glances from the few other passengers. At Tower Bridge Hotel the tram slowed to a crawl, allowing the conductor to leap down and switch the points. Five minutes later the young couple alighted at the deserted market and soon they were back in the tumbledown streets which led off from the main thoroughfare. Ironmonger Street was quiet and nearly empty, but a few older folk were chatting on their doorsteps in the fading light. They glanced at Connie and Michael as the two walked by and exchanged knowing looks. At the entrance to Jubilee Buildings they stopped and stepped into the darkness. Connie moved close to Michael and put her arms around his neck. They kissed long and passionately and when they parted Connie rested her head on his chest. Her thoughts were racing. She wanted to take him to her flat; she wanted to talk intimately with him and allow his searching hands to explore her yearning body. She felt she was ready to taste the fruits of passion and emerge unchaste and it would be something she could recall in the months ahead when they were apart. But she hesitated. They would have to pass the Bartletts' flat. Connie sighed and turned her head to his and their mouths touched, gently at first, then with a passion which left them both breathless. He searched for her neck with his mouth, and the movement which started at her ear and ran down to the top of her shoulder sent delicious thrills along her spine. His hands caressed her body and a shiver ran through her whole being. It was becoming too tempting and she caught his wrists. 'Don't, Mick,' she groaned. 'I'm scared.'

Michael kissed her ear again. 'Don't be scared, Con,' he murmured. 'I fancy yer like mad. Let's go ter yer flat.'

Connie tensed. Her good sense told her to say no, but her passion was overwhelming her and she was fighting to keep control of her feelings. He was leaving soon and it would be many long, lonely months before she would see him again. She took his hands in hers and motioned for him to be quiet. They walked carefully up the wooden stairs, and as they passed the Bartletts' flat Connie held her breath. She could hear dance music coming from the wireless but to her relief the door stayed closed. As they walked lightly along the fourth floor landing Connie reached into her handbag for the key and glanced nervously at the flat opposite hers. The elderly couple who had taken over Mrs Walker's flat were hardly ever seen, but at that moment the grey-haired Annie Riley opened her door to put the milk bottles out and she looked up, startled.

'Gawd, yer scared me, gel!' she cried out. 'I wondered who it was creepin' along the landin'.'

Michael gave the old lady a sheepish grin and she looked at him closely before straightening the door mat and closing the door with a bang.

Inside number seven Jubilee Buildings Alf Riley was dozing in his favourite chair. The *Star* newspaper was draped over his legs and his mouth hung open. Annie shook him and he awoke with a start.

'Wassa matter?' he mumbled as he moved his legs and grabbed at the arms of his chair.

''Ere, Alf. I've jus' seen that Morgan gel goin' in. She's got a sailor bloke wiv 'er.'

'What d'yer want me ter do about it?' Alf moaned.

Annie gathered up the newspaper lying at her husband's feet and puffed as she straightened up. 'I was only tellin' yer. I bet she's 'avin' a right ole game now that mother of 'ers is away.'

Alf rubbed his hand over his bald head. 'It's no concern of ours. She's got the right ter take who she wants in ter 'er flat. I dunno what yer worried about.'

'I ain't worried,' Annie said, sitting down opposite him. 'I ain't even surprised, really. 'Er muvver wasn't much good. She was always bringin' blokes back. Ole Mrs Walker told me some tales about 'er.'

'Gawd Almighty, woman!' Alf said irritably. 'Yer woke me up ter tell me the kid's takin' a sailor in there, an' now yer goin' on about 'er muvver. That's the trouble wiv the people around 'ere. They're always mindin' everybody's business but their own. Kate Morgan might 'ave bin on the game. So what? As long as she didn't interfere wiv anybody else she 'ad the right ter bring back anybody she wanted to. Now go an' put the kettle on an' let me get back ter me doze.'

Annie gave him a withering stare before going out into the kitchen.

'Silly cow,' Alf mumbled to himself. 'I wouldn't 'ave minded goin' back there myself!'

Across the landing in number eight Connie was preparing supper. She cut thick slices from a crusty loaf and spread them with a coating of margarine, and then began to look through the kitchen cabinet for the hunk of cheese and some tomatoes. Michael was standing beside her, waiting for the kettle to boil, his eyes constantly appraising her tall slim figure, and he noticed how her blond hair fell across her forehead as she leant over the table to slice the tomatoes. The kettle started to spurt steam rings and he stared down at the fresh tea leaves in the bottom of the teapot.

'P'raps she won't say anyfink, Con,' he said reassuringly.

Connie shrugged her shoulders. She wasn't concerned now about the Rileys. It was nice to be alone with Michael and to be able to prepare a meal for them both. At that moment she was not going to let anything worry her or mar the evening. Tomorrow might be different, but tonight she was going to feed him, spoil him, and let him make love to her . . .

Bright sunrays pierced the net curtains and shone down into the bedroom. Connie turned over on to her side and squinted at the alarm clock on the chair beside her bed. She could hear the sound of running water coming from the scullery and she sat up quickly, her eyes darting to the pile of clothes just out of her reach. Michael's naval uniform was lying over a chair and she could hear him washing at the stone sink. Connie slipped out of bed and dressed quickly, her eyes watching the scullery door. As she was buttoning up her blouse Michael walked into the room. He was stripped to the waist and his face and upper body glowed from the application of cold water. He smiled sheepishly, a hint of a question showing in his large eyes. Connie quickly turned away to make the bed and then nodded in the direction of the mantelshelf clock.

'It's past nine. Are yer gonna be late?' she said, avoiding his glance.

'It's okay, Con. The train don't leave till eleven,' he replied, grabbing his shirt from the back of the chair.

Connie walked out into the scullery. 'I'll put the kettle on and do some toast,' she called out.

Michael moved over to the window and glanced down into

the early Sunday street. It was deserted and he glanced up at the clear sky before going to sit down at the kitchen table. Soon Connie brought over tea and slices of thick toast and the two ate in silence. They were both feeling a strange awkwardness, and it was Michael who spoke first, hesitantly.

'Yer didn't regret last night, Con, did yer?'

She smiled wanly and dropped her eyes to the chequered tablecloth. ''Course I didn't. I was jus' scared.'

Michael nodded and sipped his tea in silence. He knew that last night had been difficult and that Connie hadn't enjoyed his lovemaking. He cursed his lack of experience. When he glanced up he found her looking at him.

'Look, I'm sorry if it didn't work out, Con. I s'pose we was both scared really. I should 'ave 'ad somefink wiv me.'

She stared down at the tablecloth, her little finger moving the crumbs into a pile. 'It's okay. There's no 'arm bin done. They say it never 'appens first time anyway.'

He nodded again and leaned back in his chair, his eyes fixing on her. Connie tried to avoid his gaze. She felt embarrassed and increasingly edgy under his scrutiny. She looked up at the mantelshelf again.

'Mind yer time, Mick,' she said quickly.

Michael stood up and put on his hat. Connie went over to the chair beside the bed and picked up his service raincoat. For a moment they stood facing each other, not knowing what to say or do. Suddenly he reached out and held her shoulders as he kissed the side of her mouth.

'I'll write soon as I can,' he promised.

Connie watched sadly from her front door until he had disappeared around the lower landing. She felt no elation, no sense of fulfilment, only disappointment as she went back into the room and sat down heavily on her bed.

* * *

Long, hot summer days and sultry nights continued throughout July and August and, as the daylight hours gradually shortened and the evenings became cooler, a wind of change seemed to be stirring Ironmonger Street from its torpor. At the Armitage factory Gerald announced that he would be leaving the family business to join a company which was owned by his father-in-law. Peter Armitage had been expecting it for some time. The brothers had become virtual strangers to each other over the years and, when Joe Cooper finally achieved his objective in getting the management to accept a trade union workforce, Gerald's defeat had been final. Young Robert Armitage took over his uncle's position, and the factory owner breathed a huge sigh of relief. It seemed certain to him that in the not-too-distant future the country would be plunged into war, and it was a great comfort for him to know that his only son would be exempt from call-up.

Robert's mother Claudette was happy, and for her own reasons. She came from country stock and was a leading light in the functions of Kelstowe village. It was her dearest wish that her only son would one day marry the Marchants' daughter Eunice and she was sure that the two were already on very good terms. Now that Robert had settled into the business his friendship with Eunice might flourish. The Marchants were landowners and City stockbrokers. A union with their only daughter would no doubt ensure a lucrative position in the City for Robert. The one cloud on Claudette's horizon was Robert's evident disinclination to settle down. It irked her that he still seemed to retain some of those radical ideas he had picked up at university. But she believed he would come to see the error of his ways and one day get around to asking for the hand of the Marchant girl. To that end Claudette planned and schemed.

* * *

In September a strange incident took place in the street, which was discussed on all the doorsteps, and quickly became known as the 'Mulligan Affair'. It concerned a genial giant of an Irishman by the name of Danny Mulligan. Danny was a chimney sweep who regularly cleaned the chimneys in Ironmonger Street. September was a busy time for Danny, as it would soon be the season for roaring fires. The Irishman had a pair of hands as big as dinner plates and a beaming smile that was a flash of white in the middle of a blackened face. He pushed a barrow around the Bermondsey backstreets and sold his bags of soot to a boot polish factory over the water in Poplar. Danny came from a large family and now he had a large brood of his own. He was a God-fearing man who attended mass every Sunday with his family in tow.

One Monday morning Danny Mulligan had the misfortune of being asked to sweep the chimney at number one Ironmonger Street, the home of the Toomey family.

It was mid morning when Danny arrived at the Toomey's house and proceeded to hang up a heavy sack over the parlour fireplace. He screwed the circular brush on to the first of the flexible poles and thrust the contraption into the chimney. It was obvious to him that the house had never seen a chimney sweep by the large amount of soot he dislodged. He screwed on more poles and finally the easing pressure told him that the brush had emerged from the top of the chimney pot. Danny thought it strange that Marie Toomey and her daughter should stand watching him while he was working. Normally he was left alone to get on with the job, but on this occasion the process of sweeping a chimney seemed somehow to fascinate the large woman and her wickedly smiling daughter.

Danny sat back on his haunches. 'Right. That's it,' he said with a puff. 'Can yer go outside an' see if the brush 'as come frew?'

As Marie went outside to check, the Irishman removed the heavy sacking and carefully began to shovel up the huge amount of soot into a large bag. He was aware that Lillian was still standing there looking at him in a peculiar way and he began to feel a little uneasy. Suddenly she turned and walked out of the room.

After a short while Marie came back in. 'Yep, it's okay,' she said with a grin. 'It's stickin' straight up.'

Danny frowned to himself as he began to pull the brush back down. 'Right. That'll be 'alf a crown, missus,' he said.

Marie grinned even more at the chimney sweep as he carried the bag of soot out into the passage. 'Yer better see our Lil,' she said, pointing to the door halfway down the passage.

Danny opened the door and looked in. Lillian was lying naked on the bed with her hand behind her head, and she winked at him.

Danny winced. He could not believe his eyes.

'We've got no money,' she said unconcernedly. 'Wanna come ter some arrangement?'

Danny's eyes turned to slits. 'We certainly can,' he said, and went back into the passage.

Lillian was lying there expectantly when the sweep came into the room carrying a large bag. Without ceremony he emptied the bag of soot on to the nude figure. Lillian spluttered, jumped up from the bed and rubbed her eyes while Danny hurried out of the front door laughing. He put his equipment on to his barrow and started off down the turning as the nude and blackened figure ran after him screaming obscenities.

For Danny Mulligan the morning had been unprofitable, but he was pleased that the temptation of the devil had been surely resisted and he knew he would feel much better at confession.

* * *

A few weeks after the 'Mulligan Affair' the Ironmonger Street folk learned of a tragedy that had long remained hidden in their midst. At first things seemed no more untoward than usual, but gradually people began to realise that something very strange was happening when the oilshop remained closed until late in the morning on more than one occasion during the weeks of September. Misery Martin seemed loath to open at all and when his regular customers were short-changed and short-weighed the word went around that the shopowner was going off his head. When Mary Brown popped into Misery's shop one Saturday morning for two-penn'orth of hearthstone and a pint of vinegar he turned her away with a shake of his head. 'Right out of it,' he growled.

'There's some right be'ind yer,' Mary pointed out.

Misery turned without a word, wrapped up a block of hearthstone in newspaper and held out his hand for the money.

'What about me vinegar?' she asked grumpily.

'What vinegar?'

'The vinegar I jus' asked yer for,' Mary said, getting more angry.

Misery Martin grabbed the empty bottle from the counter and took it to the back of the shop. Mary could see him at the barrel. When the bottle was filled to overflowing he made no attempt to turn off the tap. Vinegar ran down the bottle and into the spillage tray. Still he did not turn off the tap. The vinegar was now running across the floor and Mary called out to him. 'Oi! You asleep? Look at the mess!'

Misery came back to himself and turned off the tap. When he banged the filled bottle down on the counter Mary saw a distant look in his rheumy eyes.

'You all right?' she asked.

''Course I'm all right. What d'yer ask that for?'

'Yer don't look well.'

'I'm all right. I told yer I'm all right. What yer waitin' for?'

'Well d'yer want me ter pay yer, then?' she asked in disbelief.

Misery Martin's strange behaviour became the talking point of the street and, when one of the youngsters returned from the shop with a pint of paraffin instead of vinegar and another lad ran back to say that Misery was banging nails in his counter and mumbling to himself, the street folk decided that enough was enough. Some of the women got together and Joe Cooper was delegated to approach the oilshop owner.

'What am I s'posed ter do?' Joe asked them. 'The man needs a doctor.'

The women were adamant and Joe reluctantly agreed to call into the shop. He found Misery sitting on an upturned box behind the counter with his head in his hands, mumbling loudly to himself.

'What's the matter mate?' Joe asked quietly.

Misery did not answer. Instead, his shoulders suddenly heaved and he began to cry.

Joe walked round the counter and put his hand on Misery's shoulder. 'C'mon, mate. Let's get yer upstairs. Yer need a doctor.'

Misery did not resist as Joe led him up the stairs, and when they reached the landing the shop owner stood with head bowed. Joe opened the door facing the stairs and recoiled in horror at what he saw. He walked slowly into the room and looked around in bewilderment. The tattered curtains were drawn and the stale-smelling room was lit by dozens of thick candles which stood in dirty saucers. One wall was covered with faded photographs of a young woman who smiled down into the room. A vase holding coloured paper flowers was standing on the mantelshelf, and beside the vase there was a small framed photograph of two young people posed together outside a building. The smart young man wore a flower in his coat lapel and the pretty young girl was holding on to his arm. In the centre of the room the table was laid for two. Cobwebs covered the plates, knives and forks, and beside one of the plates there was a small parcel tied with ribbon. In one corner of the room there was an unmade camp bed with a chair placed at the head. Misery Martin slumped down on the dirty blanket, his head in his hands, his eyes staring down at his feet. As Joe backed towards the door, hardly able to take his eyes from the scene, he caught sight of the little photograph on the wall above the bed. It was of the young girl but, unlike the other photos, it was draped in black velvet.

'The poor bastard!' he whispered aloud as he left the room and hurried down the stairs to fetch the doctor.

Chapter Thirteen

Connie got dressed quickly. It was Monday morning and she had slept through the alarm. The kettle seemed to take an eternity to boil, and the toast burnt under the gas-stove grill. Outside the window she could see the rain falling from a leaden sky, and down in the street the milkman was pushing his heavy cart over the slippery cobbles. One or two people hurried along beneath umbrellas and she saw the local policeman talking to old George Baker at his front door. Outside, everything was the same as usual but for Connie the morning was different. She felt excited as she scraped the carbon from the toast and spread a thin coating of marmalade over the two thick slices. The tea was hot and she glanced again anxiously at the clock as she blew on the cup. Up on the mantelshelf was Michael's latest letter to her and in it he said that he might be home by Christmas. The holiday seemed a long way off to Connie and she stared at the letter as she finished her toast. In two weeks' time she would be seventeen and at that moment she felt much older. Robert Armitage was returning after a spell away from the factory and today she would see him.

The canteen was hot and steamy and a pile of potatoes awaited Connie as she took off her wet coat. The short dash across the street had been enough to soak her and, as she dabbed her hair on a towel, Dot came over and pointed to the sacks of cabbages in one corner.

'Yer'll 'ave ter get that lot done before yer lay the managers' table, Con. That bleedin' Emma ain't showed up this mornin'.'

Connie began peeling the potatoes. Without Emma chattering away incessantly, Connie was able to gather her thoughts, and it was with a feeling of excitement that she recalled the conversation she had had with Robert before he left. He had been very attentive whenever he saw her and often asked about Michael. Connie remembered how this time he had made much of the fact that her boyfriend would be away for quite a time, and had suggested that if she was feeling lonely she might like to go to a show with him when he got back from his business trip. Robert had made it clear that it would be merely a friendly evening out and she would have nothing to reproach herself for. Connie had been taken aback by the invitation and said she would let him know as soon as he returned. She thought that it could be asking for trouble to accept his offer, but she knew it would be hard to refuse him. She had tried to keep her distance since Michael had left but Robert always seemed to be around. He was good looking, and she found his easy, relaxed manner very appealing. Her legs would feel like jelly whenever he talked to her, and many nights she had lain awake in her bed thinking of him. It was not right, she told herself, she should be thinking of Michael. Nevertheless she was eager to see Robert again.

Connie looked at the diminishing pile of potatoes and realised that she had been peeling them with a vengeance. Life was very boring at the moment. During the days there was the grind of the factory canteen and in the evenings the often uncomfortable time spent at the Bartletts' flat. Helen and Matthew argued a lot because of the constant shortage of money and Molly had grown resentful of Connie's relationship with Michael. Occasionally the two cousins went for short walks, but the spinal jacket Molly wore made it difficult for her to go out very far without discomfort. At the pictures it was the same. Molly became more irritable, and Connie had to bite on her tongue to stop her making some retort that she would regret. Worst of all, there were the regular visits to the sanatorium. She would always come away feeling sad and depressed. Kate was becoming less talkative, and it was obvious to Connie that her mother was getting weaker. She had never told Kate about Michael and it had been an agreement between Connie and the Bartletts not to mention anything to Kate until she was feeling better. The Rileys had obviously not said anything to the Bartletts about Michael going back to the flat and for that Connie was grateful. So Robert was the one bright thing in her mundane existence.

As the morning wore on Connie became more anxious. She knew that to agree to Robert's suggestion of an evening out might well mean the start of a relationship that she could regret. It would be hard to resist his good looks and charming ways for long, she felt sure. Connie thought hard about her predicament, and she realised that she might not have been so mixed up and confused had she not taken Michael back to her flat that evening before he left. Her childish expectations of ecstasy had been let down when she had let him make love to her. Her face flushed with the recollection. It was the first time she had ever made love, and she had been anxious for her breathless need to be sated. Michael had never been with a woman before, and his fumbling and inexperience had left her unsatisfied, cheated of fulfilment. She had told him that it had been good, but he had known that she was lying, and his repeated words of concern had only irked her.

Her thoughts were interrupted when Dot called over to her.

'Leave the rest o' the veg. I'll finish it. You'd better get that table laid.'

At ten minutes past midday Robert looked in at the door and spotted Connie setting the places. 'Hello, young lady. It's nice to see you again,' he said brightly.

Connie flushed with embarrassment and smiled at him. ''Ello. Did yer enjoy yer trip?' she said awkwardly.

Robert thrust his hands deep into his trouser pockets and hunched his shoulders. 'It wasn't bad. I was in Birmingham at an engineering exhibition. We're thinking of putting some new machinery in the factory.'

'Oh,' was all Connie could muster, and Robert smiled.

'It's all boring stuff. Did you give some thought to what we talked about?'

'About goin' out?'

'Yes . . .'

Connie looked down at the table. 'I don't fink I should.'

Robert touched her arm gently. 'Look. There's a good musical show up town. Do you like musicals?'

Connie had never been to a show but she nodded. 'Yes I do.'

'Well then. What about tomorrow evening?'

It was wrong, she knew, but she couldn't say no to him. He looked totally disarming. His boyish smile made her feel breathless with excitement, and she looked into his pale-blue eyes and swallowed hard. 'Yes, okay,' she said.

Claudette Armitage put the telephone down with an exaggerated display of petulance. 'Really, Peter. I do think Stewart should have ordered the marquee by now,' she began. 'After all, he did agree. I can't be expected to do everything myself. There are the drinks and the buffet to see to, and I suppose Reverend Jones will be asking me to organise the home-made jam competition again this year. It's too much, really it is.'

Peter grinned to himself as he stayed hidden behind the evening paper. Claudette was working herself up into one of her hysterical moods, and those required very special handling. 'You're quite right, dear. You can't be expected to do it all,' he said in a tone of concern. 'In fact the fête would be an absolute disaster if it wasn't for you.'

His sympathetic words soothed Claudette somewhat and she sat down to consult her notebook once more. 'Now let me see,' she whispered to herself. 'I must phone the Marchants tomorrow. They'll need time to make arrangements. I wouldn't like Eunice to miss the day, now that Robert is back.'

Peter puffed silently behind his paper. He had always considered Clarence Marchant to be an unmitigated bore. He drank too much for a start, and he usually managed to upset one or two of the elderly lady committee members with his bawdy comments. He was also prone to ogle the young girls with his bleary, lecherous eyes. His long-suffering wife Mabel was so wrapped up in her charity work at the fête, that she didn't seem to notice her husband's boorish behaviour or, if she did, she pretended not to. Yes, Major Clarence Marchant was insufferable, Peter decided, switching his thoughts to Eunice, the Marchants' daughter. It was obvious to him that Robert partnered her at the fêtes only out of good manners and he knew, too, that his son was bored to distraction with the whole rigmarole. Peter secretly wished that Claudette would be more observant – her role of matchmaker was one function she would do well to relinquish.

During the evening the notebook was consulted thoroughly and a few more ticks placed against names. Claudette made at least a dozen calls and Peter watched with amusement as his wife performed, her repertoire ranging from thinly disguised irritation to gushing patronage. She was in her element and loving every minute of being the fête organiser. In fact, she was elected every year, and she invariably accepted with a contrived show of reluctance. 'I'm sure someone else could do a much better job than I,' she would say demurely.

'But you always do such a tremendous job, Claudette, and it all goes off so smoothly,' the Reverend Jones would always reply.

All the committee members around the vestry table would nod their heads and allow Claudette to breathe a sigh of relief. 'All right then. If you insist.'

Peter dreaded the day when the rest of the committee did not insist. The annual fête was the highlight of his wife's social calendar.

For Claudette, the evening had been reasonably successful. The usual volunteers had been recruited. The jam ladies would be eagerly competing for the coveted silver jam pot, and Miss Harcourt would be on hand again this year with a thunderingly good aria. The Waverley sisters had already started making woollen egg muffs, tasselled tea cosies and long woollen bedsocks. Cyril Thomas, landlord of the village pub, had been pressed into donating a barrel of ale, and old James the village postman had agreed to go through his musical spoon routine. Yes, it was fairly encouraging. Must have a word with Robert though, she thought, looking over to her husband who was nodding off in his armchair.

'Peter, will Robert be coming home this evening?' she asked loudly.

'No,' he yawned. 'Robert's going to see the Lupino Lane show at the Adelphi. He told me he'll be staying over in London with a few friends.'

Claudette pulled a face. 'I do hope he realises the fête's this weekend. I don't want him making other arrangements.'

Peter dutifully said he would remind him. He wished he was in a position to make other arrangements himself, instead of having to escort the Waverley sisters to the home-made jam table and wait while they nibbled on jam-smeared wafer biscuits and deliberated for what would seem an eternity.

The evening traffic was heavy, with drivers hooting and cursing as they were held up by trams and buses stopping and starting. Tired horses held their heads low as they plodded homewards, their carts slowing the traffic to a crawl. Weary office workers streamed over Waterloo Bridge and, down below the iron girders, beneath the noise and bustle, the quiet river flowed swiftly on to the open sea. The autumn night was already lit by a yellow moon which appeared low in the sky downriver. On the bridge the slow traffic began to move a little and the taxi driver slipped into the near side, ready to pull up by the Strand. His passengers sat, comfortable and warm, in the back. The young man was reclining with his arms folded, occasionally glancing at the expression on his partner's face. The young girl was wide-eyed and attentive to everything around her. It was the first time she had travelled in a London taxi cab and the prospect of seeing a real live show excited her. Robert smiled and pointed to the huge stone building which ran along the river front.

'See that place,' he said suddenly. 'It's Somerset House. We're all in there somewhere. It's where they keep a register of births, deaths and marriages.'

Connie followed his eyes. She could see lights twinkling downriver and the laughing, mocking face of the rising moon. A momentary panic gripped her as the promise she made to Michael flashed into her mind. *I won't go on any dates, Mick*, and she paled.

'You okay?' Robert asked, concerned.

Connie smiled. 'It's exciting. I've never bin in a taxi before.'

The cab driver pulled into the kerb and the two passengers got out. Robert handed over the fare and waved the change away.

'The theatre's not far from here. We can get a drink first if you'd like,' he said turning to take her arm.

At the door of the pub Connie hesitated. 'I'm not old enough ter go in a pub,' she said, looking at Robert with worry showing in her eyes.

He grinned. 'I was forgetting. Anyway, I don't suppose anyone would realise you're under age. Come on, you can have a lemonade or something.'

Connie ran her hand down her hair and compressed her lips nervously as they walked in. Her lipstick tasted scenty, the small daisy earrings were nipping her ear lobes and her high-heeled shoes were pinching slightly. It was a nuisance trying to look grown-up, she decided.

They sat in a corner sipping their drinks. Connie's eyes flitted around the room and she felt as though she were in another world. People stood at the bar, many of the men wearing evening suits and bow ties, some of the women in long dresses that touched the floor and others in fur coats or with fur stoles draped over their shoulders. All the women wore lots of make-up and Connie marvelled at how beautiful they all looked. It was like a gathering in one of those films at the Trocette. Connie half expected someone to burst into song at any minute, or dance along the bar. Looking at all the well-dressed ladies she felt shabby in comparison and her eyes dropped down to the table.

Robert was watching her carefully and he sensed she was ill at ease. He wanted to tell her that for him she was the most beautiful girl in the room. Her hair shone and hung down over her shoulders in a golden sweep. Her eyes seemed as blue as the sea and her smooth, flushed face reminded him of a Greek goddess. Her hands were clasped in her lap and she sat straight and taut. He could see the fullness of her young breasts beneath the tight coat and the slope of her slim shoulders. Her small ears peeped out from between strands of hair and he wanted to kiss her shapely red lips. Instead he picked up his drink and drained the glass.

Later, they walked across the busy Strand and up to the lighted front of the Adelphi. Connie clutched a small handbag under her arm and subconsciously slipped her free arm into his as they entered the foyer. The scene that met her eyes made her heart pound. She felt out of place as she looked around nervously and Robert smiled reassuringly.

'Just relax, Connie. All you've got to do is sit back and enjoy the show.'

She smiled sheepishly. 'Those women look really nice, don't they?' she said, glancing at a party in fur coats.

Her escort looked over, then back to her. 'So do you,' he said quietly.

She looked away from his deep, enquiring eyes feeling as though she were a Cinderella being escorted to the ball by a handsome prince. She would have him all to herself, but then the clock would strike midnight and the dream would fade. She would be back waiting at the table dressed in her apron and silly hat. He would smile like he always did and she would think about him as she cleared the plates away. The days would be the same as they always were, and the nights would be spent dreaming about the ball, and her charming suitor. Connie felt a lump rising in her throat as she walked into the darkening auditorium.

Helen Bartlett sat in the armchair beside the low fire, busily darning one of Matthew's socks. The wireless was on and the soft, melancholic music from a string quartet drifted through the flat. Molly sat in the other armchair, her head buried in a book. Occasionally she fidgeted and Helen could hear her daughter's uneven breathing. Matthew had gone to bed early after an argument and Helen worked swiftly with the large needle, her mind still preoccupied with the angry words they had said to each other. It was her fault that the argument had started in the first place, she knew. Matthew had been unlucky at the labour exchange that morning and, instead of giving him a few words of encouragement, she had niggled away at him until a row erupted. It was becoming a common occurrence and Helen was very aware that she had become short-tempered of late. It seemed to her that their whole existence had become meaningless. She had married Matthew with high hopes of building a happy life with him. At the beginning the desire to have children had been strong, but in the first five years of her married life Helen had been disappointed. When she had finally become pregnant it seemed her cup was full, her prayers had been answered. Until the traumatic experience of Molly's birth. Her disability had been hard to come to terms with, and it had been made even more difficult by Matthew's reaction. But together they had overcome their burden of grief and anger at the unfairness of it all and they had tried for another child. It had never happened. Then Matthew had fallen out of work and it made him more and more morose. He struggled to earn a few coppers at the markets to eke out his dole money, and Helen knew only too well that it was her morning cleaning job which kept their heads above water. Their problems only seemed to be getting worse and it was all becoming more than she could handle. Helen was nearing fifty and already her hair was showing streaks of grey and her face was becoming lined and gaunt. Her love life with Matthew was now practically non-existent. She knew how it upset him when she constantly spurned his advances but she felt repulsed at the thought of allowing him to make love to her. His show of frustration only added to her disgust and the rows increased.

Her daughter's difficulties were also eating away at Helen. Molly's physical problems were growing as she got older, and she was becoming harder to handle. She had become embittered and sullen. Even Connie, who had always been able to cheer her up, was finding it difficult to reach her. To make matters worse, Kate seemed to be losing the will to live. She showed no desire to talk on visiting days and it agonised Helen, and she had decided to visit her sister only once a month. Even on those infrequent occasions she came away from the sanatorium feeling very depressed.

There seemed to be no light at the end of the tunnel, nothing to expect except the drudgery and the constant struggle to make ends meet. Helen dropped the sock in her lap and leaned back in the chair as she closed her eyes.

The full moon hung over Bermondsey. Robert had stopped the taxi at the Bricklayers Arms and as they passed the shuttered shops he looked at Connie.

'Thanks for your company. I've really enjoyed this evening,' he said with a smile.

'So 'ave I, Robert. The show was wonderful. You sure I looked okay?'

'Connie, you looked perfect. I was proud to be your escort.'

'I was glad yer asked me, ter tell yer the truth,' she said.

'I wanted to. I think you're nice company. We must do it again sometime soon.'

Connie hesitated before answering. It would have been so easy to say yes. He was very good looking and exciting to be with. He had an easy manner which helped her to feel confident and self-assured. Just being with him made her forget everything. He had introduced her to another world she had not realised existed outside of films and story books. It would be quite easy to give herself to Robert, she thought. But it was wrong even to think of a serious relationship with him. They were so different. Robert did not come from the working class; his world was not one of backstreets and tenement buildings, pawnshops and poverty. And he could not be expected to understand the ways of working-class people, with their very different hopes and aspirations and their fierce pride. Connie was surprised by the beginning of a vague anger within her, and she wavered. 'I'd like ter go out with yer again sometime, Robert, but I don't think I should,' she said slowly.

'Why not, Con? We've enjoyed tonight, haven't we?'

'Too much. That's what I mean. I like yer company but I've got a boyfriend. It wouldn't be fair while 'e's away.'

They had turned into the maze of backstreets and ahead they saw the factory gates looming up in the moonlight. 'Well, here we are,' he said smiling.

They stopped at the entrance to the buildings and he looked into her eyes. 'Say you'll let me take you out again soon, Connie. I'd like to, really I would.'

Connie looked up into his face and saw something there in his eyes that promised her so much, and she felt her legs go weak. He held a key to her heart and if she was not careful her little world could come tumbling down around her. She wanted to throw caution to the wind and draw him into her world, but something deep down inside her told her to resist. 'I'll 'ave ter fink about it,' she said weakly.

He bent his head and took her gently by the shoulders as he kissed her tenderly on the cheek, then he turned and walked away. She stood there in the entrance to the tenement block, her eyes following him until he disappeared in the darkness. Her stomach was turning over with a mixture of elation and dread. She felt like a fly caught in a web, trapped by his kiss. She could still feel it on her cheek and the pressure of his hands on her shoulders. Connie turned and ran quickly up the dark stairway to her lonely flat.

Chapter Fourteen

The village of Kelstowe was tucked away in the Weald of Kent. It boasted one pub, a post office, a general store, and a crumbling sixteenth-century church that was in imminent danger of falling to the ground. Kelstowe was privileged in having a very active and influential fund-raising committee that, led by Claudette Armitage, had organised a summer fête for more years than they cared to remember. Moneys earned from the various fête activities went to the Holmesdale Home for the Elderly in nearby Canterbury. The summer fête was also seen as a way of perpetuating the traditions of village life and almost all the villagers made a point of attending the function. The Kelstowe fête had become famous locally and it was praised by some, and blamed by others, for being the prime catalyst of local matrimonial entanglements, and disentanglements. It also provided enough scandalous gossip to last until the following year.

Kelstowe was thrown into confusion in 1935 when, without warning, a piece of masonry the size of a half crown had landed on the head of Beatrice Waverley, the eldest of the Waverley sisters, just as she was leaving church one Sunday evening. Beatrice had felt the weight of the masonry as it fell on to her new bonnet, and when a trickle of blood ran down into her eye she fainted away. Doctor Spanswick was called from the Three Pheasants to administer to her, and two cold compresses and one stitch later he had zipped up his black bag and returned to his place in the snug bar. Reverend Jones was later summoned to the Waverleys' cottage at the edge of the village and instructed to pay more attention to those hooligan choirboys of his. Throwing stones was to be expected of those London guttersnipes, not of village church lads, the Waverleys were quick to point out. The Reverend Jones was at pains to reassure them that his choirboys did not throw stones and it had merely been a piece of dislodged masonry which had flattened Beatrice Waverley and ruined her new bonnet. The sisters were not to be pacified and they had demanded that a full inspection should be carried out forthwith to ascertain the level of danger to parishioners.

Reverend Jones was in a quandary. A full survey would cost money and his bishop would most certainly raise Cain, but the Waverleys were members of the village committee and as such they would command strong support. He realised he would have to talk to the bishop, and he fretted at the thought of it. At the first opportunity the elderly cleric confided in his dutiful wife Christina. It was she who gave him the answer which he felt would go a long way to pacifying the bishop.

'Why don't you get the survey done, and when the cost of renovation is worked out, get your committee to raise the restoration funds at the fête. After all, Bernard, it *is* their church.'

'But the fête is organised to raise money for the Holmesdale, dear.'

'Well, organise another fête in the autumn, dearest. It shouldn't be that difficult.'

Reverend Jones met the bishop and got approval for a full and expensive survey to be carried out without delay. The results were staggering. The church was in danger of falling down in a pile of dust unless major restoration work was started immediately. The Reverend took the news to the committee and after much wrangling he managed to win approval for an autumn fête to raise the £5,000 needed. Every year since then the autumn fête had stood in front of the summer function as the main event on the village social calendar.

Everyone was expected to rally to their church, even if they omitted to respond to the elderly at Holmesdale. Claudette Armitage made a point of reminding everyone that the west wing of Kelstowe Church was in a dire condition and for that reason the autumn fête should be enthusiastically supported this year and every year.

In Ironmonger Street the tumbledown houses and the grim Jubilee Buildings were not fortunate enough to have dedicated sponsors and, when heavy rain seeped through broken roof slates and penetrated the decayed pointing on the brickwork, the street folk realised that their homes were in danger of falling down on top of them. When the rent collector called in the street one Monday morning he was besieged by angry tenants. Pleas for him to look at the dampness and state of disrepair were ignored and his excuse that he was only employed to collect rents only served to inflame the situation still further. He was surrounded by an irate group who threatened all manner of unspeakable things if he did not report the condition of the homes to his superiors. The rent collector realised that Ironmonger Street was not any old street, and its reputation was not to be taken lightly. With a sense of foreboding he relented and promised he would do what he could. He left the street with old George Baker's threat ringing in his ears.

'If we don't get somebody down 'ere right away yer better

not show yer ugly face in our turning next week, Jacko.'

On Friday morning two smartly dressed characters arrived with clipboards and rolled-up plans of Ironmonger Street. They knocked on the doors and introduced themselves as surveyors from Vine Estates.

When they knocked at number three they were met by Mary Brown holding a handkerchief up to her running nose. ''Bout time,' she spluttered. 'These bleedin' 'ovels are killin' us. I'm off sick, me ole dad's in bed wiv the flu, me kids 'ave both got snotty noses, an' there's Mrs Cosgrove along the street. 'Er an' 'er ole man are both in bed wiv the flu. It's bloody disgustin'.'

The men nodded their heads sympathetically and wrote on their clipboards. 'Can we look around please? We won't be long.'

Mary stood back and allowed the surveyors into her home. She watched while they tapped the walls and prodded the rotten plaster, then she followed them up the stairs and into George Baker's bedroom. The old boy was sitting up in bed, a blanket drawn around his frail shoulders.

'Who the bloody 'ell are you?' he croaked.

'It's all right, Dad. It's the men from the lan'lords.'

George eyed the visitors suspiciously. 'Well it's about time yer come an' 'ad a look. I've lived 'ere fer nigh on firty years. Me an' my missus – Gawd rest 'er soul – brought our family up 'ere. We ain't never missed payin' the rent in all that time, an' what 'ave we 'ad done in the way of repairs? I tell yer what. Sweet bugger all, that's what. An' I tell yer somefink else. If nufink's done bloody quick we're all gonna get tergevver an' make this 'ere street out o' bounds ter your bleedin' rent collector. Now give that bit o' news ter Vine Estates.'

Mary patted her father's back as he went into a fit of coughing and the surveyors beat a hasty retreat.

* * *

153

The Kelstowe autumn fête got off to a very good start, with Miss Harcourt reaching a top 'C' and the piano player Christina Jones hardly striking a wrong note as she struggled with Puccini's 'The Prince'. Old James came next and, although he dropped the spoons on two occasions, his attempts to rattle out 'Colonel Bogey' received enthusiastic applause. The church hall then became silent as Claudette stood up and issued a passionate plea for everyone to give generously to the restoration fund. She took the applause with her usual aplomb and then flitted theatrically amongst the gathering to milk the plaudits for her efforts in organising the fête.

Outside in the garden things were beginning to hot up. Visitors strolled into the marquee and sampled the ale. The Waverley sisters stood behind a table selling their egg muffs and long woollen bedsocks and, unseen by anyone, two young lads slipped into the marquee and one of them dipped his grubby finger in a jam exhibit. Major Marchant had also been sampling, and he became more loud-voiced with each glass of ale. Mabel Marchant chose to ignore her husband's behaviour and strolled around the tables with her daughter Eunice holding on to her arm.

Eunice was tall and inclined to stoop. Her eyes blinked owlishly behind her spectacles, and her dark hair was tied back with a pink ribbon which exposed her rather large ears. Her one redeeming feature was her smile. When she parted her lips she exposed perfect teeth and her face lit up. As she walked beside her mother Eunice was not disposed to smile, however. Her father was rapidly becoming drunk and already attracting disapproving glances from the Waverley sisters.

Inside the church hall Claudette was getting anxious. Peter had not yet arrived, nor had Robert. The jam tasting is due in ten minutes, she groaned to herself, studying her watch. Peter knows very well it's his job to accompany the Waverley sisters and to take notes. It won't do. He knows how I insist on keeping to a schedule. Then there's Eunice. She'll be looking for Robert to escort her throughout the day. The girl obviously thinks highly of him. Why, oh why doesn't Robert realise she's set her sights on him? He could do a lot worse than marrying into the Marchant family. All right, maybe the girl isn't a raving beauty, but she has class and breeding and she would make a perfect partner for Robert. It's about time he settled down instead of gadding around with those loutish college friends of his. Maybe he doesn't like girls? Maybe he – no, the idea's preposterous. Why ever should I think a thing like that? she asked herself.

When Peter strolled into the hall Claudette immediately grabbed him by the arm. 'Really, Peter. You do cut things a bit fine. Come on, let's get the jam tasting started. By the way, where's Robert?'

Peter shrugged his shoulders. 'I left him in the Pheasants. He said he'll follow on later.'

Claudette puffed out her cheeks in exasperation. 'I don't know what Eunice is going to think. I've already told her Robert will be pleased to be her escort.'

Peter looked at his wife and shook his head slowly. 'You shouldn't have told her that, Claudette. You've no right to act as matchmaker. Robert will do his own choosing when he's good and ready. If you ask me I'd say he hasn't the slightest intention of settling down just yet. You must leave him alone, dear. He'll do things in his own time.' But Claudette was already walking away from him.

The home-made jam contest soon got under way. Peter stood aside as the Waverleys spread dobs of jam on to wafer biscuits and nibbled away before whispering their findings to him. The sisters were walking slowly along the line of jam pots when suddenly they stopped and exchanged shocked glances.

The eldest Waverley turned to Peter with a disgusted look on her face. 'We can't sample that one!' she exclaimed. 'It's been tampered with!'

Peter saw the distinct imprint of a small finger and he suppressed a smile. 'Of course you can't, Miss Waverley,' he said sucking his cheek.

The onlookers exchanged sly grins and suddenly a loud voice rang out. 'Whassa matter there?'

Peter turned to find himself confronted by the inebriated Major. He leaned away from the man's beery breath and pointed to the jam. The Major swayed unsteadily on his feet and looked down at the fingerprint.

'Good Lord!' he said, blinking at the Waverleys. 'Someone's sco-scotched the contest! No one leaves the tent!' he bawled.

Eunice shrank back into a corner and wished the ground would open up and swallow her. Mabel walked over and took her husband's arm. 'Come away, dear. Let the ladies get on with it.'

Clarence leered and swayed backward. 'Sabotage! That's what it is. Damn sabotage!' he spluttered.

More people began to converge on the jam table to offer advice and, during the confusion, Robert walked into the marquee. He was immediately approached by Claudette. 'The Major's had too much to drink, Robert. I think it's upsetting Eunice. Go and see if she's all right, will you, dear?'

Robert groaned to himself and walked over to where the Marchants' daughter was sitting. 'Hello, Eunice,' he said cheerfully.

'Oh, Robert. Father's getting awfully drunk. I feel so ashamed, I wish I could die.'

He looked down at the forlorn figure and tried to look concerned. 'It's nothing to worry about, Eunice. Your father's just a little tipsy, that's all. He's not hurting anyone.'

'He's hurting me,' Eunice blurted out, and she dabbed at her eyes with a lace square.

At that moment there was a loud crash and Robert looked over to see the Major lying across the jam table. The jam pots were strewn about and, as Clarence was helped to his feet, his blood-red face contorted in a lop-sided grin. 'Damned bloody sabotage,' he said with deliberation. 'This is a case for Sexton Blake.'

The Waverley sisters were protesting vehemently. 'That's it. The contest is over. Come, Gwen. I think it's time we left.'

Claudette was fluttering around in a panic. 'All my hard work has been in vain,' she cried to anyone within earshot. 'What could have possessed the Major? It's so unlike him to get that drunk.'

Outside the marquee the village postman sat on an upturned box and tried to focus his bleary eyes on the departing Waverley sisters. His head was swimming and he was having difficulty in rolling a cigarette. His pal George Simpson had only sampled two glasses of ale and he had gone home in a worse state than he did after a skinful at the Pheasants on a Saturday night. Mabel Marchant was worried. She had got used to her husband's drunken antics, but on this occasion he had only consumed a few glasses. His behaviour had upset Eunice and Claudette Armitage was furious, she could tell. She must apologise for Clarence. Whatever would the Reverend Jones think?

Unknown to Mabel, the venerable cleric was having difficulty in making himself understood. He had popped into the fête earlier that day and sampled the ale, intending to go back to the function after he had supervised the cleaning up operation. The problem was, he was feeling just like he did on that occasion long ago when he had over-indulged at the end-of-term party at theological college. His eyes were rolling around and words came out jumbled. Mrs Brown and two of her friends had volunteered to clean the church thoroughly and make sure it was tidy, and when their vicar staggered up and asked them in garbled English to 'sweep the pews out of the church and dust the aisle' they thought he must be ill. Mrs Brown's friend Alice had other views. 'He's sozzled,' she said. 'Probably been at the communion wine.'

Back at the fête Claudette was trying to salvage something from the day. Miss Harcourt agreed to do an encore and James the postman was being sought for another rendition on the spoons. Robert had agreed to escort Eunice home and they had managed to get the Major out into the fresh air. Peter was trying to look serious as his distraught wife dabbed at her forehead. 'The shame and humiliation of it all,' she groaned. 'I'll never do another fête, Peter. I swear I won't.'

Her name was called and, as she turned, Claudette saw one of the committee ladies hurrying towards her. 'We've located James,' the woman said breathlessly.

'Oh splendid. Get him to . . .'

'It's no use, Claudette,' the woman cut in. 'He's asleep in the middle of the flower bed.'

'I can't believe it,' Claudette wailed. 'What's happening to everyone? Have they all become alcoholics overnight?'

Worse news was to follow. Mrs Ackroyd looked in to say that it was unlikely they would see the vicar any more that day. According to her friend Alice, he had cracked up and drunk all the communion wine and was now snoring his head off in the front pew.

The unintentional perpetrator of the disaster was leaning across the counter of the Three Pheasants, engaged in a conversation with Doctor Spanswick. 'Personally, Doc, I never have the time to go to the fête now. It's not my cup of tea anyway. It drives me crackers listening to all that gossip and tittle-tattle all day long. None of it's interesting. Hardly any of 'em use the pub anyway.'

The old doctor shifted his position on the bar stool and chuckled. 'Oh come on, Cyril, it's not that bad. Their motives are good. Think of all the money they raise.'

'It's not the principle I object to,' Cyril went on. 'It's the way they go about it. They'd be better off having a get-together in my pub with a few collecting boxes. And we'd all be able to have a proper drink instead of a few sips of that watery sherry the Waverleys get from God knows where. Mind you, the fête committee talked me out of a barrel of best ale for the infernal event, though I dare say the old Major's been enjoying most of that. Well, at any rate my soul will rest easy, Doc.'

The barrel of ale donated by Cyril Thomas had already been placed out of bounds by the fête committee, and Claudette vowed that the landlord of the Three Pheasants would have some pertinent questions to answer. 'This ale is positively lethal,' she told the shocked ladies.

Harris and Beamish brewers would have had to agree. They had distributed thirty barrels of it before the mistake was discovered. The ale was in fact a rogue batch that had fermented and frothed until one pint of the stuff was enough to knock the most experienced drinker bandy. Twenty-nine barrels had been recovered by the brewers and one was given up as lost. The dishonest drayman, who had appropriated the remaining barrel and sold it to the less-than-honest Cyril Thomas, would soon have to prepare himself for the publican's wrath.

Robert Armitage walked back slowly to his home on the edge of Kelstowe. The day had been one he would sooner like to forget. The fête had been livened up by the lethal ale, it was true, but he had not enjoyed being forced to chaperone and nursemaid the designing Eunice Marchant. When he walked her home she had asked him in and when he declined, saying that he had to get back, she had played the innocent aggrieved. Her head snuggled against his chest, she told him how dependable and strong he was. Robert did his part by consoling her but the situation threatened to get out of hand when, with great expectations, the Marchants' daughter had removed her glasses. Robert had managed to escape by saying his throat felt sore and he must be going down with something. He felt a little guilty for the deception as he strolled along with his hands tucked into his trouser pockets but he felt there was nothing else he could do. He had no desire to entangle himself with Eunice, no matter what his mother wanted. His immediate plans concerned someone else, and his thoughts turned again to Connie. She had been in and out of his thoughts all week. She had charmed him with her rough accent and naive honesty, and her shy, innocent personality had intrigued him. She was a rough diamond, he thought. A glittering jewel in drab and lustreless surroundings, claimed yet not owned. He desired her, wanted to win her, to be with her more than anything. He realised it was the first time he had felt this way about a girl. Connie may come from the other side of the street, but it made no difference to him. It was something that had just happened, something he couldn't explain to himself, let alone to his family. They obviously expected him to find a girl from within their own social circle, or at least a girl with an impeccable background who would be considered acceptable. Well life wasn't like that. He had found someone he cared for and wanted to be with, and his parents were going to have to get used to the idea.

Chapter Fifteen

Rain beat against the window pane and in the distance thunder rolled. The clock beside the bed said nine o'clock and Connie turned over. It was Saturday morning and her seventeenth birthday. The warmth of the bed claimed her and the cards that had come through the door stayed unopened on the rough mat in the passage. She had heard the letter box sound earlier and guessed that Helen had put the cards through the door on her way to work. As she snuggled down, Connie heard heavy footsteps on the stairs and along the landing and the letter box rattled again. The room felt cold as she climbed out of bed and gathered up the envelopes from the mat. Back in bed she opened the two unstamped ones first. One was from Helen and Matthew, and the other from Molly. One of the stamped envelopes bore her mother's spidery handwriting.

The card contained the message: 'To Connie, with fondest love, Mum'.

Connie put the open card down on the chair beside the bed and stared at it sadly for a few moments. She was due to visit her mother on Sunday and had not expected her to post the card. It was an unexpected gesture. Connie turned her attention to the remaining envelope and inspected the handwriting. It was in a flourishing style and the postmark was smudged and illegible. Puzzled, she opened the envelope and removed the card. It was from Robert, and below the words 'Happy Birthday' he had written the message, 'To my special friend. I have two tickets for the best show in London. Please say yes. Robert'. She hugged it to her chest happily.

Later that morning, when Connie took the weekly shopping into the Bartletts, she was given two small parcels which were wrapped in brown paper.

'Go on, Con. Open 'em up,' Molly laughed.

Connie sat down in the chair beside the table and tore the wrappings from the first parcel. Inside was a green woollen cardigan which Helen had knitted.

'Cor! Fanks Aunt 'Elen. It's jus' what I wanted,' she said, jumping up and kissing the embarrassed woman on the cheek.

'Go on, Con. Open mine,' Molly said eagerly, sitting down at the table facing her cousin.

Connie removed the paper and took out a small tortoise-shell powder compact. Her eyes lit up and she cuddled Molly. ''Ow did yer guess I needed a compact? It's beautiful.'

The Bartletts' daughter cupped her chin in her thick fingers and grinned, her round face lighting up and her large eyes fixed on her embarrassed cousin. 'I reckoned yer might need a compact, now yer courtin'.' Helen and Matthew exchanged glances and Connie flushed slightly as she recognised the way Molly emphasised the last word. What would they think if they knew I'd been dated by the factory owner's son, she thought. Molly was staring at her with a strange look in her eyes. Behind her cousin's happy expression there seemed to be a look of sadness and envy. Connie understood her and pitied her without anger. Poor Molly was going through a difficult time. She was looking for a suitable job while, at home, all around her there were arguments raging. And Connie knew there would be precious few chances for Molly to meet someone who would love her as she deserved to be loved.

Connie had stayed with the Bartletts awhile, helping to clear away the dinner things and giving Helen a hand with the household chores. She felt better by helping out. The family had been kind to her and Helen said that Molly always became more cheerful after her visits. In the afternoon Connie went to her flat and, as she opened the front door, she saw a small plain envelope lying on the mat. Intrigued, she tore it open and removed the single sheet of paper. Her heart leaped as she read the message.

Dear Connie,
I hope you liked the card and have had time to think about my offer. It really is a very good show. Consider it as a birthday present. Please say yes. If so, meet me at the Bricklayers Arms tonight. I'll be there at 7 pm.
Looking forward to seeing you then.
Robert.

He must have knocked earlier and got no answer, Connie reasoned. Or maybe he got someone to deliver the note. Whatever, it was sudden and exciting. He was not willing to take no for an answer, but she must say no. It wouldn't be fair to Michael if she accepted the offer. Besides, Robert would think she wanted the relationship to blossom. No, it was too risky. But he was so persuasive and good looking and the combination was something Connie knew she couldn't resist. All right, it was one thing to fantasise and to succumb to fanciful dreams, but it was another thing entirely to start going out regularly to shows with the factory owner's son. She was not his kind and it was altogether too dangerous. It wouldn't hurt him to wait in vain – after all, she could have something else planned that evening. He was being too presumptuous – she wasn't one to come running, and he had better realise it.

* * *

The clock on Connie's mantelshelf showed fifteen minutes past the hour of six. The wireless was playing and the soft music lulled her into a state of quiet calm. The fire burned brightly and windy noises in the chimney told her it was going to be a cold night. She had washed and done her hair, using a hard brush to pull out the tangles and bring out the golden sheen. And now she added a touch of face powder from the compact Molly had given her, then slipped into her best dress and put on a precious pair of silk stockings. Before putting on her high-heeled shoes Connie breathed on the black patent leather and polished it on a towel. She had carefully brushed her winter coat and hung it behind the door. The music became more dreamy and as Connie looked at the clock once more she felt wicked. Why had she tried to fool herself? Why pretend? The young man who would be waiting for her that evening was not going to be disappointed. She knew it was something she couldn't fight; she felt too attracted to him. He had made her feel beautiful and grown up. He was sophisticated and worldly – and he seemed to want to be with her, when he could have any woman he wanted. She shivered with excitement and anticipation. What if he wanted to make love to her? Would he take her in his arms and love her with the passion for which she had always longed? Bring her the ecstasy and fulfilment she had not experienced with Michael? Poor Michael. She knew now she would never love him, and she hoped that he would accept his loss quietly, and that he would want to remain a dear friend. She knew though that she was being optimistic. He was bound to feel hurt and betrayed.

As she put on her coat and closed the front door behind her Connie knew she was entering into a game of subterfuge and deceit. Earlier she had gone down to tell Helen that one of the girls at work had invited her round to a party that evening and she would most probably be back late. Molly had seemed disappointed that her cousin would not be spending the evening with her but had tried to disguise her chagrin. Now, as Connie hurried down the dark wooden stairs and paused to check her stocking seams before stepping out into the cold night air, she felt a tightening in her insides. It was madness. Sheer madness to allow herself to walk knowingly into a situation which would almost certainly change her life dramatically.

As the orchestra struck up for the finale and the cast took their curtain calls to rapturous applause, Connie sat enthralled. A thick glossy programme lay on her lap along with the small box of chocolates. Robert glanced around at her and, as he smiled, she glimpsed the whiteness of his even teeth. Her eyes travelled over his face and she looked again at his clean-shaven jaw and rather unruly fair hair. Connie caught the faint aroma of what she guessed to be an aftershave, as he reached over and gently squeezed her hand. He looked debonair in his dark grey suit and his large-knotted blue silk tie, and the collar of his white shirt almost glowed in the darkness. His eyes seemed to challenge hers, and Connie looked away quickly at the sea of colour on the stage. As the final curtain fell, the auditorium lights went on. People made their way from the theatre and out into the windy night. Robert took her arm as they left the warm building and walked down to Trafalgar Square and up into Charing Cross Road. The air was crisp and the streetlamps bathed the pavements in golden light as he led her along a small dark road and into Leicester Square. Taxis and buses thronged the thoroughfare and theatre-goers were mingling with sightseers and pleasure-takers. The blaze of light seemed to make it less cold, although Connie shivered and pulled her coat collar up around her ears as they strolled along to

Piccadilly Circus. Robert suddenly steered her towards a narrow alley and she gave him a quizzical glance. They stopped outside a dimly lit restaurant and he turned to her. 'Hungry?' he asked.

She shook her head and tried to see into the restaurant through the steamy windows.

'It's a nice place, Con, very good food. I often come here when I'm in the West End. Even if you're not very hungry we can at least get warm.'

She allowed him to steer her into the cosy interior and immediately a waiter approached them. He seemed to know Robert and after a few mumbled words which Connie could not catch the waiter led them into a secluded corner.

The table for, two was partially hidden from other customers by a bamboo screen. A large-leaf plant had grown up from a huge pewter pot and its tendrils had woven themselves in and out of the knotted poles. Olive-green leaves hung limply over their heads, their undersides lit strangely by a thick red candle set into a gun-metal holder on the centre of the table. The white tablecloth hung down around the edges and as the two sat facing each other, sipping hot thick tomato soup, they exchanged coy glances.

Robert had spilt some of the soup on his chin and he dabbed at it with a napkin square. Connie was terrified in case she should spill her soup on the spotless tablecloth and she ate slowly. It was the first time she had eaten out in a posh restaurant and it fascinated her how the waiters managed to carry so many plates at once. She thought they looked Italian or maybe Spanish. They all seemed to have sleeked-down, jet-black hair and expressionless faces. Presently one of the waiters came over and removed the empty soup bowls. He came back immediately with fresh plates and knives and forks. Connie was overawed by the whole procedure. The menu was difficult to understand and Robert helped her to order. The grilled plaice seemed to be the most straightforward choice and Connie agreed quickly with Robert's suggestion.

They chatted together as they ate the main course and Connie wondered whether or not she should eat the sprig of parsley which had been placed on the side of her plate. Robert had left his, so she left hers, too. The wine had been opened and Robert partially filled the two glasses. He looked amused as she sipped the wine and pulled a face. 'It tastes sort o' sharp,' she remarked, thinking that it was nothing like the bottling-store wine.

He smiled broadly, captivated by her innocence. His eyes appraised her, and he noticed how her hair shone in the light of the candle. Her blue eyes remained wide open with controlled excitement, and her expressive lips curled and made tantalising shapes as she chatted about the show. As he stared at her facing him in the flickering light, excitement grew within him. Connie saw the desire in his pale eyes and she felt her cheeks growing hot. He dropped his gaze and they finished the meal in silence.

They had been in the restaurant for some time. Ice-cream had followed the fish course and they were now sipping their coffee. Connie marvelled at the tiny cups and she felt clumsy as she lifted the coffee to her lips. Robert took a silver cigarette case from the inside pocket of his coat and took a tipped cigarette from it. Connie had never seen him smoke before. He had never smoked in the factory as far as she could recall and she watched as he lit the cigarette and blew a cloud of smoke towards the ceiling.

Suddenly his hand reached across the table and rested on hers. 'Have you enjoyed tonight, Connie?' he asked earnestly.

She nodded quickly. 'It's bin wonderful. I've never experienced anyfing like this.'

His face became serious. 'You know how much I like being with you, Con. I've not stopped thinking about you. You know that, don't you?'

She was very aware of his hand touching hers and she looked into his eyes. The look in them made her feel weak and fragile. It was inevitable. She had known all along that he wanted her. She had known the first time he had taken her out, and it both frightened and excited her. For a moment she wanted to get up and run from the table, out into the dark night. She wanted to get lost in the crowds and allow herself time to get back to reality. This was wrong, very wrong, and yet she could not move. His hand sent an urgent message into her very being, and she trembled inside.

'I know, Robert,' she said, in a voice she hardly recognised. 'I've known all along.'

'We're good for each other, Con,' he whispered. 'We should be together.'

Needle-pricks of warning pierced her mind and she hesitated. Robert saw the sudden look of concern on her face and he reached across the table for her other hand.

'Listen, Connie. You shouldn't think that anyone has claims on you. Happiness is not always easy to come by. If you really want to be happy you sometimes have to make certain decisions. At times those decisions aren't easy to make. Don't shut me out of your life, Connie. I want to be part of it. Can you understand?'

His hands held hers on the table and his touch seemed to make everything all right. At that very moment it didn't matter to her that she was being deceitful and unfaithful to Michael. All that mattered was the young man facing her across the table. She felt she was experiencing for the first time what sexual desire really meant. With Michael she had been left wondering how much love had not yet touched her. How much better it could have been with him if they had not been so rushed, so fumbling. Michael had gone away and left her with memories only of what might have been. Here and now, she was in the company of someone who desired her and made her feel weak with longing. There was magic in the moment. It mustn't end, she told herself, not yet.

Out in the cold night the crowds had thinned. Connie had no sense of time. She nestled close to him as his arm encircled her waist. The lights still shone brightly and traffic rumbled past. They had taken a narrow pathway which led out into Charing Cross Road and suddenly she was in his arms. He kissed her eager mouth and his arms pressed her to him firmly and tenderly. The kiss was over quickly and they started to walk on slowly. Connie realised it was the first time she had tasted his lips on hers.

The night was becoming colder. Hoar-frost was forming on the pavement and as the two reached Trafalgar Square they looked down into the almost deserted area where the fountains played and the sitting lions guarded the tall stone column. Robert's coat collar was turned up against the wind. His pace was slow and measured and Connie slipped into step with him. Their bodies moved together as they skirted the Square and started back into the Strand. It was still rather busy as they passed Charing Cross Station. It was then that Robert spoke.

'Will you stay with me tonight, Connie?' he asked her urgently. 'I need you.'

'Where can we stay?' she asked, her voice trembling with emotion.

'Just say you will.'

'Yes, yes,' she whispered.

They reached the Strand Palace Hotel and without hesitation Robert guided his companion through the swing doors into the warm interior. 'Leave everything to me. It'll be all right,' he said softly.

As they reached the reception desk Robert turned to Connie, a smile playing in the corner of his mouth and said loudly, 'Don't worry, dear. We'll get the first train tomorrow morning.'

The night clerk gave Robert a strange look. 'Can I help you, sir?' he said in a tired voice.

'We'd like a double room for one night, please.'

The clerk spun the register. 'Is there any luggage, sir?'

'No,' Robert replied unconcernedly. 'My wife and I are passing through London. We can't catch our connection tonight.'

Connie felt uneasy. Robert had handled it all so calmly. Maybe this was where he usually took his girlfriends. No, of course not, she reasoned. It was just his confident manner. He had been the same in the restaurant. Everything he did was handled with supreme confidence. Even when the night clerk gave him what Connie thought was a disbelieving glance she noticed that Robert did not falter. She watched as he signed the register and reached for his wallet, then he smiled reassuringly at her as they waited for the porter to arrive to show them to their room.

At last they were being escorted along a thickly carpeted corridor and taken up to the fourth floor in a metal-walled lift. The elderly porter was dressed in dark trousers and a yellow-striped waistcoat. He hummed tunelessly to himself as he led the couple to their room. He had seen it all before. His powers of observation had become highly developed over the many years he had been in the hotel's employ. He had given the couple no more than a casual glance, yet he had noted certain details. The young man was probably well off: his suit was expensive and his manner confident. He was no stranger to hotels, but it was all new to the young lady. She looked uneasy, even scared. Can't be more than eighteen, he guessed. She was not wearing a wedding ring and there was no luggage, no overnight bag. The young lady's clothes were clean and tidy but not expensive. She seemed too scared to say much in case she said the wrong thing. Poor kid. She would most likely live to regret this night. Then maybe not. Ah well. ''Ere we are, sir, madam. There's a bell if yer require room service. A very good night ter yer both.'

The early morning light filtered through the heavy curtains and Connie opened her eyes. Robert lay beside her, his right arm folded across his chest. His left arm was beneath her neck and as she moved her head he grunted and stirred. Gently she slipped her legs over the edge of the bed and reached for the large bath towel that was lying on the floor beside the bed. Quickly Connie wrapped the towel around her and peered out into the street below. There was no clock in the room but she realised it must still be early. One or two taxi cabs drove past and a few people ambled along the wide thoroughfare. The morning was bright and she could see the white coating of frost on the roof tops opposite. She looked back into the room at Robert's slumbering body and then crept out into the bathroom. Soon she was under the jets of steaming water and she closed her eyes and held her face up to the shower head. It felt glorious just to stand there, letting the hot water run over her body. It was much better than the tin bath at her flat and even the local baths, she thought, as she began to lather herself with the scented soap in the dish.

It had been a wonderful night, and he had been a wonderful lover. Connie had found him gentle and considerate and she had experienced a pleasure that was new and exciting. She now felt a real woman, and she smiled warmly to herself.

171

Robert had been careful, too, and she remembered the act of love with a deep sigh. He had reached for her in the darkness and joined with her gently at first and then with an urgency that brought her to a climax that lingered and then died slowly. It was a feeling she had only dreamed about, and as she stepped from the shower and towelled herself dry Connie could not help but make the comparison. The night spent with Michael had left her feeling irritable, drained of passion and unfulfilled; this morning she felt light, almost as if she were floating, and her body tingled.

Robert was awake now and he watched her as she walked back into the bedroom with the towel wrapped lightly around her. He climbed out of bed and without any show of self-consciousness took her to him and kissed her gently.

'God! But you're beautiful, Connie,' he gasped as he squeezed her to him.

'So are you,' she whispered. 'You'd better get dressed. You're temptin' me again, Robert.'

The young man released her and smiled as he sauntered into the bathroom. Connie could hear the water running as she dried her long hair on the towel. He must be very experienced, she thought. Did all young men carry those French Letters around with them? Michael didn't use anything, although she hadn't thought too much about it before. The girls at work always said that you didn't get pregnant the first time. The older women had said otherwise and she remembered worrying over her next period, but she had taken comfort from the fact that sex with Michael had not really been completed. With Robert it had been perfect, and she was grateful that he had been careful. For herself, she had entered into the love-making with little thought of what might happen. Everything else had been forgotten. Now, in the light of day, she had time to reflect on last night. Robert might think I'm easy, she mused. After all, I've only been out with him twice. Her sudden doubts were interrupted as he came back into the bedroom. He dressed quickly and sat on the bed, watching as she tied her still damp hair back with a strip of black ribbon.

'We'd better get down to breakfast, Con. I'll get us a cab after and drop you home, okay?' he said with a loving smile.

She nodded. Right at that moment everything was okay with young Connie Morgan.

Chapter Sixteen

The train rattled on through the winter countryside as Connie stared thoughtfully out of the carriage window. The trees had lost their leaves and they bent against the keen wind. The fields had been ploughed up and the hay gathered in for winter feeding. Above, the grey overcast sky shut out the sun and spread a gloomy light over the barren landscape. The only other occupant of the carriage had been an elderly gent who had alighted at the last stop, leaving Connie alone with her thoughts. How much would her mother's condition have worsened? she wondered with a sinking feeling. The last time she visited the Bartletts had travelled with her and on that occasion her mother had been even less talkative than usual. Connie was glad she was alone today. She wanted time to sit quietly and think things over. It seemed that her life had suddenly become full of questions and quandaries. Much had happened during the past month, and she wanted time to gather her thoughts into some sort of order. Robert had added a new dimension to her life, but it would bring her problems, too. Very soon Michael would be home on his Christmas leave, and she realised it was going to be very difficult. She was feeling apprehensive about what might happen, but she knew that she would just have to take things as they came. Robert had told her during the cab journey home that he wanted to see her as

174

often as possible and, when she mentioned Michael's leave, he had become quiet and thoughtful. When she got home she had been plied with questions. Helen had looked at her in a funny way, as if she could read her mind. Connie resented the prying questions and she recalled the look on her aunt's face when she told her that she had stayed at her friend's house all night.

The train pulled into the station and Connie picked up the bag of fruit by her side and stepped down on to the platform. The wind was biting and she pulled up the collar of her coat as she left the station and began to walk along the long country road to the sanatorium. It took twenty minutes to reach the red-brick building which was set in its own grounds and surrounded by sheltering trees. As she walked along the gravel drive Connie began to sense that something was wrong. She had a bad feeling in the pit of her stomach and in her mind she saw a picture of her mother on her last visit. It was as though she was giving up the fight. Her eyes had stared blankly, and she had hardly spoken.

As she entered the building and hurried up the wide stone staircase to the first floor, Connie knew that today her mother would be worse. Her high-heeled shoes sounded loudly on the marble-floored corridor, and when she entered the doorway to the ward the nursing sister was waiting. It was the same sister who Connie often spoke with during her visits, and on this occasion she barred her way. She smiled kindly and took the young girl's arm.

'Can you come into the office for a moment please, Miss Morgan?'

Connie's heart sank as she followed the sister into a small room.

'Sit down, my dear,' the sister said quietly, moving a chair around.

'Me mum?' was all Connie could muster.

'I'm afraid your mother has taken a turn for the worse. We've put her into a small private room. The doctor is with her at this moment. If you'd like to wait here I'll ask him to have a word with you as soon as he's finished.'

'Is she dyin'?' Connie found herself asking.

The sister looked at the young girl with large gentle eyes. 'The doctor will talk to you soon, my dear.'

One of the nurses put her head around the door and beckoned the sister. Connie found herself alone in the room and she clasped her hands tightly and stared down at the whiteness of her fingernails. The room was quiet and peaceful and she glanced around. Over the small desk was a picture of Christ wearing a crown of thorns, and at the back of the desk a bunch of wilting red roses stood in a glass vase. Connie looked up again at the picture and shivered.

'Please don't let 'er die,' she whispered aloud.

It seemed to Connie she had been waiting for ever when the door opened and a tall grey-haired man entered. Connie started to get up but he put his hand on her shoulder and then sat down facing her.

'You are Miss Morgan? Katherine Morgan's daughter?'

Connie nodded, her eyes open wide.

'I'm Doctor Phelps. You're aware that your mother is suffering from Pulmonary Tuberculosis,' he said in a very soft voice. 'I'm afraid her condition has worsened. You see my dear, this disease affects the lungs but in your mother's case her heart is also weak. I must ask you not to stay too long.'

'Is she dyin', doctor?'

The doctor looked at his fingernails. 'She's very ill. We're doing all we can, but you must be prepared, child.'

Connie stood up quickly. 'Can I see 'er now, please?'

The doctor nodded. 'The sister will take you to your mother. Don't tire her by staying too long.'

'I won't stay long,' Connie promised, and she walked quickly out into the corridor and fell in step behind the ward sister.

Kate Morgan lay propped up against the pillows, her hands resting above the bedclothes. Her thin face wore a ghostly pallor, and her faded eyes were sunken. She turned her head slightly as Connie entered the room and bent over the bed.

''Ello, Mum,' Connie said softly, her eyes filling with tears. She reached out her hand and touched her mother's gently.

''Ow's my Con?' Kate whispered, her tired eyes searching her daughter's face.

'I'm fine, Mum. 'Ow yer feelin'?'

Kate closed her eyes briefly as if in answer and Connie sat down beside the bed, watching the shallow rise and fall of her mother's chest. She noticed the small gold locket which rested on her thin neck, and she began to fight back tears. She knew the locket had a special meaning for her mother; it had always hung around her neck, except on certain occasions when it had been taken, in dire necessity, to the pawnshop. Now the locket was shining brightly against the wan skin, and as it rose and fell it caught the light and glistened.

'I've brought yer some fruit, Mum.'

Kate nodded. Her hand lifted from the bedclothes and her bony finger pointed to the locker beside the bed. 'There's money – in there. Take it, Con. It's no use ter me.' Connie shook her head but her mother's hand waved impatiently. 'Don't argue, child. Take it.'

Connie went around the bed and opened the locker. There was a small open envelope lying on the shelf. She removed it and saw the money. Kate's eyes had now closed and her breathing was very shallow.

'Mum?'

There was no answer. Connie backed away from the bed and became aware that the sister was standing behind her.

'Your mother's sleeping,' she said. 'I should leave now, my dear. We'll contact you if there's any worsening of her condition.'

Connie walked out into the long corridor and dabbed at her eyes with a handkerchief. The sister walked along the corridor beside the young girl, and as they reached the ward office she turned.

'I wonder if you could spare me a moment, Miss Morgan?'

Connie followed the sister into the office and stood while she slid open one of the desk drawers.

'This came for your mother yesterday. One comes every month. There's money inside. I know because your mother asked me to open the last one. I usually post the reply off for her. You see, she has to sign the receipt. She's too ill to be bothered with this. As you're her next of kin, maybe you could do it?'

Connie nodded as she took the letter and tore it open. Inside were five one pound notes, a stamped-addressed envelope and a slip of paper. Connie signed the receipt and put it into the envelope. Her eyes narrowed as she read the address. It was destined for the Armitage factory in Ironmonger Street.

Connie walked back along the road to the station, miserable and depressed, but like a dull ray of light through the darkness of her despair questions began to form in her mind. She had known for a long time that her mother received a regular sum of money, and she had once been told it came from insurance. Connie had had no reason to question her mother's explanation, but now things were different. Why should the money come from the Armitage firm? What was the connection? Kate had never said anything about her father working there. There must be some reason for the firm to make the payments. Maybe Aunt Helen would be able to help her get at the truth. There were questions that had to be answered. Connie thought about the time when she had first seen her birth certificate and asked about the blank space where her father's name should have been. Her mother had refused to answer her questions, dismissing them impatiently with the excuse that it wasn't important. Why was there so much mystery surrounding him? What was the reason for her mother's refusal to talk about him? Connie knew that her mother was slowly slipping away from her. If the secret of her father died with her she would have no family left, apart from the Bartletts. If her father was still alive, then she surely had the right to know his identity, however bad he had been, whatever he had done?

During the trip back to London through the drab winter countryside Connie felt upset and confused. She was desperate to get at the truth, but would the knowledge bring her any peace? Maybe the whole thing should stay buried and forgotten. Connie was lulled by the gently rocking train and the clacking of the wheels and she glanced around the carriage. The other four travellers, two elderly ladies and a young couple, were leaning back against the head-rests. They all seemed to be absorbed in their own private thoughts. The young couple were holding hands and one of the elderly ladies was nodding off to sleep. Connie's thoughts turned to the brief conversation she had had with her mother and she felt her throat tighten. She closed her eyes tightly against the threatening tears and sighed deeply.

Early winter dusk was settling down in Dockland as Connie reached Ironmonger Street. She went directly to the Bartletts' flat and when Helen let her in she could see by Connie's serious face that Kate was worse.

Matthew brought Connie a cup of tea and they all gathered

around to talk to her. Tears dripped into the cup as Connie choked out the words.

'She's very weak, Aunt 'Elen. They said it's 'er 'eart. The doctor told me ter be prepared fer the worst.'

Helen rested her hand on Connie's shoulder. 'I've kept yer fire goin', luv. You go up an' 'ave a nice rest. I'll pop in ter see yer later.'

She stood up and put the empty cup down on the table. Connie felt Molly's warm hand slip into hers and she felt the reassuring pressure as her cousin looked up into her eyes. It was the way it had been in the past, when they were tiny children. Whenever the grief or the anger became too much they had always been there to comfort each other. Connie felt that the old bond between them had been renewed, and her eyes shone through her tears as she looked at her cousin.

The high wind rattled the windows and shook the doors in the dilapidated Jubilee Buildings. Connie sat in her easy chair beside the fire and re-read Michael's last letter. It was written in a bold hand and he spoke mainly about his shore leave in Ceylon. The last few paragraphs, however, caused Connie to bite her lip. They were passionate lines, saying how much he hoped they could get to know each other better while he was home. She knew she would have to tell him. It wouldn't be fair to deceive him. She would have to make him understand. After all, Michael was a sailor. He would most likely spend three quarters of his time overseas and he couldn't expect her to stay at home all the time he was away. It was natural that she would be asked out. Michael was sensible. He would understand. It would upset him, yes, but he would get over it. She would tell him it was better to be honest with him than not to say anything and deceive him while he was away. As she rehearsed the words in her mind they sounded plausible enough, but she knew in her heart that Michael would not be so understanding. He had his pride and he would see her as being a cheat and disloyal. God! Why must everything be so complicated?

There was a knock on the door and Helen came in. She looked tired and drawn. Her shoulders sagged and her hair was screwed up untidily on the top of her head and secured with pins. She sat down heavily and puffed.

'Those stairs crease me. I mus' be gettin' old.'

Connie secretly agreed. Her aunt had aged considerably during the last couple of years. Worries and troubles had taken their toll and Connie could not help but make the comparison between Helen and her own mother. Although the two were of different complexion and the shapes of their faces were different, their features had somehow mellowed into a sameness. Time and deprivation had closed the gap between them. Connie smiled sympathetically and got up to put the kettle over the gas.

'Wanna cuppa, Aunt?' she asked.

Helen waved her back into the chair. 'I've jus' 'ad one, Con. I've only come up fer a chat.'

Connie raked the fire and added a few small knobs of coal. 'I've bin sittin' 'ere finkin' about me mum. She looked really bad when I saw 'er.'

Helen stared into the rising flames and watched the smoke spiralling up the chimney. 'I thought she looked very ill the last time I saw 'er,' she said softly. 'Yer gotta steel yerself, Con. It can only be a matter o' time now.'

'I know, Aunt. I'm prepared fer the worst. I only wish me an' mum 'ad got closer. She shut me out at times. I sometimes fink she was ashamed o' the way she was. She 'ad no reason ter fink that, Aunt 'Elen. I love 'er. She's me mum after all.'

Helen leaned back in her chair and gripped the arms until her knuckles whitened. 'Yer muvver loves yer in 'er own way, Connie. She's always tried ter spare yer the troubles she's 'ad.

181

She was always tellin' me when you was little that she didn't want you ter turn out like 'er. She was always out wiv fellers. When she fell fer you she wasn't married. Yer know that much, don't yer?'

Connie nodded. 'Mum always called 'im "yer farvver". That's the way she always spoke of 'im. I've seen me birth certificate an' there's nufink on it about me dad. It was always the same when I asked questions. Mum said 'e was dead an' not to bovver 'er. I don't fink me dad's dead, Aunt. I fink me dad's alive somewhere. I'm gonna find out fer sure one day.' She paused. 'By the way, I wanted ter ask yer somefink. Did yer know the money me mum gets every month comes from the Armitage firm?'

Helen looked surprised. 'No, I never.'

'Mum gets it in a letter every month. She was too ill ter sign fer it this month an' the sister of the ward asked me if I'd do it fer 'er. It was a shock when I found out where the money comes from. The only fing I can fink of is that me dad worked there once an' the firm pay the insurance money.'

Helen stared at Connie. She wanted to blurt out the name of the girl's father, but she remembered the oath Kate had made her take all those years ago. If Kate's daughter wanted to find out about her parentage that badly then at least she should try to help her without breaking her vow to Kate.

'Firms don't pay out insurance money, Con,' she said slowly. 'Very few people are lucky enough ter be insured. Those that are get their money from the insurance companies, not the firms they worked fer.'

'What could the money be fer then, Aunt?'

'I don't know, Connie. I really don't know.'

Connie pinched her bottom lip between her thumb and forefinger as she stared into the flaring coals and Helen studied her for a few seconds.

'Michael's comin' 'ome soon, ain't 'e?' she said suddenly.

The young girl nodded. "E should be 'ome on the twentieth. It's only ten days' time.'

'It'll soon go round,' Helen said.

Connie wanted to pour her heart out about her new love and the problems it was bringing, but she knew it was not the right time. She decided to change the subject. 'Molly seems better lately, Aunt.'

Helen allowed herself a brief smile. 'The brace she's wearin' seems to 'ave 'elped a bit. I don't like 'er sittin' around the place though. She gets so bored. The labour exchange is tryin' ter get 'er fixed up wiv a suitable job, soon as she gets the okay from the 'ospital.'

'What about Uncle Matt?' Connie asked.

Helen shrugged her shoulders. 'The debts are worryin' 'im, I know they are. What wiv Christmas an' all. 'E'll get a few more coppers at the markets, but even wiv 'is dole money it won't get the fings we need this year.'

'Ain't Uncle Matt's firm openin' up again, Aunt?'

Helen shook her head. 'Nah! It went out o' business. It's a shame really. My Matt's a good French polisher. 'E's tried 'is best ter get a job in the trade, but there's not much call fer French polishers round 'ere. Most o' the cabinet makers are over the water. 'E's tried over there, too, but they take on all the local people. They get to 'ear of the jobs first, yer see.' Coals fell in the grate and Helen stretched. 'Oh well. I'd better be gettin' back. I'm feelin' tired an' I've gotta get up early.'

Connie bade her aunt goodnight and locked up when she had gone. The difficult and upsetting day had weighed heavily upon her and, as she tossed and turned in her bed, mixed up thoughts were twisting in her mind. Maybe Robert would be able to tell her about the money? She must ask him as soon as the opportunity presented itself. Before sleep overtook her, Connie said a silent prayer for her mother.

That same evening a conversation took place in the Kentish village of Kelstowe between the two men of the Armitage family, both sitting before a log fire. The smell of boiling resin from the pine logs filled the large oak-beamed room. Peter clutched a glass of Scotch whisky while his son Robert toyed with his near-empty wine glass.

'It's no good, Father, I've got to get away. I'm feeling stifled in the village. Mother's still trying her best to get me married off to that dreadful Marchant girl, and everyone I meet asks me about when Eunice and I are going to set a date. I think mother must have made it all look too obvious.'

Peter had a serious look on his face. 'Is it certain, the flat?'

'Oh yes. It will be available after Christmas and it's mine if I want it, and I do. I'd be close to work. After all, Great Dover Street is only five minutes from the factory, and I'd have some privacy.'

'Away from Eunice Marchant, eh?' Peter grinned.

'And the village, Father. It's all getting on top of me lately.'

Peter looked at his son closely. 'Is there a girl somewhere in all this, Robert?'

The younger Armitage shifted uncomfortably in his armchair. 'Now you've asked, it so happens there is.'

'Someone in London?'

'Yes, Father. It's a girl I met at the factory.'

Peter's face took on a puzzled frown. 'The factory?'

Robert nodded. 'I'd planned to tell you both. You'll have to know sooner or later, though what mother's going to say when she finds out I hate to think.'

'Go on, Robert.'

'It's Connie Morgan, Father.'

Peter stared incredulously. 'Connie Morgan? You don't mean that young girl who serves at the table?'

'The very one.'

'But she's a factory girl. She's only . . .'

'She's only what, Father? Only working-class? Only a Cockney girl with no breeding? Would you prefer me to marry someone like Eunice Marchant? I can't build a marriage around dinner parties and who's currently in favour with God knows who. Surely you know me better than that. Christ! I'd expect mother to adopt that attitude, not you.'

'Listen, Robert,' Peter began. 'We both have your welfare at heart. It's natural we want the best for you, and for that reason alone I think it's about time you learned a little of our family history. First though, you'd better fill your glass, and fill mine while you're at it. What I'm going to tell you is not very pleasant, to say the least.'

Connie heard the distant rattle of a train and the low note of a hooting tug as she tossed and turned in her bed. She felt desperately tired but sleep somehow eluded her. Pale moonlight entered the room and lit up the cracked ceiling. It played on the rickety dressing table and cast its shadows around the small bedroom. Down in the deserted street a cat dislodged a dustbin lid and the loud clatter was followed by a caterwaul. Connie leaned over and glanced irritably at the alarm clock on the chair beside her bed. It showed ten minutes past the hour of twelve. Slowly tiredness overtook her and she fell into a troubled sleep. She could see the misty figure of her mother standing in front of the mirror and brushing her long fair hair.

'You must be good, child. I 'ave ter go out,' Kate said, her face smiling mockingly.

Connie stared down at the small figure who sat upright in a

high-backed chair. The child was crying silently and tears dripped down on to her crumpled white dress.

'No Mummy, no!' she sobbed.

'Hush, child. I 'ave ter go,' her mother said, her face taking on a stern look.

Now Connie was alone in the room. She sat stiffly in the high-backed chair, unable to move as the room closed in on her. She could hear the continual thumping noise that seemed to come from within her. It became louder, and suddenly she was fighting for breath. With a jerk she sat upright and threw back the bedclothes. Her body was bathed in perspiration and, as she fought to recover her breath, Connie heard the rat-tat again. Draping a blanket around her shoulders she hurried to the front door. The policeman had a lighted torch clipped onto his shiny belt and his pale face stared down at her. He brushed a clenched hand across his bushy moustache and cleared his throat.

'I'm sorry, Miss. It's yer muvver. She died a few hours ago.'

Part Two

Part Two

Chapter Seventeen

It had stopped raining, although thunder rolled in the distance and flashes of lightning lit the dark sky. The young woman walked quickly along the sodden pavement, her footsteps sounding loudly in the quiet street. She hurried up the half dozen steps and used a key to let herself into the house. Her arrival did not go unnoticed by the two elderly women who stood talking on the doorstep of the adjoining house. The larger of the two women, Gert, slipped her hands into the sleeves of her coat and jerked her head in the direction of the black-painted front door.

'That's 'er. That's the one I was tellin' yer about, Freda. She don't look any older than my girl. She's bin comin' 'ere every weekend. Mind you, it's none o' my business, but it makes yer fink, don't it?'

Freda nodded. 'Some o' these young girls are shameless. If it was a girl o' mine I'd kill 'er, I'm sure I would.'

The large woman leaned forward, her eyes darting up and down the turning. 'I've seen 'er leave 'ere on Monday mornin's. 'E goes out later.'

'What's 'e like, Gert?' the little woman asked, her curiosity aroused.

''E's quite a nice-lookin' fella as it 'appens. 'E's well mannered an' keeps 'imself to 'imself. I ain't 'ad much occasion ter talk to 'im, 'cept ter pass the time o' day, but I reckon 'e fancies 'imself a bit. 'E talks posh an' 'is suits ain't from the fifty-shillin' tailors, that's fer sure.'

'I s'pose 'e's one o' them solicitor blokes. There's a lot of 'em livin' round 'ere, Gert.'

Gert shook her head. 'No, I don't fink so. All that lot carry briefcases. I've never seem 'im wiv a briefcase. I reckon 'e's got a business or somefink. I reckon 'e's werf a few bob by the look of 'is clobber.'

Freda folded her arms. 'It's scand'lous the way some o' them carry on.'

'Yer right there, Freda. It's disgustin' what some of 'em get up to.'

Unaware that she was being discussed by the two women, Connie climbed the stairs to the first-floor landing and let herself into the flat. After lighting the gas fire she took a towel and rubbed at her long blond hair. The fire soon warmed the room and she turned her attentions to making a pot of tea. Robert would be home soon and she wanted everything to be just so. She felt happy in a way she had never felt before and she luxuriated in the warm, comfortable feeling inside. He had made her feel wanted and needed, and she knew she loved him desperately.

The clock on the mantelshelf struck seven and Connie stretched out her stockinged feet and wriggled her toes in front of the glowing fire. The last few months had been terrible. When her mother died it had left her feeling desolate. She had been expecting it, but the rat-tat on the door and the sight of the policeman standing there in the early hours of the morning had left her shaking violently. At the funeral Helen had been overcome with grief and had almost collapsed at the graveside. Connie remembered walking back to the chapel behind her aunt and uncle. Helen had seemed to have suddenly become frail and aged and she leaned heavily on Matthew as they walked along the gravel path against a biting wind. A few days after the funeral Helen had gone down with influenza and had lost her cleaning job. Matthew had been doing very little portering on the side and money was short. As for Molly, she had seemed immune to all the misery around her and seemed unaffected by the death in the family. She had, after all, never been close to her Aunt Kate. Her attitude had been reserved throughout.

It had been a terrible end to the year. And then, only the day after the funeral, Michael came home on leave. She recalled how he had been sympathetic to her feelings of grief at first, but his attitude had changed very soon. He was no doubt eager to prove himself after his last attempt at lovemaking, and he voiced the opinion more than once that life had to go on and it was no good becoming too morbid. Connie remembered how angered she had become. She had wanted to explain to him that it wasn't just grief and emptiness that assailed her. It was more than that. Her thoughts were now centred on someone else: a person who had entered her life and who made her feel like a woman and who had become so close to her that every minute of the day she wanted to be by his side. How could she tell Michael that she had found the love she had never dreamed possible with someone else? She had been quite unable to bring herself to tell him the truth. Michael had become upset and angered at her refusal to talk about getting engaged. Her weak excuse that she was too young had only incensed him and they had rowed constantly during his leave. Connie recalled how he had tried to kiss her with passion and how her lack of response had only angered him more. He had left her in tears of frustration at her dilemma, and he had spent part of his leave drinking with his mates.

Then there was the last evening of Michael's leave. He had

been drinking heavily and was in a foul mood. They had been to the pictures and had walked home in stony silence. The recollection of what happened next filled her with anger and sadness. Michael had forced himself upon her, kissing her roughly and clumsily attempting to arouse her. She had recoiled from his actions and pushed him away. His face had turned white with rage and he raised his hand to her. Their eyes met in burning anger and he suddenly slumped back. They both knew it was all over and he turned without another word and walked unsteadily out of the street.

A key in the lock and the front door opening and closing cut short her recollections. Robert's footsteps sounded on the stairs and he entered the flat, his face showing relief.

'Hello, darling. I was hoping you'd be here.'

She went into his arms and let him squeeze the breath from her body. Their lips met in a lingering kiss, and she felt the comfort and protection that only he could bring her.

'I only just caught the train. The next one wasn't for another two hours,' he said as she nestled her head against his chest.

'I'd still be 'ere, Robert. Yer know I would. Now sit down and let me get yer a nice cuppa,' she said, smiling at him.

Robert took off his coat and threw it over a chair and then slumped down beside the fire. 'I couldn't get out of it, Con, I had to go. You know what it's like when it's family.'

'Did it go all right?'

He ran his fingers through his fair hair and clasped his hands behind his head. 'Mother still isn't happy about it. Her plans for me have come rather unstuck, but I managed to convince her that it's my life and I've got to run it, not her. She seemed to think my taking a flat was tantamount to disowning my family. There were a few tears, but it was all right. She saw it my way in the end.'

'What about yer farvver, Robert?' she asked.

Robert sighed deeply and stretched out his legs.

'Father was okay,' he answered. 'He could understand why I needed to get away. In fact, he thought it might be better for me to become a little more independent. Nice of him, wasn't it? Anyway, I'm glad it's over. Things were getting a little strained at home.'

Connie smiled sympathetically and then hurried into the kitchen. Soon she came back with the tea, and as they sat facing each other Connie eyed him over her cup. She understood how he must have felt. She had faced a difficult situation within her own family just a few weeks ago. Helen had called in to see her and had seemed anxious to have a quiet chat with her. Connie vividly recalled what had been said.

''Ow yer gonna manage now, girl?' Helen had asked. 'I mean, yer muvver's money paid the rent. Now that's finished what yer gonna do?'

'I'll manage, Aunt 'Elen. I've got some of Mum's money put away, an' I'm gonna look around fer anuvver job. The lan'lord said I could take over the flat, as long as the rent was paid regular.'

Helen pursed her lips. There was another question she wanted answered. She was aware of Connie's break up with Michael, and lately the girl had become very secretive about her comings and goings. She wasn't eighteen yet and now that her mother was dead it was only right that the young girl should have someone to watch out for her welfare.

'We don't see much of yer at weekends, Con, an' ter be honest, I'm concerned at yer stoppin' out on Saturday nights,' she said quietly.

Connie felt her face flush. She realised it was no good continuing with the deceit. Her aunt had been like a mother to her for as long as she could remember. She had a right to know the truth.

'I don't know 'ow yer gonna take this, Aunt 'Elen,' she answered, looking her squarely in the eye. 'I can't go on keepin' yer in the dark. I've not said anyfing before, 'cos I know 'ow yer worry. I fink the world of you an' Matt, as well as Molly. Yer my family, so I'm gonna tell yer. I've got a fella, an' I fink the world of 'im too. 'E's got a flat an' that's where I spend me weekends. I love 'im, Aunt 'Elen.'

The elder woman looked hard at her niece. How like her mother she was. There was the same look in her eyes, the same tone in her voice that defied criticism and the same mannerisms and attitudes. It was uncanny. It seemed to her that the girl was already following in her mother's footsteps, and if she was not careful she would make the same mistakes. There was one big difference between Connie and her mother, and of that Helen was sure. Kate Morgan's daughter had compassion. It showed in her eyes, and it was apparent in her close friendship with Molly. The girl was overflowing with love. She lacked her mother's hardness, and it could be her downfall.

'Do I know 'im, Con?' she asked.

''Is name's Robert Armitage. 'E's the factory owner's son, Aunt.'

Helen looked shocked. 'Christ! Yer know what yer doin', gel? They're not our kind. That crowd live in a different world to us.'

Connie returned her stare. 'Listen, Aunt 'Elen. I know it's not gonna be easy. We don't talk the same an', like you say, we're worlds apart, but Robert makes me feel good. 'E don't ask me ter change or alter the way I talk. 'E's 'avin' a bad time wiv 'is family over me, but it don't stop 'im goin' wiv me. I'm not gonna give 'im up, Aunt. 'E means too much ter me.'

Helen averted her eyes from her niece's burning gaze. 'I only want yer ter be 'appy, gel. That's all I want fer yer. If yer sure in yer mind that 'e's the one, I won't try ter put obstacles in yer path. I'll say one fing though. Be careful. Don't make the same mistakes yer mum made.'

Connie reached out and touched Helen's arm. 'Don't worry, Aunt. I know what I'm doin'.'

Helen smiled and leaned back in her chair. 'So that's why you an' Michael split up.'

Connie's face was serious. ''E knew there was somebody else, I'm sure. I didn't tell 'im about Robert though. I jus' couldn't bring meself ter tell 'im.'

Helen was silent for a while, and then she asked, ''Ave yer spoke ter Robert about the money yer mum was gettin' from the firm?'

Connie shook her head. 'Yes, I asked 'im about it, but 'e said it was an arrangement made years ago wiv mum an' Robert's gran'farvver. That's all 'e knew.'

'It all seems very strange ter me, Con. Is Robert tellin' yer the truth?'

'I believe 'im, Aunt.'

Helen stood up and straightened her pinafore. 'Don't ferget what I said, Connie. Be careful. We don't want you gettin' yerself in trouble. I remember when yer mum got pregnant. She was goin' ter get an abortion, but a girl out o' John Street 'ad 'ad one a few weeks before an' she was found dead in a flat over the butcher's in Bermondsey Lane. Whoever done it must 'ave panicked when the girl started bleedin' an' left the poor cow ter die. It was in all the papers. I fink that made yer mum's mind up not ter go through wiv it. Don't forget ter look after yourself, Connie.'

Night had fallen, and in the cosy flat in Great Dover Street the two young people faced each other across the table. The meal was finished and they sat drinking coffee and chatting happily.

Outside it was raining again and the wind was rising. They fell silent listening to the record playing.

Robert was thinking of the meeting he had had with his father before Christmas. Until then, his knowledge of the arrangement between Kate Morgan and the firm had been the same as Connie's, and the truth had shocked him. He had been told the whole sordid story and had reluctantly agreed with his father that Connie was not to be told anything, even though she had questioned him about the money. Kate Morgan's silence had been bought all those years until her death. It would serve no purpose to let her daughter into the secret after Kate had agreed never to tell anyone. Nevertheless, he didn't like deceiving Connie.

The gramophone record finished and Robert got up to turn it off. He came back and took Connie's hand as they nestled down together on the well-padded sofa, her head resting in the crook of his arm, and her hand lying across his chest.

'You 'appy?' she asked dreamily.

In answer he kissed her gently on the top of her head and she sighed.

After a few moments Robert said, 'Connie, I've been thinking. Wouldn't you like to give up your work?'

'Give up work?'

'Yes. You could stay here. I've money enough. You wouldn't have to worry about clothes and things. I could give you everything you'd need.'

She pulled herself upright and glared into his blue eyes. 'You listen ter me, Robert Armitage. I'm not goin' ter let you keep me. I wanna earn me own money. It's important to a girl. I wanna be able ter buy fings wivvout 'avin' ter keep on askin' you.'

He saw the indignant look on her face and he grinned widely. 'I want to take care of you, buy you things. I love you, Connie.'

'You are takin' care of me,' she replied. 'You could always buy me a little present once in a while, but I wanna be independent an' earn me own money, Robert, so let's 'ear no more of it.'

'Okay,' he said, with mock seriousness. 'I'll never mention it again.'

They became quiet again. Connie's head was resting against his chest and she listened to the steady thump of his heart.

Suddenly she looked up into his eyes, as if reminded of something. 'Do yer fink there's really gonna be a war?'

'What made you ask that, Con?'

'I dunno. There's a lot o' talk about a war. If there is, will yer 'ave ter go away ter fight?'

'Don't let's talk about war,' he said, squeezing her hand. 'It's not the subject I want to get into on a cosy Saturday night when I'm entertaining my lustful mistress.'

Connie looked up into his smiling blue eyes. 'Is that what yer see me as, a lustin' mistress?'

Robert laughed loudly and she felt the rumble in his chest. 'You're my lover, my mistress, my scarlet woman. You're sharing my secret bedchamber, did you not know? Be warned. To spurn my advances could mean the Tower.'

Connie did not laugh at Robert's jest. 'You fool,' she whispered as she snuggled closer to him and closed her eyes. It felt good just to be with him, but she could not still her thoughts. She remembered the first time she had gone to meet him and the feelings which ran through her then. She did not want to suffer the heartache and pain her mother must have endured. She wanted to make these magic moments last, and keep him, against the pressures of his family and the temptations of other more sophisticated women. Robert hadn't spoken of the future. He hadn't talked about marriage or even mentioned getting engaged. He had remained light-hearted and casual about their affair. It was as though he saw their relationship as one to savour for the moment. He avoided mentioning what was to come in the days ahead and laughed off her fears and apprehensions. Maybe he saw the future and feared it? Maybe he shared her fears and refused to face them, lest the realisation spoil their treasured moments together. She felt him slide his hand from beneath her neck and she watched him go to the fire. He came back and bent over her. She felt his strong arms around her as he lifted her from the sofa and she nestled against him, feeling the warmth of his body as he carried her to the bedroom.

The gusting wind and the heavy beating rain were forgotten as the lovers moved closely together. Their lips met in the darkness and their hands explored each other's hot bodies. As the night wore on their spent, exhausted bodies finally moulded together in a dreamless slumber.

The year was young, with early spring buds showing and light rains spattering the branches of the trees as they began to come back to life. In Ironmonger Street the April showers fell on to old, leaky rooftops and against brick walls which were cracked and crumbling. Upstairs rooms became sodden, and water dripped down from the stained ceilings. The dampness penetrated the plaster of the tiny parlours and caused the wallpaper to bubble and peel, and the angry tenants of Ironmonger Street decided that enough was enough. They gathered together in George Baker's front room on a Friday evening and listened while Joe Cooper said his piece.

'Now we all know why we're 'ere, folks, so let's get down ter business. First of all, we know what 'appened last time we complained ter the rent collector.'

'Sod all, that's what,' George piped in.

'Be quiet, Dad. Let Joe finish what 'e's got ter say.'

Joe looked at the old man. 'You're right, Pop, sod all! We know they came round an' stuck a few slates on the roofs, an' they plastered up a few cracks in the walls, but it was only a sweet'ner. It ain't stopped the water comin' in my 'ouse, an' it ain't stopped the water gettin' in your places eivver. No, I'm afraid unless we all stick tergevver an' demand a proper renovation job, we'll all end up floatin' out o' the street.'

There was a knock on the door and Mary came back into the room with Mrs Cosgrove holding on to her arm.

''Ere, make room fer Clara,' she said.

They made the old lady comfortable in an armchair and Joe then put his proposition to the group.

'Right, now this is what I reckon we should do. When that soppy-lookin' git of a rent collector comes round on Monday we all tell 'im ter piss orf, 'cos we ain't gonna pay 'im any rent.'

Clara Cosgrove chuckled. 'I was gonna tell 'im that anyway.'

'Good fer you, Clara,' Joe exclaimed.

'Wait a minute, Joe,' Mary's husband said, 'that's a bit strong, ain't it? They could give us all notice ter quit. Where we gonna live, out in the street?'

Joe looked across at him. 'Now listen, Frank. You work in the docks. You know yer don't get anyfink unless you're prepared ter fight fer it. If we all stick tergevver an' nobody pays their rents on Monday, Vine Estates are gonna start finkin'. We'll give 'em somefink ter fink about on top o' not payin' the rent. We'll call in the *South London Press*, an' we'll lobby the councillors. Anuvver fing we can do is ter call in the council doctor. 'E can put a bit o' pressure on. Once the ball starts rollin' the lan'lords will 'ave ter do somefink.'

'Yeah, like chuckin' us all out,' Lizzy Conroy piped in.

'Well I fink Joe's right,' said George. 'We gotta do some-fink. These places'll kill us all 'fore long.'

Mary patted her father's head. 'Now don't get yerself all worked up, Pop. Yer don't want anuvver turn like last time, do yer?'

'I'm all right, gel. Don't fuss. I fink we should listen ter Joe. 'E's talkin' sense.'

Frank held out his hand. 'Jus' look around. There's sixteen 'ouses in this turnin'. 'Ow many of us 'ere? If we're gonna stop the rent we've all gotta do it. The Toomeys won't go along wiv us, an' nor will Widow Pacey.'

'Nor will Muvver Adams. She'd be too worried over 'er moggies,' someone else chimed in.

Joe held his hand up for silence. 'Right. Now this is what we gotta do. First fing termorrer we get a delegation ter see all those who ain't 'ere ternight. We'll put it to 'em, then we'll take a count. If the majority ses they're fer a rent strike we'll meet the rent collector when 'e comes round on Monday an' tell 'im ter piss orf. That way nobody can back out o' the strike. What d'yer say?'

There was a general nodding of heads and Joe smiled. 'Are we all in agreement ter stop our rents till they fix up our 'ouses?'

Everyone nodded and Frank looked at the stocky figure of Joe. ''Ere, Joe. There's nine of us present, an' there's only sixteen 'ouses in the street. We've got a majority, ain't we?'

'No, we gotta do it right, Frank,' Joe replied. 'There can only be one vote fer each 'ouse'old.'

George gave his son-in-law a scornful glance, then looked up at the tenants' leader. 'Yer got my vote, Joe,' he rasped.

'Anybody against?' Joe asked.

There was silence, interrupted only by the gentle snoring of Clara Cosgrove.

'Okay then. We got six votes fer a strike. If we get anuvver three, we tell the collector what ter do,' Joe said.

'We're wiv yer, Joe,' Mary shouted.

'Yeah, right in the bloody work'ouse,' mumbled Lizzie Conroy.

''Ang on a minute,' Joe shouted as the gathering prepared to leave. 'What about the delegation? Who's gonna come round wiv me termorrer?'

'I'll come round,' George said.

'Oh no yer don't,' his daughter cut in. 'Yer not up to it. Let somebody else go round.'

'I'll come wiv yer,' said Lizzie Conroy, hoping she might be able to dissuade the rest of the tenants.

'I'll come, too, Joe,' Mary said.

'Yer'd better be careful when yer call on the Toomeys, Joe,' George joked. 'That girl o' theirs'll 'ave yer trousers orf, give 'er 'alf a chance.'

'Don't worry,' Joe laughed. 'If it goes our way we'll give 'er the rent collector as a bonus.'

Chapter Eighteen

The belief that war was inevitable was becoming strong in everyone's mind. Newspapers carried large banner headlines proclaiming the events in Europe, and the inside pages recounted the worsening situation in many parts of the world. The international situation was followed very closely of course by the Horseshoe domino club members. Pints of ale at their elbow, the two spokesmen resumed their habitual debate.

'I tell yer, Bill, it's bloody disgustin'. Everywhere yer look there's trouble. Now take Spain.'

'I don't want it, Tel.'

'C'mon, all jokin' ter one side, it's 'orrible what's goin' on out there. Did yer see those pictures in the *Daily Mirror* of the bombin' out there? It's the bloody German air force what's doin' it.'

'Yeah I did as a matter o' fact, Tel. I bin readin' all about it. They call 'em the Condor Squadron. Ole Franco called 'em in. I mean, 'e's a bloody Fascist 'imself, ain't 'e? Terrible what they're doin' ter those towns. If we go ter war wiv Germany they'll be bombin' us. Bloody trainin' in Spain, that's what the bastards are doin'.'

'D'yer fink it will come to it, Bill?'

'Stone certainty, Tel. I mean ter say, they've got Austria, an' they're 'avin' a go at Czechoslovakia. Everybody's flyin'

202

around signin' pacts. Sooner or later we're gonna get involved.'

'Long as they keep our pub out of it, Bill. I don't fancy that Kraut beer.'

'Yeah, it's lookin' bad. Anyway, let's change the subject. It's gettin' me depressed. It's your turn I fink, Tel. I'll 'ave a pint o' the same.'

In Hyde Park, crowds gathered every Sunday morning to listen to the orators, some of whose recent forecasts of how things would move in Europe were proving correct. Other speakers continued to plead for their own pet causes, and one fiery character pronounced, as he had done for the last fifteen years, that the end was nigh. First-time visitors to Speakers' Corner were often given directions to the spot by a ruddy-faced constable with a busy moustache who clasped his hands over his corpulent middle as he added, 'It's the place where they go from the sublime ter the Gor blimey.'

In the April of 1938 the events abroad were forgotten for a time as the folk from Ironmonger Street faced their own troubles. The delegation met as planned early on Saturday morning and began door knocking. At number eleven, Widow Pacey answered the knock on the door and stood, arms folded, as Joe and Mary argued the case for a rent strike. Lizzy Conroy, the other delegate, remained silent and she was secretly pleased at Widow Pacey's response. She had listened intently, her tired eyes flitting from one to the other. Widow Pacey had been a widow for a number of years; her only source of income was from bagwash collections and deliveries which she made on a battered old pram with wheels that squeaked for want of a drop of oil. People in the street paid her sixpence for a round trip to Maxwell's, the local laundry in Long Lane, a journey she made in all weathers and, as she slowly walked along the street with the pram piled high, the local youngsters would talk in whispers of all the horrific stories they had heard about her. Widow Pacey's children had all left home and, as far as anyone could recall, they had never once returned to visit their ageing mother. She was a proud, deep woman who always stood her ground and on this occasion she could not be moved.

'No. Count me out. This place might not be the best place ter live, but it's better than none at all.'

The delegation's entreaties were dismissed with a short wave of her hand. 'I can't stand 'ere argufyin' wiv yer,' she said. 'I got me washin' ter collect.'

At number twelve they had a success. Ada Halliday wanted to go even further. Her eyes blazed as she said, 'We ought ter tar an' feavver the bastard when 'e comes round!'

''E only collects the rents, Ada. 'E ain't ter blame,' Lizzie replied, realising that the rent strike was looming closer now.

As they approached number fifteen, Mary screwed up her round face. 'Bloody 'ell! I can smell the cats' piss from 'ere!'

Mrs Adams greeted them with a curt reply. 'No fanks. I got me animals ter fink about,' she said, closing the door abruptly.

It was later that Saturday morning when the delegation realised it was facing failure. Only one other tenant had backed the strike. Doreen Richards' daughter Bella was ill with pneumonia, and her mother was convinced that their living conditions were to blame. There was one more house to visit and it had been left until last.

Joe paused at the front door. He shrugged his broad shoulders and ran his fingers through his thick greying hair. 'Oh well. I s'pose we'd better give it a try,' he sighed.

Toby Toomey opened the door of number one and stared absently as Joe began to speak. Lizzie was trying not to look too happy, but she was already confident of the outcome.

When Joe finished Toby scratched his head and looked a little thoughtful.

'I'd better go an' see if Marie agrees,' he said.

Marie came to the front door, an apron tied around her waist and her dark hair hanging loosely around her pale face. Joe repeated what he had already told Toby and when he had finished Marie's face lit up.

''Ere, Lil. Come down 'ere. We're all goin' on strike,' she called out.

Lillian Toomey hurried down the stairs and joined her mother at the front door. Her large brown eyes bore into Joe and she gave him a crooked smile. 'A strike?' she said in a deep voice. 'That'll be nice. 'Ere, are you the organiser, Joe? I've always admired forceful men.'

Mary glanced at Joe and saw that he was almost squirming under Lillian's smouldering gaze. 'Well that's it,' she said loudly. 'It's a strike!'

Lizzie concealed her disappointment at what she considered to be a bad result. The Toomeys had surprised her by their enthusiasm. The whole family must be stupid, she mused. They don't seem to know what day of the week it is. They soon will when they get thrown on to the street.

As they walked back along the turning Joe could hardly conceal his pleasure at having won the first round of the battle. Mary was also grinning widely. Lizzie was more serious-faced. She was worried about what her husband had said. He had tried to dissuade her from going to the meeting in the first place. He did not like Joe, and expressed the view that he was a trouble-maker and a Bolshevik. 'If we do get into a war it'll be people like 'im who'll cause trouble, mark my words.'

Lizzie would have been more surprised had she listened in to the conversation which was taking place at number one that very minute. Marie Toomey was grinning widely as she waved the piece of paper in front of her sheepish-faced husband. 'This bloody letter can go in the dustbin now. We'll owe more than four weeks' rent by the time we're finished. But they can't chuck us out now the rest of the street ain't payin' their rent. It'll be more than they dare do.'

Toby nodded, and his daughter Lillian smiled at her reflection in the mirror as she applied another layer of rouge to her red cheeks. Marie screwed up the notice of arrears and prodded Toby in the chest with her forefinger.

'You'd better get that pram fixed. You've got a reprieve. I want you out collectin' soon as possible, an' don't ferget what I said. No lumber – no food. Okay?'

Toby stood up without replying and grabbed the oil can as he walked out into the backyard.

Connie had made up her mind to leave Armitage's as soon as she could. It was getting difficult to wait on the table now that the secret of her relationship with Robert was out in the open. It seemed to her that the management's eyes followed her every move, and Peter Armitage had taken to looking at her in a strange way. It was as though she had become an embarrassment to the factory owner and it worried her. She had already confided in Robert about her feelings and he had said she shouldn't let it worry her. Connie felt that he showed a slight sign of relief, however, when she told him she was looking for another job. It must be difficult for him, she mused, what with his family's attitude, and the fact that her presence in the canteen was a constant reminder to them.

But another problem was still causing her considerable concern. She had come no nearer to solving the mystery of the money her mother had received from the firm. Robert had not been able to shed any light on the subject and she had decided to try another approach. Recently she had found out that the matronly looking woman who sat next to Peter Armitage at the table was his secretary. Dot had said that Alice Jones was an old employee who had been with the company in the time of George Armitage and she seemed a pleasant woman who was ready with a smile and always polite and friendly. Connie reasoned that Miss Jones might well have been involved in the arrangements to get the payments to her mother sorted out in the first place, and it might be worth approaching her about it. Miss Jones had taken the trouble to express her sympathy after the funeral, and it had been the start of a rapport between them. They often exchanged a few words and pleasantries at lunchtime, and Miss Jones had on more than one occasion indicated her irritation towards Peter Armitage by a secret flick of her eyes in his direction and a sly smile. Connie decided to bide her time until she had a chance to catch the woman alone.

The opportunity presented itself one Monday morning. It was nearing midday and Connie was just finishing laying the table. Miss Jones suddenly walked into the room and handed her an envelope.

'Would you put this beside the boss's plate, dear,' she asked. 'It's a birthday card and we've all signed it. It might help cheer the old goat up a bit,' she giggled.

Connie took the envelope and propped it up against a glass, glancing at the well-groomed woman. 'Would yer mind if I asked yer somefink, Miss Jones?'

Alice Jones patted her permanent wave theatrically. 'Call me Alice, dear. It sounds less formal. Now, what is it you want to ask me?'

Connie hesitated. 'It's . . . it's about me mum. I was wonderin' if . . . if yer know anyfink about the money she got from the firm?'

Alice bit on her lip. It was a subject she did not want to discuss in the firm's canteen, especially as it was almost lunchtime. She looked over her shoulder before answering. 'Look, dear. I can't talk to you now. They'll all be down soon. It would be best if we talked outside of working hours really. You're welcome to come round to my place, if you'd like to. I don't live far away. My house is just off the Old Kent Road.'

Connie nodded. 'I need ter talk ter yer as soon as possible, Alice. It's important ter me.'

Alice patted her hair again with the palm of her hand. 'If it's that important you're welcome to come round tonight, if you want to.'

'I'd like to, if you're sure you don't mind,' Connie said hesitantly.

'Of course I don't mind,' the older woman said, fishing into her handbag. 'Look, here's my address on this envelope. If you can manage around half-seven it'll suit me fine.'

Connie nodded as she took the creased envelope and slipped it into her apron pocket. Suddenly the day seemed much brighter.

The day had started badly for Gordon Harris and it could only get worse, he decided. At nine o'clock precisely he presented himself to the manager of Vine Estates and was motioned into a chair. Norman Wallburton raised his bulky figure from behind the desk and paced the room.

'Now look here, Harris. I'm rather concerned about that little business in Ironmonger Street.'

The rent collector felt his heart sink, and he bit on the inside of his cheek. That bloody turning will be the death of me, he thought.

'Number one, Ironmonger Street,' the manager went on. 'They owe four weeks' rent. How come you allowed the arrears to build up?'

Harris took a deep breath. 'Ah, yes. The Toomey family.

Well you see Mr Wallburton, it's like this. Toomey has been ill. His wife promised me faithfully that the rent arrears would be cleared up today. In fact, I'm going round to Ironmonger Street this morning.'

The manager grunted. 'I don't like these arrears building up, Harris. In future, if any tenant in that particular street slips, even for one week, I'll want to know why. Is that clear?'

Harris nodded. 'Don't worry, Mr Wallburton. It'll be all right. You can take my word for it. Toomey told me he's going back to work this week and not to worry. The rent will be paid up to date.'

The bulky manager of Vine Estates looked over his thick-rimmed spectacles at his pale-faced subordinate. 'What exactly does this Toomey do for a living, might I ask?'

Harris swallowed hard 'He's a collector.'

'A collector?'

'Yes. He collects scrap iron and things.'

'Scrap iron!? You mean the man's a totter?'

'Well, sort of.'

The manager sat down at his desk and glared at the rent collector. 'I hope he doesn't store scrap iron in his house?'

'No, he collects and delivers directly.'

'What does he use for these collections, a horse and cart?'

'No, a pram,' Harris mumbled.

'A pram!? Good God, man. No wonder he's in arrears. Now you get straight round there and get that rent. Oh, and make sure our totter friend isn't storing that scrap of his in the house. It's against the law.'

Gordon Harris left the estate office and walked slowly down the Old Kent Road. There was no doubt about it, he mused, collecting rents was not a job for the faint-hearted, especially when the round took in Ironmonger Street. He thought about the times he had been verbally assaulted, propositioned, confronted and, worst of all, ignored in that scruffy turning. Even the factory owner had been pelted with rotten apples by the kids as he drove into the street. Then there was the oilshop on the corner. The kids had driven poor old Jerry Martin into Colney Hatch and no one wanted to buy the shop. There was the rag shop on the opposite corner as well. Once every blue moon it opened up for the purpose of loading bags of rags on to a lorry and then it promptly closed again. Vine Estates did not own the premises and no one seemed to know the identity of the shop owner. It was a mystery. Now, on top of everything else, he had heard that Vine Estates was negotiating to purchase Jubilee Dwellings. God! he thought. If that deal goes through I'll have to give the job up and try something else. Anything would be better than facing another load of moaning tenants every Monday morning.

As he turned into Tower Bridge Road and walked past the market stalls Gordon Harris could sense trouble. The feeling increased as he turned off the thoroughfare and weaved his way towards the dreaded turning. When he reached the corner of Ironmonger Street he knew he should have reported in sick that morning. There was a whole line of people spread across the turning.

'There 'e is,' someone shouted.

The rent collector could see the broad-shouldered figure of Joe Cooper approaching him with his hands thrust deep into his trouser pockets and a stern look on his round face.

'Sorry, pal. Yer can't come in the street. Yer barred.'

'What do you mean, I'm barred? I've got rents to collect – and arrears,' Harris added with forced bravado.

'Well we're not payin' any rent until your precious Vine Estates does somefink about our 'ouses.'

'That's right,' piped in Mary Brown. 'Our 'ouses are a

bloody disgrace. We've got water pourin' in the roofs an' the walls are soppin' wet. It's bleedin' scand'lous.'

Harris put his black book under his arm and scratched his head. 'Well I don't know what I can do about it. I'm only employed ter collect the rents.'

The Ironmonger Street folk milled around him in a threatening manner and George Baker hobbled up, leaning heavily on his walking stick.

'Now listen, mate,' George said. 'We ain't payin' no poxy rent, so yer can go back an' tell yer guv'nor we want somefink done pronto, or we might jus' come round an' set yer bloody office alight. Got it?'

The collector had got the message. He had caught a glimpse of Toby and Marie Toomey grinning triumphantly in the background. He turned on his heel and walked away with cheers and jeers ringing in his ears.

Connie sat with the Bartletts listening to Helen's account of the confrontation at the street entrance that morning.

'You should 'ave seen Mary Brown an' 'er farvver standin' up ter that rent collector,' she said to Matthew. 'Joe Cooper was up the front – as usual. Anyway, they ain't payin' their rents till somefink's done. I dunno what Joe an' Mary were doin' there. They must 'ave lost a day's pay. I can't imagine the firm givin' 'em time off fer anyfing o'that sort.'

Matthew slumped down in his chair and hooked his thumbs through his wide braces. 'That Joe gets 'imself mixed up in everyfing. I bet 'is missus ain't very 'appy.'

Helen shrugged her shoulders. 'Joe's always bin the same. I don't know 'ow 'e finds the time, what wiv Sadie bein' stuck in a wheelchair.'

'What's wrong wiv 'er?' Connie asked.

'She caught polio years ago. Shame really. She was a good-lookin' woman. You wouldn't reco'nise 'er if yer'd seen 'er then. Very smart she was. Funny, they never 'ad kids. Always out tergevver, like a couple o' love birds they was. It's different now though. She don't stop naggin' 'im. I fink 'alf of it is that cousin of 'ers. She's always in the 'ouse, so I've 'eard. She's prob'ly poisoned 'er mind against Joe.'

'Why don't Joe chuck the ole bat out?' Matthew asked.

'I s'pose 'e's glad she's there. It gives 'im a break. 'E was always at meetin's, but I don't fink 'e goes ter many now.'

Matthew glanced at Helen. 'You seem ter know a lot about Joe Cooper.'

'It's only what I'm told,' she countered.

'Well I don't fink they're gonna get away wiv not payin' the rent. They'll send the bailiffs round.'

Helen turned her attention to a pair of Matthew's torn trousers and Molly buried her head in a magazine, sensing that another row between her parents was likely. The clock on the mantelshelf struck seven and Connie realised it was time for her to leave. She had not mentioned that she was going to see Alice Jones. Better wait until I know something definite, she reasoned.

Connie had gone back to her flat before she left for her appointment. She could hear raised voices in the flat below and she felt a concern for Molly. Her cousin had taken to reading as an escape from the unpleasant atmosphere and Connie was, once again, finding it difficult to communicate with her. Molly had become even more withdrawn and less willing to talk. Connie guessed that her relationship with Robert had something to do with Molly's attitude. She had been a little off-hand when she had learned about Michael Donovan, and now when they had one of their rare chats together Molly would go quiet at the mention of Robert's name. Connie sighed as she glanced into the mirror. She did not want to shut her cousin out of her life. They had always been very close and she wanted Molly to share in her happiness. Maybe it was inevitable that they should grow apart. Maybe it was unreasonable to expect Molly to be happy for her. After all, there was little happiness in her own life, only the knowledge that she was trapped inside a misshapen, ailing body. It was all so unfair. Connie sighed heavily as she closed the door behind her and hurried down into the quiet street.

Chapter Nineteen

The Old Kent Road was quiet that evening. The shops were shuttered and the traffic had died down. One or two trams clattered past and a pair of tired horses pulled an empty hay-cart along beside the kerb. Connie reach the Dun Cow public house and took the envelope from her handbag. She showed the address to an elderly gent who was lounging against a sand bin smoking a clay pipe, and he directed her to a little backstreet a short way from the pub. Potter Street was made up of neat terraced houses which stretched along both sides of the turning. Steps led up to the front doors, and more steps afforded entry to the basement areas. Number twenty-six had a highly polished front door and a brass knocker and letterbox. Connie climbed the steps and as she lifted the door knocker she saw the lace curtains move in the downstairs window. The door was immediately opened by Miss Jones who smiled at her and stepped back for her to enter. The passage was carpeted and just inside the front door there was a hat stand on which a long bevelled mirror hung. Alice glanced at her reflection and touched her well-managed hair before showing Connie into the front room.

'Would you like a cuppa?' she asked.

Connie shook her head. 'No fanks. It's nice of yer ter see me.'

Alice motioned to an armchair. 'Sit yourself down, girl. Let me take your coat.'

While Connie was making herself comfortable Alice put the coat on a hanger and hung it behind the room door.

'Now then. How can I help you?'

Connie clasped her hands in her lap and looked down at her toes. 'I'm tryin' ter find out about the money me mum received from Armitage's all those years right up till she died,' she said directly.

'Didn't your mother tell you anything about the money, dear?'

'No. Every time I asked 'er she said it was me dad's money. I never knew 'im. Mum told me 'e was dead and that was all I needed ter know.'

Alice looked at the pretty girl sitting facing her and felt sorry for her. She had known Kate Morgan and had learned quite a lot about her from the works' gossip. It couldn't have been easy for this girl growing up. As she studied her Alice could not help but notice how like her mother she was: there was an uncanny resemblance. Alice crossed her legs and straightened her skirt.

'You think I might know about the money?' she asked.

Connie nodded. 'Well I thought you bein' the guv'nor's secretary you might 'ave arranged it.'

The older woman smiled kindly. 'Look. Let me get you a cup of tea and then we'll have a chat.'

Sounds came from the kitchen and while she was waiting Connie looked about the room. The two armchairs were covered with a floral-patterned material and against the wall facing the fireplace was a matching sofa. In the centre of the room there was a square dining-table with an embroidered sash spread across the middle. A bowl of fruit stood in the centre of the table and the arrangement reminded Connie of

Christmas. The walls were papered in a leaf-pattern and various pictures of landscapes were hung around the room. One different picture took Connie's eye. It was of a guardian angel standing over two young children. There was something about that particular picture that reminded her of the sister's room at the hospital. The painting was hung in a wide gilt frame and like the others it was suspended from a wooden picture rail that went around the walls. A gas fire stood in the hearth and above the high marble mantelshelf there was a mirror shaped like a butterfly. A rearing iron horse was perched at each end of the shelf and in the centre there was a large chiming clock with an ebonised base. The whole room looked clean and everything seemed in place. Heavy curtains hung at the side of the window and the lace covering the window panes looked freshly laundered. Connie was feeling slightly ill at ease.

Alice came back into the room with two cups of tea balanced on a wicker tray. She handed one cup to Connie and then sat down in the chair facing her with a sigh.

'There, that's better,' she said, stirring her tea with some deliberation. 'First of all, Connie,' she continued, 'I know you've a right to know about the money, now that your mum's passed away, but you must realise that although I might not be able to help you much, what I do tell you is confidential. I'm in a position of trust, and I wouldn't like Peter – Mr Armitage – finding out that I'd been talking to you.'

Connie nodded. 'I promise nobody at the firm will find out anyfink from me, Alice.'

Miss Jones took a sip from her tea and put the cup down on the occasional table at her elbow. 'I remember when the payments started, because I had to arrange it with the pay office. Old George Armitage authorised the money when he was the boss. It was only three pounds a month at the beginning, but it was increased to five pounds a month later. I remember when I first made the arrangements because it was just after the firm's outing to Southend. It was the first and last outing the firm ever had.'

'What year was that, Alice?' Connie interrupted.

'It was the summer of twenty-three. That's over fourteen years ago. How time flies.'

Connie was eager for the woman to get on with it and she fidgeted in her seat.

'As I was saying,' Miss Jones went on. 'It was the year of the outing. I didn't go myself. I don't like Southend, and I'm not one for social outings. Anyway, just after the outing your mother left the firm. Rather sudden it was, if I remember rightly. A few weeks later I was ordered to arrange the payments. Your mother was to receive the money by post every month. I wasn't taken into George Armitage's confidence, Connie. I never knew what the money was for.'

'You say me mum left suddenly? Did yer know why?'

Alice picked up her cup and took another sip before replying. 'Well, there was a lot of talk at the time. I couldn't get to the bottom of it, but it was something to do with Gerald Armitage.'

'Gerald Armitage?'

'Yes. He was the younger brother. He left the firm before you started. He was a nasty piece of work. Fond of the girls and always upsetting someone or other. I heard Gerald got drunk and caused trouble at the pub in Southend. Your mother was involved in some way, so I heard. She was very upset apparently. As I said, she left soon after. The following week I think it was. That's all I can tell you, Connie.'

'If the money started in twenty-three I'd 'ave bin three years old at the time,' Connie said thoughtfully.

'I don't think the money had anything to do with your

father, dear. If your mother never told you what the payment was for I don't see how you're going to find out now. All I can suggest is for you to talk to those workers who went on the outing. Some of them still work at the firm. They might be able to throw some light on the mystery, although, as I say, it was a long time ago.'

'How can I find out who was on the outin', Alice?'

'I might be able to help there,' Alice volunteered. There's some old photographs up in my office. They were taken at the pub in Southend. There's a group photo amongst them, I'm sure. Look, I tell you what. I'll sort them out and get them to you as soon as I can. How's that?'

Connie stood up. 'Fanks very much, Alice. I really appreciate you 'elpin' me. I've jus' gotta find out about the money. It's bin worryin' me ever since mum died.'

Alice helped Connie into her coat and showed her to the door. 'Don't worry. I'm sure you'll be able to get to the bottom of it, dear.'

Once out in the street Connie sighed deeply; the mystery surrounding her mother's life seemed to be getting more and more complicated.

The Sunday evening was balmy, with just a hint of a breeze stirring a couple of toffee wrappers at their feet. They walked arm in arm through the park and heard vague brassy sounds drifting over from the distant bandstand. Above, the trees were displaying their new leaves, and through the thickening foliage they caught a glimpse of the scurrying clouds. The two walked slowly, their steps measured and their bodies touching. From time to time they exchanged glances, passing silent messages with their eyes and smiling to each other in the quiet fading light. A couple was walking towards them, the woman pushing a pram and the man walking beside her carrying a large shopping bag. The only other person on the gravel path was an old man with a walking stick who had nodded to the lovers as he passed slowly by. Away in the distance they saw the redness rising over the tree-line and above it the diminishing shades of gold that reached up into the heavens.

The girl sighed, a deep lingering sigh as she squeezed his arm. 'It's so peaceful, Robert. Doesn't that cut grass smell luvvly.'

'Yes. I love this place. It's like standing on top of London. When you look down on the river you can sense all the noise and bustle going on, but up here it's like being in the heart of the country. You can breathe fresh air and almost hear the quietness. You can leave the ugliness and the squalor down below and forget everything.'

Connie stared into his pale-blue eyes and thought she saw a distant look there. 'You seem serious, Robert. I'll give you a penny fer yer thoughts.'

He grinned nonchalantly, but inside his head there were thoughts that he could not reveal. Thoughts which crowded his mind and gave the lie to what he had been saying. The beauty of the surroundings could do nothing to dispel the nagging fear that before much longer the country would be plunged into war. He felt it strongly, and the fear was steadily growing. It plagued him and affected his thinking. He imagined the destruction and carnage there would be, and could envisage nothing but sorrow and darkness ahead.

'I'm sorry if I seem serious, Con,' he said after a while. 'I was just thinking how peaceful it is here, when you consider all the trouble and strife that's going on in the world.'

Connie laid her head against his shoulder as they strolled along. 'Are yer worried about a war, Robert? You was mumblin' somefing about war in yer sleep last night.'

'No, of course not,' he replied quickly.

Connie was not to be put off. 'If it is worryin' yer, tell me. We're s'posed ter share everyfink, so yer said.'

They had just passed a park bench and Robert stopped suddenly and steered her towards it. 'Let's sit down awhile, Connie. I suppose we'd better talk about it.'

The couple with the pram passed by without a glance in their direction and when they were out of earshot Connie touched his arm. 'I knew there was somefink troublin' yer,' she said as they settled down on the slatted seat. 'Yer keep gettin' that funny look in yer eyes. It frightens me.'

He held her hands in his and looked into her worried eyes. 'Look, Con. I love you very much. I can't possibly tell you just how much. I want to be with you always. Nothing else matters to me. What scares the living daylights out of me is the thought of a war. A war that would part us, and maybe I'd never see you again.'

Connie felt her eyes glaze. 'Even if there was a war we would still be tergevver, wouldn't we? I mean yer wouldn't 'ave ter go away an' fight, would yer?'

'You mean that with me being a factory manager I'd be exempt?' he said with a sudden hardness in his voice. 'Yes, I would, but can't you see I couldn't just carry on in the factory while everyone else was going off to fight. I couldn't live with myself.'

She pulled her hands away suddenly and sat up straight in the seat. She glared at him, her eyes burning into his. 'You make me so mad when yer talk like that. It's all men fink of, goin' away ter fight. It strikes me yer want there ter be a war, jus' so yer can go off an' get yerself killed or somefink.'

'You don't understand, Connie. It's not like that at all. I don't want to go and get killed. It's just that ... oh let's forget it.'

She looked into his troubled eyes and her arms went out to him. 'Yer mustn't go away an' get yerself killed or badly wounded, Robert. I couldn't live wivvout yer. Yer mus' know that by now. I love yer terrible.'

He took her to him and they held each other close. No words were spoken as they clung together. Finally their bodies relaxed, and he took her by the shoulders and leaned back until she was at arm's length.

'I'm sorry, Con. I've frightened you. Look, it's just me. All this warmongering has been getting to me. I don't think there'll be a war, honest. Now let's forget all about such talk. Come on, there's a nice place I know down near the pier. We can sit on the veranda overlooking the river. If you're good I'll buy you a beer,' he joked.

They walked in silence down the steep path which led to the park gates. The evening traffic noise sounded loud after the quiet of the serene surroundings they were leaving, and as they crossed the busy road and walked leisurely down to the river they heard the harsh tone of the pleasure boat's horn as it pulled away from the pier. Along the walkway they passed tired children who were being ushered home, and lovers like themselves who strolled arm in arm, oblivious to everyone around them. They found the riverside inn and Robert squeezed his way to the counter. The pub was quite busy, with a mixture of visitors to the area and local folk who sat around in small groups and cast curious glances at the strangers as they arrived. Robert finally managed to get served and then led the way out on to the veranda. They found a seat by the rail and sipped their drinks as they took in the view. Downriver they could see the sweep of the Thames, flowing in a wide curve around the Isle of Dogs. Crane arms reached up to the darkening clouds and upriver the distant stone of Tower Bridge was bathed in light as the setting sun painted the heavens in shades of red and gold. The last pleasure craft was nearing the pier at Greenwich and across the water dark wharves loomed mysterious and ghost-like. Connie glanced at her lover and saw that now familiar look in his eyes. There was nothing she could say or do to smooth away the fear and concern he was feeling. She felt inadequate, unable to reach into him and bring him any comfort. If war did come she would lose him, she felt sure. He was determined to go away to fight.

Night was settling in and the sound of an accordion drifted out on to the veranda. The haunting strains of 'Moonlight Bay' seemed to float across the water and blend with the swish of the ebbing tide. The two lovers had been silent for a while, absorbed in their secret thoughts and content to sit and watch the night creeping in around them. Connie began to notice the middle-aged couple who had come out on to the veranda and sat down opposite her. The woman took some snapshots out of her handbag and passed them to her companion who put his glasses on to study the prints. Connie was suddenly reminded of the large envelope she had received that Friday morning. Alice Jones had slipped it to her before the rest of the management had arrived for their lunch. That evening Connie had pored over the photos of happy people who wore funny hats and held their glasses of beer up to the camera. One large photo showed the group standing beside the charabanc, and it was this photo which had interested her most. The photo was fourteen years old and most of the people in it were unfamiliar. She could pick out her mother, however. She stood between a young-looking Joe Cooper and a young woman who looked very much like Mary Brown. One other figure caught her eye. He was smartly dressed and the only member of the group who wore a tie. From what Miss Jones had told her Connie took him to be Gerald Armitage. There had been no opportunity so far to talk to the secretary about the people in the photograph nor to show it to Helen, but she was determined to follow up the lead as soon as possible.

'You're quiet, Con,' Robert said, squeezing her hand in his.

She glanced briefly at the couple who were giggling like young children over the snapshots. 'I was jus' finkin',' she said quietly. 'Let's get a photo done of us tergevver, Robert.'

The past week had been a time of feverish activity for the Ironmonger Street strike committee. The *South London Press* had been alerted and they had sent a reporter down. Joe Cooper had met with Mary Brown and her father George to draft a letter to the Bermondsey Doctor of Health. One or two local councillors who had been sympathetic to Joe's activities in the past were also contacted and they pledged their support. As for the rent collector, he had not been seen around since he was sent packing. Lizzie Conroy's fear that the bailiffs would arrive with the police did not materialise. Joe knew that it was only a matter of time before the bubble burst, and he passed the word around. 'Be on yer toes. It's gone too quiet.'

All was not quiet in the Vine Estate office that Friday morning.

The portly manager Norman Wallburton had summoned the agitated rent collector into his office and proceeded to read out the riot act. 'Look, Harris. You're employed to collect rents, not to be a bearer of bad bloody tidings. No rents collected are bad bloody tidings indeed. I won't have tenants telling the landlord that they are not going to pay their rents. Good God, man! It's the tail wagging the dog. I won't have it, d'you hear?'

Gordon Harris heard right enough. The bellowing voice hurt his ears. One thing you won't be having, he thought, and that's the rents.

'I said, did you hear me?'

'I heard you, sir. Trouble is, there's a nasty crowd in that street. It's got a bad name y'know.'

'A bad name!? I'll give it a bad name before I'm finished with Ironmonger Street. I'll have the lot of them thrown out,' Wallburton spluttered, sitting down heavily in his padded chair and wiping his perspiring forehead with a large handkerchief.

Harris looked at his hot and bothered manager. I'd like to see you face that rabble, you fat, overgrown slob, he thought. That lot would eat you for breakfast. I'm out there taking my life in my hands, and there's you sitting on your fat arse giving stupid orders. You make me sick.

'Harris!'

'Yes, sir?'

'Get the rest of your rounds done and I'll talk to you again next Monday morning.'

'Yes, sir.'

On Friday afternoon another visitor was shown in to the Vine Estate office and Norman Wallburton got up to greet him.

'Hello, Frank. How are you?'

The tall, stooping figure of Councillor Frank Salmon reached out and took the manager's clammy hand. 'I'm well, Norman. I hear you've been having a confrontation with some malcontents?'

The manager pulled up a large leather-bound chair and motioned the councillor into it. 'My collector had the confrontation, Frank. Seems the bolshy bastards over in Ironmonger Street have organised a rent strike, would you believe?'

Councillor Salmon crossed his legs and proceeded to scratch his shin. 'Yes, Norman, I know. That's the purpose of my visit. I've been contacted by the strike leader and, being their ward councillor I'm obliged to mediate.'

'Mediate? They've got to pay their rents, Frank. All right, I grant you there're problems with repairs, but let's face it, those places are nearly eighty years old. It costs a small fortune these days to keep them in good repair.'

Frank Salmon nodded. 'I sympathise with you, Norman, but we've got a problem here. The local press are on to it. They'll make capital out of this rent business. I've also been talking to the council doctor. He showed me a letter he'd received from the Ironmonger Street people only this morning. It's a bad time for that sort of publicity, especially after the diphtheria outbreak over on Conner Street a few months ago.'

'What can I do, Frank? I've got a business to run. Those houses have already been patched up once.'

Councillor Salmon scratched his leg again. 'How long have we known each other, Norman?' he said.

'Quite a number of years now, Frank.'

'Well then, trust me when I say I'm thinking of both our interests in this matter. Like yourself, I'm a businessman. I make it a point of knowing just what's going on in the borough. I happen to know that your company is negotiating the purchase of Jubilee Dwellings. I also happen to know that the property is owned by the Granthams and that Lady Grantham is planning to leave for America shortly and wants to complete the deal as soon as possible.'

Norman Wallburton toyed with his paper knife. 'You're certainly well informed, Frank,' he said a little archly.

'As I said, Norman. It's my business to know, and I find my lodge meetings can be very informative. However, there's one other little bit of information which might interest you. At the last Housing Programme Meeting, Jubilee Dwellings was mentioned as a prospective site for council housing development. Nothing was decided, I hasten to add, but at next week's meeting we'll be voting on the sites for selection. Point is,

Norman, will the council bid for that particular land, or will the idea be vetoed? Let's look at it objectively.

'Vine Estates agrees to carry out a renovation exercise on the Ironmonger Street houses. The council committee then abandon plans to include the Jubilee Dwellings site for future house building, and we all come out of this with our credibility intact. I say we, because my credibility is at stake. I've been put up to champion the Ironmonger Street tenants' cause. They'll be looking to me for a result.'

Norman Wallburton suddenly felt that his options were being squeezed. 'Suppose Vine Estates decides to defer the repairs, Frank?' he said. 'Suppose we decide to compete with the council for the land?'

Frank Salmon's mouth twitched into a ghost of a grin. 'Let's talk about Mr Knight for a minute or two. Basil Knight owns the lead mills in Crown Street. He also owns the foundry in Dockhead and a saw mill down in Rotherhithe. Talk to his employees about their wages and conditions of work and you'll find out that Mr Knight is about as popular with his work force as a boil on the arse. He's not too popular with the unions either, nor the council Labour group. The man is a Midas and a skinflint.'

'I'm not with you, Frank,' the estate manager said frowning.

'All right then, let's talk about one of your major share-holders, Miss Audrey Kenwood. The shares are registered in her maiden name. Audrey Kenwood happens to be Mrs Basil Knight.'

The estate manager's mouth hung open and his eyes popped.

'That's right, Norman. I think we can draw our own conclusions,' Frank Salmon went on. 'If the local rag gets hold of that tit-bit they'll have a field day. What's more, the council would fight tooth and nail to obtain that site if it becomes general knowledge that Basil Knight might well be pulling the strings at Vine Estates. As for those houses in Ironmonger Street, one or two of our radicals on the council might even set the ball rolling for a slum clearance order just to get at Basil Knight. As I said, Norman, those lodge meetings of mine are very informative.'

The portly estate manager had sagged in his chair. 'Tell me, Frank. Do you think you can operate a veto at the next meeting?'

'No problem at all, Norman. There are certain other members of the committee who belong to my lodge. All I need from you is a promise that you'll start repairs, and a letter of intent when I give you a written assurance that the site is safe. How does that sound?'

'I need to take your offer to the board, Frank. I don't envisage any problems.'

'No, I didn't think you would, Norman,' the councillor grinned.

Chapter Twenty

Spring gave way to a hot dry summer and in the backstreets of Bermondsey the stench from the drains mingled with the reek of the tanneries and the sour smells from the local vinegar factory. In the Tower Bridge Road market, fruit and vegetable stalls were piled high with produce, and the smells mingled with the sweet aroma of cakes from the bakery and the meaty odour coming from the pie shop. Behind the market a sweet, scented smell from the jam factory drifted through the backstreets as another consignment of Seville oranges went into the giant presses. Further along the Tower Bridge Road the air began to carry a hint of sour river mud from the Thames and the sharp, peppery tang of ripened hops as they were transported to the brewery, an ancient establishment that sprawled alongside the waterfront. In Tooley Street a myriad different flavours came from the docks and wharves as various commodities were transferred from small freighters and flat-bottom barges into the warehouses and on to lorries and carts. Impatient car-men cursed the sweating dockers and stevedores, while weary horses pulled against the shafts as whips cracked over their backs. Amongst the drab buildings, dingy railway arches and tumbledown streets of Bermondsey, there was an intense, feverish activity.

In Ironmonger Street, the recent renovation of the terraced

houses caused much comment amongst both tenants and gossips. In the Horseshoe public house two elderly regulars were expounding on the subject.

'I don't know about you, Bill, but I reckon the lan'lords got a right kick up the arse. Let's face it, those 'ouses was fallin' down. They 'ad ter do somefink.'

'Well, if the people didn't stop their rents, Terry, the lan'lords would 'ave let the 'ouses fall down, that's what I say.'

'That's right, Bill. After all, they couldn't chuck 'em all out fer not payin' the rent, could they?'

'Maybe not, but I fink there's more to it than meets the eye. I reckon the tenants 'ave got a shock comin'.'

'What, yer mean they'll put the rents up?'

'That's right, Tel. The bastards'll get their money back some way.'

Terry sucked on his unlit pipe and glanced up at the landlord of the Horseshoe. 'It's jus' like 'im,' he said, jerking his thumb at the bar counter. ''E sticks a bit o' shitty wallpaper up an' gives the place a lick o' paint. Then 'e gets a few new chairs in, tarts up the gaff, an' what does 'e do next? Puts a penny on a pint. Bloody skinflint. I dunno why we drink 'ere, Bill.'

'I tell yer why we drink 'ere, Tel. When we get pissed we can fall out of 'ere an' straight in our front doors, that's why.'

The victorious rent strike committee was discussing the recently completed renovation.

'Well at least the rain won't come in now, George.'

The old man nodded as he filled his stained clay pipe. 'Yeah that's right, Joe. We showed 'em, didn't we?'

Mary had just finished putting her youngest to bed and was studying a knitting pattern. 'All I 'ope is, the bleeders don't up the rents,' she said.

Joe picked up the chipped china mug and took a swig of his tea. 'Well accordin' ter ole Frank Salmon, we ain't gotta worry about that. 'E reckons providin' the arrears gets paid up we're okay. Mind you though, they'll 'ave a problem gettin' the back rent from the Toomeys, that's fer sure.'

'They'll 'ave ter send Lill out on the game,' George piped in.

'Well all I can say is, I 'ope she 'as more luck this time. Remember the turn out wiv Danny Mulligan?' Mary laughed.

Connie Morgan had left the Armitage factory and started work at a leather firm in the Tower Bridge Road. Brockway and Sons was busy on a government contract and quite a few of the locals had managed to get work there. Connie found the job interesting. She was moved around the factory, working as a stitcher, gluer and cutter, and packer, which she liked best of all. The girls were a friendly bunch, mostly about her own age and she felt happy. She and Robert usually went out twice a week, sometimes to see a film, or if the weather was nice they would take long walks and occasionally visit a restaurant for an evening meal, and she continued to spend her weekends at his flat. Although she was not yet eighteen, Connie now had the body of a mature woman; she was full-breasted, with shapely hips and long, slender legs. Her blond hair shone and her pale-blue eyes sparkled with happiness and good health. Her impish sense of humour had endeared her to the rest of the girls at the factory, and she was always being asked to accompany them to parties and various other events. Most of the time Connie declined their offers with as much grace as possible. The girls knew of her relationship with Robert and secretly envied her. Often he would meet her from work and, as they walked off arm in arm, Connie felt a warm glow inside as she noticed the other girls' envious glances and heard their bawdy remarks.

The summer days continued to remain hot and dry, with only the occasional shower of rain. Connie's quest for information about her mother's past had reached a dead end. She had had a conversation with her Aunt Helen, who was surprised to learn that there had been some sort of trouble at the firm's outing.

'Well as far as I can remember, yer mum never told me anyfing about it, Con. As a matter o' fact I didn't see very much of 'er at that time. She was always out an' about.'

When Connie showed her the photos of the outing, Helen studied them and identified certain people. She was apprehensive about Connie approaching them, however.

'Yer can't go askin' questions ter the likes of Joe Cooper and Mary Brown, can yer?' she asked. 'They're neighbours. Yer wouldn't want them knowin' all yer business. That's Joyce Spinks standin' be'ind yer muvver, Con. She still works at the firm an' she's bound ter talk if yer ask 'er awkward questions. It's difficult. I don't know 'ow yer gonna get round it. I mean, yer jus' can't go up ter people an' say, "What 'appened ter me mum at the outing?" Not unless yer prepared ter tell 'em about the money. The only person in that photo yer could ask is 'er there,' Helen said, pointing to a grinning, plump-faced woman standing in the background. 'That's Norma Cantwell. She was yer muvver's best friend fer years. In fact I know they used ter go out quite a lot tergevver. I fink they shared a few blokes as well. Trouble is, I don't know what 'appened to 'er. I remember yer mum sayin' Norma left the firm ter get married. Gawd knows where she is now. She might even be dead fer all we know.'

Connie had agreed that it was out of the question to ask any of the neighbours. She felt frustrated that there was nothing else she could do, and she hoped that some time in the future she might be in a position to find out the whereabouts of Norma Cantwell.

The days grew shorter as the summer passed, and in

September an international crisis flared up. Hitler had turned his attentions towards Czechoslovakia. War now seemed very probable and the Prime Minister Neville Chamberlain flew out to Munich to see the German dictator. The ensuing flurry of political activity was viewed with growing concern and a special meeting was called in the Horseshoe.

The pint at Terry's elbow was forgotten as he laboured the point. 'But yer can't go on chasin' back an' forwards after that bloody second-rate paper-'anger. It ain't dignified. All it is is bloody appeasement. What ole Chamberlain should be doin' is layin' the law down, instead of dashin' around like a tit in a trance kissin' 'Itler's arse. I mean, look what's goin' on 'ere while the silly bleeder's back an' forth. There's barrage balloons goin' up an' down in the sky like Punch an' Judy. There's shelters goin' up, an' san'bags everywhere yer look. They've mobilised the ARP, an' what's more, they're diggin' trenches in the bleedin' parks. Bloody nice, ain't it?'

Bill nodded sadly and picked up his pint. 'I fink yer right, Tel. They're talkin' about evacuatin' the women an' children now. Did yer see it in the paper last night? Bloody scand'lous. I dunno about 'ang the Kaiser. They should 'ave strung ole Schickelgruber up before 'e got too big fer 'is boots.'

Terry watched as his partner gulped at his pint and he took a swig from his. 'It makes yer fink, Bill,' he said, wiping his lips with the back of his hand. 'I see they're settin' up all these air-raid shelters in factories an' ware'ouses. I wonder if they'll set one up in Courages' brewery?'

At Speakers' Corner in Hyde Park there were angry scenes as the subject of Czechoslovakia was debated. Many people felt that the Czechs were being sold out by Britain, and others argued that it was not realistic to get into a war over a small country which most people knew nothing about. Tempers rose and fists flew as large crowds gathered to hear the speakers.

One particular orator remained impassive throughout as he announced to a motley crowd that 'The end was nigh'.

'Yer've bin sayin' that fer years,' screamed a scruffy looking individual in a grubby white mackintosh.

The speaker was not to be put off. 'Seek redemption, friend, or you'll perish in the fires of hell.'

'Perish yerself, yer bloody idiot,' the scruffy one growled.

'Take up the Scriptures, my friend. Study the word of the Lord.'

'I ain't yer friend,' the heckler screamed out.

'Go on, mate. You tell 'im,' someone shouted.

The scruffy man was becoming heated and his feet did a nervous shuffle. 'I've studied the Bible. I know what God said.'

'Well pay heed, my friend, for the Lord said you should turn the other cheek to the aggressor.'

'Oh no 'E didn't. God said yer take an eye fer an eye. That's what 'E said.'

'An' a nay for a nay,' shouted Paddy McGuinness.

The orator gave the big Irishman a withering look. 'You're mocking the Scriptures, Paddy. I hope your priest forgives you.'

'Heavens above!' Paddy cried out, with mock seriousness. 'I'm with you, sor. The end is nigh, I grant yer. Now listen ter Paddy McGuinness me lads. We'll never witness the end. It'll come like a thief in the night. It'll take us in our beds. 'Tis the truth I tell yerse.'

'Go an' boil yer socks, yer bloody maniac,' someone shouted.

The scruffy man in the white mackintosh had heard enough. With some of his thunder stolen he departed to heckle another speaker. Paddy meanwhile took out his battered timepiece and consulted it. Realising that the pubs had opened and it was high time for a pint of Guinness he, too, departed, allowing the meeting to return to sensible debate.

233

* * *

In the backstreets of Bermondsey life went on as usual, but now everyone seemed to be more inclined to chat on their doorsteps. Children still played out on the cobblestones and chalked on the pavements. Young lads chopped up apple boxes and sold the splintered sticks at front doors. Young girls skipped in and out of a turning rope and made up songs to dance to under the watchful eye of their worried mothers and in the pubs discussions went on about the seemingly inevitable war.

It was early September when Connie Morgan got her part-time job. She had befriended one of the girls at the leather factory, Jennie French. Jennie's parents ran the Dolphin, a family pub in Salter Street which was situated behind the Old Kent Road. Their part-time barmaid had got herself pregnant and had left. Jennie felt that Connie would be an ideal replacement and when she approached her parents they seemed keen on the idea. Connie thought about the offer. She was struggling on her factory wages and badly needed some extra money. It would mean three nights' work during the week, which still allowed her two evenings to see Robert. When Jennie took her friend to see her parents they were impressed. The landlord of the Dolphin was not too concerned that Connie had no knowledge of pubs and, while she waited in the bar with Jennie, he and his wife talked it over.

'I'd sooner get 'em green. The old 'ands are more likely ter dip the till. Long as she's polite ter the customers an' serves a good measure we should be okay. We'll soon teach 'er the trade. The only fing that worries me is 'er age. She said she's not eighteen till November. We'll 'ave ter be careful the brewery don't find out.'

Dora French gave a dismissive wave of her hand. 'She looks more than eighteen ter me, Bill. Who's ter know she's not? I'm sure the girl won't go blabbin' 'er age about.'

'All right, Dora. You put 'er on 'er guard an' we'll see 'ow she performs. You tell the girl she's got the job. I've gotta change a barrel over.'

When Neville Chamberlain returned from Munich, waving a piece of paper and declaring 'Peace in our time', the folk in the Bermondsey backstreets breathed a deep sigh of relief. Some folk were saddened, however. They felt that the Czechs had been betrayed and the deal with Hitler had only delayed the war. Bill and Terry were hard at it in their favourite corner of the Horseshoe.

'They've bin done down, Tel. There's no ovver word for it. Fancy doin' a deal wiv that mongrel 'Itler. It's bloody disgustin'. No, mate. We've sold those poor bastards down the river, an' we're gonna be sorry. We should 'ave learnt our lesson from the last turn out.'

'Yer right, Bill. I remember years ago when old 'Arold Simpson was alive. 'E was always goin' on about 'angin' the Kaiser. If 'e was alive terday what would 'e be sayin' about Adolf bloody Schickelgruber?'

'Trouble is though Tel, that 'Itler ain't nufink like yer Kaiser. 'E's got the bulk of the German people be'ind 'im. 'E's even promised every family out there a car in the future.'

'Go on wiv yer. 'As 'e really?'

''S'right, Tel. Strike me if 'e ain't. I read about it in the *Telegraph*.'

''Ow comes you bought the *Telegraph*? They don't sell that paper in our paper shop.'

'I didn't buy it, yer berk. It was wrapped round a bit o' plaice me ole woman got fer me tea. Interestin' article though.'

'Sounds a bit fishy ter me, Bill!'

Bill ignored the quip. ''Ere, Tel, I was finkin'. I bet ole 'Enery the Eighth is turnin' in 'is grave, don't you?'

Terry's face screwed up in puzzlement. 'What yer talkin' about?'

'Well I mean ter say, those trenches they're diggin' in 'Yde Park an' Regents Park. It's crown property, ain't it? It was 'Enery the Eighth what made 'em royal property. 'Ow would you like it if some geezer come along an' started diggin' your property up?'

Terry grinned. 'The only park land I've got is me winder box, an' me moggie digs that up every night. Mind you I'll wring the flea-bag's neck next time it claws up me geraniums.'

'I tell yer what, mate.'

'What's that, Bill?'

'All this talkin's givin' me a thirst. 'Oose round is it?'

The days got shorter and winter fogs began to roll in from the river. The backstreet folk waited in for the coalman while their elder children took prams up to the Old Kent Road Gas Works for bags of coke. The local kids also scoured the area to search the roadworks. Some of the roads were being re-laid and there were often discarded tarry logs for the taking. People struggled to clear their Christmas loans and the shops began to put up their festive decorations. Seasonal work meant that many folk who had been unemployed throughout the year managed to get a job. One of the lucky ones was Matthew Bartlett, who found a job as a factory labourer with a manufacturing tailors in Tooley Street. The firm had secured a government contract for military uniforms and needed more workers. It was not the type of work he was used to but Matthew was getting desperate. His earnings at the East End market had been a pittance and the lack of money was a major cause of tension in the Bartlett household. Luckily, Molly had also managed to get a job through the labour exchange. She was employed as an assembler of electrical components at a small factory in the Old Kent Road. The work was tedious but there were other young girls with physical disabilities working alongside her, and it made Molly feel less miserable. Helen had recovered enough to return to her early morning cleaning, and she felt happier than she had been all year.

Connie had celebrated her eighteenth birthday with a night up West. Robert had taken her to see a film and then they had visited a little restaurant in Dean Street for supper. For a present he had given her a tiny gold locket and chain. The evening had been romantic and he had been very attentive. They had returned to his flat in Great Dover Street and during their conversation he had let slip something which caused Connie considerable anxiety. They had been chatting happily when Robert mentioned his university days.

'There was always something going on at the college,' he said. 'I got involved with a crowd who were mad on flying. They used to take lessons and I became interested. In fact I did some flying myself. We all used to go to an airfield at weekends, weather permitting, to do a few sorties. I never progressed very far. I mean, I didn't go solo. Then it was the exams, and back to the family and the business. If war had been declared I suppose it would have been the RAF for me, Con.'

'S'posin' there is a war, Robert? Lots o' people still fink it'll come ter that.'

'Don't worry your pretty little head over it,' he said grinning. 'There'll be no war, believe me.'

Connie wanted to believe him, but she felt deep down inside that her happiness would somehow not last. It was a feeling that constantly attacked her insides and sent shivers running through her whole body. Only when she was in his arms did she feel totally secure. His caresses took the ache away and she drew new strength from his presence. When she was alone again, she worried about the future, and of one day losing him.

The recent war crisis had been affecting the Cooper household. Joe's wife Sadie had made it clear that if there was a war she would not stay in London.

'I couldn't stand it,' she groaned. 'I'd sooner kill meself.'

'Don't talk stupid,' Joe retorted. 'You'd 'ave ter put up wiv it jus' like everybody else.'

'It's all right fer you, Joe. I'm stuck in this chair. 'Ow could I manage?'

'Yer manage now, don't yer?'

'No fanks ter you. If it wasn't fer Cousin Constance I don't know what I'd do,' she said, dabbing at her eyes. 'Yer never 'ere. If it's not one fing it's anuvver. Yer always dashin' off ter bloody meetin's. Yer never give a thought ter me. I could be dyin'. It wouldn't make any difference. Yer'd still go off ter yer bloody meetin's.'

Joe puffed out his cheeks and got on with polishing his boots. It was better to ignore her outbursts, he thought. As long as she paid heed to that cousin of hers he'd be wasting his time trying to reason with her. Constance was an embittered, wicked woman who had ruined her own life by her nasty attitude. Her husband had run off with someone else and she had taken to unburdening herself on Sadie. She was always around, he mused. She had grown to hate all men and seized any opportunity to poison her cousin's mind against him. Sadie could not understand that it was Constance who was driving him out of the house. He could not bear to be in the same room as the woman. The trouble is, Sadie won't have a word said against her, he thought ruefully.

'Me sister Rosie said I could go an' stay wiv 'er if the 'vacuation starts,' Sadie went on.

'There's not gonna be any evacuation now,' Joe replied.

'Well if it does all blow up again, I'm off. Yer'll 'ave ter look after yerself. I couldn't stand it 'ere,' she moaned.

Joe bit his tongue. The way things had been for the past few years maybe it would be a good idea if she did go and stay with her sister, he thought. At least there would be no more rows. It would also mean he'd see the back of that bloody interfering cousin of hers.

Chapter Twenty-One

The village of Kelstowe lay under a thick carpet of snow. A full moon shone down on the quiet hamlet and lit up the large red-brick house which stood at the end of the deserted lane. Inside the lounge Claudette Armitage sat beside a brightly burning log fire. The heavy velvet curtains were tightly drawn against the inclement weather and a stack of sawn pine logs rested next to the stone fireplace. Around the large room there were sprigs of mistletoe and holly, and in one corner a Christmas tree reached up to the huge oak beams. The tree was lit with tiny lights and strands of silver tinsel hung from the branches. At the base there were parcels, wrapped in festive paper and tied with coloured ribbon. The high wooden mantelshelf was bedecked with Christmas cards, and to one side of the fireplace a tall lamp-stand afforded a pleasant, pinkish glow. Claudette sat looking distastefully at her husband who was snoring in the leather-bound armchair facing her. She reached for the glass of sherry at her elbow and drained the contents.

There had been words between them and she felt angry. Peter did not seem to grasp the situation. Either that or he didn't care. It was bad enough Robert leaving home and taking a flat in London, without him consorting with that factory girl. Worse still, he did not seem to have been put off by what his father had told him. Peter had weakly taken it in his stride and merely shrugged his shoulders. He should have taken a much harder line. After all, he had to consider their good standing in the village. For him to add to the hurt by suggesting to Robert that he bring this girl down to spend Christmas at their home was most inconsiderate, to say the least. Surely he could have envisaged the embarrassment it would cause? The girl was from a working-class background. How could Robert be so silly? He must have realised the implications of getting involved with a girl of that sort. There were many girls he could have chosen; girls like Eunice, who came from respectable and prosperous families. It just didn't make sense. It was too ridiculous.

Peter stirred in his chair and Claudette got up to add another log to the fire. Her irritation increased when her husband yawned and settled down again. It was just like Peter to ignore the situation. He should be more concerned about his son's welfare, if nothing else. This girl's mother had caused the family enough trouble without her daughter throwing herself at their son. That Kate Morgan woman had led Gerald on and then had made the family pay for his indiscretion. The girl would do the same if she got the chance, it was obvious. Another scandal would be too much to bear. Surely Peter could understand the dangers? Why was Robert being so naive? He must realise there could be no future with this factory girl. Well if Peter wasn't going to do anything about it, she would have to – somehow.

In the Bartletts' flat the curtains were drawn tightly against the cold night. Molly sat with Connie in front of the fire, their chairs positioned so that their stockinged feet rested on the brass fender. On Monday evenings Connie normally went out with Robert, but on this occasion he had gone to see his family to make arrangements for the Christmas visit. Connie was pleased to have the opportunity to stay with Molly. They had not spent much time together lately and it had caused her some concern.

'This is nice, Con. D'yer remember when we used ter sit an' chat fer hours about all sorts o' fings?' Molly asked her with a coy smile.

'Yeah I do. It was nice, wasn't it? I'm sorry I've neglected yer, Molly.'

'It's okay, Con. I know yer got it bad,' Molly said giggling.

'I do love 'im, Molly. 'E makes me feel ever so good.'

'Will yer marry 'im one day?'

'I dunno. Maybe I will – one day.'

'Don't it worry yer, sleepin' wiv Robert an' yer ain't even engaged?'

'It did at first, but it don't seem that important now. The problem is Robert's family. I'm sure they don't like 'im goin' out wiv me. I s'pose Robert wants ter let fings settle a bit before 'e springs an engagement on 'em.'

'Sounds like 'is family are real snobs, Con. They should be glad fer 'im. You're better than any o' them upper-class girls.'

Connie smiled and wriggled her toes. Molly seemed more cheerful than she had for a long time, and Connie was glad of the chance to sit talking intimately with her. She glanced at her cousin and saw how pale she was. Her short, thick body seemed to have become more misshapen and her head appeared to be resting directly on her hunched shoulders. As Connie studied her she noticed how Molly's eyes had grown larger in her thin face. They appeared to glow darkly with a sad defiance and as she stared into the fire they reflected the flames.

'It don't worry me all that much,' Connie said, placing her hands behind her head. 'I s'pose Robert's family will get used ter me in time.'

There was silence for a while, then Molly said, 'D'yer fink I'll ever get a fella, Con?'

''Course yer will.'

'I don't fink so. I've come ter realise it jus' won't 'appen. I know I'm different an' there's nufink can change it. When I was younger I used ter cry meself ter sleep some nights, wishin' I was like you. You're nice-lookin' an' yer can always get a fella. I used ter be jealous of yer, Con. Is it wicked ter be jealous of yer best friend?'

Connie felt a lump rising in her throat. ''Course it ain't wicked. I fink yer very brave, Molly,' she said, her voice faltering.

'I'm not brave. I'm jus' resigned ter the way fings are. I know I can't change the way I look. It used ter upset me when people stared, but it don't worry me now. I've got used to it. 'Ere. D'yer remember when we worked in the bottlin' stores? Michael Donovan always smiled at me an' I really wanted ter get talkin' to 'im. I jus' couldn't though. I tried ter kid meself 'e fancied me, but I knew 'e was only bein' nice. I was glad when 'e started chattin' you up, Con. Really I was. Sounds funny don't it?'

Connie could find nothing to say. She puckered her lips and stared into the fire, reminded of her time with the young sailor.

''Ave yer seen anyfing of 'im since yer split up, Con?' her cousin asked after a while.

Connie shook her head. 'No. I'd like ter see 'im, jus' fer ole time's sake. I don't fink I'd be able ter talk to 'im though. I'd be too embarrassed.'

The fire had started to die and Molly shovelled more coal on to the embers. Outside the wind was getting up and the windows rattled. The two sat in silence for a while, watching the violet-coloured flames spurt from the smoking coals. Presently Molly got up to poke at the fire and when she had settled herself once more she said, 'You lookin' forward ter meetin' 'is family, Connie?'

'Not really. I'm gonna feel terrible, 'specially the way fings are. I expect they fink I'm a right little tart.'

'Why should they fink that?'

'Well, they must know why their son got 'is own flat. It stan's ter reason.'

'Let 'em fink what they like, Con. Yer as good as them. All right, yer might not speak wiv a plum in yer mouth, but it ain't the talkin' what counts, it's the doin'.'

Connie laughed aloud as she saw the look on Molly's flat round face. 'You're gettin' ter be a proper little philosopher. It's all those books yer bin readin'.'

Molly grinned. 'Well, it makes me so mad. Me dad's always goin' on about fings like that. 'E reckons we're as good as anybody.'

''Ere, Molly. Talkin' about yer dad. 'Ow's fings wiv 'im an' yer mum?'

Molly held her crossed fingers out in front of her. 'Since me dad got that job 'e's bin much better. I ain't 'eard 'im an' mum arguin' at all lately. They even went ter the flicks tergevver. They ain't done that fer ages.'

'What about you, Molly? D'yer feel better fer workin'?'

'Yeah, sort of. It's not a bad job. It gets a bit monotonous at times, but they're a nice crowd o' girls there. One or two of 'em are even worse than me. Poor Barbara comes ter work in a wheelchair. At least I can walk ter work. I 'eard that the guv'nor gets money from the gover'ment ter take on people like us. By the way, 'ow's yer barmaid's job goin'?'

'Oh, it's okay. I'm gettin' used ter servin' beer an' chattin' all the customers up. Jennie's mum an' dad are pretty decent too.'

'D'yer get asked out a lot, Con?'

'Not really. They're all too drunk ter notice me 'alf the time.'

Molly yawned and Connie got up to stretch her legs. She crossed to the window and eased the curtains aside. Down below in the empty street a white blanket of snow covered the cobblestones and the grey slated roofs. A full moon shone down into the little turning, giving the snow a bluish tint. Long shadows reached out from the factory gates and climbed up the yellow brick walls of the houses opposite. The cold glow from the lone gaslamp flickered up and then faded, its light paling in the radiance of the bright round moon high up in the heavens. For a time the ugly looking factory held the young woman's gaze. How many secrets were locked away behind those ugly iron gates? she wondered. How many ghosts were roaming around inside the darkness of that old red-brick building?

The Christmas Eve train chugged through the white countryside and finally slid noisily into Kelstowe station. Outside in the station forecourt Connie and Robert climbed into a waiting taxi-cab and were driven the couple of miles to the Armitage home. Connie was feeling apprehensive about meeting Robert's mother for the first time. Her stomach knotted up and she shivered. Robert took her hand in his, aware of her feelings. It was something that had to be done. His parents had to be made aware that he was serious about the girl. He felt uneasy about the confrontation but he gave her an easy grin as he looked into her blue eyes.

'It'll be fine, you'll see,' he said reassuringly.

When they reached the house Robert paid the driver and took her small case. Connie slipped her arm through his as they walked up the snow-cleared path to the front door. Robert's knock was immediately answered by his father. He smiled as he beckoned them in, and the warmth made Connie's face glow red as she slipped out of her coat and straightened her dress.

'Have a good journey down?' Peter asked them.

'We had a carriage to ourselves,' Robert answered.

Peter took their coats and hung them on the tall coatstand. Claudette appeared from the lounge and smiled graciously.

'So this is Connie,' she purred, taking the young woman's hand in a limp grasp. 'Do go in.'

Connie followed Robert into the large lounge and glanced quickly around, her eyes wide with surprise. Everything seemed so perfectly placed, she thought. The giant fireplace caught her eye and she could smell the bubbling pine resin. Robert took her hand and steered her into the long settee, seating himself beside her.

Peter Armitage walked over to a cabinet and picked up a bottle. 'Right. Now what about a sherry, Connie?'

'Yes, please,' she answered, giving Robert a brief glance.

'I'd love a Scotch and soda, Father. Easy on the soda. It's a cold night out there,' Robert said, winking at Connie.

Claudette had left the room, saying she wanted to check all was well in the kitchen. Peter brought over the drinks and sat down in his favourite armchair, his eyes on Connie as she sipped the sherry.

'How's the new job?' Peter asked presently.

'It's all right fank you, Mr Armitage. I've got used to it now,' she replied.

'You can always come back you know,' he said, grinning.

Connie began to settle down and her stomach eased. The factory owner had always been courteous to her when she worked in the canteen and now he was trying to encourage her to relax. His wife had seemed very starchy and formal, however. Her smile had seemed forced, although it might just have been her way. Connie decided she would just have to see how things developed.

Out in the kitchen Claudette fussed around Mrs Goodyear. 'We'll sit down at eight, Amy. Is that all right?'

Mrs Goodyear took the Dover sole from beneath the grill and gently prodded it with a fork. 'It'll be ready by then, Mrs A. I'll just check the pudding.'

Claudette watched thoughtfully as Mrs Goodyear took a large china bowl from the steamer. Her mind was on other things. She had been taken aback when she first saw the young woman who was holding on to her son's arm. She had to concede she was very pretty. Her hair shone in the light and her eyes had a sparkle. Claudette could see why her son had been attracted to the girl.

'That's it. Everything's ready,' Amy said, glancing at Claudette and noticing the faraway expression on her face.

The meal passed smoothly. Connie had become used to eating out with Robert and she managed to use the correct spoon for the soup. The fish course was followed by steamed pudding and, during the whole of the meal, Peter talked lightly about the weather, the factory output, and the recent visit of the Prime Minister to Germany. It seemed to Connie that he was attempting to monopolise the conversation, preventing his wife from saying very much. Connie was pleased. She could sense the hostility in Claudette, although on the surface she was polite and attentive. When Amy had cleared the last of the plates Peter leaned back in his chair and lit a cigar. Robert declined the proffered cigar box, preferring a Craven A which he took from his silver cigarette case. Amy brought in coffee and then went back into the kitchen to face the huge pile of soiled crockery.

The two men had left the dining room to go to Peter's study for a brandy or two. Connie sat at the table with Claudette, watching her hostess as she poured out fresh coffee from a tall china pot into minute cups.

'One or two, dear?' Claudette asked, holding the sugar tongs delicately between her thumb and forefinger.

'Two, please.'

Claudette passed the cup to Connie and leaned forward on the table, her arms making a bridge and her fingertips touching. 'Tell me, Connie. How long have you known Robert?' she asked, looking at her intently.

'We've bin tergevver for about a year now,' Connie replied.

'Robert tells me you live in Bermondsey. Quite near the factory, I understand.'

'Yes, that's right. I live in Jubilee Dwellings. Next door ter the factory.'

'It doesn't sound a very nice place to live. What are the dwellings like? Do you have electricity?'

'The street's gas-lit. There's no electricity, except in the factory.'

'Good God! It must be terrible,' Claudette said, pulling a face. 'Are they very old, these dwellings?'

Connie's mind went back to the time the men came into the Bartletts' flat to fit an extra gaslamp. When they lifted the floorboards to lay the piping Molly had pointed out the carved signature of the original carpenter. Beneath the name Isaac Smith was a date. 'Yes, they are old,' Connie answered. 'The dwellings were built in 1862. That was the year of Queen Victoria's Silver Jubilee. I s'pose that was why they called 'em Jubilee Dwellin's.'

'Good Lord!' exclaimed Claudette, taken off guard by the unexpected answer. 'Do you study history?'

'I read quite a lot,' Connie replied, remembering that it was Molly who had told her about Queen Victoria's Silver Jubilee. She hoped that Robert would hurry back soon.

Claudette toyed with her cup for a while. Suddenly she said, 'Are you and Robert going steady? I mean, are you planning to get married one day?'

'I can't say. Robert 'asn't asked me – yet,' Connie said quickly.

The woman of the house studied her fingernails. 'I understand from Peter that your mother once worked at the factory?'

Connie felt her stomach knot. 'Yes, she did.'

Claudette fiddled with her spoon, removing an imaginary coffee dreg from her cup. 'Peter was telling me about the arrangement made between Robert's grandfather and your mother. You know about that, of course?'

'Yes, I do.' Connie was surprised at Claudette's frankness.

'You know why the money was paid to your mother?'

'No. When I asked me mum I was told it was from me dad,' Connie replied.

Claudette's mouth parted in a ghost of a smile and it did not go unnoticed by Connie. She felt sure that the woman knew the reason for the payments and her mind started to race. Maybe it was the right moment to try a little bluff, she thought, fixing Claudette with her eyes.

'Robert told me 'e doesn't know anyfink about the money, but I'll know pretty soon. As a matter o' fact I'm goin' ter see somebody who worked at the factory the same time as me mum. She was a good friend of 'ers. I know she'll be able ter tell me what I want ter know.'

The older woman leaned forward as though she was about to say something when Robert and his father walked back into the dining room.

'Hello. You two still here?' Peter remarked. 'I would have thought you'd have taken your coffee into the lounge.'

'We were having a cosy chat,' Claudette purred, glancing at Connie, who was silent.

* * *

The cold winter moon shone through the parted curtains into the bedroom and played on the pink counterpane. Connie lay on her back with her hands clasped behind her head. She could see the snow-covered branches of the cedar tree through the leaded window and distant stars peeping through the moving clouds. It had been a tiring evening, with Peter continuing to talk away lightheartedly. It was after midnight when Claudette had pointed out that Connie looked tired and suggested that maybe she might like to go to bed. Sleep would not come, however, and as she watched the swaying branches of the cedar tree and saw its shadow dancing on the ceiling Connie felt wide awake. She was certain in her mind that Claudette knew the reason for the payments. The truth was written on her face, and Connie felt that she would have learned something had their conversation not been interrupted. It Claudette knew, then it was almost certain the rest of the family knew, too. That would mean Robert had either lied to her or he had been kept in the dark by his parents. Connie's mind went back to the meeting she had had with Alice Jones. She had doubted that the payments had anything to do with her father. If she was right then it could only mean that the money had bought her mother's silence. But for what? It had either been offered or demanded and the thought troubled Connie. Her mother might have been a bit wild in her young days, but she had been a proud woman. It seemed unthinkable she would have demanded money from the firm without a very good reason. Maybe there would be an opportunity to carry on the conversation with Claudette. The woman obviously knew something.

Connie felt her eyelids at last begin to grow heavy. She turned on her side and let her head sink into the lavender-scented pillow. She did not hear the door creak open and shut, nor the words that were whispered in her ear. She did not know Robert was in the bed beside her until he began gently stroking her hair as he moved his body close to hers. She opened her eyes and saw his face next to her, smiling in the pale moonlight. Her arms reached for him as he kissed her neck and her ear and sought her open mouth.

'I needed you, Con,' he whispered.

'Hold me,' she said, her voice coming out husky.

The wind whistled and powdery snow lifted from the swaying tree. She caught his hot breath on her face and felt his warm body against hers. She closed her eyes and let his kisses and his caresses shut out the cold night.

In the bedroom at the back of the house Peter Armitage snored noisily, his sleep fortified by the brandies he had consumed during the evening. Claudette lay awake, her eyes gazing at the ceiling, her thoughts centred around the man who had on certain occasions come to her bed and loved her with a sensuous passion she had never experienced within her dull, monotonous marriage. Her lover was wild, unpredictable, wicked even, and so unlike his staid brother. She would protect him out of her love for him. She would do what had to be done to shield him. She heard the landing creak and then the sound of a door closing. Claudette glanced at the illuminated clock beside the bed; it showed two-thirty. Her lips compressed and she pushed her elbow into the snoring figure at her side. Peter grunted and turned over. It had become silent again, and in the darkness Claudette schemed.

Chapter Twenty-Two

On Boxing Day Connie and Robert decided to catch the late afternoon steam train to London Bridge. The ancient taxi left the house and slithered over the fresh snow as it journeyed through the quiet village. At the station the driver followed the tracks in the snow and brought his battered vehicle to a stop, mumbling to himself as he searched his pockets for change. The tip helped to gratify him and he drove off, blowing on his cold hands. Robert took Connie's case as they walked along the platform looking for an empty carriage. Few people seemed to be on the train and when the two finally settled themselves in the warm compartment Robert lit a cigarette.

'I know I shouldn't really say it, Con, but I'm glad that's over. My father does go on a bit, and as for my mother, she's not happy unless she's fussing over something or the other. How about you? Was it very difficult?'

'No, it was very nice,' Connie lied. 'I was very nervous at first but yer dad made me feel at home.'

'What did you think of Mother?' he asked, grinning broadly.

'I fink I was a bit scared of 'er. When I first saw yer mum I thought she reminded me of the 'eadmistress at our school.'

Robert laughed. 'She'd be pleased about that.'

Connie looked out at the snow. 'Don't dare tell 'er I said that.'

Robert squeezed her arm. 'Don't worry, I won't say anything. I'm sure you made a big impression.'

The guard blew his whistle and the train jerked away from the station. Robert glanced at Connie and said, 'You seemed very quiet in the taxi. I thought there might be something wrong.'

Connie forced a smile. 'There was nufink wrong. I was just wonderin' about what they said about me after we left.'

'They liked you a lot,' Robert said casually. 'I could tell.'

Connie glanced out of the carriage window as the train rushed through the bleak countryside. Robert would have been shocked if he had heard her conversation with Claudette. Or would he? She suddenly wondered. She looked at Robert and saw that his eyes were drooping and his head was rolling slightly with the motion of the train. She studied his finely cut features and realised how childlike he looked. His small, straight nose twitched occasionally and she noticed how long his eyelashes were and how his fair hair curled at the ears. His head was slipping down towards her shoulder and Connie looked back out of the window as the train passed quickly between fields covered in snow. Her thoughts went back over the past two days and she shuddered.

Christmas morning had begun with a cooked breakfast of poached eggs, bacon and mushrooms. When they were finished they had all exchanged presents. Robert had given her a gold bracelet and she had given him a thick woollen cardigan which he was now wearing. Robert's parents had given her a silver hairbrush and comb, and she had presented Peter with cigars and Claudette with a tortoiseshell hand mirror. Connie had been helped in her choice of presents by Robert, who solved the problem by saying that his mother had broken her favourite mirror – perhaps by bringing it down a little too heavily on his father's head! They had attended the morning church service, trudging through the snow and stopping on the way to exchange pleasantries with their neighbours and friends. Connie recalled that it was the first time she had been inside a church since she was a small child and the Christmas service seemed to go on for a long time, and then there were more handshakes and introductions afterwards in the church-yard. Connie was glad when they arrived back at the house and she felt the warmth of the welcoming log fire. The table had been laid in the dining room: Claudette had served the vegetables from silver dishes; and Peter had expertly cut the huge turkey. It was the first time Connie had tasted turkey and it reminded her of chicken, which was the usual Christmas fare at the Bartletts' home.

The day passed pleasantly enough, she thought, with Peter showing off his collection of gramophone records which he played on an upright machine. After a tea of mince pies and cream cakes, Peter suggested they play cards. Connie smiled to herself as she remembered how Robert had tried unsuccessfully to teach her how to play whist. Later they listened to the wireless and she had drunk two glasses of sherry. It was well after midnight when the Armitages retired to bed, leaving her and Robert alone together. Connie nestled closely to Robert, his arm around her, cuddling her to him. She had stared into the burning logs and imagined that they were alone in their own house watching the fire dying before he swept her up into his arms and carried her up to their bedroom. They had kissed goodnight on the landing and she had gone to her room hoping he would come to her again, but she had fallen asleep as soon as her head touched the pillow and slept soundly until morning.

There had been no opportunity to talk to Claudette during Christmas Day, but on Boxing Day morning Claudette had suggested to Robert that he might like to accompany his father to the Three Pheasants for a lunchtime drink. Connie knew then that Claudette was eager to pick up the threads of their conversation. She was not to be disappointed, for as soon as the men had departed Claudette made coffee and suggested they sit beside the fire for a cosy chat. Connie watched while her hostess fussed over the chair cushions and then brought in the coffee pot and crockery on a silver tray. Placing the utensils at her elbow, Claudette made herself comfortable and looked closely at her companion.

'If I remember rightly, you were saying that you expected to learn something from this get-together you've arranged?' she began with very little hesitation.

'That's right.'

'Problem is, you're talking about a long time ago, my dear. Memories fade and the truth sometimes becomes distorted.'

Connie watched while Claudette poured the coffee. 'I thought about that,' she said quietly. 'Fing is, there was more than one person in my street who worked wiv mum at the factory. I intend ter talk to 'em all in time. Then I should be able ter get ter the truth. That's all I want, Mrs Armitage.'

'Of course you do, my dear,' the elder woman said, passing over a filled coffee cup. 'You have to remember though that the truth will hurt.'

'It might not,' Connie replied.

'It will, my dear. Believe me it will.'

'Yer can't know that,' Connie said, eyeing the woman with a puzzled frown.

'Oh, but I do,' Claudette said quickly.

'Yer mean yer know all about the money?'

'Yes, I do.'

'Will yer tell me?' Connie asked, her eyes fixed anxiously on her hostess.

'I will, providing I have your assurance that you won't say anything to Robert. You see my dear, Peter and I have never felt it necessary to mention the reason for the payments to him because it all happened a long time ago. The arrangement was between Robert's grandfather and your mother, and it was purely their business. If my son felt he had been excluded it might affect his trust and faith in us. He would think he had been treated badly, and I don't want that to happen.'

'I won't say anyfink, I promise,' Connie said earnestly.

The fire began to burn low and the coffee cooled as the two women faced each other in the lounge. Connie sat with her hands held tightly together in her lap and Claudette leaned forward in her armchair.

'It was at the firm's outing to Southend back in 1923,' she began. 'During the evening the charabanc stopped at a public house on the way home. Most of the workers were more than a little drunk by that time, including your mother. There was a lot of merry-making and she got talking to one of the locals. Later she was seen leaving with him. Peter's brother Gerald was responsible for everyone's welfare on the day, and he was worried by your mother's absence when it was time to leave. Anyway, he went off to look for her and finally found both your mother and this local man lying together in a field behind the pub. When he called out that it was time to leave the man became abusive and Gerald was threatened as he tried to remonstrate. In the process your mother accidentally fell into a ditch. She wasn't badly hurt, just a few bruises and cuts. The man who was with her attacked Gerald, who fought him off and then helped your mother back to the pub. A member of the staff helped her to get cleaned up and then the charabanc left. Most of the people on the outing were very drunk and no one was aware of what had happened. Apparently your mother slept throughout the whole of the journey home.

'On the next Monday morning she went to see Robert's grandfather and said she had been attacked by Gerald on the outing and intended going to the police to tell them he had tried to rape her.'

Connie gasped. 'I can't believe me mum would do such a fing! It's not true!'

'I warned you the truth would hurt, dear,' Claudette said, crossing her legs. 'Of course, it came as a terrible shock to Grandfather. Gerald had already told him about the accident. He tried to dissuade your mother from going to the police but she was adamant. "You'll have to pay to keep me quiet" were her very words.'

'I can't believe what I'm 'earin'. She wouldn't do that! I know she wouldn't!' Connie exclaimed. She was clenching her fists tightly.

'Listen, my dear. You told me yesterday that when you approached your mother about the money she told you it was to do with your father. I think you realise that it wasn't true. If there was nothing to hide then your mother would surely have told you about where the money came from and what it was for.'

Connie was silent, her eyes filling with tears as Claudette went on. 'Your mother told Grandfather that she could not continue to work at the factory after what had happened and as she had a young child to support it was only right that the firm should look after her financially. The arrangement they came to was that a sum of three pounds would be paid to your mother every month. The payment was increased a few years later to five pounds.'

'But it doesn't make sense,' Connie blurted out. 'Why didn't Gerald defend 'imself? 'E could 'ave gone ter court an' told 'em 'is version. I'm sure 'e would 'ave bin believed before me mum.'

Claudette leaned back in her chair and sighed. 'You don't understand, Connie. Let me try to explain. At the time Gerald was going through a bad patch. He had marriage problems and his wife had decided on a separation. If he had gone to court the bad publicity might have influenced his wife into seeking a divorce, even though he was innocent. Gerald was desperate to save his marriage and felt he couldn't take the chance of defending himself in public. There was another consideration also. Back in the 'twenties businesses were struggling to stay alive. Contracts were hard to come by and the firm was at that time negotiating an important contract against very fierce competition. Newspapers would have reported the case. Publicity of that sort might well have cost the firm a great deal. Anyway, a document was drawn up in which your mother agreed not to proceed further with her allegations and the firm promised to pay her a regular sum for the whole of her lifetime. That money bought her silence. I think you should let it stay that way. Talking to anyone about what happened all those years ago will only cause you more grief. Let it stay buried, my dear. It's the only true course, believe me.'

Connie's hands came up to her ashen face and she stared incredulously at Claudette. 'I just can't believe it,' she gasped in a whisper.

Claudette stood up and put her hand on Connie's shoulder. 'Just leave it buried, dear. It's best that way. Really it is.'

The train clattered on towards London and Robert slept soundly. Connie sat staring out into the approaching night, deep in thought. What she had heard from Claudette had shocked and angered her. She did not believe her. There had to be another reason for the money, she told herself. Her mother had been a little wild in her time but she would never have stooped to getting money in that way. There had to be something else. Claudette had seemed too well informed about the whole series

258

of events. It was as though it had all happened yesterday, the way she told it. If the woman was lying, who was she protecting? Was it Gerald or was there some other person involved? Questions flooded into her troubled mind. Why wasn't Robert told anything? He was an adult. One day he would take over the factory. Why should his parents keep the secret locked away from their son? Maybe Claudette had lied about that, too. Maybe he knew and was sworn to silence, or was just trying to be protective by saying he did not know the reason for the payments. She was now more determined than ever to find the woman Helen had pointed out in the photograph. She had been a close friend of her mother. Maybe she would be able to tell her the truth.

The white countryside had given way to bricks and mortar. Dark factories and houses flashed past, their chimneys belching smoke from roaring fires. Robert was rousing himself and Connie nudged him gently.

'We're nearly there,' she said, watching him as he shook his head and rubbed at his eyes. The train slowed into the station and came to a juddering halt with a loud hiss of steam. It was dark as they hurried along the platform. Connie yawned and held his arm as they passed through the ticket barrier.

'You look tired. Do you want me to take you straight home, Con?' he asked.

'I don't want to be on me own ternight, Robert. I wanna stay wiv you.'

He led her to the taxi rank in the station forecourt, his arm around her waist. 'Let's go home, Con,' he said softly as he opened the door of the taxi and helped her in.

Snowflakes danced in the cold wind as the cab moved along Borough High Street. They sat close holding hands, her head resting against his shoulder. Robert gazed out at the flurrying snow and caught sight of a discarded placard leaning against a shuttered shopfront. 'PEACE OR WAR' it read in bold black letters.

It had been a quiet Christmas in Ironmonger Street. There had been virtually no incidents that would have added to the turning's already dubious reputation, and in the local pubs the customers went home without much persuasion when time was called. George Baker had drunk too much on Christmas Eve and was helped back to his house by his son-in-law and Joe Cooper, who took hold of the old man's arms and steered him along through the thickening carpet of snow.

The Bartletts stayed at home with their daughter. Matthew had managed to clear up his Christmas Club and had found the money for a large chicken and presents for Helen and Molly. There was not enough money left for a visit to the pub but Matthew was content. It might have been worse, he thought. His job did not pay very much, but it was better than standing in the freezing cold with bundles of shoelaces and cards of collar studs throughout the week for a few coppers. Helen was feeling content, too. There had been a better understanding between them lately. Matthew was much less inclined to argue with her now that he had found a job, and Molly had become less withdrawn once the rows had stopped. Helen's only concern was for Connie. She was becoming more like her mother as time passed, in looks as well as attitudes. She had become defensive about her relationship with the factory owner's son, and disinclined to talk about her staying out at weekends. It worried Helen that Connie was sleeping with him. It would be terrible if the girl fell for a child the way her mother had.

It had been a quiet Christmas, too, for Toby and Marie Toomey. Toby had managed to get his battered pram operational once more with the aid of an oil can and a ball of string. He had been out collecting scrap which he stored in the shop next door, alongside the bundles of rags and old newspapers. He had saved enough money to clear up the rent arrears and pay the rent on the shop, but the scrap merchants had finished early this Christmas and did not call to clear his stock on Christmas Eve. Marie had given her dutiful husband a mouthful of abuse for his lack of foresight, which had left them almost penniless. Their daughter Lillian had decided that sitting at home and listening to her parents arguing all through Christmas was unthinkable. She had to do something and as she put her make-up on Lillian had already made up her mind. She would go back to her old haunt down in Rotherhithe. It had been profitable in the past, and at this time of year there would surely be a few seamen ready to pay for some company. She had left the house early on Christmas Eve and caught the tram to Surrey Docks Station. The Windjammer was packed and Lillian took stock as she entered the public bar. A few hefty blond seamen stood in one corner talking excitedly and in another corner she spotted one or two of the girls she had socialised with during her adventures in the area. A large redhead noticed her and came over.

''Ello, Lil. What yer doin' down 'ere?'

''Ello, Bel. I'm slummin' again. Fings are quiet in Bermon'sey. I'm lookin' fer a nice big seaman wiv a pocket full o' dosh.'

Bella laughed aloud. ''Ere. See that big geezer over by the pianer? I went wiv 'im last night. 'E's a Swede. Go on, give 'im a pull. I've jus' tried me luck again ternight but I fink 'e likes new faces.'

'Bloody 'ell,' Lillian said, grinning. 'I don't mind a big-un but 'e looks like King Kong.'

'Don't worry about 'im, Lil. 'E's a babe. I took 'im 'ome last night an' told 'im 'ow much I charge, an' yer know what?

'E give me an extra couple o' quid jus' ter tiggle 'is toes. I tell yer, Lil, I've bin asked ter do some weird fings in me time, but that topped it all.'

Lillian took out a small mirror from her handbag and studied her face. 'What's 'is name, Bel?' she asked.

''E's called Sven. Go on, Lil, try yer luck.'

The big Swede was standing apart from his noisy countrymen, his round face impassive as he stared into space and his massive hand clamped around a pint glass.

''E looks pissed, Bel,' the Toomey girl remarked.

''E's okay. That's 'is natural look. Go on, chat 'im up then. Yer better 'urry up if yer goin' to. Fat Sara's got 'er eyes on 'im,' Bella whispered, nodding towards the counter.

Lillian glanced over and saw the big woman standing with her back to the counter and one foot resting on the brass rail. 'She still about, Bel? I thought she retired years ago.'

'She did,' Bella replied. ''Er ole man's turned pimp. 'E's put 'er out again.'

Lillian had caught the Swede's eye and she gave him one of her seductive smiles. He smiled back, displaying gold front teeth. Winking at her friend, the Toomey girl sauntered over to him and said in a low voice, ''Ello, Sven. Gonna buy me a drink, then?'

His large blue eyes widened and he took a fistful of notes from his coat pocket. 'Ja. Drink. You fetch, eh?'

Lillian took a pound note from the screwed up wad and turned to see Fat Sara blocking the way to the counter. 'What yer doin' round 'ere, Toomey? Out o' yer manor, ain't yer?'

Lillian smiled sweetly at her rival. 'It's a free country, Sara. I'm toutin' fer a bit o' business.'

'Not in 'ere yer don't,' Sara growled, her eyes flashing.

'Why, you got the monopoly then?' Lillian replied, hands on hips.

Fat Sara prodded the Toomey girl in the chest with a fleshy forefinger. 'Listen, darlin'. Me an' the girls from Riverside Street work this patch. We ain't gonna stan' by an' see business snatched from under our noses. Not by a skinny prat like you, so piss orf an' get yer business somewhere's else.'

Lillian made a grab for the prodding finger and bit on it. Sara gave out a yell and thumped her rival in the eye with her clenched fist. Lillian staggered back and fell into the arms of the big Swede.

'You get drink, ja?' he grinned.

'Oh, no, she won't!' screamed Fat Sara, shaping up with her fists.

Lillian lunged forward and grabbed at the woman's long dark hair. Customers backed away and a loud voice shouted out from behind the counter. 'No fightin' in 'ere, girls! Outside fer punch-ups!'

The two women had fallen to the floor in a scratching, screaming heap. Sara was under the lighter contestant and was getting the worse of the exchange. Lillian had grabbed her rival's ears and was pummelling her head on the bare floorboards. They were finally separated by the Swede who grabbed the back of Lillian's coat and hoisted her up like a baby. Fat Sara saw her chance as she struggled to her feet.

'I'll kill the whore! Let me at 'er!' she screamed, rushing forward.

Sven was ready and with his massive hand held out he stopped Sara in her tracks and shoved her backwards against the counter. Sara's scrawny looking pimp rushed across with a beer bottle held up in his fist. He tried to bring the bottle down on the Swede's head but he was stopped by two large seamen who grabbed him and threw him bodily over the counter. There was a sound of breaking glass and then the cross-eyed pimp's bloodied head appeared from behind the bar. A few young dockers jumped into the fray and suddenly the whole public bar of the Windjammer was filled with a fighting, sprawling mass of bodies. The landlord and his helpers tried desperately to break up the brawl, only to be engulfed in flailing fists, bar stools and any other object that came to hand. As customers hurried for the door they were confronted by a saintly looking lady in a blue bonnet who held a collection box in one hand and a bundle of papers in the other.

'Get your copy of God's paper,' the lady called out, holding up the *War Cry*.

A body came spinning out through the open door and landed in a heap in the gutter. The man picked himself up painfully and staggered back into the fray. A tall, elderly man wearing the Salvation Army uniform took the paper-seller by the arm and pulled her away from the door.

'I think the customers are previously engaged, Matilda. We should perhaps try the saloon bar, don't you think?'

Lillian had managed to disentangle herself and she staggered out into the night air. The street lamps seemed to spin above her and as she tried to focus her one good eye she fell against the wall of the pub. When she had composed herself a little she walked unsteadily away in the direction of Bermondsey. She had only gone a short distance when the sound of heavy footsteps grew louder behind her. 'You wait, ja?' a booming voice called out.

Lillian turned and saw the dishevelled Swede hurrying towards her. His shirt was torn and he had a thin line of dried blood on the side of his face. The large man beamed at her.

'You come have drink on my ship. Ja?'

She smiled at him and took his arm. 'C'mon, Sven,' she said. 'Let's go an' tiggle yer toes. Ja?'

Chapter Twenty-Three

During the early part of 1939 posters were pasted up everywhere, informing people of their nearest gas-mask fitting station. When the Civil Defence men arrived in the Tower Bridge Road market with the posters Solly Jacobs put down the sharp knife which he used for gutting the fish, wiped his bloodied hands down his apron and called out to Bernie Cornbloom.

'Watch the stall fer ten minutes, Bernie. I fancy a pint.'

Solly spotted Joe Cooper, who was sitting alone in the Jolly Compasses moodily contemplating his near-empty glass of ale. 'You seen them posters what they're puttin' up, Joe?' he asked.

Joe nodded. 'I've bin sittin' 'ere finkin' fer the last 'alf hour. It's all gonna blow up soon, I'm sure it is. The Krauts 'ave nicked Czechoslovakia, they've warned us that Poland's next, an' we've promised we'll 'elp the Poles. What else d'yer expect, Solly?'

The fishmonger walked over to the counter and returned with two pints of ale. 'I've bin finkin', Joe. I'm gonna put me name down fer the ARP.'

Joe grinned. 'What kept yer? I 'ad me name down last week fer the street warden's job. They've told me I've gotta be in charge o' the shelter.'

265

'What shelter?' Solly asked, scratching the side of his face.

'Why, the one they're buildin' in the basement o' the Armitage factory. They started last week. Yer wanna see what they're doin'. They've stuck great big concrete supports under the roof an' sandbagged the entrance up, an' they've put a gas blanket over the door. Next week they're gonna bung a toilet in, an' a water tap. The people are likely ter move down there lock, stock an' barrel, what wiv the state o' the 'ouses in Ironmonger Street.'

In July Connie Morgan took her very first holiday away from London. She left Paddington with Robert on the Cornish Riviera Express and travelled to Penzance. From there they took a taxi to Lamorna Cove, a tiny fishing hamlet a few miles from Land's End, and booked into a small hotel high up on the rocky hill overlooking the bay. From the bedroom window shadowed by large trees they could see the green hills which sloped down to the small sandy shore and the cold, sparkling Atlantic. The lovers had registered as Mr and Mrs Wilson and, to prevent speculation, Connie wore a thin gold band on the ring finger of her left hand. The owners of the hotel were curious nevertheless. Mrs Lampton was convinced that the couple were honeymooners.

'They're very much in love, Claude,' she whispered to her husband. 'They hardly take their eyes off each other, and she's just a child.'

'You're a soppy thing, Eveline. Don't you go indulging them now. They may be lovers wanting to escape from something or other, so leave them alone. I know how inquisitive you can be.'

The weather stayed fine for the week, with cloudless skies and a hot sun that caused the sea to shimmer. They ran hand in hand along the sand and bathed in the sheltered cove. They took long walks up into the hills and lay together in the cool green grass. When the sun slipped down in the western sky and long shadows crept along the cove they strolled leisurely along the harbour wall and listened to the wash of the incoming tide. The lovers dallied there until the heavens turned velvet black and star patterns lit the night. They looked up at the crescent moon and their minds were serene, away from the fearful feverishness of preparation for war. They did not speak of the parting they both knew would now be inevitable, and they savoured and lived for the moment.

When the sun rose again and peeked through the curtains of their bedroom they would get up quickly and wander back to the harbour wall and stand at a discreet distance from the local artists. They watched their brushstrokes as they slowly captured the rolling, shimmering sea, the rising grey cliffs and the many shades of green which reached up to the deep-blue sky. They ate their lunch of freshly caught crab with salad in a small café that was cut into the rocks, or they strolled down to the Smugglers Inn and took their lunch there in the company of leather-faced fishermen who sat around in small groups, discussing the weather and smoking stained clay pipes.

At seven o'clock each evening they dined at the hotel, sitting in a window seat and glancing at each other over a vase of wild flowers. Connie sometimes looked down at the gold band around her finger and wished secretly. Robert, as though reading her thoughts, would reach out and take her hand. The evening meals were served by Eveline who missed nothing, and she would remove her matronly figure to the kitchen and speak of young love to her perspiring husband as he stood over the hot ovens and tended the steaming pots.

Later, as the moon climbed high in the sky and the night owls hooted, the lovers lay in each other's arms. Connie was aware of the token band around her finger as he took her to him and loved her. She felt pleasure and deep satisfaction, and with it the knowledge that whatever happened in the future, however tortuous and twisted their fate would be, she would always remember the glorious week they had spent together in that romantic Cornish cove.

In August in the markets and pubs and workplaces the only real topic of conversation was the coming war.

The Dolphin in Salter Street was busy one Tuesday evening. It was darts night and the visiting team from the Horse and Groom had brought quite a few supporters. Connie and Jennie were serving drinks in the public bar and during the matches the two were kept very busy. Bill French the landlord usually took Tuesday nights off and his wife Dora served alone in the saloon bar. As the evening wore on and the two teams became more excited the barmaids found little time to talk to the customers. It had grown very noisy, with cheers ringing out every time a winning dart was thrown. Regular customers got irritated as the visiting team and their supporters elbowed their way to the counter and impatiently shouted for service. Jennie was used to the hustle and bustle but Connie found it very nerve-wracking and she was glad when Dora looked in on her and suggested she should do a spell in the saloon bar where it was much quieter.

It was nearing closing time when Connie resumed serving in the public bar. The visiting team had lost the match and most of them had left to get a last drink back at the Horse and Groom. A few remained, and one of them, an elderly man with grey hair and a thick moustache was leaning on the counter, sipping his pint of ale. Connie had become aware of his interest in her. He seemed to be watching her closely and, when she went to serve a customer next to him, he smiled at her. Connie became uneasy. He was studying her every action, and when he finished his drink and beckoned to her she felt her face flush. As she took the empty glass and pulled on the beer pump she could feel his eyes on her.

'I bin watchin' yer, luv,' he said as Connie put down the filled glass and picked up the half crown. 'Yer ain't Kate Morgan's kid, are yer?'

'Yes, I am,' she replied with surprise, looking into the man's faded blue eyes.

'I knew it!' he exclaimed, slapping the top of the counter with a bony hand. 'I bin clockin' yer fer a while now. Yer the spittin' image of yer muvver. 'Ow is she? I ain't seen 'er fer ages.'

'Me mum died two years ago,' Connie said quietly.

The old man's face showed shock and he sucked his lips. 'I'm ever so sorry, luv. I didn't know.'

'It's okay,' Connie said, passing over his change. 'Was you a friend of 'ers?'

'I worked wiv yer mum at Armitage's years ago,' he said, looking down at his pint.

'It must 'ave bin a long time ago. Me mum left there in 1923.'

'I know,' the man replied, taking a swig from his glass. ''Ow time flies. We used ter 'ave some good ole laughs at that factory.'

'Did yer go on the firm's outin'?' Connie asked.

'Yeah. What a day that was!'

Connie leaned her elbows on the counter. 'I remember me mum tellin' me there was some sort o' trouble on that outin'.'

The old man stroked his stubbly chin. 'I did 'ear of a bit o' bovver, but ter tell yer the trufe I was too pissed ter remember much after dinnertime.'

Dora called for last orders and Connie found herself busy once again. When time was called and Dora rang the bell,

Connie managed to pick up her conversation with the grey-haired old man as he finished his drink.

'Did yer know that woman who was me mum's best friend?' she asked. 'They was always tergevver.'

'Yer talkin' about Norma Cantwell? Yeah, that was 'er name. 'Er an yer muvver was like two peas in a pod. I fink they left the firm tergevver as well.'

Connie looked hard at the man. 'Yer don't know what 'appened to 'er I s'pose? I fink it's only right she should know about me mum dyin'.'

The old man stroked his chin again. 'Well as fer as I know, she used ter live in Birdcage Lane orf the Old Kent Road. Mind you, they've pulled a lot o' that turnin' down now.'

'Fanks fer the info,' Connie said, smiling at him. 'If yer do get any news of 'er whereabouts, give us a look in, will yer?'

'Sure fing, luv,' he replied, buttoning up his overcoat.

Connie watched him leave as she began to collect the empty glasses. It was a chance meeting, she thought, but somehow she must have been meant to bump into him. Now she had a lead to follow, however. She wondered whether it was time she confided in her Aunt Helen. She would be angry at being kept in the dark for so long, but the story Claudette had told her last Christmas had been something she could not bear to talk about, not even to her aunt. She hoped desperately that somehow she would be able to find this Norma Cantwell first, for she might be able to tell her what had really happened.

Towards the end of August army reserves were being called up and an alliance pact was signed with Poland. On the first of September Warsaw was bombed as German troops marched into Poland. In the Bermondsey backstreets people took the news with calmness, even relief that the uncertainty was now over. They knew it meant war. At the Armitage factory the word went round that as they were engaged on war work the factory would be evacuated to the country.

'I can't go ter the bleedin' country,' Lizzie Conroy moaned. 'Who's gonna get me ole man's food?'

''E'll find somebody ter feed 'im an' wash 'is dirty socks, I'm sure,' Mary Brown quipped.

Joyce Spinks shed a few tears as she confided in Mary. 'We ain't gonna be 'vacuated, are we? I'd be worried about Arfur. 'E can't do a fing fer 'imself.'

'Don't worry, Joyce. They can't 'vacuate the factory, an' we won't be able ter go neivver. We'll be stuck 'ere same as usual wiv all this bloody war work ter do, you mark my words.'

Lizzie spotted Joe Cooper coming down between the machines. 'Oi, Joe. What's the latest?' she called out.

'I dunno, Liz, 'cept that they're evacuatin' children, accordin' ter the wireless.'

'Oh my Gawd!' Lizzie gasped, putting a hand up to her mouth.

As Friday wore on slowly the rumours were spreading fast and furiously. The sound of the pounding machines played on the workers' frayed nerves and finally one of the machinists found it all too much. She suddenly let out a piercing scream and dashed along the gangway, her hands help up to her ashen face. Joe Cooper made a grab at her but she dodged past him and ran screaming from the factory and out along the little turning. George Baker was standing at his front door, leaning heavily on his walking-stick and he saw her dash past. The tallyman who had just reached George's door watched her run off down the street and he looked back enquiringly at the old man.

'It's the factory,' George said, with mock seriousness. 'It sends 'em all that way in time.'

'Good God!'

271

'Yeah, it's true,' George went on. 'They've bin known ter crack up wiv the noise an' put their 'eads under the presses before now. They come out lookin' like flat red lollipops. It don't 'alf make a mess!'

The tallyman was beginning to feel queasy and with a shiver he turned and left the turning in rather a hurry.

George smiled to himself. The collector had forgotten to ask for the weekly payment.

Later, when Mary came in from work on that Friday evening, the family had an urgent discussion.

'What about yer two kids, Mary? Yer gonna send 'em out o' London?' her father enquired.

'What yer reckon, Frank?' Mary asked, looking anxiously at her husband.

'I dunno, girl. I don't like the idea of sendin' 'em away. Yer know what young Jimmy's like. 'E's only six. It's a dead cert 'e'll pine. June's that bit older but she's gonna fret too, it's only natural.'

They both looked at George, who raised his gnarled hands helplessly. 'Don't ask me. It's your decision. If it was me though, I'd keep 'em roun' me. What's ter be will be.'

'I fink we'll wait,' Mary said finally. 'We'll see 'ow fings turn out. Okay, Frank?'

George settled down in his chair and filled his pipe. He could hear the children's laughter coming from upstairs and he grinned to himself. It would be miserable without the kids about the place, he thought.

''Ere, Dad,' Mary said with her hands on her hips. 'What's this money doin' on the mantelshelf? Ain't the tallyman bin?'

'Yeah. We was 'avin' a chat an' 'e must 'ave fergot all about the money.'

Mary shook her head slowly. 'All this talk of war seems to 'ave turned everybody upside down. We 'ad one o' the girls

272

go berserk terday. She run out o' the factory screamin' 'er 'ead off. Joe Cooper said she run up the street like the devil was after 'er.'

George Baker puffed on his pipe. 'Did she?' he asked innocently.

There had been little work done that day in the leather factory. Everyone was preoccupied, including the management. Some of the girls discussed the possibility of going along to the recruiting office to join one of the women's services. Connie could think only of her coming weekend with Robert. Unless he had changed his mind, he would be volunteering for the airforce, she thought. This would be the last weekend together for some time, and she wanted it to be very special.

When she got home that evening Connie went straight to the Bartletts' home and found her aunt alone.

Helen had a worried look on her pale face. 'Ain't it terrible? I've jus' bin listenin' ter the wireless. There's fousands o' kids gettin' 'vacuated, Con. It's made me feel ill jus' 'earin' it all.'

Connie slumped down in the armchair. 'It was the same at work terday. It's all everybody talked about.'

Helen walked out to the kitchen. 'I'll get yer a cuppa. I've got one made. Molly an' Matt'll be in soon.'

The dark day had worked strangely on Connie and she had decided to unburden herself while she was alone with Helen. She had kept the story Claudette had told her to herself for almost nine months now and she needed to confide in her aunt, now that her recent attempt to find Norma Cantwell had come to nothing.

The two women sat facing each other in the armchairs, their cups of tea held in their laps. Helen listened intently while Connie related what Claudette had told her and when the girl had finished she shook her head slowly.

'I wish you'd 'ave told me sooner, Con. You shouldn't leave us out in the cold. We're family. We're the only family yer've got, girl. Don't shut us out. Yer mum used ter do that an' it stopped us bein' really close.'

Connie looked into her aunt's tired eyes. 'I know I should 'ave told yer long ago, Aunt 'Elen, but I was 'opin' ter get ter the bottom of fings before I worried yer all. Yer've got enough on yer plate. Trouble is, when I went round ter find this Norma an' saw the street 'ad bin pulled down I knew I was at a dead end. I wanted ter prove that Robert's muvver was lyin'.'

'Listen, Connie. Yer don't 'ave ter convince me,' Helen said sharply, anger showing in her eyes. 'Kate was me sister. She would never do what that woman said she done. All right, we know the firm was payin' 'er fer some reason, an' it might 'ave bin ter keep 'er quiet, but whatever 'appened it must 'ave bin somefink bad. Yer mum wouldn't 'ave invented it.'

'What do we do next, Aunt? 'Ow do we find this Norma Cantwell?'

'Yer gotta be patient, girl. All right, nobody knows where she's gorn to, but we've got a photo of 'er. Then there's that old man yer said yer talked to. 'E might come back wiv some news.'

'That's pretty unlikely, Aunt.'

'Yer never know, Con. It was only fate 'e saw yer in the pub. If yer meant ter get ter the bottom of it all it'll 'appen, you'll see.'

'I 'ope you're right, Aunt. I always hoped the money me mum got was really from me dad. Now I know it wasn't. I don't s'pose I'll ever find out about 'im, but I'm determined ter get ter the truth, about the money at least.'

Helen pursed her lips. She felt a great sadness at having to bear the burden her sister had placed upon her. She wanted to shout out the man's name and put Connie's mind at rest. It was so unfair, but it was Kate's wish. Even when she had been very ill and knew that she would not recover, Kate had still insisted that the secret should be kept.

Footsteps on the landing interrupted her thoughts and she got up from her chair as Molly and Matthew walked in together.

'News is bad, luv,' Matt said as he took off his coat and hung it behind the door.

Molly sat down heavily in the armchair, her breathing coming quickly. She smiled wanly at Connie and when she had recovered she kicked off her shoes and sighed deeply.

'Is there really gonna be a war, Dad?' Molly asked.

'Seems it's certain now, luv. It's no good pretendin'.'

'Will yer 'ave ter join up, Dad?'

'No. I'm too old. I might 'ave ter do war work though. Our firm's talkin' about gettin' exemptions fer us, 'cause o' the gover'ment contract we're on. I jus' gotta wait an' see.'

Molly glanced at her cousin and then looked back at her father. 'The girls at work were talkin' about London gettin' bombed. Couldn't we all go away somewhere safe, Dad?'

Matthew ran his fingers through his greying hair. 'I wish we could,' he said quietly. 'Trouble is, there'll be nowhere ter go. We might escape the bombin', but we can't leave the country. In any case, people like us ain't got nowhere ter go. All we can do is grin an' bear it, like always.'

Helen came into the room with the teapot. 'Now wash yer 'ands, Molly. You, too, Matt. War or no war, yer gotta eat. What about you, Con? Wanna stop fer tea? It's saveloys an' pease pudden.'

Chapter Twenty-Four

It had been a special weekend. On Saturday evening Connie cooked a meal and Robert opened a bottle of red wine. They sat together in the quietness of the flat and talked casually and light-heartedly, avoiding the thing that worried them most. They lay in each other's arms and, as Robert stroked her long blond hair and she felt his hands gently caressing her body, she tried to stifle the ache that welled up from deep within her. Soon he would be gone, she knew. The thought of being without him was hard to bear. He was her whole life, and without his strong arms around her and his gentle words of love, life would not be worth living. Somehow she had to bear it, however painful. She must wait for him to return to her. She had to be strong, like her mother must have been. He must carry her love with him so that wherever he went, whatever dangers he faced, the knowledge would sustain him and bring him back safely.

Robert slept soundly, his even, shallow breathing hardly moving his chest. Connie twisted and turned, her sleep spoiled with mixed-up dreams. They awoke late and had hardly finished breakfast when the news came over the wireless that the Prime Minister would be speaking to the nation. They listened in silence as the flat, cultured voice spoke of how he had striven to preserve peace and that now, despite all his efforts, the country was at war with Germany. His voice dragged on painfully and, when Robert finally got up and turned off the wireless, Connie saw the set expression on his face and the sadness reflected in his ice-blue eyes. She knew that all the speculation was over. She felt calm, even relieved that the challenge was there for her to take up. She had to be brave now. There must be no tears, no regrets. He would surely leave her, but it would not be for ever. Their times together in the days ahead would be short and treasured. One day they would meet again and never be parted.

The unearthly wail of the air-raid siren broke the silence, and they looked down into the Sunday street below. People were running along the thoroughfare, their eyes searching the skies. Mothers clutched their babies and held on desperately to their youngsters as they ran for the shelter in the square opposite.

Connie gripped Robert's arm. 'What shall we do?' she asked him, her voice trembling.

He put his arm around her waist. 'Don't be frightened, Con. They're probably just trying out the sirens. We might as well stay here, at least for the time being.'

They sat together at the window as the sound of the siren died to a moan. There was a deathly silence outside. The street was now empty, save for a lone mongrel who cocked his leg against a tree then trotted off unconcernedly. A police car suddenly dashed past, and then it was silent again.

As soon as the Prime Minister's speech ended, Ironmonger Street came to life. Front doors opened and people spilled out on to the pavements. Windows in the buildings were thrown open and eyes looked down at the commotion below. Outside number one the Toomeys stood together, Toby with a distant expression on his narrow face, Marie sobbing and being comforted by her daughter Lillian. The Bakers and the Richards stood talking in a huddle while Widow Pacey stood alone in her doorway, her arms folded and a defiant look on her face. When the siren sounded the street folk looked fearfully towards the clear blue sky and then hurried through the factory gates and down the steps into the stale-smelling basement shelter. People ran from the buildings. Alf Riley held his shaking wife by the arm and they were followed by the Smiths, the Carringtons and the Argents. The wail died and the little cul-de-sac became empty and quiet.

The basement shelter in the Armitage factory had become full of shaking, fearful folk who sat around on the hard wooden benches and talked in low voices. Lizzie Conroy took out her knitting and found she was dropping more stitches than she picked up. George Baker had left his false teeth in the cup and he sat making funny faces, to the delight of his two young grandchildren. Mother Adams sat fretting over her cats, and Doris Richards held her arms around her daughter Bella. Joe Cooper stood in the doorway, wearing his steel helmet which had the words ARP stencilled on it and carrying his service gas-mask pack over his shoulder. With him stood Mary's husband Frank who was looking around at the assembled street folk.

''Ere, Joe. Ole Clara Cosgrove ain't 'ere,' Frank said suddenly.

'Bloody 'ell!' Joe exclaimed. 'I bet she didn't 'ear the siren. C'mon, Frank, we'd better see if she's all right.'

The two men hurried to number, twenty and knocked loudly on the door. Joe bent down and put his mouth to the letter box. 'You all right, Clara?' he called out.

'She's fell asleep, it's a dead cert,' Frank said, looking up at the sky anxiously.

Joe fished his hand into the letter box and pulled out a

string with a key tied to the end of it. 'C'mon, Frank, let's go get 'er.'

The two men entered the house and walked into the front parlour. Clara Cosgrove was seated in her favourite armchair, her hands folded in her lap and her mouth hanging open.

Joe shook the old lady gently and she awoke with a start. 'Gawd! Yer frightened the bleedin' life out o' me. What's wrong?'

'C'mon, Clara. We're tryin' the shelter out,' Joe said, taking hold of her arm.

'Leave me alone, sod yer!' she growled. 'There's me 'avin' a nice nap an' you two come in 'ere playin' silly buggers. Now piss orf out.'

'The warnin' went, Clara. We come ter take yer ter the shelter.'

'D'yer mean the war's started?'

'That's right, Ma,' Frank said softly.

Clara reached beneath her pinafore and took out a small lace handkerchief with which she dabbed at her eyes. 'So it's all orf again, is it? They'll never learn, will they? I'm sure it was gettin' gassed in the last war caused my Fred ter peg out the way 'e did. Well I tell yer somefink. I don't care what 'appens. They're not gettin' me down that bloody shelter. I'd sooner stay 'ere in me own 'ome, 'cos the way I see it, when yer number's up there ain't much yer can do about it. Now you two go on back ter the rest of 'em. Tell 'em Clara Cosgrove is 'avin' a little nap 'an don't wanna be disturbed. 'Ere, an' tell 'em all not ter make too much noise as they come past me winder, okay?'

'Okay, Ma,' Joe said, looking at Frank and jerking his head towards the door.

* * *

The long, even tone of the all clear brought people out on to the street once more. The sun shone down from an almost cloudless sky as people stood about at their front doors and children came out to play. Later Tony Armeda pushed his ice-cream barrow into the turning and became busy, scooping dabs of yellow cream on to large wafer cones. Children gripped their pennies and jostled for position at the front of the queue.

'I'm first! I'm first!'

'No you ain't. I was 'ere first.'

'Donna push! Yer knocka da barrer over. Waita yer turn, you all geta served.'

'Gissa tupp'ny one, Tony.'

'Me, too, Tony.'

The big Italian reached down yet again into his metal drum and came up with another scoop of ice-cream. The kids jostled each other as more gathered around the gaily painted barrow, pennies clutched tightly in their sweaty palms. Cooking smells drifted out from open front doors and men started off up the turning dressed in their Sunday best, caps askew and white silk scarves knotted around their necks. Public houses filled and urgent discussions were quickly begun.

'It won't last long. I give it six months. It's a big game o' bluff,' Terry said, hooking his thumbs through his braces.

'I don't fink so, Tel. I reckon it's gonna be a nasty turnout. You've only gotta look at what 'appened in Spain. Look at the bombin' what went on out there.'

'Yeah, but them there Republicans didn't 'ave any planes, Bill. They couldn't fight back. If the Germans bomb us we're gonna retaliate, stan's ter reason.'

'I 'ope you're right, Tel. 'Ere, gonna get anuvver drink in, I feel like gettin' pissed.'

* * *

Evening shadows lengthened in the thoroughfare below as Connie sat with Robert in the quiet flat. The wireless was switched on and soft orchestral music drifted through the room. There had been urgent broadcasts all day warning people to read the notices that were going up in public places. People had been urged to register their children for evacuation and advice was given on how to cope in the event of a gas attack. Prayers were broadcast and then sombre music had played once more. Connie rested her head on his shoulder. 'When will yer go?' she asked.

'I'll go along to the recruiting office first thing tomorrow, Con. There's no point in waiting.'

'Will yer 'ave ter go straight away?'

'No, they'll send for me. I'll get a medical first.'

'What will yer parents say, Robert? They'll be upset, won't they?'

He nodded his head slowly. 'I think they expect me to volunteer. Dad used to point out the value of managing production in a factory which was on a government contract, but he knows I couldn't sit out the war in the factory. I'd go mad, Con.'

'You are mad,' she smiled sadly. 'Yer could stay 'ere wiv me. Yer don't 'ave ter go away an' fight.'

He did not answer as he stood up and walked over to the window. He looked down into the deserted street. It was the first night that the blackout was in force and it was complete. No lights shone out and passers-by lit their way with shaded torches. The distant rumble of thunder and a brief flash of lightning seemed like an omen to him as he stood gazing into the darkness.

Connie walked over to him and put her arms around his tense body. 'Come away from the winder, Robert. Close the curtains an' put the light on. I don't like the dark.'

He bent his head and found her lips. She pressed herself to him, aware that time was short. There was so much she wanted to say and so little time. She clung to him and felt his hands gently stroking her back.

'I love you, Connie,' he whispered. 'Will you wait for me?'

She nodded, unable to speak as tears filled her eyes and a lump rose in her throat. He stepped back and took her hand as he led her away from the window.

'I want to say something, Con,' he said, pulling her down beside him on the sofa. 'You must know I love you. I want to spend the rest of my life with you. No, don't say anything. I've wanted to ask you if you'll marry me, but I couldn't bring myself to say the words. I've been convinced for some time now there'd be a war and it wouldn't be fair to you. I could get killed and you'd be a widow before you'd got used to being a wife. But now that it's happened . . .'

'Yer shouldn't fink like that,' she said, her voice trembling. 'I've got a stake in us, too. We could get engaged. Ask me, Robert. Just ask me,' she urged him.

He took her to him and looked into her blue eyes. 'Will you marry me, Con?'

'Yes! Yes!' she gasped, pulling his head down on to her open lips.

The country was in its first week of war and in the shops and at the markets trade was brisk as people bought up blackout material and rolls of gum-backed paper to protect their windows against blast. Cinemas and dance halls closed, along with sports stadiums and public meeting places. Vehicles drove at night with their headlights shielded and the streets became dangerous places for everyone in the blackness. Police and street wardens began to patrol the back turnings, and the call to 'Put that light out' became a very familiar cry. Whole schools were evacuated with their teachers, and many thousands of parents said goodbye to their offspring as trains and coaches took the youngsters to the supposed safety of the countryside. For children who stayed in the capital there were few schools that remained open, and they ran wild in the streets to the chagrin of the local bobbies. News bulletins came with monotonous regularity and the government announced that all young men between the ages of eighteen and forty-one would be liable for call-up.

Robert Armitage had volunteered for the RAF and, after a medical, he was called up almost immediately. Connie attempted to fill the void in her life by spending most of her spare time with the Bartletts. On Tuesday and Thursday evenings she worked at the pub, and when she was asked if she would like to work on Saturday evenings Connie jumped at the chance. The atmosphere at the Dolphin was pleasant enough and she found the work helped her to get over her parting from Robert. He wrote to her regularly and in his letters he spoke of going off to flying school very soon. In the pub young faces were missing as the first batch of eligible men in their twenties received their call-up papers. Pub parties became a nightly occurrence as fresh-faced lads and their anxious parents drank together on the eve of conscription. The lads were invariably treated to a free drink and a fond kiss on the cheek by Dora French, who remarked to her husband, 'They're only kids, Bill. Most of 'em ain't started shavin' yet.'

'They'll grow up soon enough, Dora,' he replied. 'There'll be a few gaps along the counter before this war's over, mark my words.'

The first days of war passed without the expected air attacks, and people began to get used to the defence preparations that had appeared everywhere. Sandbags and posters, first-aid posts and street shelters were in evidence all across London, and travellers carried their gas masks with them on trains and on the buses and trams. Foodstuffs were becoming scarce and the government issued ration books prior to announcing a food-rationing system. The street blackout became a problem as the days grew shorter. People struggled home from work through dark streets and accidents became commonplace.

For the Ironmonger Street folk the blackout did not pose too many problems as most of them worked locally, but for Toby Toomey it became a source of some considerable embarrassment. He had set out on a cold Monday morning in September determined to have a good day. The pram was holding up well although the wheels had started squeaking again, and as he left the turning Toby decided to try Rotherhithe. He had often pushed his battered old pram through the backstreets around the Surrey Docks and the people there knew him. It was quite a walk, but trade had dried up locally and he thought it would be worth the effort. By midday his conveyance was filled with bits of scrap iron and bundles of old newspapers. Mrs O'Shaughnessy had offered him an old tin bath and Mrs Carter wanted him to take her bug-ridden mattress away, but Toby had to remind the two women that it was a pram he had and not a horse and cart.

The sun had come out during the morning and the wind had dropped. Toby decided to eat his sandwiches down by the water. There was a riverside pub he knew where the landlord wasn't too fussy who he served, providing they could pay, and he would be able to stow his pram within sight. Once he had not taken such a precaution and the local kids had stolen the wheels off his pram for their box-carts. Toby parked his contraption in the alley at the back of the pub and walked in the back door. He ordered a pint of ale and sat out on the veranda where he ate his sandwiches of boiled bacon, keeping one eye on the day's collection of old rubbish. The sun felt warm on his face and the smell of the river mud drifted up as the tide began to ebb. He could see the Norwegian timber ship moored in mid-stream and the busy dockside cranes dipping and swinging as pine and spruce sets were lifted from the holds of the Scandinavian ships berthed in the Surrey. The beer tasted good and Toby sifted through his pockets. There was just enough for another pint and, glancing at the laden pram beneath the veranda, he felt he had earned it.

The usual clientele had left the pub and the landlord closed and bolted the front doors before settling down to a drink with a few docker friends. The veranda had been cleared of glasses and no one had noticed the frail figure in the scruffy overcoat who was snoring quietly in the corner. The parked pram had been spotted however, and a discussion was taking place.

'What's this fing doin' 'ere then, Alan?'

'I dunno,' said the smaller lad, biting on a large cooking apple. 'Somebody who's in the boozer, I s'pose.'

'Don't be silly,' his friend said, kicking the wheels. 'The pub's shut. It's afternoon.'

'P'raps somebody's left it 'ere, Tom. It's all ole junk,' the third lad said, kicking the brake off.

The two lads looked at Tom, waiting for their leader to make a decision. 'Gissa bite of your apple, Alan, then we'll ditch this ole junk.'

The sun had gone off the river and an easterly wind blew along the estuary. Toby woke up with a start and shivered. For a few moments he looked around, wondering where he was. When he had pulled himself together and walked unsteadily into the public bar four pairs of eyes stared at him.

'Where the bloody 'ell did you come from?' the landlord said, his hands on his hips.

'I'm sorry, mate. I was sittin' out on the veranda an' I must 'ave fell asleep,' Toby said yawning.

'This pub's bin closed fer over three hours. Yer must 'ave bin in a coma.'

'Sorry, mate. I done a lot o' collectin' this mornin' an' I come over tired.'

'What d'yer collect then?' one of the dockers asked, smiling at his pals.

'Scrap iron an' fings. I got a pram outside,' Toby replied, scratching his thinning hair.

The landlord stroked his chin. 'D'yer take carpets?'

Toby wondered how he was going to manage another item on his already overloaded pram, but he thought it better not to antagonise the beefy pub owner. 'Yeah, I'll take it out o' yer way, mate,' he said cheerfully.

'C'mon then. It's in the passage. I'll let yer out that way.'

Toby followed the landlord and saw to his dismay that the rolled-up carpet was over eight feet long. He went red in the face as he lifted it, and with the help of the publican he managed to hoist it on to his shoulders. This bloody thing must weigh a ton, he groaned to himself as he staggered around the alley to where he had left his pram.

'Oh Gawd!' Toby gasped. 'The bastards 'ave nicked it.'

He dropped the carpet roll on to the cobbles and looked around. There was no sign of his pram. He walked over to the riverside wall and winced as he looked down at the muddy shore. The battered old pram was lying upside down at the bottom of the flight of stone steps which led down from the walkway. The larger bits of scrap iron were sticking out of the oozing mud but the smaller pieces had sunk below the surface. Toby hurried along to the steps and clambered down to where his contraption was lying. It took all his strength to pull it out of the sticky, clinging mud and drag it up on to the walkway. Toby went back down to the shore and tried to recover bits of iron, but he had little success. The scrap was stuck fast. His boots were covered in mud and his socks had become sodden.

'Bloody 'ell,' he groaned aloud. 'Marie'll kill me.'

People turned and stared at the spectacle as Toby Toomey pushed his mud-covered pram along in the kerb with the carpet roll placed lengthways on top. His overcoat and boots were caked in mud and two of the wheels were buckled. It was getting dark and there was still a long way to go. By the time Toby had reached Dockhead it was pitch black. As he rounded a curve in the road he felt a bump and heard a stream of cuss-words.

The uniformed figure at his feet stared up at Toby with a murderous look in his eye. 'Yer knocked me orf me bike, yer scatty git. I'm gonna nick yer fer pushin' a pram wivvout due care an' attention,' the constable growled as he retrieved his helmet and reached for his notebook.

'I'm very sorry, mate. I . . .'

'Don't you "mate" me, yer bloody idiot. Now what yer got ter say fer yerself?'

'Well, I 'ad a couple o' pints an' I fell asleep yer see, an' . . .'

'Right,' the constable barked, licking his pencil stub. 'Drunk in charge of a pram on a public 'ighway, fer starters.'

A sorry, tired and totally dejected figure walked into Ironmonger Street to face the wrath of his beloved wife.

'We'll all end up in the bleedin' work'ouse before long!' Marie screamed at him. 'Yer bin out all bloody day long an' all yer've collected is a pissy, moth-eared carpet that stinks o' dog shit an' two buckled wheels. Look at the state o' yer. Where did yer find the carpet, in the poxy river?'

Chapter Twenty-Five

1940 began with the worst winter for over forty years. Parts of the River Thames froze over and trains became stranded. Road transport was thrown into chaos as horses and vehicles slipped and slithered over the iced-up cobbles and tarmac. Car-men wrapped their nags' hooves in sacking and road vehicles were fitted with wheel chains in a battle against the elements. Coupled with the perilous blackout regulations the bad weather caused many accidents and resulted in delays and shortages of supplies to shops and factories. The misery was compounded by the introduction of food rationing. Bacon, butter and sugar were now in short supply and people had to register with particular shops. During the first Christmas of the war, shortages had begun to be felt and now the situation was beginning to get worse.

Christmas had been a time of reunion for Connie and Robert. They had spent just four days together before he left for pilot training, and during that time they had visited a jeweller's shop at the Elephant and Castle where Connie chose a ring. It had a single white diamond mounted on a platinum shoulder, and when they walked out of the shop and she felt the weight of it on her finger Connie wanted to shout aloud to everyone that she was now engaged. It was during their short time together that Connie had insisted they each get a photo done for the other to keep. They picked a photographic studio in the Tower Bridge Road and it was on the way there during Christmas Eve that she spotted Michael Donovan. He was in uniform and accompanied by a young woman who was holding on to his arm. Connie felt her face flush as they drew near.

He smiled at her with his easy grin. ''Ello, Connie. 'Ow yer keepin'?'

'I'm fine, Michael. Er . . . this is Robert.'

The men shook hands and Michael turned to Connie. 'This is my wife, Beckie.'

The dark-haired young woman held out her hand. 'So you're Connie. Michael told me about yer. I'm pleased ter meet yer.'

Connie took the girl's hand, her face showing surprise. There was an embarrassing silence, and Robert asked, 'When are you due back, Michael?'

'Day after Boxin' Day. 'Ow about you?'

'Same day,' Robert grinned. 'What are you on?'

'Destroyers. Are you aircrew?'

'Not yet. I'm pilot training.'

'So yer gonna be a flyer then?' Michael grinned. 'I prefer the water meself.'

The women looked at each other and Beckie's eyes raised in feigned impatience. ''Ere we go,' she said, smiling.

Michael pulled the collar of his topcoat up around his ears. 'Sorry, we've gotta dash. We're off ter get Beckie's Christmas present.'

''E's buyin' me a coat,' the girl said, looking adoringly at her husband.

Michael grinned sheepishly. 'Oh well, duty calls. All the best, an' a merry Christmas.'

Robert glanced at Connie and saw the distant look in her

eyes as she watched Michael and his wife walking away. 'Come on, Con,' he said quietly. 'Let's get those photos taken.'

The bitter winter persisted throughout February and, when the weather finally broke at the beginning of March, a new tribulation was foisted upon the Toomey family. An envelope was pushed through their letter box and when Marie read the contents she screamed out for Toby, 'Get yerself down 'ere. We got troubles.'

'Whassa matter, luv?'

'Read this,' Marie growled, holding out the sheet of paper.

'You read it, Marie. Yer know I can't see wivvout me glasses.'

'Well it's about time yer got yerself anuvver pair. They've got plenty o'cheap glasses at the market.'

Toby sat himself down in the tattered armchair and looked up at his irate wife. 'What's it say, luv?'

'We've gotta give the shop up,' she said, her arms akimbo.

'Do what!' he gasped.

'This letter's from Uncle Bert. 'E ses the shop's bein' took over by the ARP fer a warden's post. It's ter do wiv the defence regulations.'

'Christ! They can't do that, Marie.'

'Well they've bleedin' well gorn an' done it. You'll 'ave ter get yer stuff out o' there by next week, it ses 'ere.'

Toby scratched the top of his head and stared dejectedly into the fireplace. It was bad enough having to scrounge a living by totting, without having nowhere to store all his scrap and old newspapers. At least the shop had been a decent place to dump it. The rent wasn't much either. Uncle Bert had been generous, but then it had rather suited his purpose. Certain items which had fallen off the back of lorries and horsecarts were often secreted beneath sacks of rags and bundles of old newspapers. Marie's uncle is a carney character, Toby admitted to himself. No notice was ever taken when the lorry called to remove the scrap, and certain other items, too. Yes, Uncle Bert was carney, although his keeping on about not letting anyone know Toby was renting the shop was a bloody nuisance. It made it difficult, having to cart all the scrap iron and bundles of rags and papers into the shop through the backyard. Uncle Bert had emphasised the need for secrecy to Marie, and he had made himself crystal clear.

'Look 'ere, luv,' he said, 'if yer neighbours know yer ole man's rentin' that shop they're gonna get curious. They're not stupid. They know that what 'e does don't run ter payin' rent on a shop. Somebody's only gotta open their trap ter the wrong person, like the local bobbie, an' I'm gonna be in trouble.'

Marie had been staring at Toby as he sat slumped in the battered armchair. 'Well, what yer gonna do about it? I ain't 'avin' that rubbish o' yours stuck in me yard. Yer better sort somefink out 'cos I don't want our Lil upset. If she brings a fella 'ome an' 'e sees bits of old iron stuck in the passage 'e's gonna fink the Toomeys are a load o' scruffs.'

Toby scratched his head thoughtfully. He felt he was getting too old to push that creaky old pram around the back-streets. Maybe he should give up being a totter. It would be nice to get a steady job and put his tired feet up in the evenings, instead of having to sort through the day's collections and bag up all those stinking rags. Perhaps there was work going at the factory. Maybe they needed a nightwatchman? It can't be very hard being a nightwatchman, he thought. After all, it's only watching the place. Be a chance to get away from Marie and her acid tongue, he mused, his face breaking into a smile.

'Oi! What yer sittin' there grinnin' like a Cheshire cat for?'

Marie shouted. 'Fings won't get sorted out while you're stuck in that chair.'

'I was finkin', Marie.'

'Bloody 'ell! You surprise me.'

Toby stared dejectedly into the fire. Perhaps he should really get things sorted out, like waiting until Marie was asleep and then crowning her with the flat-iron. He could wrap her up in one of those old pissy carpets and dump her in the river. When folks asked after her he could say she had run off with a tallyman. No, it wouldn't work. Lillian would smell a rat. Oh well, it was nice thinking about it anyway.

During the early part of April Germany seized Denmark and invaded Norway. British troops were fighting at Narvik before the month was out, and in May German troops marched into Belgium and Holland. Churchill was now Prime Minister of a coalition government and his rousing speeches were inevitably discussed in the Horseshoe.

'Well at least 'e ain't tryin' ter pull the wool over our eyes, Tel. 'E's puttin' it to us straight.'

'Yeah, I grant yer that, but it frightens the life out o' my ole woman, Bill.'

'Yeah, it's the same wiv my ole dutch, Tel. It's playin' on 'er nerves. The ouvver night she woke me up screamin'. "There's a bloody parachutist sittin' on our chimney pot," she shouts out. Bleedin' nightmare she was 'avin'. I said to 'er, "Don't worry, girl. I'll go down an' light the fire. That'll do the trick." She turns over an' five minutes later she's snorin' 'er bleedin' 'ead orf.'

'Yer gotta admit though, Bill. It's gettin' bad.'

'Yeah it is. So's this beer.'

'Fancy anuvver one?'

'Might as well, Tel.'

A few days later, on Saturday the first day of June, everyone in the Dolphin public house in Salter Street was talking about the war. The news was bad. The remnants of the British and French armies were being taken off the beaches at Dunkirk and repeated wireless bulletins had reported that casualties were very high. Connie and her friend Jennie were serving in the public bar and they could both feel the tension. It seemed unusually quiet that evening. Normally the pub pianist would be banging out the latest tunes, but tonight he sat at the counter with his chin resting on his cupped hand. Tubby Jackson's son was somewhere in France and the anxiety was written all over the old man's face. There was no laughter in the Dolphin that evening, only subdued conversation and occasional words of encouragement for the piano player.

It was around nine o'clock when the pub door opened and a tall, fair-haired young man in airforce uniform moved the blackout curtain aside and stepped into the smoky interior. He looked around the bar sheepishly and was immediately spotted by two old ladies who were sitting near the door.

''Ere, May. Who's 'e?'

''Ow the bleedin' 'ell should I know, Nora.'

''E's a nice-lookin' bloke, May. Makes me wish I was twenty years younger.' May Sanders watched as he squeezed through towards the bar counter. ''E's an orficer by the looks of 'im. I wish it was me 'e was lookin' for.'

Nora Matthews chuckled. 'We're gettin' ter be dirty ole cows, May, ain't we?'

'Dirty nufink. It's only natural ter notice a bit o' prime beef when you've 'ad ter put up wiv scrags o' mutton.'

'I know what yer mean, May. It does seem strange in 'ere now all the young men 'ave bin called up. Poor ole Tubby looks worried out of 'is life. 'E dotes on that son of 'is. Then there's Mrs Argrieves. She looks terrible. Mind you though, that son of 'ers don't fink nufink of 'er. All the time I've bin comin' in 'ere I ain't never seen 'im buy 'er a drink.'

'Still, blood's thicker than water, Nora. It's only natural fer 'er ter be worried, even though 'e is a bit of a cow-son.'

Connie had just finished serving a customer when she spotted Robert. He had reached the counter and was watching her, a wide smile on his handsome features. Connie gasped and ignored another customer as she hurried over to him. She noticed how his cap was pushed back from his forehead and how his blue eyes lit up as he smiled.

'What yer doin' 'ere, Robert?' she said joyfully. 'Yer didn't say yer was comin' on leave.'

'I didn't know myself until a few hours ago. I've been given a forty-eight-hour pass. I thought I'd look in and surprise you.'

'C'mon, Con, I'm dyin' o' thirst,' one of the customers called out.

Robert grinned as he put a ten shilling note down on the counter. 'I'd like a Scotch, if you've any left.'

'C'mon, Connie girl, don't eat 'im,' the waiting customer said to roars of laughter.

Connie felt her face redden and she quickly poured Robert a whisky.

Jennie came over and touched her arm. 'Don't your fella look smashin' in that uniform. I could fancy 'im meself.'

Connie smiled as she handed over the drink and watched as he took a sip. 'I was gettin' worried, not 'earin' from yer,' she said quietly.

'Sorry, Con,' he said, pushing his cap farther back on his head. 'I've got an operational posting. First thing Monday morning.'

'Is it near London?' Connie asked, her eyes studying his pale features.

He put his finger to his lips and made an exaggerated

movement with his eyes left to right. 'It's classified, I can't say.'

Jennie had been hovering nearby and she nudged her friend. 'Ain't yer gonna introduce me prop'ly, or are yer keepin' 'im all ter yerself?' she asked finally.

Connie giggled and before she could speak Jennie held out her hand. 'I'm Jennie. I used ter see yer when yer met Connie at the factory. Trouble was she wouldn't let any of us get near yer. If yer ever get fed up wiv our Con I'm always available.'

They all laughed, to the chagrin of the still waiting customer. ''Ere you two. If yer don't serve me soon I'm gonna climb over the bleedin' counter an' 'elp meself.'

Jennie raised her eyes to the ceiling. 'All right, all right. I'll serve yer. Jus' give yerself a chance.'

'Give meself a chance? I'm dyin' o' thirst an' there's you two natterin' away wiv Flash 'Arry over there. Who is 'e anyway?'

'That's Connie's fiancé. 'E's a pilot,' Jennie said, glancing in Robert's direction.

The customer's face relaxed. ''Ere, Jen. See if the lad wants a drink.'

Jennie pinched the old man's cheek playfully. 'Leave 'em alone, Jerry. Yer can buy me one instead.'

Robert had struck up a conversation with some of the regular customers as Connie continued serving, occasionally glancing coyly in his direction.

At ten o' clock Jennie caught Connie's eye. 'You'd better get yer fella out of 'ere before ole Benny bores 'im ter death. Go on, I can manage.'

Connie squeezed Jennie's arm. 'Fanks a lot, Jen. It's one I owe yer.'

She put on her coat and beckoned to Robert, whose hand was being furiously pumped by the inebriated Benny, and he nodded back. The two lovers walked out into the chill night air, Connie gripping his arm tightly and resting her head against his shoulder as they came out from the backstreet into the Old Kent Road. No lights shone out as they made their way along the street. A pale moon shone down wanly, its beams catching the tramlines and making them glow eerily. At the junction they passed the white stone library building and continued into Great Dover Street. Very few people were about, and as they neared Robert's flat the moon had become obscured behind heavy clouds. Large spots of rain stained the pavement as they hurried up the stairs to the front door and let themselves into the dark passage. They climbed the flight of stairs and entered the first-floor flat just as the first roll of thunder sounded. Lightning flashed across the dark sky and rain beat against the window panes. Connie pulled the blinds while Robert lit the gas fire and then turned on the light. He looked around, his eyes taking stock.

'You've been busy I see. It's very nice.'

Connie smiled. 'I come up 'ere now an' again. I like ter keep it nice an' tidy.'

They looked at each other, searching for something to say. The long period apart had made them both feel awkward. He suddenly held out his arms and the barrier between them disappeared as she rushed forward and kissed him. It was nice to feel his body against hers again and for a time no words were spoken. Slowly he reached his hands up to her face and then gently stroked her white neck. His fingers found the buttons of her coat and soon she could feel his cool hands slipping around her slim waist. He pulled her to him in a strong embrace and their bodies moulded together.

'God! I've missed you, Connie,' he gasped, his lips moving against her tiny ears.

'I've missed you, too, Robert. I've missed your love an'

your touch. I've dreamed about yer lots an' lots.'

They moved away from the heat of the fire and Connie slipped off her unbuttoned coat. He threw his cap into a chair and took off his topcoat. She saw the white cotton wings sewn above his breast pocket as she returned to him. They settled down in the comfortable settee and he put his arm around her shoulders and pulled her close to him. Her fingers followed the raised shape on his chest and she sighed.

'Will yer be flyin' straightaway, Robert?'

'I'm to report to Tangmere,' he answered. 'I'll be flying Hurricanes.'

'Where's Tangmere?'

'It's in Sussex. I'm not supposed to say anything, so keep it to yourself, Con.'

'Mum's the word,' she grinned, her lips brushing his cheek.

The room was warm and cosy and the heavy curtains deadened the sound of the rain as it beat against the windows. They sat in front of the hissing gas fire as the mantleshelf clock chimed the hour of midnight. Connie noticed how serious Robert looked as his finger traced a circle on the back of her hand.

'Are yer worried about the postin'?' she asked.

His face relaxed slightly as he smiled. 'No, angel. As a matter of fact I was thinking about you.'

'Oh, an' what about me?'

'Connie. How long have we known each other?'

'Forever,' she laughed, moving her head from his shoulder and looking into his soft blue eyes.

He sighed deeply and squeezed her hand. 'Do you believe I really love you?'

'Of course I do,' she whispered. 'What's troublin' yer, Robert?'

He sat up straight and looked directly at her. 'Listen, Con.

We share this flat and you know that one day we'll be married. In the time we've been together you've only met my mother on that one occasion, the Christmas before last. I've never taken you back, and you've never mentioned it or asked me why. I've wondered about that.'

Connie looked down at her hands. 'Let's face it. We both know your mum don't see me as an ideal choice for a daughter-in-law. We come from different sides of the street. It's never worried you, an' ter be honest I don't fink your dad worries too much eivver, but your mum can't accept it. That time I met 'er I could tell. It was written all over 'er face. It doesn't worry me, but what does worry me is the upset it's causin' you.'

He lifted her head gently and gazed into her sad eyes. 'There's something else, too, isn't there?' he said quietly.

She looked away. 'There's nufink else, Robert.'

He leaned back heavily in the settee and sighed. 'Before I met you this evening I went to see my parents. I told my mother I couldn't go on holding things from you if we were going to be married.'

'What fings, Robert?'

'The real reason why your mother was paid that money.'

Connie's eyes hardened. 'You've known all along?' she asked, raising her voice.

He reached out and took her firmly by the shoulders. 'You've got to understand, Con. I was trying to save you from being hurt. My father told me before we both went down for the Christmas. He asked me to promise not to say anything to you. I kept that promise because of the way I feel about you. You did the same for me. You promised my mother you wouldn't say anything to me, remember?'

'Yer mean yer know what your muvver told me that Christmas?'

'Yes.'

He saw the puzzlement in Connie's eyes as he relaxed his hold on her. 'Let me explain,' he began. 'When I told my parents I was going to tell you what I knew there was a blazing row. My mother told me what she had said to you when you were alone with her. It seems she was protecting Gerald. She told me that you were intending to meet someone who might well be able to tell you why your mother received those payments and she said she had concocted the story to protect the family name. Those were the words she used.'

A distant roll of thunder sounded and the rain continued to beat faintly against the window as the two sat before the fire. Connie looked at Robert anxiously.

'You were only two years old when it all happened,' he went on. 'It was at the firm's outing to Southend. My uncle Gerald was told to organise the event by my grandfather who was running the company then. Apparently there was a lot of discontent amongst the workers at the time and grandfather thought it might help to calm the atmosphere. Anyway, the outing went off well until the charabanc stopped at a pub on the way home. Everyone was pretty drunk by that time, including Gerald. He saw your mother sitting alone in a corner of the pub and she was crying. From what I understand she had recently broken off a relationship and was feeling pretty low. Uncle Gerald took advantage of the situation by plying her with drinks. Later he followed your mother out of the pub and when she was in a secluded spot he forced himself on her. At first your mother thought he was joking, but when it started to get out of hand she asked him to take her back to the pub. It was then that my Uncle Gerald raped your mother.'

Connie gasped and her hand came up to her mouth. 'My mum was raped!?'

He nodded slowly. 'Afterwards he warned her not to say

anything or he'd make it bad, not only for her but for a few other workers he was out to get. He also said that he would deny everything and that his word would be taken before that of a slut. I'm sorry, Con. That was what he said. Most of the workers were drunk and none of them knew what had happened. The next Monday morning your mother saw my grandfather and she told him everything. She told him that she was going to the police and under the circumstances she would have to leave the firm immediately. Of course Uncle Gerald was confronted by the old man and he finally broke down and admitted everything.

'My uncle already had a reputation for being a womaniser. There was some scandal at the time about him and another woman, and that was the reason for his marriage being in a bad way. My grandfather knew all about his reputation and wasn't going to have the wool pulled over his eyes. Uncle Gerald knew that, too. He knew he couldn't get away with lying to his father, and so he confessed everything. It was exactly as your mother told it. Grandfather George was a persuasive man as well as being very shrewd. He could see the harm it might do to the company should there be a court case. He was also worried about his son, even though what he had done was inexcusable, and he wanted him to get his marriage sorted out. He begged your mother not to go to the police. He reminded her of the duty she had to you and that if she kept quiet he would pay her a regular sum for the rest of her life. Father told me that your mother was a proud woman. Grandfather George knew that, so he agreed to her demand that an agreement be drawn up with a special condition. The firm would pay a regular sum for your mother's silence, and would guarantee continued employment to a certain worker who was facing dismissal because of his trade-union activities. The old man knew that it allowed her to feel she had retained her self-respect. Your mother kept that silence. My grandfather knew she would honour the agreement. So did my father. The ironic thing is, if only my mother had listened to them she wouldn't have worried about you finding out, and she wouldn't have needed to slander your mother's name. It was a terrible thing to do.'

For a while Connie found it difficult to talk. Finally she looked at Robert, her eyes wet with tears of sadness and relief. 'Fanks fer tellin' me, Robert.'

He looked down at his feet in embarrassment. 'I'm glad I did. Your mother must have been some woman. I'm sorry I never knew her.'

Connie smiled wanly. 'Yes, she was, Robert. By the way, did the firm keep their promise?'

'You mean about keeping the worker on? Yes they did. You know Joe Cooper who lives in your street? Well he's still working for the firm, thanks to your mother.'

The storm had abated and the rain was now a steady drizzle. In the little flat in Great Dover Street the two lovers lay contentedly in each others' arms. Connie felt that a heavy weight had been lifted from her shoulders. At last she knew the truth, thanks to Robert. She was also very much aware how the same fierce pride which had kept the silence about Gerald had kept another silence too. It was going to be virtually impossible to find out who her father was. Maybe one day, somehow, she told herself as sleep overtook her.

Chapter Twenty-Six

During the first week in June the last of the British and French soldiers had been taken from the Dunkirk beaches. The weather was now sunny and warm and early summer flowers were in bloom. Around the coastline the incoming tide lapped against concrete tank traps and flowed over buried mines. Along the length of the south coast people walked along the promenades beside fences of barbed wire, pill boxes and sandbagged fortifications, while the opposing armies gazed towards each other across the narrow English Channel. On the tenth of June Italy joined the war on the side of Germany and immediately there were assaults made on the Italian community and their properties. In Bermondsey a group of young men broke into Tony Armeda's premises and smashed his barrow before setting light to the shed where Tony made his ice-cream. The young Italian narrowly escaped death by jumping from his bedroom window after the fire spread to his house. Shops owned by the Italian families were smashed and one or two owners were badly beaten up.

Great Britain had now become an island under siege and folk stared up at the sky, fearing an airborne invasion at any minute. Wireless broadcasts gave out depressing bulletins as more ships were reported sunk. Casualty lists got longer, and the government warned everyone to be prepared for air raids.

In Jubilee Dwellings the neighbours got together and decided to use the ground-floor flats as shelters should there be an attack. Some of the folk were against the idea and made up their minds to use the factory shelter, even though it would be overcrowded. Annie and Alf Riley said that they would never be able to stand the factory basement and they would take their chances in the buildings. But others disagreed, including the Bartletts.

Matthew had been adamant. 'If a bomb caught these dwellin's they'd collapse like a pack o' cards. Let's face it, 'Elen, they're fallin' down as it is.'

Alf Riley put up a different argument. 'What about that bleedin' factory? Look at all that machinery over yer 'ead. What chance would yer stand over there?'

A few of the older folk in the dwellings were fatalistic in their approach to the dilemma. Mrs Hawkins summed it up by saying, 'If yer gotta go, then yer gotta go, no matter where yer are. I'm gonna stay in me bed, an' if the good Lord wants me 'E knows where ter find me.'

In the summer of that year Bank Holidays were cancelled. Factories on war work extended their hours and many work places were operating seven days a week. Cinemas, dance halls and other places of entertainment had been closed at the outbreak of war, but they were soon re-opened. During the summer of 1940 they were all very crowded as people sought an escape from the ugly reality that surrounded them.

In Ironmonger Street the folk were constantly reminded of the war as sandbags were stacked against the rag shop and telephones were installed. Toby's secret storehouse had now become an ARP post. The little oilshop opposite remained closed. It had been shut since Jerry Martin went into the mental hospital and, for the street folk, it had become a memorial to the grumpy old character. The paint had peeled from the shutters and the name over the door had faded. Some of the street kids said the place was haunted and they frightened each other with tales of demons and ghouls.

'Go on, I dare yer.'

'I'm not scared.'

'Go on then, look frew the letter box.'

'Don't want to.'

'What yer scared of, ghosts?'

'Nah.'

'Bet yer scared of ole Wider Pacey. She goes in there an' sleeps in a coffin.'

'I'm not scared o' nufink. I'll look frew the letter box.'

Two little lads walked boldly up to the shop and one peered gingerly into the dark, dank interior. 'Cor! It looks like a skelinton in there. You 'ave a look.'

'No fanks. I can't stan' skelintons.'

'Skelintons can't 'urt yer. They're only rattly ole bones.'

'Ghosts can. Jimmy Brown said there's a ghost livin' in there.'

'C'mon then, let's try an' bump in the Trocette. It's better than searchin' fer ghosts an' fings.'

Connie had gone to Waterloo Station with Robert on Monday morning. She found the parting very hard. On previous occasions when they had said goodbye she knew it would only be a matter of time before they were united again, but this time Robert was going away to join a fighter squadron. She realised she might never see him again and, as he left, she tried to burn the moment into her anxious mind. He seemed relaxed, almost debonair as he took her to him, kissed her gently on the mouth and then climbed aboard the early train. He was wearing his cap at a jaunty angle and his fair hair was brushed back, partially covering his ears. His pale blue eyes were smiling calmly at her, mocking her anxiety as the train moved slowly away from the platform. She turned and said a silent prayer as she walked back to the main concourse, her mind trying desperately to record for ever his expression and his whispered words of love. Connie suddenly felt very alone and frightened. She wondered what the future held, and what might have been had she never met him. Her thoughts turned to Michael Donovan and how surprised she was when she had seen him in the Tower Bridge Road last Christmas Eve. It was the first time she had set eyes on him since they had parted in anger. She recalled her confused feelings on seeing him. In the space of a moment memories of their happy times together and how they had turned bitter had been brought back to her. She had been very surprised when she learned that Michael was married. It must have been a whirlwind romance, she thought, but they seemed suited to each other and she hoped for Michael's sake that they would be happy.

That same evening Connie talked with Helen. Her aunt was visibly shocked on learning the truth about her sister. She was also hurt that Kate had not taken her into her confidence.

'That's the way she was, girl. Your mum kept too much to 'erself. We could 'ave all rallied round if she'd 'ave bin more open wiv us all. It's what families are for. You remember what I was sayin' ter yer, Con. Don't yer leave us out in the cold, child.'

'Don't worry, Aunt. You, Matt and Molly are the only family I've got. I shan't ferget.'

Helen smiled briefly and then her face became serious. 'Whatever possessed that Gerald to attack yer mum the way 'e did? It must 'ave bin the drink. Some men are like that when they're boozed.'

Connie was reminded of her own experience when Michael had come near to hitting her. 'Robert said that Gerald's marriage was in a bad way. I s'pose it didn't 'elp any.'

'That's no excuse for what 'e done, Connie.'

The young girl sat in silence for a while. 'Auntie,' she said finally. 'I didn't see any document from the factory when we sorted through mum's fings. I wonder what become of it?'

'Well it must be somewhere. Yer mum wouldn't 'ave left it wiv anybody else, would she? Are yer sure it's not in the back of a cupboard or in a drawer?'

Connie shook her head. 'I've searched everywhere. It's nowhere ter be seen.'

'Maybe yer'll come across it, Con. I've got nufink 'ere of yer mum's.'

The young woman pinched her bottom lip between her thumb and forefinger. 'I was finkin' the ovver night, Aunt. What 'appened ter mum's gold locket? I never saw 'er wivvout it, unless it was at the pawnshop.'

Helen stared down at her clasped hands. 'It went wiv 'er,' she said quietly. 'She thought the world of that locket. I thought it best if it was buried wiv 'er.'

Connie reached out and touched her aunt's hands. 'Yer did right. She would 'ave wanted it that way, I bet,' she said gently.

The long summer days wore on with the fear of an invasion ever present in people's minds. Church bells were now silent on Sunday mornings and folk dreaded to hear them while the war lasted, for they knew that if they did it would not be a call to worship, but a call to arms against an aerial invader. There was also a stark reminder of how hideous the war might become: tops of pillar boxes were painted a yellowish green, and the colour would change should the paint be exposed to poison gas. People carried their gas masks around with them everywhere, and posters were on display all over, warning of what to do in case of gas attacks. More young men were called up and their jobs were often filled by women. Many Bermondsey men were employed at the docks and wharves and were excused from registering for military service, but there were men in their early thirties and forties who waited anxiously for their turn to come.

Toby Toomey was in his mid fifties but that didn't stop his wife from worrying.

''Ere, Lil, 'ave yer seen this?' Marie asked, handing a copy of the *Daily Mirror* to her daughter. 'It ses 'ere that older men will 'ave ter register in the near future.'

'Dad won't 'ave ter go, will 'e, Mum?'

''E might 'ave to, later. Fings ain't lookin' too good.'

Lillian laughed. 'Imagine Dad in a uniform – an' wiv a rifle. Gawd! 'E'd be shootin' 'is mates instead of the Germans.'

Marie hid her grin. Toby could not be trusted with a pram, let alone a lethal weapon! she thought. Even the magistrate had said he was a danger to other road users when he had fined him twenty shillings after that incident with the copper. If they called him up and gave him a gun he'd be a menace to the whole British army. Toby was worried himself, but it was not over being conscripted. Most of the scrap metal was being collected for the war effort and his only source of income at the moment was from bundles of old newspapers and rags. He had considered at one time hiring a barrow and branching out into bottles and bones. Old Jerry seemed to do all right out of it. Trouble was, a barrow was heavier to push than a pram, and the smell of old bones wasn't exactly pleasant. Then there were the flies. They didn't seem to bother old Jerry, but then nothing ever did. Maybe it would be better to conveniently lose the pram the next time around and go into war work? Maybe they'd send him to the north of England, or even Scotland. At least it would be a change not to be on the receiving end of Marie's rough tongue when he stacked his papers and rags in the backyard. Better still, he could volunteer to be a full-time air-raid warden. Just imagine walking the streets in a tin hat and keeping an eye on the blackout!

'Oi you! Put that light out! D'yer want me ter report yer? – Sorry Mr Toomey, sir. It won't 'appen again, honest. – Well all right, but I'll be keepin' an eye on yer, just in case. – Fank yer, Mr Toomey. Fank yer, sir.'

Toby's stern voice carried in from the backyard and Marie shook her head sadly. The man's losing his marbles, she told herself.

'Is that you talkin' ter yerself again, Toby?' she shouted out.

'I was jus' readin' out loud, luv,' he answered grimacing.

'Well get them papers bundled up instead of readin' 'em. We ain't paid no bleedin' rent again this week.'

In the middle of August the Battle of Britain was raging in the skies. Daily newspapers carried reports of heroic action and mounting losses. Hurricanes and Spitfires roared off from fighter stations in Kent and Sussex to meet the German air armadas and people watched as tracer trails scarred the clear blue sky. Along the coast folk could see planes fall into the sea and crash into the rolling green downs. They would see an occasional billow of white as a pilot escaped from his stricken aircraft and floated down beneath a mushroom of silk. News placards carried reports of the losses on both sides as though they were scores in a game. Everyone was filled with a strange excitement, as they knew that the battle was a fight for their very survival. If the battle was lost then an all-out invasion would be inevitable. Pubs were packed each evening and people pored over the latest newspaper stories and headline banners. In the Dolphin the piano was sounding loudly as a happy Tubby Jackson banged down heavily on the ivories. His son Joey had been plucked from the beaches unharmed. For Mrs Argrieves however, the news had been bad. Her son Billy was lying seriously injured in a military hospital. And for Connie the days and nights were fraught with uncertainty and fear. There had been no news of Robert since his last letter the day before the battle started. However, there was news of a local lad who was serving on a destroyer in the North Atlantic and it was tucked away inside the Saturday evening edition of the *Star*.

''Ere, Dora. You seen this?' the landlord of the Dolphin called out.

'What's that, Bill?'

'It ses 'ere a local lad's won a medal. Listen ter this. "Able Seaman Michael Donovan of Bermon'sey 'as bin awarded the DSM fer bravery at sea." It ses, "Able Seaman Donovan stayed at 'is post despite bein' wounded an' 'elped ter save a badly wounded comrade while under fire." Fancy that.'

Connie's ears picked up at the mention of Michael's name. 'Does it say if 'e's okay, Bill?' she asked quickly.

'Doesn't say, Con. Why, d'yer know 'im?'

'I used ter work wiv 'im a long time ago,' she answered.

The battle of Britain continued to rage and still there was no news of Robert. Late on Saturday evening Connie walked home feeling worried. She let herself into her flat and pulled the blackout curtains before lighting the gaslamp. Later, when she sat sipping her tea she noticed the lighter square patch on the grubby wallpaper. Puzzled, she got up and went over to look more closely. She saw that a picture she had hardly ever noticed had fallen from the wall and was wedged behind the sideboard. As she retrieved it Connie saw that the glass was broken. She spread out a sheet of newspaper on the table and gently eased out the larger pieces of glass. The sepia photograph in the ebony frame was of her mother as a young child. She wore a white dress that was buttoned high in the neck and she was standing beside a jardiniere which held a sorry-looking aspidistra. For a while Connie stared at the photograph and then she turned the frame over. The dusty string was till intact. She walked over to the wall and saw the large nail was also still in place. There seemed to be no reason why the picture should have fallen from the wall, and she shivered as she stared down at the back of the picture. A square of thin cardboard had been placed over the back of the frame and was held by a drawing pin in each corner. Connie could see that the picture backing had been dislodged by the fall and a piece of white paper was protruding from one edge of the cardboard. Carefully she prised the pins away and lifted the backing. 'July 30th, 1923' was written in faded pencil at one corner of the folded sheet of paper. She opened it up and sat down beneath the gaslamp. It was the agreement, worded just as Robert had described and signed in a flourishing style by George Armitage and by the small, neat hand of Kate Morgan. The two signatures were side by side, and beneath the words 'in the presence of' was the signature of Fran Collins.

Connie heard the clock chime one and then two, but sleep would not come. She could not understand why the picture frame should have fallen from the wall and thoughts rushed through her mind as she lay staring up at the dark ceiling. It seemed to her almost as though her mother was there in the room with her, and she felt strangely calm and rested. Connie remembered it was only a few weeks ago that she had given up all hope of finding out about the money, and now she knew. Then there was the document. She had searched high and low without success and now the paper lay on the chair beside her bed. She could sense a growing kinship with her dead mother, a kinship she had yearned and prayed for but had never found during her mother's lifetime. Connie had tried for hours to work out how the picture could have fallen, but now it seemed unimportant. She knew with a profound certainty that she had been somehow destined to follow the path she was now treading. She remembered experiencing the feeling once before when she had first set out to meet Robert. The realisation did not frighten her, and she turned on to her side and buried her head in the cool pillow.

Chapter Twenty-Seven

The sun's rays lit the room and Connie stirred. She realised she had slept late, and she was about to leap out of bed when she remembered it was Sunday morning. The sound of the street children carried up to the quiet room and she heard the vendor's cry as he pushed his barrow laden with shrimps and winkles into the turning. Connie turned over and stretched. She had promised to go down to the Bartletts' flat for breakfast that morning and the clock showed fifteen minutes past nine. She got up and washed at the scullery tap. The cold water took the remaining tiredness away and it was not long before she was tapping on the door of the flat below. As soon as Molly opened the door the appetising smell of bacon frying reached her. The front-room table was laid for breakfast and a low fire burnt in the grate against the morning chill.

Helen came into the room smiling. 'Take yerself a seat, Con. Breakfast won't be long.'

Connie sat down at the table facing her cousin. ''Ow are yer, Molly?'

Her flat round face broke into a cheerful smile. 'Guess what, Con?'

'What?'

'I'm gettin' promotion! I've bin put on inspections an' it means five shillin's a week extra.'

'That's smashin'! What's inspections?'

Connie's cousin laid her short thick hands on the blue checked tablecloth. 'Well yer see, when the resistors an' condensers are soldered in place I've gotta check 'em wiv a special meter. It's a responsible job but our forelady finks I'm pretty reliable.'

'So yer are,' Connie said with emphasis. 'Yer'll be forelady next!'

Helen came in carrying a large dish full of fried rashers which she shared out on the four plates. Matthew followed her in with a flat tray. 'Make way fer the chef,' he grinned, sliding a ladle under a lightly fried egg.

Soon the four were sitting around the table to a breakfast of eggs, bacon and tomatoes. Helen held the loaf of bread against her as she neatly cut thick slices and passed them around. Matthew opened a packet of margarine and spread a thick coating on his slice.

'What d'yer fink of our Molly gettin' a rise, Con?' he said, cutting his slice in half and dipping one piece into his soft egg.

'Molly jus' told me, Matt. 'Ow much 'as she gotta give up out o' the rise, four an' sixpence?' Connie joked.

Helen laughed. 'We've told 'er ter start a savin's book. If she saves all 'er rise fer a year she could end up bein' a moneylender.'

Matthew got up and took the large china teapot from the hearth. As he filled the cups Connie looked around at the family. They were relaxed and happy. Helen had a little colour in her cheeks and Molly looked cheerful. Matthew joked a little as he poured the tea and when he spilled a little on the clean tablecloth Helen tapped his hand playfully. Connie felt happy for them. They had experienced some bad times and now things seemed to be looking up.

After the meal was finished Connie helped her aunt to do

the washing up while Matthew and Molly took a morning stroll to the paper shop. While they were alone Connie took the opportunity to show Helen the document.

'I was cleaning the picture and it slipped out of me 'ands,' she lied, aware of her aunt's superstitious nature. 'That's 'ow I found it.'

Helen wiped her hands on a towel and put on her glasses. 'Well I'll be!' she exclaimed. 'Fancy ole Fran bein' a witness.'

Connie stared at Helen. 'Why Fran Collins, Aunt?'

'Ole Fran was the one who 'eld yer by yer ankles an' smacked the breath o' life inter yer, Connie. 'Alf the muvvers in this street 'ad Fran Collins ter fank fer deliverin' their kids. I can understand why yer mum picked 'er ter be a witness.'

'Wasn't that the lady they 'ad the big funeral for, Aunt 'Elen?'

'That's right, luv. When ole Fran was buried all the street turned out. She was a lovely lady. Most of the women round 'ere didn't 'ave two pennies ter rub tergevver. They couldn't afford a doctor so they called on ole Fran Collins. She knew 'er job too. They wasn't always easy births. Lots o' mums worked till the last minute an' sometimes the 'eavy liftin' they done got the baby's cord twisted. Ole Fran 'andled plenty o' them cases. People paid 'er, but most often she 'ad ter wait months fer the money. Fran never complained though, and when she passed away everybody lined the street ter pay their respects. Quite a few of those mourners still owed 'er a few bob, I'll be bound.'

Towards the end of August ports and airfields in Southern England were being bombed, and wireless bulletins reported scattered raids on Midland towns. German bombers even reached the eastern suburbs of London and the Bermondsey folk held their breath. Everyone knew how important the docks and wharves were, as well as the rail networks and freight yards. They were all obvious targets and people knew that it was only a matter of time before the onslaught began. Anti-aircraft guns were positioned in Southwark Park and on suitable open spaces near the River Thames. Cars and vans were commandeered and adapted for carrying stretchers, and all first-aid and wardens' posts were on a constant alert. The summer sky over the centre of London remained peaceful and, high above dockland, barrage balloons floated gently in the breeze at the end of their steel hawsers. In the look-out posts, nervous eyes stared downriver for the first signs of aircraft, but only seagulls drifted and wheeled above the moving cranes and turning tides.

It was the last day of August, a warm Saturday afternoon, when Robert drove into Ironmonger Street. The kids were playing on the cobblestones and the street folk stood by their front doors chatting to their neighbours. Connie heard the throaty roar of the engine and the toot of the horn and she hurried to the open window. Robert answered her wave as he sat behind the wheel, surrounded by curious, toffee-smeared children who stared at the controls and giggled as he revved the noisy engine. The street folk nodded knowingly and watched as the young woman ran from the buildings and stepped in beside the uniformed figure. With a toot-toot of the horn to scatter the inquisitive children he swung the car around and roared off, leaving a cloud of blue smoke rising in the little backstreet.

Connie sat beside him resting her hand on his leg, her golden hair flying in the wind as the car accelerated along the Old Kent Road. Her eyes watered and she ducked her head below the tilted windscreen as Robert glanced at her, a boyish grin breaking out on his handsome features.

'What do you think of it?' Robert shouted above the noise

of the engine, patting the dashboard with his gloved hand.

Her answer was swept away in the wind as the open-top sports car gathered speed up Blackheath Hill. Houses and factories were gradually left behind and fields were beginning to spread out around them. Connie held her hand up to her hair and occasionally glanced at Robert as he manipulated the gears and roared past slower-moving vehicles. She could see the small piece of cloth in blue and white diagonal stripes which was pinned above his breast pocket.

'Is that the medal you told me about in your last letter?' she asked loudly.

'It's the clasp. I've got the actual medal in a box,' he shouted with a grin.

They had been travelling for some time when he suddenly swung the car on to a side road and slowed down through the village.

'Another fifteen minutes should do it,' he said, squeezing her hand in his as they left the sleepy hamlet behind.

It had all happened so quickly. There had been no news of him for more than three weeks and, with daily newspapers carrying stories of air battles and mounting losses she had feared for his safety. Then the letter had arrived, and now they were together again once more. Connie felt apprehensive at the prospect of meeting his parents again after such a long time. Robert had said in his letter that they had planned some sort of celebration, but he went on to say that he would make his excuses as soon as possible and maybe they would be able to spend the night in one of the nearby inns. Connie guessed that the family feud must have healed and she wondered how she would feel on seeing Claudette again, and how she would be received.

The sun was setting and the sky was gloriously aflame as they drove into Kelstowe. The red brick house was just as she remembered it and, when they climbed from the car feeling stiff and wind-swept, the Armitages came out quickly to greet them. Peter shook Robert's hand vigorously and Claudette hugged her son tightly, much to his embarrassment.

Peter kissed Connie on the cheek and took her arm. 'It's been a long time since we've seen you, Connie,' he said kindly. 'I can see you're taking very good care of our son.'

Claudette had composed herself and she glanced briefly at the Morgan girl. 'Let's go inside,' she said. 'There are a few people who want to congratulate our hero.'

'Good Lord!' Robert gasped, looking helplessly at Connie.

People were crowding around, eager to pump his hand. A chorus of 'For he's a jolly good fellow' rang out and he gazed sheepishly at the sea of faces. Connie tried to stay at his elbow as well-wishers slapped him on the back. Drinks were flowing and she found herself holding a glass of sparkling champagne.

Major Clarence Marchant made a beeline for her and held out his hand. 'Hello, my dear. So you're the pretty little thing young Robbie has kept from us, what?'

Connie smiled at the portly major and looked around desperately to where Robert was standing.

'Drink up, me dear. That's Bollinger '29. Plenty more where that came from,' the major said, brushing his military moustache with a forefinger.

Connie found the bubbles made her want to sneeze as she took a sip of her drink and over the rim of the glass she saw a tall, thin young woman eyeing her intently. The girl wore tortoiseshell spectacles and her hair was pulled back tightly, which gave her a rather severe appearance. The major was eyeing her too as she drained her glass.

'Let me get you a refill,' he slurred.

As Clarence Marchant walked away unsteadily the bespectacled young woman came over. 'I'm Eunice

Marchant,' she said, holding out her hand. 'Isn't it marvellous about Robert. Five victories in just two days. Everyone is so proud of him.'

Connie smiled. 'So am I.'

Eunice stared over her glasses at the Morgan girl. 'Robert and I have known each other for a long time. I suppose he's told you about me?'

'No, I'm afraid not,' Connie replied, looking in Robert's direction.

Eunice's face clouded and she pushed her spectacles up on to the bridge of her nose. 'We were almost engaged at one time, you know.'

'I didn't know,' Connie said, smiling gently and holding out her ring finger. 'We got engaged last Christmas.'

Eunice looked disapprovingly at the diamond ring. 'You'll have to watch him, dear. Robert can be a terrible flirt, as most of the girls around here will tell you.'

'I'll watch 'im, Eunice. I'll watch 'im real close,' Connie said with a hint of malice now in her tone.

The Waverley sisters came over and introduced themselves and they were followed by the Reverend Jones, while Eunice drifted away to find her hero. Connie became immersed in a constant stream of chatter and her eyes sought out Robert.

A tall, stooping figure came over to her, his white hair sprouting out from a large head. His eyes were dark and brooding, and his clothes seemed shabby beside the rest of the guests. He took her arm without introduction and smiled at the Waverley sisters. 'Now then Beatrice, Gwen, we mustn't tire our lovely guest, must we? Come, my dear. Let me show you the garden. I can assure you it is a wonderful place,' he said with mock pomp.

Connie looked at him in surprise and let herself be guided out through the French windows into the cool of the evening.

'Just smell those roses,' he said to her. 'Aren't they gorgeous? And the jasmine. It's at its best this time of day.' He waved his arm in a grand gesture toward the flowerbeds.

The tall stranger was still holding on to her arm and she glanced at him with some puzzlement. He caught her look and smiled, his dark eyes lighting up. 'I'm sorry, my dear. I should have introduced myself before stealing you away from that unmitigating rabble. My name is Spanswick. Leo Spanswick. I'm the local physician, family counsellor and father confessor to these people. I saw you looking rather bewildered and, if I may say so, rather frightened, so I took it upon myself to become your knight in shining armour. Let us walk on, my child, unless you wish to go back and rejoin our friends?'

Connie smiled sweetly at him. She felt strangely at ease in his company and, as they strolled along the path which led between the well-tended lawns, he took out a large briar and tapped it against his thigh. 'I hear you and Robert are engaged, Connie. You don't mind me calling you Connie, do you?'

'That's me name,' she said lightly. 'And yes, we are engaged.'

'Good for you. By the way, you know you've upset the apple cart somewhat. I noticed one or two pairs of eyes cast enviously in your direction.'

'Yer mean Eunice? She did mention about 'er an' Robert.'

'Her and Robert nothing, child. You've no doubt heard of marriages made in heaven? Well in this instance the Marchants and Claudette Armitage were conspirators in what I would say was an attempt to create a boardroom marriage.'

Connie looked at him with a puzzled frown, and he chuckled. 'Money, my dear, money. The amalgamation of two business concerns through the manipulation of young love. Isn't it terrible?'

Connie smiled and he touched the side of his nose in a

confidential gesture as he guided her towards a garden seat at the end of the path. They sat down and she watched as he pulled out a grease-stained tobacco pouch and flipped the stud catch with his thumbnail.

'Yer seem ter know a lot about Robert's family, and the Marchants, doctor – should I call yer doctor?' she asked.

'Leo will do fine, my dear. Yes, I consider myself to be pretty well informed, but then I brought young Robert into the world and, after all, I am the village doctor. It's hard to keep any secrets out of the endless rounds of gossip in our tight little community,' he said with a wry smile.

'Sounds like where I live in Bermon'sey,' Connie replied.

She watched with interest as Leo packed the bowl of his pipe with dark stringy tobacco. There was something about the man she found fascinating. He seemed to find it very easy to talk to her and his manner was very charming. He reminded her of an actor delivering well-rehearsed lines. He did not stutter or pause, and the way he moved his hands was almost theatrical. He lit the briar carefully and when he was satisfied he leant back and glanced up at the evening sky.

'Do you want to go back, young Connie?' he asked.

She shook her head. 'No, it's peaceful 'ere. I dare say Robert 'asn't even missed me yet.'

Leo chuckled. 'I take it you two intend to get married soon?'

'We're gonna wait, Leo. I want us ter get married as soon as possible, but Robert finks we should wait, what wiv 'im bein' a pilot.'

Leo puffed out a cloud of smoke and studied the glowing bowl. 'I'm afraid we're living in a dark age, my dear. The whole world seems to have become one gigantic lunatic asylum. Too many young lives are being thrown away.' He sighed and seemed to think for a moment. 'Anyway, enough of the war,' he said dismissively. 'Now where exactly did you say you live?'

'Bermon'sey. It's near the docks.'

'Oh, I know where Bermondsey is. I spent my younger days in Stepney. I did my medical training at the London Hospital in the Whitechapel Road. You might call me a lapsed Cockney – or a talkative old fogey.'

Connie touched his arm. 'I find yer very nice. After all, yer did save me from our Eunice an' those ovver two ole ladies.'

'And we mustn't forget the Reverend Jones,' he said with a comical frown.

'Are yer married, Leo?' she asked suddenly.

The doctor's eyes widened as he stared in the direction of the large rose bush. 'My wife died more than five years ago.'

'I'm very sorry, I shouldn't 'ave asked.'

'It's quite all right. It's an innocent enough question, after all,' he said with a smile. 'As a matter of fact my wife is buried in the village churchyard. She came from this village. We met in London many years ago and I came here for the wedding. It was to be a brief stay but I never left. Yes, I've lived in Kelstowe ever since.'

Connie glanced at him and watched his white hair moving in the gentle breeze. He suddenly seemed a sad figure, resigned to loneliness and memories. He must have really loved his wife and be missing her terribly, she thought. It showed in his eyes. The rose bush moved as the breeze freshened and she gave a little shiver.

'Come along, Connie. We don't want you catching cold while you're in the care of the village doctor, do we?' he said with a chuckle.

As they walked back into the house Robert came over and put his arm around her slim waist. 'I was getting anxious,' he said. 'I thought our doctor had spirited you away.'

Leo laughed. 'Twenty years ago and you would have had a fight on your hands, young whippersnapper. I've been known to resort to fisticuffs in honour of the prettiest girl in the room.'

'Why fank you, dear sir,' Connie laughed, and she planted a kiss on the old man's cheek.

'Careful, Robbie lad,' Leo whispered. 'I can see the major's on his way over.'

Clarence Marchant held a filled glass in each hand as he staggered up to them. 'I'm afraid the "War Department" has had to leave, Robert,' he slurred. 'She's taking our Eunice home. Nasty touch of migraine I fear.'

'You be careful with those drinks, Clarence,' the doctor said. 'Remember that ulcer of yours.'

The major gave the doctor a lopsided grin as he staggered off to find Gwen Waverley and Robert winked knowingly at Leo.

'Connie and I are going to take our leave now,' Robert said to the doctor. 'Thanks for taking care of her. I'll be in touch.'

The men shook hands warmly and Connie planted another kiss on the old man's rough cheek. The two passed amongst the guests and as they moved out into the hallway Robert's parents said their goodbyes. Connie could see the anxiety in Claudette's eyes as she hugged her son.

As Peter Armitage clasped Robert's hand Claudette turned to Connie. 'I can see that Robert is happy, and that makes us happy, too.'

Connie drew back a biting reply. Instead she stared hard at the woman and said quietly, 'Goodbye, Mrs Armitage.'

Robert took Connie's hand and they walked away towards the car. As they roared away into the gathering darkness Connie saw his parents waving from the front door. She felt light-headed and glowing inside as they sped through the country lanes. She wanted to forget that Robert would soon be back in the air and might never return. She wanted tonight to be special, one they would both remember through the days and nights ahead, however long and however lonely they might become. Her head rested on his shoulder and she closed her eyes. The shielded headlights picked out the road ahead and Robert brushed the strands of her golden hair from his face. He could feel her sweet breath on his cheek and his heart was heavy.

Chapter Twenty-Eight

The chill of an early September morning gave way to a pleasant warmth as the sun got up over the rooftops and shone down on the busy Tower Bridge Road. The market traders were already putting the finishing touches to their displays as the first of the shoppers stopped for their vegetables and fish. The beetroot lady was standing behind a pile of produce that she had boiled the night before, and Cheap Jack had tipped the final box of tuppenny items on to his already overloaded stall. In the pie shop the large containers behind the marble counter were crammed with steaming mashed potato, and crusty hot meat pies were gouged out of the baking trays. Parsley liquor bubbled in the huge copper bowl, and on the freshly scrubbed marble tables pewter pots of salt and pepper stood beside pint bottles of vinegar which had been expertly laced with spices and cloves. Soon the customers would arrive with their laden shopping baskets and bags and the women would kick off their pinching shoes as they tucked into pie and mash or a basin of stewed eels. The youngsters would arrive, too, with dinner money clutched tightly in their sweaty hands. Other children would saunter into the bustling market and casually glance under the traders' stalls and barrows in search of empty wooden boxes, whilst in the adjoining backstreets their confederates slipped out of their homes with choppers concealed under tatty jerseys to claim suitable pitches.

In the market, the traders were used to the usual Saturday morning ritual.

''Ere, mister. Finished wiv yer box?'

'No, I ain't. Now piss orf out of it.'

''Ere, mister, yer've only got a few more apples left in that box. Shall I give 'em ter yer?'

'Leave 'em where they are an' get out o' the road or you'll get knocked right up in the air if a tram comes.'

'We ain't 'urtin' nobody, mister. We only want empty boxes fer firewood.'

''Ere, take it an' piss orf.'

One or two young lads had perfected a more devious way of obtaining the empty boxes. When the shoppers were gathering thickly around a particular stall a small lad would crawl under the display and pass out boxes to an accomplice. Very often the boxes would not be empty and some woodchoppers were able to exchange apples and tomatoes for cigarette cards and glass marbles. On a good day the pennies earned would pay for a plate of pie and mash, a cheap seat in the cinema, and maybe two ounces of sticky toffees. On Saturday the seventh of September it promised to be a good day. Trade was brisk and the woodchoppers were eagerly engaged in earning their pennies. The sun shone from a cloudless blue sky and even Solly Jacobs was humming to himself as he wrapped up his customers' fresh herrings, sprats and portions of plaice in sheets of newspaper.

Joe Cooper had said goodbye to his wife Sadie that morning. She had left London to stay with her sister in Devon and, as he walked through the factory gates, he was whistling to himself. Joe went down the few steps into the dark shelter and turned on the lights. There were now enough wooden benches to accommodate the street folk and he had managed to scrounge a couple of trestle tables and a tea urn. Two toilets had been fitted and there was a cold-water tap in one corner. Beside the entrance he had placed a few buckets of sand and a stirrup pump. Joe scratched his head as he looked around. Everything seemed to be in order. He moved a few benches further away from the doorway then walked back out into the afternoon sun.

The day had gone well. Now the market traders were getting ready to pack away and children were called in to their tea as the sun began to move down in the sky. In the Bartletts' flat the wireless was switched on and lazy Hawaiian music filled the room. Connie was helping Molly to wind a skein of wool and Matthew dozed in the armchair. Helen sat darning a sock and hummed to the strains of 'Sweet Liani'. Every now and then Matthew mumbled in his sleep and Molly looked at her cousin and giggled. Suddenly the wireless crackled and went silent. Helen put down her darning and turned her head sideways. The girls heard it, too. It started as a rumble and grew into a steady drone.

'Wake yer dad, Molly,' Helen said, a frightened look on her face.

The wail of the siren and the crash of anti-aircraft guns shattered the quietness and drowned the sound of the approaching planes. People were out in the street. They could see the aircraft now and the shell bursts around them. Joe Cooper was blowing on his whistle and shouting for everyone to get under cover. People stood as though transfixed as the tight formation of bombers flew in. The sound of exploding bombs became deafening and a rising pall of black smoke filled the sky.

'It's the Surrey! The bastards are bombin' the Surrey!' old George Baker croaked, leaning on his walking stick.

People hurried through the factory gates and down into the

shelter as the sky turned black. Flames were rising hundreds of feet into the air and the roar of guns rose to a terrifying crescendo. Joe stood by the entrance and shepherded the street folk down into the darkness. He wore his steel helmet and carried a gas mask pack over his shoulder.

'C'mon, girls. Take it easy now. Mind yer step,' he said, trying to control the tremor in his voice. 'C'mon, Toby, 'old on ter Marie's arm.'

Mary Brown's husband Frank carried young Jimmy while Jane hurried along at his side. Mary held on to the protesting Clara Cosgrove. 'Now, don't worry, Clara,' she said calmly. 'It's all right in 'ere. Once we get yer settled I'll make yer a nice cuppa.'

'I told yer straight, Mary. I'd sooner stay in me own 'ome. Ain't it bleedin' all right? I was jus' standin' at me door talkin' ter Muvver Adams when I 'ears this noise. I didn't know what ter fink. Gawd 'elp us, Mary.'

George Baker's daughter helped the angry old lady down the steps and into a seat near the door. Marie Toomey was sitting nearby, her face a mask of fear, but she forced a smile in Clara's direction.

'Who's she lookin' at?' the old lady growled.

'Now c'mon luv, don't upset yerself,' Mary said, taking Clara's hands in hers. 'She's only tryin' ter be friendly.'

Clara grunted and pursed her lips tightly as she gave Marie Toomey a hard look. The shelter was packed and young children were crying as the noise of the air raid increased. Joe left the refuge and ran up the street to the warden's post. Inside the dusty shop men were manning the phones and one of them beckoned to the street warden as he entered.

'It's the Surrey, Joe! It's gettin' a terrible pastin'!'

Joe shook his head. 'That place is stacked full o' timber. The bastards 'ave picked the right target.'

'Yer tellin' me,' the man replied. 'There's a general call gone out ter the fire brigade. They're askin' fer reserves ter come in from outside o' London.'

'Christ! It mus' be bad, Bill.'

One of the men put down his phone and came over. 'I've jus' bin talkin' ter the area control. Apparently the roads are cut off down town. They said the whole place is afire. Gawd 'elp those poor bleeders. The bridges are blocked an' there's no way they can get to 'em.'

Cigarettes were passed around and Joe took a deep drag on his Goldflake. 'I fink most of our street are down in the shelter. We even got ole Clara out of 'er place. She's a cantankerous ole bitch but I fink she was glad ter get out o' the 'ouse.'

The roar of guns continued and the wardens' post shook. Plaster dust fell from the ceiling and a telephone rang. Bill Johnson picked up the receiver and his face took on a serious look.

'There's anuvver wave of bombers comin' in,' he shouted above the noise as he replaced the receiver.

They could hear the sound of fire bells and the dull thump as more explosives landed on the stricken docks. Outside the evening sky had changed to a dull red as the Surrey burned. Black smoke drifted upriver and hung like a huge storm cloud over the whole of dockland. The reflection of the roaring inferno flickered on the hanging black pall and a smell of charred wood filled the air. Joe stood in the doorway and stared up at the angry sky. It was like nothing he had ever seen before. The heavens were ragged, charred and nightmarish. From where he stood he could see the tips of the flames licking the ever-growing smoke clouds which were swiftly turning day into night. He could hear the drone becoming louder as a fresh wave of bombers approached their burning target and the explosions shook the ground beneath his feet.

Connie sat beside the Bartletts in one corner of the shelter, her arm around her cousin's shoulders. Molly was sobbing quietly as she bit on her handkerchief. 'I'm scared, Con. We'll all be killed.'

Connie pulled her closer. ''Course we won't. We're safe in 'ere. Everybody's scared though, Molly, it's only natural. 'Ere, jus' look at all their faces. Poor ole Toby looks like a little boy who's jus' bin told off. Look at ole Clara Cosgrove mumblin' to 'erself, an' Widow Pacey. See 'ow she keeps lookin' at Muvver Adams. I bet she's sayin' to 'erself, "don't you come near me". Mind you, Molly, she does smell o' cats.'

Molly had stopped crying and was bravely trying to raise a smile. The dull thud of falling bombs and the louder crash of the local guns continued. People sat white-faced, their hands clenched and their shoulders hunched as they fought their growing terror.

After what seemed to be an eternity the noise finally ceased and the street folk started to relax. Animated conversation began as everyone waited for the all-clear signal. Connie thought about Robert and the wonderful night they had spent together in the old country pub. What was he doing now? Was he up there in the clouds with the rest of his squadron? She recalled how she had pressed him into showing her the medal he won. He told her it was the Distinguished Flying Cross and she remembered how embarrassed he got when she told him how brave he was. He had said that there were many of his friends who should have got medals before him. Connie thought about Claudette and her parting words. She had seemed different somehow. Maybe she was genuinely sorry for the story she had invented and wanted to make amends, especially now that her son was going back to war. She thought about Robert's father, and how his eyes had misted when he shook hands with his son before they left. She thought about the charming and lonely old doctor who had rescued her from the twittering Waverley sisters and the drunken major. She smiled to herself when she recalled how brazen she had been when she and Robert found themselves alone in their room above the old inn. Her face became hot as she recalled standing naked in front of him as he sat on the edge of the bed looking at her with such love in his eyes, and whispering words of endearment as he explored her eager body. It had been a truly wonderful night, and one she would treasure for as long as she lived.

The long, even wail of the all clear sounded and people hurried from the musty shelter and passed out through the factory gates. The smell of burning hung in the evening air and they saw the terrible result of the blitz on the Surrey Docks. The sky was stained dark red. The black smoke still rose high in the heavens and the street folk walked back to their front doors as though mesmerised. The sounds of fire bells clanging in the distance shattered the strange quietness and they knew that the war had finally reached them. People remained outside their houses and talked in low voices. Everyone knew that the afternoon raid was only the beginning. The terror would go on and it would get worse, and the knowledge seemed to draw the folk together. People passed around cups of tea as they stood in the street and Joe Cooper walked the length of the turning chatting to everyone. He felt pleased that Sadie had got away from London just in time. He saw the Bartletts standing by the dwellings, looking up into the sky, and he went over to them.

'You lot okay?' he asked.

Helen nodded and Matthew turned towards him. 'They say it's the Surrey Docks got it, Joe.'

The warden nodded and turned his attention to the two young women. 'What about you two? Yer wasn't frightened, was yer?' he grinned.

Connie pulled a face. 'I was.'

'So was I,' Molly said. 'I couldn't stop shakin'.'

Joe was staring at Connie. 'I expect you're worried about young Robert, luv.'

'Yeah. I 'ope 'e's all right,' she replied, returning his stare.

Joe put his arm on her shoulder. ''E's okay, luv, take it from me. I got ter know 'im pretty well when 'e was at the factory. 'E's a good 'un. 'E can look after 'imself.'

As Joe walked away Matthew turned to Helen. ''E's a strange bloke is Joe,' he said.

Helen looked pensive. 'I tell yer what. 'E's a lonely man.'

The Saturday evening sky was blood red as the German air force returned in strength. They flew up the Thames Estuary, guided by the still raging fires and made for the docks, wharves and railways. Bombs fell all over dockland and the surrounding boroughs. Factories and warehouses burned, and some little backstreets were smashed into rubble. Fire engines raced to roaring blazes, only to find that water mains had burst. Buildings fell on the tenders and hoses were cut and buried beneath tons of bricks and rubble. Rescuers toiled desperately to free people buried under the ruins of their homes, and ambulances and stretcher cars ferried hundreds of casualties to the nearby hospitals. Only the severely injured were taken to the wards. The rest of the wounded were placed in corridors, store rooms and any other space that could be made available. The Ironmonger Street folk huddled together in the factory shelter, their faces white with fear as bombs screamed down and anti-aircraft guns opened up with an ear-shattering clatter. Shrapnel fell into the yard and a thick metal nose-cone bounced over the cobbles and came to rest near the shelter entrance.

Joe Cooper and Frank Brown stood talking inside the refuge.

'The ole cow wouldn't move, Joe. Our Mary pleaded wiv 'er but she was adamant. She said she'd 'ad enough o' the shelter fer one day. What can yer do though? I mean yer can't drag 'er down 'ere, can yer?'

Joe shook his head. 'I dunno. Trouble is, them 'ouses will tumble like a pack o' cards if a bomb did land nearby. Wait till it eases off a bit an' we'll go take a look, jus' ter see if she's okay.'

Frank jerked his thumb in the direction of the Toomeys. 'Them two are 'avin' a right bull an' cow. Poor ole Toby looks like 'e's gettin' an' ear'ole bashin'.'

Marie was poking her frail-looking husband in the chest with her forefinger, her dark eyes glaring like two black coals. 'If I told yer once I told yer a fousand times about those bloody bundles o' newspapers yer got stacked up in that yard. If they catch light we'll be burned out of 'ouse an' 'ome.'

'They'll be okay, unless a bomb falls in the yard, then we'll be bombed out anyway, so it won't make much difference, will it,' Toby said with a valiant attempt at bravado.

'Don't yer get saucy wiv me, Toby. A bleedin' spark could set them bundles alight. Yer should 'ave took 'em round the bleedin' paper sorters weeks ago.'

Toby's face took on a look of resignation. 'I s'pose yer right, luv, but . . .'

'But nufink. You're just a lazy ole bastard. If it wasn't fer our Lil bringin' in a few bob we'd all starve. I fink it's about time yer got off yer lazy arse an' started earnin' some money.'

The Widow Pacey was sitting nearby and she suddenly turned towards Marie. 'Oi, you!' she shouted out. 'Why don't yer shut yer trap! It's bad enough we've all gotta sit down 'ere, wivvout you makin' it worse.'

Marie Toomey's eyes blazed as she faced the bagwash lady. 'An' what's it got ter do wiv you? If I wanna row wiv me ole man I'll row wiv 'im whenever I like, so put that in yer pipe an' smoke it!'

Widow Pacey leaned forward in a threatening manner, arms folded over her ample bosom. 'When my ole man was alive 'e'd 'ave smacked me round the jaw if I'd talked to 'im like you're talkin' to your ole man.'

'Maybe your ole man wasn't a lazy good fer nufink like 'im, so there.'

Toby's tired eyes flitted from one to the other and he shifted uncomfortably on the hard wooden bench. 'Now don't start arguin', Marie,' he whispered.

'Start arguin'. Who's arguin'? I'm jus' tellin' a few 'ome truths. Anyway, who told you ter butt in?'

'Yer ought ter give 'er a good 'idin',' the bagwash lady growled at Toby. 'That might keep 'er quiet fer a bit.'

Marie's face went purple and she pointed aggressively at Widow Pacey. 'If yer don't shut yer cake 'ole I'll shut it for yer!'

The big woman stood up on her feet and squared up with her fists. 'C'mon then, if yer fink you're up to it!'

Folk sitting around jumped up to get a better view, the bombs and the danger forgotten as they jostled for position. Joe and Frank pushed their way towards the circling women and stood between them.

'What's the matter wiv you two?' Joe said sternly. 'Ain't it bad enough the bloody Germans are knockin' the life out of us wivvout you two silly mares tryin' ter do it for 'em. Now sit down an' be'ave yerselves, or I'll chuck yer both out o' the shelter.'

Toby slumped down in his seat. Maybe ole bagwash Pacey is right, he thought. Maybe I should give Marie a pasting. I don't know though. Maybe it would be better to put some rat poison in her food. Just think, she'd be rolling all over the floor screaming out for help and I could say, 'die, you silly mare, die'. Trouble is, they'd string me up for murder. Perhaps it would be better to put a match to those bundles of newspapers when she's asleep and then just disappear. It's worth thinking about, he mused.

The night wore on, with brief periods of quiet between the thunder of the guns and the rolling explosions. The street folk tried to catch some sleep as they sat on the hard benches, their backs propped against the damp walls. Young children nestled against their mothers and babies slept fitfully as the guns opened up and more bombs fell. The cramped shelter became unbearably stuffy but when one of the men rolled up the gas blanket to let in some air the noise that carried into the refuge was loud enough to wake the babies and young children. Outside the shelter entrance, beneath a concrete canopy, Joe Cooper stood talking to some of the men. They could see flames and black smoke rising over the rooftops and the lightning-white flashes of the heavy guns lit up the empty street. At number twenty Clara Cosgrove slept on and, in a few of the ground floor flats in Jubilee Dwellings, some of the street folk were huddling together white-faced and trembling.

With the merciful dawn came the all-clear siren and tired, jaded folk walked wearily out through the factory gates, thankful that their homes were still intact, apart from a few broken windows and dislodged slates. The street folk brewed tea and listened to the wireless broadcasts. They heard of the carnage wrought during the night and the many casualties which were flooding into the hospitals. They heard the call for blood donors, and later in the morning many people went to the church; for some of them it was the first time they had gone in many a long year.

Chapter Twenty-Nine

The London blitz had been raging nightly for nearly three weeks. Bombs had fallen in the Tower Bridge Road and on the Tooley Street wharves, and one little Bermondsey backstreet had been almost destroyed by a landmine. Factories had been burned to the ground by fire bombs and the local gas works had been badly damaged. Lack of sleep and the constant strain of being under attack was taking its toll. People were becoming upset and nervous as they thought of yet another night with little, if any, sleep.

Most of the Ironmonger Street folk hurried home each night, had their tea and made for the factory shelter before the air raids started. Even Clara Cosgrove had decided reluctantly that it was probably safer than staying in her home. Every night the street dwellers rested uncomfortably on the hard benches and fell asleep where they sat, despite the noise of the blitz. Joe Cooper had organised a team of fire watchers and they took turns to keep an eye on their street. Mary Brown and some of the women organised a tea counter where a mug of tea could be bought for tuppence. The strain of shelter life was beginning to show and there were minor rows and disagreements. In an attempt to calm the atmosphere Lizzie Conroy and Ada Halliday led a nightly sing-song, with Bill Richards accompanying the singers on his ukulele. Lizzie had a strong voice and Ada could reach the high notes. The two plump, middle-aged women managed to get a good response, with a few of the folk volunteering to do a solo turn of their own. The nightly sing-songs became more melodious when Lizzie's husband brought his harmonica to the concert and one old man rattled out the tunes on a pair of dinner spoons.

For the Bartletts, shelter life brought added problems. Molly's health was beginning to suffer. Sitting for hours on the hard bench was agonising, and her breathing began to be affected by the stuffy confinement. Helen had talked to Matthew about Molly's condition and they both decided that if the raids continued Helen would try to get herself and Molly out of London. Connie was still working at the Dolphin most nights, although the pub shut early. She would hurry to the shelter at closing time and on occasions she was forced to run through the streets after the air-raid siren had sounded. Helen wanted her to leave the job, but Connie insisted that the work stopped her brooding about Robert's safety. The evening work tired her out and she usually fell asleep where she sat, even during the heaviest of raids. Only one of the shelter people never went to sleep. Widow Pacey sat in a corner, her arms folded and her eyes staring into space. She never nodded off even once and people marvelled at her resilience. Every Monday morning Mrs Pacey made two or three trips to the laundry with bags of washing piled high on her old pram, and then she made another collection on Wednesdays. People began to look at the big woman in a new light, and they admired her for the way she had stood up to the vociferous Marie Toomey.

It was Monday morning and after three weeks' of shelter life Connie felt exhausted as she settled down to work at her bench. The factory had been damaged by blast the night before. Tarpaulins had been put up to cover a hole in the wall and broken glass had been swept into one corner. The ground floor was underwater from a burst main, and there was a film of white dust over the tables and machines. All the girls looked tired and jaded as they worked, cutting the leather or glueing pieces together. The girls who operated the stitching machines were watched closely by the forelady who was terrified lest one of the girls should fall asleep and have a serious accident. Most of the work was for a government contract to produce leather holsters and binocular cases, as well as document holders and instrument containers. Posters were displayed on the walls of the factory, urging workers to toil for victory and to remember that their jobs were vital to the war effort. This morning none of the workers was paying too much attention to the posters. One or two of the girls had left their shelters to find their homes in ruins and a few tears were shed as they related their horror at being homeless and having to face the immediate future in rest centres.

It was almost midday when the serious-faced forelady came up to Connie. 'Come with me, luv. The manager wants ter see yer,' she said quietly.

Connie followed the forelady out of the workshop and along the corridor to an office which had a sheet of cardboard nailed over the damaged door glass. When she entered the room Connie was shocked to see Alice Jones standing beside the manager's desk. The forelady left and the manager got up. 'I'll see if I can get you a cup of tea,' he said, making a quick exit.

'Sit down, Connie,' Miss Jones said, taking her arm and guiding her to a chair.

'What is it!? Is it Robert!?' Connie blurted out.

Alice stood beside the chair and put her hand on Connie's shoulder.

'Peter Armitage phoned me this morning, Con. He asked me if I would come along to see you.'

'Why!? What's wrong!?'

'I'm terribly sorry but Robert's been reported missing in action.'

Connie buried her head in the woman's stomach and sobbed bitterly. 'No! It can't be! 'E can't die an' leave me! 'E can't!'

Alice stroked the young woman's hair and could feel her whole body shaking violently.

The forelady came into the room with a cup of tea. 'See if she'll drink this. I've put something in it,' she whispered.

Alice handed Connie a handkerchief. 'Dry your eyes, dear. Drink this tea, it'll make you feel better. C'mon now.'

Connie sipped the tea, tears of grief falling into the cup. Her eyes looked up appealingly to the older woman. 'When? When did it 'appen?'

'Someone from the squadron came to see Peter early this morning. I think it was the commanding officer. Robert's plane crashed into the Channel last night. One of the pilots saw his plane go down. He never got out, Con.'

Connie's face was deathly white and she stared at the floor as though in a trance. The cup shook in her hands and Alice took it from her.

'C'mon, let's get you home,' she said softly.

The Bartletts had finished their tea and they sat in silence. Molly had gone to her bedroom and Matthew was staring into the empty grate. Helen's hands shook as she tried to thread a needle and after a while she gave up. She rose and went into the kitchen where she stared at the dirty cups and plates for a few seconds before returning to the front room.

Matthew looked up as she came in. 'Shall I go up an' see if she's all right?' he asked her.

Helen shook her head. 'I've bin up twice. She's jus' lyin' there on the bed. I can't get a word out of 'er. The poor cow was sobbin' 'er 'eart out.'

Matthew sighed deeply. 'One of us'll 'ave ter go up before long. We can't leave 'er in the flat all night. We'll 'ave ter get 'er ter the shelter some'ow.'

Helen sat down and looked up at the clock. 'You go up, Matt. Maybe she'll take notice o' you.'

Matthew climbed the flight of stairs and let himself into the flat. Connie was lying sprawled across the bed, her face buried in the pillow. Gently he put his hands on her shoulders and she turned on her side. He could see her tear-stained face and red eyes as she stared up at him.

'Why, Matt? Why should Robert 'ave ter die? We was so 'appy. Why should it be 'im?'

'I don't know, Connie. All I know is, there's lots o' brave fellas givin' their lives in this war. Fellas jus' like your Robert. I know it's 'ard, luv, but yer've gotta be brave. 'E was brave, an' 'e would want yer ter be brave, too. C'mon now, luv. Wash yer face an' we'll all go over the shelter tergevver.'

'I can't, Matt. I wanna stay 'ere ternight.'

'Now listen, girl. Yer can't stop in these buildin's all night. Put some water on yer face an' come down to us. We'll wait fer yer.'

'You go over the shelter. I'm gonna stay 'ere.'

'Well if yer determined ter stay 'ere ternight we'll all stay wiv yer. We're not leavin' yer alone.'

Connie slipped her feet over the bed and sat hunched, her head buried in her hands.

Matthew touched her gently on the top of her head. 'C'mon, luv. We'll go down tergevver. C'mon, take me arm.'

* * *

The siren sounded early that night and the air raid was a particularly bad one. A bomb fell in John Street and demolished a row of houses. The Horseshoe public house was flattened and some of the shops in Tower Bridge Road had their fronts blown out. Bad fires started in the wharves and docks, and a fire bomb landed on the derelict oilshop on the corner of Ironmonger Street. Joe Cooper and Frank Brown roused the rest of the fire watchers and they raced to the burning shop.

'It's 'opeless!' Joe shouted as he dashed into the wardens' post opposite. 'The oilshop's alight!' he screamed above the noise of the guns.

'We've already reported it, Joe. Gawd knows 'ow long it'll take 'em ter get 'ere. Control's told us 'alf o' London's burnin' ternight.'

Joe ran back to the others. 'Let's get back under cover. They've phoned the fire brigade. If that fire spreads ter the buildin's we're in trouble.'

As the men ran back down the little turning they could hear the sounds of falling shrapnel and glass shattering. They stood and watched from the shelter entrance and eventually the fire tender arrived and firemen began to play their hoses on the shop and adjoining barrow sheds.

'It looks like the buildin's are okay. Let's get a cuppa while we've got a chance,' Frank shouted.

Inside the stuffy shelter the grimy-faced men stood by the urn, mugs of steaming tea held in their shaking hands.

Mary Brown came over to Joe and whispered, 'Young Connie Morgan's in a terrible state. 'Elen told me the girl's fella got killed in action.'

Joe looked over and saw Connie sitting next to Molly. The two girls were holding hands in silence, their eyes staring ahead. 'Gawd 'elp us!' he groaned. 'What a bloody shame. I was only talkin' to 'er the ovver day. She was worried out of 'er life then. What a bloody shame.'

Mary took his empty cup and dropped it into a bowl of water. 'I dunno where it's all gonna end, Joe. Jus' look at 'em sittin' there. Look at their faces. The old 'uns can't stand much more o' this, an' there's the kids. It ain't right fer 'em ter be stuck down 'ere night after night.'

Joe put his hand on her arm. 'The old 'uns can take it, Mary. They're made of iron, an' the kids'll be all right too. The way I see it, we've got some sort o' chance down 'ere, barrin' a direct 'it. Is there anuvver cuppa in that urn?'

The bombers had gone and the first light of day showed over the rooftops. Joe Cooper roused himself and stretched to ease his aching back. People around him were in various positions of fitful sleep and he noticed Clara Cosgrove had her head in her chest and was snoring loudly. As he glanced around he saw that Connie Morgan was sitting upright, her hands clasped in her lap and her eyes staring ahead. Molly sat next to Connie with her head resting on the Morgan girl's shoulder and she was sleeping soundly. Both Helen and Matthew were fast asleep where they sat.

Joe walked over and crouched down in front of Connie. 'You all right, luv?' he asked softly.

She nodded and continued to stare blankly. Joe could see how pale and drawn she was and he reached out and touched her clasped hands. 'Yer've gotta bear up, girl. Yer gotta face it, no matter what. I wish there was somefink I could say ter ease the pain, but I can't. Nobody can. All I know is, time's the greatest 'ealer. The pain will ease in time, believe me, girl.'

Connie's angry eyes met his. 'Robert's gone. I'll never see

341

'im again. You don't know 'ow much it 'urts, nobody does, so jus' leave me alone.'

Joe stood up and looked down on her grief-stricken face. 'Okay, Con. I'll leave yer alone, but jus' one fing though. There's a lot o' folk sufferin' like you. There's a lot o' loved ones bein' grieved over – an' grievin' – an' I tell yer somefink else. I lost someone once. It was someone I was very close to, an' I suffered jus' like you are now. I know 'ow yer feel, luv, so bear that in mind if yer want somebody ter talk to, okay?'

Connie's eyes filled with tears and she forced a brave smile. 'Okay, Joe.'

The wail of the all clear sounded and the weary Ironmonger Street folk emerged from the shelter to see the blackened shell that was once Jerry Martin's oilshop. The stench of charred timbers and scorched bricks filled the little turning. Fire hoses were still attached to the hydrant and two tired firemen sprayed jets of water on the smouldering ruins. Windows had been damaged and broken glass was scattered over the pavements, and overhead the morning sky was copper-coloured and darkened with smoke.

It was mid afternoon when the well-dressed figure climbed the four flights of stairs and knocked on the front door. Connie ignored the knock and continued to stare into the fireplace. When the knock was repeated she got up reluctantly and opened the door.

'I'm sorry, I was . . .' she began.

He had stepped over the threshold and removed his homburg, his sad eyes looking into hers. Without a word she hugged him and he held his comforting arms around her sobbing shoulders.

'I wanted to come. I know how you must be feeling, Connie. We loved him too,' he said.

Peter Armitage closed the door behind him and they walked into the front room. Connie composed herself and went into the scullery to make some tea. She came back with two cups on a tray and they sat talking quietly, each glad of the other's company.

'Claudette is in a terrible state,' Peter said. 'Doctor Spanswick has given her a strong sedative and I've got someone to sit with her for a while.'

They sipped their tea in silence, and then Connie said, 'Fanks fer sendin' Miss Jones round. When I saw 'er in that office I knew she'd come about Robert.'

'It was the least I could do,' he said. 'I'd promised my son that if anything happened to him I would get the news to you. It was the way he wanted it. I would have come earlier but Claudette . . .' His eyes filled and he choked back the tears. 'Robert's commanding officer told us he was awarded a bar to his DFC. We're very proud of him, and I know you are, too.'

Connie looked away from the bowed figure and stared at the small black box lying on the table. 'Is that Robert's medal?'

He nodded. 'I'd like you to have it.'

She shook her head. 'No, I couldn't. You keep it. I've got enough memories ter last me the rest o' me life. It's only right you should keep it.'

He picked up the box and slipped it into his coat pocket. 'You must come to see us soon. I'm sure Claudette would like that. I would, too.'

She showed him to the door and kissed his cold cheek as he stepped out on to the landing. 'I will come ter see yer both, Peter. Fanks fer comin' round.'

She stood on the cold landing and watched the sad figure disappear down the wooden stairs. Maybe one day, Peter, she thought. One day, when it doesn't hurt so much.

* * *

With the darkness came the raiders, and there was no respite. Each night the bombs fell and more fires raged. Each night more stories were told in the factory refuge of friends and acquaintances who had been made homeless or who had been killed or maimed. The Ironmonger Street folk began to feel that their little turning was immune to the carnage. Every night the shelter dwellers listened to the noise of the bombs and the loud crash of the guns, and they emerged the following morning giving thanks that their little turning was still intact. The street folk who had once rallied to its defence now joked about its immunity.

'Let's be fair,' George Baker said with a smile on his lips. 'That there Field Marshall Goerin' ain't gonna waste no bombs on our street. The fifth columnists 'ave told 'im the bleedin' street's fallin' down already.'

Lizzie Conroy got angry with the cantankerous old man. 'Yer shouldn't joke like that, George. Yer'll put the bleedin' mockers on the street if yer not careful.'

'Mockers nufink,' George replied, leaning on the wall and using his walking stick to sweep a large piece of glass from the pavement. 'Yer like a bloody ole gipsy, believin' in such fings.'

'You can scoff, yer silly ole bleeder. All I'm sayin' is, yer shouldn't tempt fate.'

'I ain't temptin' nufink. What I'm sayin' is . . .'

'I can't stand 'ere talkin' ter you,' Lizzie cut in. 'I've got me ole man's tea ter get.'

George watched Lizzie's departure with a grin on his grizzled features. 'Silly ole fat-arsed cow,' he mumbled to himself.

Lizzie was about to let herself into her house when Ada Halliday walked up.

''Ello, luv,' Ada said, putting her shopping basket down at her feet and rubbing her aching back. 'I jus' bumped into Mrs Argrieves down the road. You remember 'er? 'Er what used ter live in John Street. Yer know 'er Billy copped a packet at Dunkirk.'

Lizzie pulled a face. 'Yeah. Was it bad?'

'Well, Mrs Argrieves reckons 'e 'ad a bullet lodged near the spine. They took it away all right an' 'e's walkin' again, but she said 'e's sufferin' from shell-shock. She reckons 'e's gorn a bit funny.'

'Funny? 'Ow d'yer mean, funny?'

'Well, be all accounts 'e's mumblin' to 'imself an' 'e won't keep 'imself clean. Mrs Argrieves said 'e ain't 'ad a shave fer a week, an' yer know 'ow smart 'e used ter be.'

Lizzie nodded. ''Er Billy used ter get in wiv that gamblin' crowd. They used ter play cards an' dice on the corner of John Street. The police was always tryin' ter catch 'em. Billy used ter wear some smart suits. Must 'ave cost 'im a few bob.'

Ada glanced along the turning then looked back at Lizzie. 'Accordin' to 'er, all Billy's mates clubbed tergevver an' bought 'im a complete rig-out when 'e come 'ome from the 'orspital. Yeah, shoes, ties, the lot. She said 'e looked 'is ole self fer a while. Trouble is, 'e ain't 'ad the clothes orf 'is back since. Yeah, that's right. She said 'e even sleeps in 'em. The poor bleeder's gorn right down the pan. It's a bloody worry fer 'er. I did feel sorry fer the poor ole cow when she told me.'

'That's the trouble, Ada. We don't know what those boys went through out in that Dunkirk. Some of 'em won't never be the same.'

Ada picked up her shopping basket and held her back again. 'Well, luv. I must be orf. I don't wanna be late down the shelter ternight. I left it late last night an' those bleedin' Toomeys nicked me place.'

Lizzie took her foot from her doorstep. ''Ere, Ada. Before yer go. Don't that Morgan girl look ill. I 'ardly reco'nised 'er when I see 'er the ovver day.'

'Well it's only natural, ain't it. She was goin' wiv that fella fer some time. 'E seemed such a nice chap. Always very polite when 'e see yer out. It's a bleedin' shame. All right, 'e wasn't one of us, but she thought the world of 'im. You could tell that when yer see 'em out tergevver.'

Lizzie nodded. 'Ain't she gettin' like 'er muvver in looks? I fink she's the spittin' image of 'er.'

'Well I 'ope she don't take after 'er muvver, Lizzie. That Kate Morgan did love the fellas.'

Lizzie grinned. 'Don't we all? Chance would be a fine fing, what wiv my ole man. If 'e caught me lookin' at anuvver fella 'e'd kill me, I know 'e would.'

Ada changed her shopping bag over from one hand to the other. 'Oh well, I gotta go. I got a couple o' pigs' trotters fer me tea. I do like them with a few taters an' pease pudden. See yer down the shelter, Liz.'

'See yer, Ada.'

As dusk fell the tension grew. In Ironmonger Street the factory gates stayed open as usual and the early arrivals found their regular spot in the dimly lit shelter beneath the machine-shop of the Armitage factory. People knitted and chatted together, and some sat quietly reading. Children ran around between the wooden benches or played with their favourite toys, trying not to go too close to Widow Pacey. Mary Brown put a light under the tea urn and laid out the clean mugs. Joe Cooper arrived early and checked the fire buckets, stirrup pumps and spare sandbags. Later on that Friday evening Clara Cosgrove took her place in the shelter and, when the air-raid siren sounded and the bombs started to fall, once more Clara was already fast asleep.

Chapter Thirty

The first few days of October saw the weather turn very cold and damp. Influenza and bronchitis were rife in the docklands and many of the people in Ironmonger Street were affected. Molly Bartlett went down with a bad attack of bronchitis on the first Saturday of the month and, when Helen called in the doctor he was adamant. 'That young lady should be in bed. It's just asking for trouble her sitting up all night in that shelter.'

Helen made a decision. 'I'll stay wiv Molly an' you go over the shelter, Matt. Yer can't do anyfing 'ere.'

Matthew would have none of it. 'Yer don't fink I'd leave yer both up 'ere on yer own, do yer? I'm stayin', too. If fings get too bad I can wrap a blanket roun' the girl an' carry 'er down ter the ground floor flat. They wouldn't mind.'

Helen knew she would get nowhere arguing with him and, as she stood over the gas stove stirring a pot of soup for Molly, she worried for her daughter, and she thought of Connie who had returned to her job at the Dolphin. The raids were starting earlier now and Helen feared that her niece was cutting it a bit fine leaving the pub almost at closing time. She sighed deeply and said a silent prayer that they would be spared the bombing for just one night.

Connie found herself very busy on that Saturday evening. She preferred it that way, for the work and the noisy atmosphere prevented her from brooding too much over her tragic loss.

It was getting near to closing time when Dora French came into the public bar. 'I thought yer'd be gone by now, Con. Yer better be on yer way, just in case the siren goes early.'

Connie bid the French family goodnight and hurried from the pub. As she walked out into the Old Kent Road she took a torch from her handbag and shone the dim light down on the pavement. She thought about the Bartletts having to stay in the buildings all night instead of the shelter. She had offered to stay with her cousin but Helen would not hear of it. Maybe the siren wouldn't sound tonight, Connie thought as she picked her way carefully through the darkness. Wouldn't it be nice to curl up in bed just for one night and sleep undisturbed until morning?

She had just reached the Bricklayers Arms junction when the siren wailed out its mournful sound. Connie hurried on as the drone of aircraft became louder and flashes of gunfire lit the night sky. As she ran along the Tower Bridge Road and turned off into the backstreets the drone sounded directly overhead. The scream of falling bombs sent her scurrying into a doorway and she felt the hot blast of air rush past her as a bomb fell a few streets away. Shattered glass tinkled on to the pavements and cobblestones as Connie pressed herself into the doorway. More bombs exploded nearby and she shook with terror. The crash of guns made her clasp her ears and grit her teeth as she left the doorway and ran as fast as she could into Ironmonger Street. Pieces of red-hot shrapnel landed all around her and the factory gates seemed a mile away as she heard the scream of a falling bomb. She was thrown headlong into the gutter by the blast, the flash of the explosion momentarily blinding her. She picked herself up painfully, her head pounding, and she could see the rising flames coming from the damaged gas main in John Street. She heard running footsteps and, as Joe Cooper reached her, Connie lost consciousness.

The street was lit by red lamps and the clean cobblestones were shining in the phosphorescent glow. Connie walked in silence beside the shadowy figure of her mother. The turning was empty and the houses were in darkness. They stopped beside a door and her mother reached out for the iron knocker. Connie could see the tears on her face as the door opened and she stepped over the threshold. The young girl wanted to follow but she was rooted to the spot. She tried to hold out her arms but they were pinned to her sides. Her mother was slowly disappearing from sight and the door started to close. Connie was alone in the turning. She seemed to be drifting along and the light changed to a bright blue. It was cold and she wanted to get far away. She began to run but the street moved with her. Her breath came in gasps and suddenly she screamed. Hands were bearing down on her, squeezing the remaining breath from her body. She fought until there was no more strength left, and she saw the faces staring down at her.

'Connie! Connie! C'mon now, girl. It's all right.'

Her eyes opened wide and Connie saw Joe and Frank bending over her. She was lying on her back in the shelter and she could see the familiar trail of conduit tubing which ran the length of the ceiling. Mary was cradling her head and people were standing around, their faces all looking serious.

Joe stared down at her. 'It's okay, girl. Yer fainted when we got ter yer. The blast must 'ave concussed yer. You'll be all right. Jus' stay quiet fer a while.'

Connie looked up into Joe's large brown eyes and felt comforted. His wide friendly face was split in a relieved grin and she could see the deep lines that spread out from the corners of his eyes.

'Yer gave us a scare, girl. What was yer doin' out there? Yer should 'ave bin in the shelter long ago.'

Connie attempted a sheepish grin and winced as the pain in her head increased with the rush of blood as she sat up slowly. 'I left it a bit late leavin' the pub. I thought I'd 'ave enough time before the raid started,' she said in a faint voice.

'You're a daft 'ap'orth,' Joe laughed with an exaggerated shake of his head.

There was a short lull in the bombing and people had started to chat together. Connie sat in a corner, a mug of hot tea clasped in her still shaking hands. Mary sat beside her whilst nearby her two young children were listening to Frank as he read them a story.

'You okay now, Con?' Mary asked.

Connie nodded. 'I was scared, Mary. I thought the world was fallin' in on me.'

Mary grinned. 'Yer was strugglin' like a good 'un when Joe carried yer in the shelter. I thought yer was 'avin' a fit.'

'I was 'avin' a terrible dream,' Connie said shivering. 'It was more like a nightmare. I could see me mum but she was leavin' me an' I couldn't get to 'er. It was really 'orrible.'

Mary patted the young woman's hand. 'Drink yer tea, luv, it'll do yer good. Yer've 'ad a nasty shock.'

Connie looked up at Mary. 'I wonder 'ow me aunt an' uncle an' Molly are gettin' on? They mus' be frightened up in them buildin's on their own.'

'They'll be okay. Now drink that tea,' Mary urged her with a note of authority in her voice.

The bombs had started to fall again, and the shelter seemed to shake to its foundations. The gas blanket rustled and dust blew in. People had lapsed into silence, each alone with their secret fears. Strings of plaster dust fell from the ceiling and with every explosion the electric lights dimmed. Joe and some of the men got out the kerosene lamps and began to prime them while Mary poured more water into the tea urn. Lizzie and Ada were trying to get a sing-song going but there was little support, and the strains of the harmonica were swallowed up by the increasing noise from outside. People sat rigid with fear and some of the children started to cry as they were awakened from fitful sleep. More dust and paint flakes fell from the ceiling and the smell of carbolic coming from the toilets hung in the stuffy air.

It was after midnight when the clattering started. Joe cast his eyes up to the ceiling and clenched his fists tightly. It sounded to him as though someone with immense strength was violently shaking a sheet of corrugated iron. It seemed to last for ever and grow into a deep rumble, and then the blast from the explosion threw everyone on to the floor. People were screaming as the lights failed, and in the panic that followed some folk found themselves being trampled on. Joe picked himself up and struggled to the doorway. As he reached the yard, the sight which met his eyes made him recoil in sheer horror. There was a great gap in the buildings. Dust was still rising into clouds of white in the sudden unearthly silence. Half of Jubilee Dwellings had been reduced to a great pile of rubble. Joe could see the exposed fireplaces and the pieces of furniture balanced precariously on the remaining flooring. The part of the dwellings which was still standing had had all the windows blown out and most of the roof tiles dislodged. For a few seconds Joe stood rooted to the spot. He stared in disbelief, not knowing what he should do. As the rest of the men struggled to their feet they stood beside him and stared up at the devastation.

Joe suddenly came to his senses. 'Quick! Somebody get ter

the wardens' post fer Gawd sake!' he shouted. 'There's people buried under that lot!'

Guns were still screaming out and bombs were falling as Bill Richards ran along the street. Inside the post there was pandemonium. All the lines had gone dead. Without hesitation he ran back into the street and headed for the Tower Bridge Road. The streets were illuminated by fires which were burning everywhere and here and there jets of water shot high into the air from damaged mains and hydrants. Half a mile along the main thoroughfare he found the area wardens' post and staggered in gasping for breath.

'Jubilee Dwellin's!' he blurted out. 'They've copped it! There's people buried there.'

The fire watchers of Ironmonger Street had begun burrowing into the rubble and now and then they stopped, listening for sounds of life. Timbers were gently prised loose and huge chunks of brickwork were eased aside as the digging went on. It was almost an hour later when the lorry drove into the turning and men from the Heavy Rescue Squad rushed to help.

Joe pointed to the tunnel they had made. 'There was a sound come from down there a little while ago, but it's gone quiet now,' he said, his face a white mask.

'Take a breather, mate. We'll carry on diggin',' one of the rescuers said gently.

Joe sat down on the kerb beside Mary Brown's husband. 'I can't stop shakin', Frank. It's the first night the Bartletts 'ave stopped in the buildin's. I feel so bloody useless.'

'We done all we could, Joe. We've jus' gotta wait now.'

It was under a dawn sky when the first body was brought out. Joe slid back the blanket and saw that it was Molly Bartlett. The man holding the rear of the stretcher shook his head slowly. Soon after the body of Matthew Bartlett was dragged from under a wall of bricks. Joe Cooper's face was ashen as he pulled back the blanket to identify the body. Tears of frustration and anger fell down his blackened face as he screwed up his eyes and slumped down heavily on a pile of rubble.

'That's two of 'em gone, an' the poor sod's wife is still under that lot,' he groaned, staring at the two stretchers lying side by side in the middle of the street.

There was a sudden call for silence. The rescuers stopped digging and crowded around the shored-up tunnel. Joe picked himself up and hurried over to the men. He saw their leader standing by the tunnel, his head held sideways and a stern look on his dust-streaked features. They could all hear it now. It sounded like a mournful whine coming from far away. The sound made Joe's flesh creep and he gazed helplessly at the rescuer beside him. The man rested his large hand on the warden's shoulder and motioned to the shelter.

'We'll call yer when we reach whoever it is. Yer can 'elp us by tryin' ter find out 'ow many are likely ter be under the rubble,' he said.

'I can tell yer that now, mate,' Joe replied. 'Most of the people who used ter stay on the ground floor got scared and started usin' the shelter in the factory a few nights ago. There's only a woman by the name o' Bartlett, a Mr and Mrs Riley, an' an ole woman called 'Awkins. They're the only ones unaccounted for.'

The man nodded. 'All right then, we'll give yer a shout soon as we can.'

Joe watched as one of the rescuers slid down into the tunnel. Another man followed him in and the rest of the men stood quietly waiting. The street warden turned towards the factory gates. His heart went out to the grief-stricken young woman who sat alone in the shelter, and silent tears ran down his gaunt face. How much more grief was the girl expected to suffer?

The all clear had sounded and exhausted, ashen-faced folk had emerged from their refuge to stand horrified at the sight of the stricken dwellings. They watched silently as the sun rose up over the chimney pots and they shivered in the cold sunlight as the ambulance drove back into the street. The shocked street folk caught their breath as a stretcher was carried down from the rubble. They could see old Mrs Hawkins, her head swathed in bandages, waving her hands in protest. 'I can walk, sod yer! Put me down I tell yer!'

'It's okay, Ma. Jus' lie quiet. You'll be all right,' the rescuer said as he held her shoulder.

Another stretcher was rushed up to the tunnel, and soon they carried Helen Bartlett down. A doctor clambered along beside the stretcher, his small black bag held in his bloodied hand. 'Careful!' he cried out to the bearers. 'Keep the stretcher level, she's badly hurt.'

Joe trailed along behind them, his eyes lowered towards the cobblestones. He looked up as the injured Helen Bartlett was placed in the ambulance and he shook his head at the questions thrown at him. His thoughts were centred on the young Morgan girl who was being restrained back in the factory shelter. Mary Brown had broken the news to her and she had physically to hold her down with the help of Ada Halliday. Now he had the task of telling the young girl that her aunt had been brought out from the rubble barely alive.

As the red sun climbed up overhead the service began. A small wooden cross was placed on an altar of bricks, and the congregation stood throughout the sermon. Instead of a church floor beneath their feet there were only cobblestones strewn with debris, and the roof above their heads was the cloudy autumn sky. No hymns were sung and no collection boxes were passed around on that Sabbath morning. The cassocked figure stood perched on a mound of rubble, his sombre voice echoing eerily in the shattered street. He spoke of the courage of rescuers and of the forebearance of those who mourned. He raised his arms to the heavens as he asked the congregation to join him in prayers for the departed souls of the victims and he thanked God for the deliverance of the survivors. Above, the cold sun gave no heat, and as the gathering mumbled 'Amen' a new fall of rubble sent a cloud of dust rising into the air. The priest climbed down and walked sorrowfully from the turning with his head bowed. He clutched the wooden cross in his hand and held the New Testament under his arm. As he turned out of the street he heard from somewhere behind him a pitiful cry of torment.

Later the exodus began. The tenants of Jubilee Dwellings were taken to a nearby rest centre with the exception of Connie Morgan. She had been given a strong sedative and was sleeping in Ada Halliday's bed. In a little church hall a few streets away lay the bodies of Matthew and Molly Bartlett, alongside those of Annie and Alf Riley. The local hospitals were filled to overflowing and many victims of the night's bombing lay in draughty corridors or in makeshift wards. Among the casualties admitted to Guy's Hospital was Helen Bartlett. She lay in a coma, her back broken and both her legs smashed. In the locker beside her bed was a small handbag which she had been holding on to when the rescuers found her. Back in the little street that George Baker had said was invincible a pathetic stack of furniture and bits and pieces stood in a heap beside the huge pile of rubble. The part of Jubilee Dwellings which remained standing would never again be a home for the Ironmonger Street folk. Walls were showing huge cracks and all the window frames had been blown out on to the cobbles below. Chimney pots lay amongst a showering of roof slates, and a rope cordon had been thrown along the pavement beneath a crazily balanced chimney-stack which was in danger of toppling at any minute.

The street was strangely quiet on that Sunday afternoon. Mercifully, the little houses opposite Jubilee Dwellings had escaped serious damage, apart from broken windows, loosened front doors and dislodged roof slates. Plaster had fallen from the ceilings and soot filled the rooms, but the structures remained intact. Women cooked their lunches on gas stoves which were operating on half pressure and they fetched their water from a hastily erected stand-pipe at the end of the turning. The men had left the street earlier and walked sadly past the heap of rubble that was once the Horseshoe. They drank beer in unfamiliar surroundings and returned to find their dinners still not ready. The street folk took to their beds later that afternoon to catch up on sorely needed sleep and Ada Halliday, loath to awaken Connie, slumbered in her favourite armchair. Outside the wind rose and whisked spirals of brick dust along the cobblestones. At the end of the turning the Armitage factory gates remained open, and they rattled noisily on their heavy chains.

Part Three

Part Three

Chapter Thirty-One

A stocky figure with greying hair walked purposefully through the hospital gates with a young woman holding on to his arm. She wore her long blond hair tied back with a black ribbon and her once proud shoulders slumped. Her eyes were ringed with dark circles and her pretty features were pale. She started to lag and the man beside her slowed his pace as they crossed the forecourt and entered the main building. The wind had dropped and spots of rain started to fall from a leaden sky. In the distance a roll of thunder announced a coming storm. The man was silent as he guided his companion up the wide stairway and squeezed the hand which rested limply on his arm. They were stopped at the entrance to the ward by a stern-looking matron.

'I'm sorry. Visiting time finished over an hour ago.'

The girl stared blankly at her feet and the Ironmonger Street warden nodded. 'We've come ter visit Mrs 'Elen Bartlett. We were told she's on an open order.'

The matron's face relaxed a little. 'Oh I see. Are you the next of kin?'

'This 'ere young lady is. She's the only relative,' Joe said, looking at Connie.

The matron motioned to a side room. 'I'm afraid Mrs Bartlett hasn't regained consciousness yet, but you're both welcome to sit with her. Would you like a cup of tea?'

Connie swayed back on her heels and Joe gripped her arm tightly. 'The tea would go down a treat, luv.'

The elderly matron raised her eyebrows stonily and turned away, her crisp apron crackling as she walked swiftly along the dimly lit corridor.

Joe was aware of the noise his boots made on the tiled floor as he led Connie into the side room. The two looked down on the still figure and Joe caught his breath. Helen Bartlett had aged considerably since he had last seen her. Her hair was now completely white and her eyes were sunken, the dark circles around them conspicuous against the pallor of her face. Helen's breathing was very shallow and her hands were white and streaked with blue veins as they lay motionless outside the raised bedclothes. Joe turned his shocked gaze to the young woman at his side but he could see no emotion in her eyes as she looked down at her aunt. Joe eased his companion into a chair beside the bed and he drew up another seat at the other side. They sat in silence: Connie staring at her comatose relative and Joe studying his tightly clenched hands.

It seemed an age before a nurse came into the little room carrying two cups of tea. Before she left the nurse pulled the blinds and lit a green-shaded light above the bed. In the strange glow Helen's face seemed to become almost transparent and the dark circles around her eyes became more prominent. It was very quiet. From somewhere in the distance came the muted sound of a passing train, and footsteps tapped faintly along the tiled corridor outside. They had been sitting in silence for over an hour when Joe got up quickly.

'C'mon, darlin'. We can't do anyfing. Let's go 'ome.'

Connie stood up without saying anything and walked to the door, her shoulders sagging and her head bowed. Joe followed her out into the corridor and took her arm. Still Connie did not speak. She walked along as if in a trance, and her hand felt as light as a feather on his supporting arm. They walked out into the night air and at the gates Joe stopped and clasped the girl's shoulders gently.

'Now listen, kid,' he said softly. 'Yer gotta pull yerself tergevver. Yer wanted me ter bring yer 'ere, an' yer ain't said one word since we left the street. Yer can't go on bottlin' it all up. Let go, Con. Scream, shout, or 'ave a good cry, but don't go on torturin' yerself by keepin' it all inside yer.'

For a few moments Connie stared into his large brown eyes, then slowly she fell against his body. Tears fell on to Joe's collar as the young woman sobbed bitterly, her head resting against his chest. He patted her back gently and whispered encouraging words as they stood beside the huge iron gates. Presently he slipped his hand under her chin and raised her head.

'C'mon, luv. Take me 'ankey an' dry yer eyes. There's a pub just along a bit. We'll get yer a stiff drink. It'll do yer good.'

The saloon bar of the Sadlers Arms was almost empty and Joe Cooper led her to the table farthest from the counter. When Connie was seated he ordered two brandies and as she sipped hers the young woman's eyes screwed up and she gasped for breath. Joe touched her hand.

'Go on, finish it up. It'll steady yer nerves,' he said.

Connie looked at her companion. 'I'm gonna lose 'er,' she said. 'I'm gonna lose 'er jus' like I've lost everybody else who's ever meant anyfing ter me. Why, Joe? Why?'

For a second or two he could say nothing. He felt the lump rising in his throat and he swallowed hard. 'I wish I could tell yer, Connie. Gawd knows, yer've suffered more grief than anybody should 'ave to. There's nufink I can say, nor can anybody else fer that matter. No amount o' talkin' can ease yer pain, luv. All I can say is, yer not alone. Yer've got friends.

Yer've got the folk in the street. We're yer friends. Yer can always count on us, girl.'

Connie's eyes were now dry and she laughed bitterly. 'I can't afford ter get too close ter people, Joe. Not any more, I don't. There was me mum. I loved 'er dearly, even though she could never show 'er feelin's ter me until she was very ill. I really only got close to 'er when it was all too late. I lost Robert. We were gonna be married an' I lost 'im, too. Then there was Aunt 'Elen an' Uncle Matt an' Molly. They gave me all the love in the world, an' now Uncle Matt an' Molly are dead, an' Aunt 'Elen is layin' in that 'ospital wiv a broken back an' both 'er legs all smashed up. She'll die an' leave me, I know she will.'

Joe fought back the tears that came to his eyes. 'She won't die, Connie. Yer aunt's a fighter. She'll pull through, honest.'

Connie stared down at the table for a few moments and then she reached out her hand and squeezed his. 'Fanks fer bringin' me ter the 'ospital, Joe, I 'ad ter come, even though it wasn't much use.'

'Don't yer be so sure,' Joe said quietly. 'I fink yer aunt knew you were there beside 'er, even though she was unconscious. When she wakes up she'll know you came in ter see 'er, you mark my words.'

'I 'ope so. I 'ope you're right, Joe.'

With the night came the bombers. The shattered backwater behind the Tower Bridge Road was lit up as anti-aircraft guns spat out shells and explosives fell on the nearby docks, wharves and railways. The roar of battle shook the factory shelter and terrified the street folk as they huddled together and prayed for their lives. There was no relief. Throughout the long night the bombing continued and no one slept. The knowledge that their much maligned and newly ravaged little turning was still in the front line had made everyone aware that their lives could be snuffed out just like their neighbours from the Dwellings. Mary Brown was nervous as she handed out mugs of tea, and the voices of Ada Halliday and Lizzie Conroy, the shelter duo, were a little unsteady as they tried valiantly to entertain their neighbours with songs. The Toomeys were sitting unusually close together staring glumly at the floor, and Widow Pacey had taken up her usual position against the wall, her arms folded and her eyes unblinking. Outside, beneath the concrete canopy, Joe Cooper and some of the menfolk stood ready with sand buckets and stirrup pumps in case incendiary bombs fell on the little houses. They watched fearfully as the flashes of battle lit up the mountain of rubble, the ruins of the oilshop and the charred gates of the barrow sheds. They cast their eyes skywards and watched the bursting shells and the white pencils of light which searched the heavens for the enemy bombers. Tiredness and anxiety had worn down the strongest of them and, as the explosions grew louder and the guns crashed suddenly, they would start like hunted animals. As the long hours of the night dragged past the drone of aircraft would diminish and then become louder as fresh raiders appeared overhead. The sickly sweet smell of cordite and the acrid smell of burning timbers carried into the little turning. Sounds of fire bells were drowned beneath the din of battle and white-hot shrapnel fell with a clatter on the cobblestones. The factory gates rattled and more roof slates slithered down from the tops of the houses with a loud crash.

The long night finally broke into a grey dawn and as the all clear echoed through the battered Ironmonger Street the sleepless shelter dwellers emerged once more. They came up from their stuffy refuge and blinked in the early morning light. One or two crossed themselves and others were overcome with emotion as they stared at what was left of the Dwellings. Ada emerged with her arm around Connie, her grey hair piled on to the top of her head and secured with a large hat pin. Ada's buxom figure dwarfed the slim girl at her side as the two walked slowly out through the open gates of the Armitage factory. The Toomeys followed behind. Marie held on to her daughter's arm and Toby trailed in their wake. Mrs Adams followed on, eager to get home to feed her cats. Widow Pacey came out last, her features set in an expression of grim determination. It was Monday morning and she knew the bags of washing still had to be taken along to the factory in Long Lane.

Not too far away from Ironmonger Street the French family came up from their shelter in the cellar of the Dolphin to find that their little street was unscathed. Bill was confident that the cellar was a much safer place during the bombing than the shelter in the church hall. He had reinforced the ceiling with thick posts of wood and installed camp beds, and he had filled buckets with sand and water in case of emergency. Although the beer cellar was cold and damp his family could at least brew tea and heat up soup on the electric grill, and the walls were thick enough to deaden a great deal of the noise. Unlike most of the local folk, the French family slept reasonably well, even though the last few air raids had been very heavy.

When Bill opened up at lunchtime one of the first customers to walk through the door was Mrs Argrieves. Her grey hair was pulled tightly into a bun at the back of her head and there was a worried look in her pale-blue eyes. She had a cotton shawl draped loosely around her drooping shoulders and she carried her purse in her hand.

'Give us a drop o' gin, Bill,' she said. 'I'm fair done in. I ain't 'ad a wink o' sleep all night.'

Bill passed over the gin and leaned on the counter facing her. ''Ow's young Billy doin', Flo?'

Florence shook her head as she picked up the glass. ''E's

drivin' me to an early grave, Bill. All 'e does is sit around the 'ouse all day. I can't get 'im ter wash or shave, an' when I say anyfing it's wrong. Gawd knows I've tried, but it don't make a scrap o' difference. When I fink of 'ow smart 'e used ter be before they called 'im up I could cry.'

The landlord of the Dolphin shook his head. 'Yer gotta remember, Flo, the lad's bin frew it. It'll take time fer 'im ter settle. I mean, nobody knows 'ow them lads suffered at Dunkirk.'

Florence downed her gin and pulled a face. 'Christ! I needed that. I dunno about my Billy, but I fink my nerves are shattered, too.'

As other customers started to come in Mrs Argrieves ordered another gin and took it to a table near the door. She sat deep in thought, the gin untouched at her elbow. Florence was feeling sorry for herself. Hadn't she been a good wife and mother? she asked herself. And what was her reward? A husband who runs off with a flighty young girl half his age and a son who was turning into a dirty, unwashed gormless tramp! What had she done to deserve such treatment? She had gone without, just so young Billy could have the things all the rest of the kids in the street had. All right, maybe he had not had a father behind him to check him when he ran off the traces, but he should still have a little more consideration for his own mother. He was always out gambling before he was called up, always dressed like a toff and never short of a bob or two, and now look at him. A miserable young git who sleeps in his clothes and finds it too much trouble to wash and shave himself. What was going to become of him?

The gin was still standing untouched on the table when Mabel Hamilton rushed into the public bar, her round face flushed and her breath coming in short gasps. 'Fank Gawd I've found yer!' she spluttered. 'Yer better get 'ome, Flo. Young

Billy's gorn stark ravin' mad. 'E's jus' chucked the tallyman down the airey!'

Florence rose and hurried out of the pub towards her house with Mabel trying to keep up with her. 'That bastard'll drive me mad. They'll end up takin' me away in a straitjacket, I know they will,' she groaned.

Mabel waddled along behind the enraged Florence as they hurried along Salter Street. A crowd had already gathered at the end of the turning.

''Old up, there's 'is muvver,' someone shouted.

Florence could see her son standing on the steps that led up to the front door. Down in the area beside the steps a figure sat on his haunches, holding a bloodied handkerchief up to his nose.

'The stupid bastard should be locked up,' the victim shouted. 'All I said was, "Is yer muvver in? She owes two weeks". 'E 'ad no right ter get stroppy.'

Billy Argrieves stood with his feet apart at the top of the steps, his broad shoulders hunched and his fists clenched tightly. His wild dark eyes stared out from a square face covered with three days' growth of beard. His thin lips were twitching. The once smart grey suit was creased and dirty, and his brown shoes were trodden down and unlaced. His filthy shirt was unbuttoned, and his dark hair hung down over his forehead. Below him on the pavement the crowd had become quiet. One or two of the onlookers were grinning as an old lady held out her hand to the sad figure.

'You should make yer peace wiv the Lord fer what yer've done, lad,' the old woman said. 'Pray ter Jesus. Pray fer yer salvation.'

Florence had reached her front door. 'Get that prat away from 'im!' she screamed. 'She'll only make 'im worse.'

Mad Lou was ushered away reciting the gospel and Florence

looked up at her angry son. 'Ain't yer got no feelin' fer yer ole mum, boy?' she said with exasperation. 'Don't yer know what yer doin' ter me wiv yer wild ways? Now get inside, fer Gawd's sake. Can't yer see they're all laughin' at yer?'

His broad shoulders slumped and tears welled up in his handsome face. 'I told 'im yer got no money, Muvver. 'E kept all on. I clouted 'im 'cos 'e kept goin' on.'

'I only asked 'im once,' groaned the tallyman. ''E's a bloody lunatic.'

'Gawd 'elp us!' Florence mumbled. 'What 'ave I done ter deserve this?'

Billy's wild eyes turned to the tallyman. 'Shut yer trap or I'll stuff the poxy book right down yer throat!' he growled.

Florence climbed the stairs and took her son by the arm. 'Now you get yerself inside, d'yer 'ear me?'

The dishevelled figure shook himself loose. 'I ain't goin' inside till 'e pisses orf out of it,' he shouted, jerking his thumb in the direction of the tallyman.

'All right, yer scatty bleeder, I'm goin',' groaned the tally-man, picking himself up and staggering up the steps into the street.

'Walk in the way of the Lord Jesus Christ,' Mad Lou shouted from the other side of the street. 'Think not of retribution. Renounce the devil and turn the other cheek.'

The white-faced tallyman scowled. He had been thumped hard and had tumbled painfully down a flight of stone steps. The idea of going through that again was unthinkable. 'Shut yer face, yer bible-punchin' ole mare,' he mumbled at her as he staggered along the street.

Billy allowed himself to be shepherded through the front door and the crowd dispersed. The bloodied tallyman had left the street only seconds before the beat constable arrived. PC Rowley had been looking forward to finishing a quiet spell of duty when he was informed that there was trouble in Salter Street. Well it looks quiet enough, he thought as he sauntered into the turning. He could see Mad Lou sitting on the kerb reading her tattered New Testament, and a couple of kids were hopping in and out of a turning skipping rope. A few people passed him carrying shopping baskets and he noticed the bent figure of the road sweeper as he pushed his stiff-haired broom along in the gutter. The constable stopped beside a lamppost and waited until the council employee reached him.

''Ello, Bonzo,' he said, rocking backwards and forwards on his size elevens. 'What's bin goin' on round 'ere then?'

Harold Scribbins lifted his head, his doleful eyes fixing the local bobbie. There were a few things which Harold disliked. One was sweeping streets, and another was the nickname Bonzo, especially if it was being used by a tricky policeman whom he disliked intensely. 'What d'yer mean, what's bin goin' on?' he asked sullenly.

PC Rowley swayed back on his heels. 'Fisticuffs, Bonzo. A punch-up.'

The irritable road sweeper's sleepy eyes blinked slowly and the beat constable could see why the local kids had named Harold Scribbins after one of their favourite comic characters.

'I 'eard there was a set-to in the street a few minutes ago,' the policeman said.

'I ain't paid ter stand around watchin' punch-ups,' Harold said, leaning on his broom. 'I'm paid ter keep this palsy turnin' clean, which is jus' like sweepin' sand orf the beach. I tell yer, before I'm out o' the turnin' it's like I've never bin 'ere, what wiv toffee wrappers an' apple cores and Gawd knows what else. When the supervisor comes round 'e finks I've spent the time scratchin' me arse. It's a bloody unfankful job sweepin' streets, 'spesh'ly round 'ere.'

'So yer didn't see anyfink then?'

'Nope.'

'What's them spots o' blood doin' on the pavement then?' the constable asked, his eyes narrowing.

''Ow the 'ell should I know,' Harold replied. 'P'raps it's red paint, or it might be ole Percy 'avin' anuvver nose-bleed.'

'Percy?'

'Yeah, Percy Axford. 'E gets a nose-bleed every time 'is ole woman catches up wiv 'im. Anyway, I can't stand 'ere chin-waggin' all day. I've got me work ter do.'

PC Rowley watched as Harold walked away, the handle of his broom pressed against his bony shoulder. 'Bloody ole fool,' he said aloud.

'Piss orf, yer nosey bastard,' Harold said over his shoulder.

That evening Jennie French came home from work saddened by the news of Ironmonger Street and her friend's anguish.

'Yer should 'ave seen 'er, Mum,' she said, her voice full of pity. 'Connie was so upset. 'Er an' Molly was very close. The ole family was. I dunno 'ow she made it in ter work terday. 'Er flat's gone, an' all 'er fings, too. Poor cow's only got the bits she's standin' up in.'

Dora looked at her husband. 'She could live 'ere fer a while, couldn't she, Bill? She's a good worker, an' if she feels obliged we could suggest she does a couple of extra turns be'ind the bar.'

Bill nodded. 'Why not? Yer've got a few bits an' pieces yer could give 'er Jen, ain't yer, an' we could fix that attic up an' put a spare bed in the cellar.'

Jennie threw her arms around her father and planted a wet kiss on his cheek. 'Fanks, Dad. You're the bestest.'

Dora grinned at her husband's discomfort and winked knowingly at her daughter. ''E ain't so bad,' she said.

Chapter Thirty-Two

The London blitz continued unceasingly. Each night the German bombers came and left behind them vast fires burning and horrific devastation. Whole streets were destroyed, factories and warehouses were left in smoking ruins, and the toll in human lives mounted. The local hospitals were filled to overflowing, and more and more people were made homeless. Nevertheless, amongst the carnage, the street markets still flourished and the traders displayed notices on their barrows and stalls vilifying and deriding the efforts of Goering's airforce to bomb the British people into submission. Windowless shops opened up for business, the trains still ran, and buses and trams still managed to operate with numerous diversions. People went to work exhausted from lack of sleep and hurried home for an early tea before going down to their refuge for the night. Rubber ear-plugs were issued to everyone and, as bunks began to be installed in many shelters and people started to take bedclothes with them on their nightly trips, it became a little easier for some to catch a few hours' sleep whilst the bombs were falling. But other problems got worse for the shelter dwellers, with lice and skin complaints affecting even the most hygiene-conscious members of the community. Scabies hit the young badly, and special clinics were set up where sorry-looking children were methodically put into a bath of hot water and scrubbed with strong soap before being painted all over with an evil-smelling lotion which stung their sore patches and reduced many of them to tears. Sties and boils plagued everyone, and the smell of kaoline poultices became as familiar in the shelters as the reek of carbolic.

For some, the nightly blitz did not pose too many problems. The French family shelter beneath their little pub was now well equipped, and room had been made for an extra bed. Jennie had persuaded Connie Morgan to move in with the family after Jubilee Dwellings had been destroyed, and most nights she managed to talk the sad figure into giving a hand in the bar. Connie tried to force an occasional smile and chat a little to the customers, but her heart was leaden and she could hardly hide her despair. Each night Connie went to the hospital straight from working in the pub to sit with her comatose Aunt Helen. She whispered words of comfort into her ear and watched for a movement or a flicker of acknowledgement, but there was none. Helen's eyes remained closed and her features were white and stone-like. There was no living sign of pain on her hollow face, and only the cage beneath the bedclothes bore witness to her injuries.

Throughout October Connie continued her nightly vigil. The pale-faced young woman, her long blond hair tied back at the nape of her neck, leaned forward in her chair and stroked the cold, lifeless hands of her aunt, willing her to open her eyes. The nursing staff, hard pressed as they were, brought in tea and tried to talk to Connie, but she stayed silent and they soon left her alone with her grief. Each night before she left the small room at Guy's Hospital Connie bent over the still figure and gently kissed her forehead, and then she hurried back to the Dolphin in Salter Street. Sometimes she would change her route and pass the little backstreet that was once her home. The rubble from the shattered dwellings had been pushed back from the pavement and the windows and roofs of the houses had been patched up. Sometimes Connie passed one of the street dwellers and she would quickly avert her eyes, avoiding any conversation. Although the painful memories were still vivid in her mind and the very sight of the ugly little turning was distressing, the Morgan girl found herself irresistibly drawn back to the place. Something told her that she should return, that her future was linked to the street. She could not understand her feelings, nor her almost obsessive desire to go back again. There seemed to be distant voices in the dark corners of her mind which urged her on, and they frightened her.

During the latter part of October 1940 the weather was unusually mild. Folk prayed for a good old pea-souper which would bring a respite from the bombing, but it was not to be. Each night the clear black sky was full of stars, and the inevitable air-raid siren screamed out. The cellar beneath the Dolphin public house held firm, and each night Connie lay awake listening to the dull explosions and the thump of the gunfire. She felt grateful to Jennie and her parents for taking her in and giving her the opportunity of spending more time behind the bar. For the few hours she was serving she could almost forget. The customers were friendly, and she was slowly getting used to their ways and their sense of humour. Jennie had proved to be a good friend. She was constantly joking with the customers and doing her best to include her friend in the conviviality, but Connie was afraid of becoming too attached to the family and she was resolved to keep her distance, determined never again to let herself go through the torment and agony of losing someone she really cared for. Maybe that was the way her mother had chosen to run her own life in the end, she thought. There had seemed to be no one really close to her. She had lived the way she wanted, and she had become a stranger even to her own sister. From what Connie had gathered, there had been many men friends in her mother's life, and one of them had been her father. Somewhere along the way things had gone wrong and the man had left. He might be dead now, and yet maybe he was still living somewhere? The only certain thing was that her mother had cut him off and refused even to discuss him. She had been a private person who had found it very difficult to show her real feelings. Maybe she hadn't always been that way, Connie mused as she lay staring up at the whitewashed ceiling. Something must have happened which had changed her mother. Maybe her own life was following the same path. Perhaps it was her inescapable destiny to suffer in the same way, to know the heartbreak of loss and end up a bitter, empty shell. Would the love she had shared with Robert be enough to sustain her for the rest of her life? Would she be able to keep herself apart from people and remain true to herself, would she never again feel the joy and agony of loving someone deeply and reaching out for love in the darkness? She remembered Joe Cooper's words. It would take time, and time was a great healer. As the sound of the explosions and crashing guns faded she would turn over, her head sinking into the soft pillow.

Salter Street had so far survived the bombing and the little pub was busy on Saturday night. Outside the wind was keen, threatening colder weather, and folk were crowding into the public bar to discuss the bombing, the food rationing and the local street gossip. One group who was discussing the recent disturbance outside the Argrieves' house was silenced by the sudden appearance of the woman herself. She walked into the small bar with her head held high. Behind her came her son Billy, who looked around sheepishly as he reached the counter.

'Go on then, son. Get yer money out. I'll 'ave a milk stout,' Florence Argrieves said, looking around with a satisfied grin on her tired, lined features.

''Ere, Bess. Look at 'er,' one of the customers whispered to her friend. 'She looks like the cat that swallered the canary.'

Bess nodded her agreement. 'I s'pose she's done a feat gettin' that son of 'ers ter smarten 'imself up. Jus' look at 'im. 'E's 'ad a shave, an' 'e's got a clean shirt on. There's even a crease in 'is trousers.'

Nora grinned. 'I s'pose yer right. She's even got 'im ter buy 'er a drink. Now that's a feat.'

Billy Argrieves pulled out a handful of coins and dropped some on the threadbare carpet as he looked at the pretty blond barmaid. 'Er . . . milk stout, an' er . . . er, pint o' bitter.'

Florence raised her eyes to the ceiling as her son spread the handful of coins on the bar and stared at Connie as she counted out the right amount. When the drinks were placed in front of them Florence took a long gulp and licked her lips appreciatively. Billy just stared down at his filled glass, a faraway look in his dark eyes.

'Well go on then, drink yer beer, it won't bite yer!' Florence chuckled, nudging her son.

As she pulled down on the beer pump Connie glanced at the uncomfortable young man at the counter. She had heard some of the stories surrounding Billy Argrieves, but it was the first time she had set eyes on him. He looked a sad figure, she thought. Once he must have been attractive, with his dark brooding eyes and small nose. His thin lips framed an expressive mouth and his dark wavy hair was unkempt, a lock hanging down over his high forehead. He was heavily built with wide shoulders and he looked tall, although it was difficult to judge his height as he slumped at the counter. Connie noticed how his hands moved constantly as he rested them out on the wooden counter. The grey suit he had on was grease-stained, although she could see it had been pressed recently. His white shirt was unbuttoned at the neck and the blue tie he wore was knotted carelessly and pulled away from his throat. Connie could see the discomfort growing in the young man as his mother spoke to him and she noticed his face redden. It made her sad to see him suffering. He was only a young man, and already he had been reduced to a physical and nervous wreck by what he had gone through.

Jennie came over and puffed loudly. 'Christ! It's busy ternight. 'Ow yer doin'?'

'I'm okay,' Connie replied as she mopped up a puddle of beer from the polished counter. 'What about you?'

Jennie grinned. 'I'll survive. 'Ere, Con. That's Billy Argrieves over there,' she said, jerking her head in his direction. 'It's the first time 'e's bin in 'ere since 'e got out o' the army. Cor, what a change in the bloke! D'yer know, us girls used ter go weak at the knees when we see 'im around? 'E was a right smart fella once. 'E wore smashin' suits an' real smart shoes an' shirts. 'E used ter knock around wiv all the local 'erberts. And jus' look at 'im now. That suit could do wiv a good clean, an' 'is barnett could do wiv a comb.'

Connie felt irritation welling up inside her. 'Maybe 'e ain't interested in poncin' 'imself up anymore. Maybe 'e don't want the girls droolin' over 'im.'

Jennie pulled a face. 'P'raps you're right. Still, yer can't 'elp noticin' the difference in the bloke.'

Their discussion was forgotten as Dora rang the bell and the customers began to be ushered out. There were lots of glasses to be washed and the tables and counter had to be mopped. Ash trays needed emptying and the carpet cleaned, and when the chores were finished they had to prepare something quickly to eat in case the air-raid siren sounded early.

Later, Jennie and Connie sat together in the upstairs room. Dora and Bill were still down in the bar counting the night's takings and their daughter took the opportunity to confide in her friend.

''Ere, Con. Yer see me chattin' ter those two well-dressed fellas in the bar earlier? Well, the tall one lives round the corner an' the shorter one is a pal of 'is. They've got a transport business down in Rotherhithe an' they was tellin' me all about this club they go ter up West. Real fancy it is. They was sayin' there's a girl in short skirt and black stockin's that goes round wiv cigarettes, an' anuvver girl that takes yer coat when yer go in. There's a cabaret as well. They was tellin' me they go up ter the club quite a lot an' they asked me if I'd like ter go wiv 'em.'

Connie looked hard at her friend. 'I'd be careful if I was you.'

Jennie dismissed Connie's caution with an easy grin. 'There's nufink ter worry about. Steve Barnett's okay. 'E told me 'e'd look after me. 'Ere, Con. What about you comin' as well? We could make a foursome.'

Connie shook her head. 'Count me out, Jen. I wouldn't be any company. Besides, I go ter the 'ospital every night.'

'That's okay. But it might cheer yer up a bit. Yer need ter get out once in a while, Con.'

Connie felt tired and jaded. Going out in a foursome was the last thing she wanted. She saw Jennie looking at her expectantly. 'I'll fink about it, Jen,' she said quickly.

Footsteps sounded on the stairs. 'Don't let on ter mum an' dad,' Jennie whispered. 'They don't go a lot on Steve Barnett.'

With the gloomy November days came a respite in the

bombing. Other large cities were now being targeted and the London raids became more sporadic. People began to sleep in their own beds again, although they would often start awake in the early hours terrified that they had heard the wail of the siren. The sixty-seven nights of consecutive bombing had left terrible scars, but Salter Street had escaped with virtually no damage except for a few missing roof slates and some cracked and broken windows. The Dolphin stayed open later than most local pubs during the evenings, and most of the time it did good business. The staff were kept busy, and Connie began to find it difficult to drag herself to work each morning. She was not sleeping very well and the dreary mornings were hard to face, with nothing but the prospect of another day of mundane tasks at the leather factory. Then there was the awful thought of sitting beside Helen's hospital bed just waiting, praying for a miracle. Aunt Helen was showing no signs of coming out of the coma. Instead she seemed to be slipping away. Connie was reminded of another time when she had felt the way she did now, when she was nursing her mother in the flat that had just been destroyed. Her life had been dreary and sad then, but at least there had been a future to dream about. Now she could see nothing to look forward to but the same desolate emptiness which she carried around inside her. It would be her twentieth birthday in a few days time, she thought, and for the first time it meant nothing to her. It would bring her no joy.

It was on Connie's birthday that the message came. Dora took the phone call late on Saturday evening and called Connie into the small room behind the public bar.

'It's the 'ospital, Con. They said you should go there as soon as possible,' she said urgently.

'Is she . . . is she . . .'

'They wouldn't say,' Dora stopped her. 'Get yer coat. I'll come wiv yer. Bill can manage the bar.'

The two women hurried through the blacked-out streets, picking their way carefully in the dim light of a torch. As they neared Guy's Hospital the pungent smell of hops from nearby warehouses filled the air. Connie held on to Dora's arm as they walked quickly through the gates and climbed the wide stone staircase up to the wards. They were met by the ward sister who took Connie gently to one side.

'Your aunt regained consciousness a couple of hours ago,' the nurse said. 'She seemed to rally for a while, but I'm afraid she's slipped back. She won't be able to talk to you, my dear. You must be prepared for the worst. It can only be a matter of time now. I'm terribly sorry.'

'Can I see 'er?' Connie asked, biting back her tears.

'Of course you can,' the sister replied, leading the way towards the small side room.

Connie left Dora standing outside in the corridor and walked hesitantly over to the bedside. She noticed a glimmer of recognition in her aunt's glazed eyes as she bent over the still figure.

''Ello, Aunt,' she whispered.

Helen blinked and a tear formed in the corner of her eye. Connie leaned over and gently brushed her aunt's ashen forehead with a soft kiss. She sat down and took her aunt's cold hand in hers. Helen blinked again and moved her eyes slowly to one side and then back again to Connie, as if in a gesture. Connie could feel the very slight movement in her fingers and she saw her move her eyes sideways once more.

'What is it, Aunt 'Elen? What are yer tryin' ter say?' she whispered huskily.

For a moment Helen's dull eyes stared up at the ceiling, and then she repeated the gesture. Connie released her aunt's hand and got up. Following the movement of her eyes she walked around the bed and, when Connie stood beside the small

378

locker, Helen blinked a couple of times. Without taking her eyes from her stricken aunt's stare Connie slowly opened the drawer. She glanced down and saw an old grey handbag lying there, and as she lifted it out Helen closed her eyes and sighed deeply.

'Yer wanted me ter take this, didn't yer, Aunt 'Elen?' she whispered.

There was no response. Her eyes remained closed, and Connie thought she could see a faint smile on her aunt's white, drawn face. A nurse who had come into the room with the sister gently led Connie out into the corridor.

After a few minutes the sister came out grim-faced. 'I'm afraid your aunt has passed away,' she said quietly.

Dora got up from the wooden bench by the wall and led the sobbing young woman out on to the dark landing. Connie did not hear her words of comfort as they descended the wide staircase and walked out slowly into the cold black street.

It was a quiet night. The air-raid siren had not sounded, and only the moaning wind invaded the silence as it rattled the window panes and whistled down the chimney. In the hearth a small coal fire was burning steadily and the room was warm and close. Connie stared down sadly at the bits and pieces from her aunt's handbag which she had emptied on to the counterpane of her bed. There was a little tortoiseshell comb, a few pennies and a new half-crown, an oval powder compact, and three keys tied together with a black shoe-lace. There was also a tiny gold pixie wrapped up in tissue paper. Connie sadly remembered the many times her aunt had said the piece would bring her good luck. With a sigh she picked up the bag to replace her aunt's effects and she felt something inside a clipped compartment which she had not opened. She snapped the catch and took out a bundle of papers. There were a couple of notes, the words written in a childish scrawl and signed 'Molly', and a faded photograph of Matthew standing with his arms folded a railway station. There were receipts and bills and, folded up in a piece of plain notepaper, there was a pawn ticket headed 'Mills & Sons'.

Connie sat cross-legged on the bed staring wistfully at her aunt's pathetic belongings, and as she touched one thing after another trying to make some sense of them her eyes filled with tears. All her life Aunt Helen had struggled against adversity. Matthew had been continually in and out of work and she had had to clean houses and take in washing until she had become exhausted. And she had suffered the terrible heartbreak of watching her only child struggle through illness and pain in her misshapen body. She had known little happiness, only worry and struggle, and all she had to show for it were a few coins and a pawn ticket. It seemed strange that her aunt had drawn attention to the bag, but there had been nothing else in the locker. Connie picked up the pawn ticket again and stared at it for a long time, alone in the silence.

Chapter Thirty-Three

For the folk of Ironmonger Street the long-awaited lull in the bombing was a chance to forsake the draughty, uncomfortable factory shelter. Old Clara Cosgrove dug out her clean sheets and made up her bed. She changed the pillow cases and put on the patchwork quilt which had not been on the bed since her husband died. She made herself a cup of cocoa and listened to the late-night play on the wireless. Clara was cherishing the thought of slipping into the clean bed that she had already warmed with two hot water bottles, and when her eyes started to droop she put down the empty mug and thought how nice it would be to get in between the fresh warm sheets. As the first light of dawn filtered through the spotless lace curtains of Clara's front room she finally opened her eyes. She felt cold and stiff, and more than a little put out. 'Sod it!' she grumbled aloud. 'I knew I shouldn't 'ave drunk that bleedin' cocoa!'

One morning Peter Armitage called Joe Cooper into his office to tell him that the Ministry was going to install bunks in the shelter, as he knew that Joe would be able to ensure they were allocated fairly. Joe was shocked to see the change in the man since the last time he had spoken to him. Gone was the upright stance and the alert manner. Now the factory owner was bowed and grey, and his suit seemed to hang shapelessly on his frail figure. The ever-present Miss Jones came into the office with some forms for Peter to sign and she had to prompt her boss into completing the task he would once have done with a flourish.

As Peter walked back into the outer office Joe glanced at the secretary. 'Is 'e all right?' he asked quietly.

'I don't know,' Alice replied. 'The poor man's still grieving, and he told me this morning his wife's gone into a nursing home. It's terrible. I feel really sorry for him.'

Joe shook his head. 'I fink 'e's aged this last few months. 'E idolised that boy of 'is.'

Alice leaned back in her chair. 'I'll never forget the day I had to break the news to young Connie,' she said sadly. 'I never want to go through that again.'

'I wonder 'ow the kid's gettin' on?' Joe said, thrusting his hands deep into his trouser pockets.

'God knows. I haven't seen anything of her.'

'Me neivver,' Joe said, rubbing his chin.

Their conversation was interrupted by Peter coming out of his office. 'I'd better sign those forms, Alice,' he said, scratching the back of his head.

Alice frowned. 'You've already signed them,' she replied, giving Joe a sideways glance.

'So I did. It's this headache. I can't seem to concentrate. Cancel my calls will you, Alice. I think it would be better if I went home.'

As Peter disappeared back into his office Alice raised her eyes to the ceiling. 'He'll go down with a bang if he's not careful,' she sighed.

In the privacy of his office Peter slumped down in his padded leather chair and dropped his head into his cupped hands. During the previous evening he had answered the telephone and heard the almost inaudible voice of Gerald's estranged wife on the other end of the line.

'It's Gerald!' she had sobbed. 'He's killed himself.'

Peter could get no more information from the distraught woman and it was left to Gerald's father-in-law to explain just what had happened. His unfortunate son-in-law had been suspected of embezzling large sums of money from the company and the police had been informed. Gerald was on his way in to the office to answer the charges when he had thrown himself under a tube train on Wimbledon station.

With Christmas near, the Toomey family had been compelled to make some changes. Toby finally lost his pram when it fell into a water-filled crater down at Dockhead, and he had decided there and then that enough was enough. The next day he presented himself at the labour exchange and was sent for a job at the pickle factory.

'Sit down will you, Mr Toomey,' the rather nervous manager said as Toby stood awkwardly in the middle of his office. 'Now, the job is rather messy, but you will be supplied with rubber boots and waterproofs. We're looking for someone who's reliable. The last man was always off sick with one thing or another. You are fit, aren't you?'

Toby nodded. 'Yes, sir.'

The manager of Hayden's Choice Pickles shuffled some papers and glanced rather sceptically at the spiky-haired character facing him. 'Now tell me a little about yourself, Mr Toomey. What was your last job?'

'Self-employed, sir.'

'What did you do?'

'I was in buyin' an' sellin'.'

'What exactly did you buy and sell?'

Toby thought for a while. 'Beds, carpets, ornaments, irons,' he said matter-of-factly.

'What sort of irons?'

'You know, ironin' irons.'

The manager's brow furrowed. 'You bought and sold household commodities?'

Toby's eyes widened. 'Yeah, an' old newspapers an' rags. Mind you, though, I never accepted pissy mattresses. Bit difficult with carpets though. When they're rolled up yer can't always see the condition they're in. Some 'ave dog shit all over 'em'.

The manager held his hands to his face and slowly shook his head. Finally he looked up. 'Mr Toomey. Are you trying to tell me you were a totter?' he asked pointedly.

'Not really,' Toby replied, grinning. 'Totters go round wiv 'orse an' carts, or barrers. I 'ad a pram – till it fell in this bloody great crater in Dock'ead.'

The manager of Hayden's Choice Pickles knew then that he should have stayed in bed that morning. He badly wanted a barrel-washer, and all the labour exchange had been able to come up with was a pram-pushing totter. Why was barrel wash-ing considered to be such a bad job? Why couldn't they send someone who had just a little credibility? he groaned to himself.

'All right, Mr Toomey. You've got the job on a week's trial,' the manager said with a sigh. 'Report to the yard foreman at eight o'clock on Monday morning.'

Toby walked from the factory grinning widely. Marie would be pleased. He had gotten himself a steady job at last. 'What do yer do fer a livin', Toby?' he said aloud, looking at a lamppost. 'I'm a barrel-washer at the pickle factory.'

A passer-by gave him a strange glance and Toby grinned in reply, shuffling his feet in a two-step before sauntering off to the nearby bus stop. The worried figure who was watching Toby's actions from his office window shook his head sadly and slumped down at his desk. He picked up a pencil and scribbled into a notepad: 'Phone labour exchange. Will probably need a new barrel-washer Monday week.'

* * *

As Christmas drew closer, the weather deteriorated. Rain-filled mists rolled up from the river and enshrouded the docks, and the German bombers did not come for nearly two weeks while the visibility was poor. Dockland folk began to visit the cinemas again, and when the Trocette showed 'Gone With The Wind' large queues stretched back every night from the box office. The pubs, too, were doing a brisk trade, and in the Dolphin both bars were always packed.

Each evening Connie put on a cheerful face and went down to the bar. But behind the mask her sadness grew. She missed Robert more and more as time went on, and her memories of him seemed to grow rather than fade. Whenever the bar door opened she looked over, half expecting him to be standing there. Voices and mannerisms reminded her of him, and whenever the newspapers published a photo of the latest flyer to receive a decoration Connie could see Robert staring out of the picture. The nights were worse. She remembered his arms around her and heard his soft voice whispering in her ear, and in her troubled drowsiness she touched the empty pillow beside her. Sleep was always slow to come and many nights she would lie wide awake until dawn, staring at the ceiling. She felt that her loneliness was beginning to tear her apart. One morning Dora French remarked how tired she looked and when the young woman told her she was having difficulty sleeping the landlord's wife gave her one of her sleeping tablets. That night her sleep was deep and empty, and in the morning a raging headache and sickness prevented her from going to work. It was then that Connie started drinking.

It began innocently enough. Old Albert Swan was propping up the counter and had been sharing a joke with Connie. ''Ere, Con, fill that up, will yer? While you're at it, pour yerself a tot.'

'Fanks all the same, Albert, but I gotta keep a straight 'ead or I'll be overchargin' yer,' Connie said smiling.

'Go on, 'ave a drink. I 'ad a nice little double up at Stamford Bridge terday. 'Undred ter six an' a nine ter two. It come to a nice few bob. You 'ave a drink wiv yer ole mate Albert. Pour yerself a whisky, it'll put a bit o' colour in yer cheeks.'

The dark spirit burnt her throat and made her eyes water but the warm glow stayed in her stomach. Before time was called old Albert Swan was looking bleary eyed and his face was flushed from his celebrating. He had managed to persuade Connie to have another drink and she was feeling a little unsteady herself. That night the drink quietened her nerves and she was asleep as soon as her head touched the pillow.

Whisky soon became a regular tonic, and when the customers included her in the round of drinks Connie would gratefully take a small nip. She found she could shake off the morning-after feeling without much trouble and soon she was sneaking a drink before she started work behind the bar. Jennie began to notice the difference in her friend. She had become more talkative and inclined to joke with the regulars. Her face seemed to become flushed as the evenings wore on and when the occasional air raid took place Connie slept undisturbed in the damp cellar. Dora had noticed the change in the Morgan girl and she mentioned it to her husband.

'I'm a bit concerned about 'er, Bill. She's very good be'ind the bar an' the customers fink the world of 'er, but she's drinkin' too much. After all, she's only a kid.'

Bill looked over his evening paper at his wife. 'D'yer fink she's 'elpin' 'erself then?'

'Of course not. She might sneak one now an' again, but they all do, don't they? No, I'm more concerned about the drinks she accepts from the customers.'

Bill folded up his paper. 'I wouldn't worry too much, luv. If they wanna buy 'er a drink it shows they like 'er. If so they'll be 'appy ter drink in 'ere instead of somewhere else. Besides, it prob'ly does 'er good. I mean, look what she's bin frew this last few months. If the drink 'elps 'er ter blot out the memories, so be it.'

Dora nodded. 'Okay, but you keep an eye on 'er,' she said, turning to Jennie. 'She listens ter you. Try ter make 'er ease up a bit. It ain't good fer a girl that age ter drink too much.'

During the Christmas week the Dolphin was packed. There had been no air raids for a few nights and everyone was hoping the bombing would hold off at least until after the holiday. Connie noticed that Jennie had been spending a lot of time chatting to a couple of well-dressed men who had been coming in the pub nightly for the past few weeks and, on Christmas Eve, the publican's daughter approached her excitedly. 'Come on, Con. There's no 'arm in it,' she urged her. 'They jus' wanna take us fer a drink when we close up. They've got a bit of a party goin' on at Steve's place. 'E only lives a few streets away.'

Connie pulled at her chin. 'I dunno Jen. I won't be much company. You go, I'll get an early night.'

Jennie laughed, 'What, on Christmas Eve? Listen, Con. You can't go on shuttin' yerself away fer ever. I know it mus' be 'ard fer yer, but yer gotta let go some time. All yer do is slog away all day at the factory an' work in 'ere all evenin'. It ain't good fer yer. Come on, go an' put yer face on. Yer can keep yer eye on me. If me dad knows yer comin' wiv me 'e'll feel 'appier.'

Connie gave her friend a wan smile. 'Okay,' she said reluctantly. 'As it's Christmas.'

Jennie's eyes lit up. 'Smashin'! You go up an' get ready. I'll finish clearin' up.'

Connie could hear cheerful voices in the street below as she sat at the small dressing table and stared at her reflection in the tilted mirror. She had drunk three whiskies that evening and the pleasant glow in her stomach had calmed her dull, gnawing ache. She noticed the little pouches beneath her eyes and the slight puffiness of her pale face. She ran her fingers through her long blond hair and sighed as she picked up the hairbrush. While she was brushing out the tangles Connie's eyes fell on the little gold locket lying beside the grey handbag. She put down the brush and gently picked up the trinket by its thin chain. It had been a shock when she had presented the ticket at the pawnbrokers in the Old Kent Road and found that the article she had redeemed for twenty-five shillings was her mother's gold locket, the one she had always worn around her neck. Connie shivered. She wondered why Helen had desperately wanted her to have the memento, and she tried to imagine what she could possibly have been thinking as she lay there in the hospital, unable to speak. If only she could have said something to explain the mysterious little inscription on the inside. Perhaps she would not have told her anything. After all, she had lied about the locket being buried with her sister's body. Connie wondered whether her aunt had been sworn to secrecy, and if she had, why the secret had been so important that she had kept it until her dying day. Perhaps Aunt Helen had wanted to leave her something out of love – the chance to find out at last who her father was.

Connie felt an intense excitement as she looked down at the tiny heart-shaped locket resting in the palm of her hand. Gently she slid her thumbnail along the side of the locket and prised it open. Once again she read the inscription which had been worked neatly on the inner surface: 'With all my love, Bonny.' For a while Connie stared down at the etching, then she snapped the locket shut. The name was unfamiliar to her. Who was Bonny? she asked herself again and again. Was he her father? Whoever he was, he must have been special for her mother to have always carried his words of love around inside the little trinket. Although she did not forget for a moment how difficult it might be for her to find her father, Connie felt that at last she had come closer to knowing him. She held something in her hand that he had touched, that he had given to her mother. She closed her eyes, as if in the dark recesses of her mind she might catch a glimpse of him. There was a sudden tap on the door and Connie started.

'Yer ready, Con?' Jennie asked eagerly as she poked her head round the door. 'The fellas are waitin'.'

The piano player was pounding away on the keys and couples were dancing together in the middle of the large room. Connie stood with a glass in her hand watching her friend being waltzed around the floor. Jennie's face was flushed and her white teeth flashed as she laughed loudly with her tall, smartly dressed partner. Around the high-ceilinged room paper chains and balloons moved in the breeze caused by the dancers and tiny coloured lights around the Christmas tree shone on the silver tinsel and pretty baubles. The heavy drapes over the windows were a deep red velvet, and Connie noticed that the carpet beneath her feet was high-piled and obviously expensive. Bottles of drinks stood on the sideboard and in a far corner there was a firkin of ale resting on a curved wooden stand. The crowded room was hot and stuffy and the open fire had been allowed to die down to a dull-glowing mound of white ash.

As she glanced casually around Connie was acutely conscious of the man's eyes appraising her. He was standing nearby, his thumb hooked into his waistcoat pocket to expose a silver watch chain that spanned his middle and supported a small silver fob. The man was swarthy and his heavy brows met above the bridge of his wide nose. He was slightly shorter

389

than her and quite heavily built. His dark eyes were deep-set and piercing, and Connie felt uneasy beneath his gaze. She knew he was studying her and she could feel her face getting hot. Like Jennie's partner Steve, the man was well groomed and acted very self-assured. He had been watching her closely since the four of them left the Dolphin and walked to the large house in Saddlers Square. Jennie had laughingly introduced him as Sammy and during the short walk to the house the swarthy character had fallen in step alongside Connie and proffered his arm. She had ignored the gesture and kept her hands inside her buttoned-up coat.

Now, as the music stopped and Jennie and her partner walked over, Connie drained her glass. Immediately Sammy reached out and took it from her hand. 'Same again?' he asked, walking towards the sideboard without waiting for her reply.

Jennie was flushed with excitement and when Steve slipped his arm around her waist she leaned against him. 'Yer enjoyin' yerself, Con?' she asked with a wide grin. 'It's a smashin' party, ain't it?'

Connie forced a smile, 'Yes, it's nice,' she lied, wishing she had not allowed herself to be coaxed into coming.

''Ow're you an' Sammy gettin' on?' Jennie asked, staring enquiringly at her friend.

'All right,' Connie answered, trying not to show her irritation as she changed her weight from one foot to the other.

Sammy came back and handed her a glass which was three-parts full of whisky. 'Drink up, it's Christmas,' he said grinning at her.

Connie caught a glimpse of his gold-edged teeth and his narrow-set eyes and suddenly she felt revolted. She wanted to run from the room out into the cold night and fill her lungs with fresh air. Instead she lifted her glass and gulped at the drink.

The musician had been to get some refreshment and was now back at the keyboard. He rubbed his hands together smartly and began playing a waltz tune. Jennie laughed happily and pulled Steve into the centre of the floor. As they danced away Sammy took hold of Connie's elbow and jerked his head in the direction of the dancers.

'C'mon, girl. Let's me an' you dance.'

She felt his bulk against her body and his hand moving along her back as they began turning around the floor. He held her tightly in his arms and she could smell his peppery breath on her cheek. Connie wanted to ease the pressure of his body against hers but his arms seemed stiff and heavy. She closed her eyes and let the fiery liquid she had drunk soak through her. Her head was swimming as he pulled her around and she bit on her lip.

Later, when the fire had gone out and the piano player had left, a few couples were left sitting around the room talking quietly. Connie leaned back in the large armchair, trying to focus her eyes. Sammy had plied her with drinks and she was beginning to feel quite hazy. She looked around the room for Jennie but she was nowhere to be seen. Her escort sat on the arm of her chair, his large hairy hand gripping a near empty glass.

Connie looked up at the man. 'Wh ... where's Jennie gone?' she faltered.

He grinned, 'She's gone upstairs.'

'Upstairs?'

Sammy suddenly stood up and grasped her hand, pulling her out of the chair. He was leading, urging her, and she could only half protest as they climbed the steep stairs. Connie could not see very clearly and her mouth had suddenly become very dry. Sammy was still holding her hand very tightly as he stopped at the top of the stairs and opened a door. She was standing directly behind him and she caught a hazy glimpse of the couple lying naked on the bed.

'Sorry, Steve!' he exclaimed, shutting the door quickly.

They moved along the landing, his strong hand squeezing hers almost painfully. As he opened another door and pulled her into the room sharp needles of anxiety pricked her befuddled brain. He turned and pulled her close, his wet lips searching for her mouth and kissing her roughly. His hands were moving over her body and she felt herself being pushed back towards the bed. She could do nothing as he kissed her face and her ears and grabbed her hair to pull her head back. She wanted to push him away but he had pinned her arms to her sides. As they fell back on to the bed, Sammy's body smothered hers. He was fumbling with her clothes and she felt his hand rub up the inside of her thigh. He was panting like an animal, his mouth open and his wide eyes glaring. She fought him, tensing her body and clenching her teeth in anger as his hand reached the top of her leg. His head was leaning into her shoulder now and his hot breath was searing her face as she felt the pressure of his fingers. A black feeling of sickness and fear possessed her and from nowhere a sudden last urge to preserve herself filled Connie with fierce strength. She freed one arm from his hard embrace and tore at his face. She felt her nails sink into his fleshy cheek and he jerked back. His body slackened and he cursed as he clutched at his face.

'Yer spiteful bitch!' Sammy snarled, hitting her sharply across the face with his open hand.

Connie fought back her angry tears as he stood up and glared down at her. She sat up slowly, drawing her legs over the edge of the bed and straightening her dress. She was completely sober now as she watched him like an animal at bay. He had moved back away from her and slumped down in a chair, dabbing at his torn face. She saw a childlike look of disappointment on his swarthy features and her fear turned to cold anger and contempt. There was no threat now, she knew. The moment of danger had passed.

Connie looked over at him. 'Fink yerself lucky I didn't scream out. Yer'd 'ave 'ad some explainin' ter do,' she said, her voice cold with rage.

'I'm sorry,' Sammy said huskily. 'I thought yer wanted it. Yer came upstairs wiv me, didn't yer?'

'Yeah I did,' Connie said, a sudden tremor shaking her body. 'Let's ferget it. Yer didn't get it all yer own way.'

Sammy touched his cheek and shook his head quickly. 'I'll go downstairs an' see if I can scrounge us a cup o' tea,' he said, going to the door and turning to face her. 'Yer won't let on, will yer?'

She looked at him with disdain. 'Don't worry,' she said with a twist of her mouth. 'I won't say nufink.'

For some time Connie sat on the bed, staring at the open doorway. When she finally got up and went downstairs she found the room empty. Sammy came in and handed her a cup of tea, and without saying anything else he had gone. A little while later Jennie and Steve came down into the front room.

'Where's our Sammy?' Steve asked, glancing around.

'I fink 'e left,' Connie said, sipping her tea.

The two lovers exchanged glances and then Jennie looked at her friend curiously. 'You two 'ad a row?'

Connie averted her eyes. 'Are yer ready, Jen?' she asked with a hardness in her voice. 'I wanna get goin', I'm tired.'

Steve followed Jennie out into the hall and Connie could hear them mumbling to each other. Jennie came back alone carrying their coats and they left the house together, walking home in silence through the dark empty streets.

Chapter Thirty-Four

On Christmas morning a north wind was blowing and the gathering clouds promised snow. Spirals of smoke rose up from leaning chimney pots and young excited voices rang out in the backstreets. At noon the Dolphin opened, and amongst the first customers was Billy Argrieves. His face was clean-shaven and bore a few cuts, as if the razor had been held in a shaking hand. His dark wavy hair had been plastered down with water and his clothes were clean and pressed. The white shirt he wore was open at the collar and his shoes were polished. He came into the public bar almost apologetically and sidled up to the counter. He stood, unsure of himself, coins clutched in his hand. People around him leaned forward and called out their orders, impatient to begin the Christmas drinking session.

Connie spotted him and came over, ignoring the other customers. 'What'll it be, Billy?' she asked.

He looked at her, his eyes widening as he scratched his forehead. 'I wanna – I wanna pint of ale, please,' he stammered, his eyes fixed on hers.

Connie took a pint glass from under the counter and smiled at him as she held it beneath the pump tap and pulled on the handle. He smiled back, baring his even white teeth, and then in sudden embarrassment he dropped his gaze to the money in his hand. When Connie placed the filled glass of ale in front of him Billy held out his palm and offered the coins to her.

'You wanna drink?' he blurted out as she took the money.

Connie smiled familiarly at him. 'Can I 'ave one later, Billy? I jus' got one, fank yer,' she said kindly.

He nodded and lifted the glass to his lips as he turned away from the counter. People were pushing their way to the bar and one impatient customer accidentally jogged Billy's arm. Beer spilled down the front of his clean white shirt and over his coat. The young man carefully brushed the drips from his front without looking up and walked to a seat by the door with his head bowed.

'What's 'e doin' in 'ere?' the impatient man asked his friend. ''E shouldn't be out on 'is own. 'E's a bloody menace.'

Connie heard the remark and her face flushed with anger.

The man's friend grinned. ''E's all right, is Billy. Look at 'im sittin' there. 'E's in a world of 'is own.'

'I dunno,' the other went on. 'Did yer 'ear about the tallyman 'e clobbered?'

'Yeah, I 'eard about it. Seems ter me the bloke asked fer it. Some o' those tallymen get a bit lippy at times.' The man picked up his glass and took a sip. 'Yer gotta understand, mate,' he said, wiping the froth from his mouth with the back of his hand. 'Young Billy Argrieves was always a bit wild. The army didn't 'elp neivver. Dunkirk ruined 'im like it did a lot o' young lads. From what I've 'eard, it was sheer bloody murder out there.'

The impatient man was mollified somewhat and he nodded his head grudgingly.

Connie found herself rushed off her feet as the customers crowded into the little bar. Now and then she looked over and saw that Jennie was preoccupied with her boyfriend who stood at the far end of the counter. There was no sign of Sammy, and

Connie felt relieved. The pub was now packed full and customers were having to wait for their orders, one or two beginning to mumble about the service and glance in the direction of the publican's daughter. Connie occasionally looked over to where Billy was sitting alone. He was staring down at his near-empty glass, apparently deep in thought. Once she saw him count through the coins he held in his hand then put them back into his pocket. Her heart went out to him and, as soon as the opportunity presented itself, Connie had a word with Albert Swan.

''Ere, Alb. Do us a faver. Can yer take this pint over ter Billy? 'E's sittin' over by the door. Tell 'im it's on the 'ouse.'

Albert pushed his way through the milling crowd and said a few words to the young man as he put the pint down in front of him. Billy looked over, a bright, nervous smile breaking across his rugged features as he held the glass up in a toast. Connie felt better and she was pleased when she saw Albert sit down and start chatting to Billy. The old man leaned forward in the chair, nodding his head as the younger man used his hands to describe something. Connie found herself staring over at the two. The stories she had heard about Billy had made him out to be a wild young man, a dangerous character who it was better not to know. He did not seem fearsome to Connie and she remembered what Jennie had said about how smart he once was, and how all the girls went weak at the knees when they saw him around. It was easy to see why, although now he looked like a lost, pathetic soul who found it difficult to enter the pub on his own and face the regulars. He was another casualty of this war who needed some understanding and friendship.

Ironmonger Street was quiet on Christmas night. The factory gates remained open and folk prayed that the siren would not interrupt their festivities. Joe Cooper had left to visit his ailing wife in the country and Lizzie Conroy had taken the frail Mrs Cosgrove into her home for the holiday. For the Toomeys the holiday was one of good cheer, and Marie was feeling optimistic for the new year. Toby had held down his job. He was on regular wages and the rent was now getting paid on time. Lillian had reason to feel happy too. She had met and fallen in love with Sandor Konetsky, a Czech serviceman who was stationed in London and attached to a labour battalion. Sandor could speak very little English and Lillian's knowledge of her boyfriend's mother tongue was limited to a few naughty words. They carried on their courtship mainly in sign language but, as the Toomey girl explained to some of her friends down in Rotherhithe, 'My Sandor is smashin' ter go ter bed wiv, an' I can understand 'im, even though I don't know what the bleedin' 'ell 'e's talkin' about most o' the time.'

Sandor Konetsky was a lonely soul who enjoyed the hospitality of 'those crazy English people' as he put it. He especially liked Marie's cooking and Lillian's preoccupation with sexual matters – in that order – and for those reasons he had omitted to tell them that he had a wife and seven children back home in Prague.

The rather set-upon patriarch of the Toomey family was also feeling pleased with himself that Christmas. Washing out filthy barrels with detergents and rinsing them with scalding water from a leaking hosepipe was not the greatest job in the world, but it had its compensations. He was left alone most of the time, and one of the women in the packing department had taken a shine to him. Occasionally she would slip him a large jar of mustard pickle or gherkins and Toby would seize the opportunity to sell his ill-gotten gains to the local transport café. The café owner sometimes drove his car into the factory yard when it was convenient and Toby promptly gave it a wash and a polish. For services rendered the café owner provided the 'head barrel washer' with a free dinner and a large slice of apple pie. Yes, life wasn't too bad, Toby thought. Marie had eased up on her nagging and he had been able to shelve his plans to do away with her – for the time being.

On the twenty-ninth of December the air-raid siren sounded early and soon the bombs began to fall again. As the night wore on the bombing grew in intensity and the fire watchers of Ironmonger Street could see a red glow rising over the City of London. Joe Cooper had returned from a miserable Christmas in the country and he ran into the wardens' post at the height of the raid.

'It's murder over the water, Joe!' one of the men shouted to him above the din. 'Control's told us the place is burnin' down! The bloody tide's right out and they're 'avin' trouble pumpin' the water out o' the Thames!'

Joe winced as a nearby explosion shook the old rag shop. 'It's a bad one ternight. They're over in force,' he shouted back.

The warden put down the phone and rubbed a grubby hand over his tired features. 'Are your crowd okay?' he asked.

Joe nodded. 'They're all right. Our two girls are gettin' 'em goin' wiv a sing-song an' we've managed ter keep the tea flowin'.'

Ted Butcher, the senior warden, leaned towards a bespectacled young man who was wearing a steel helmet a size too large. 'Talkin' o' tea. 'Ow about you puttin' the kettle on, 'Orry?'

Horace Wilson grinned owlishly and disappeared into the back room. Ted took out a packet of Goldflake and held one out to Joe. The two men sat in the dimly lit shop, their faces tired and strained. They puffed away on their cigarettes without talking and, when Horace brought in two mugs of tea

Ted stretched and puffed heavily. 'Did yer 'ave a good 'oliday, Joe?' he asked.

Joe pulled a face. 'I tell yer, Ted. I was glad when it was all over. My ole woman didn't stop naggin' all the time I was there, an' 'er sister was a right bundle o' laughs as well. Between the two of 'em they gave me the right 'ump. On Boxin' Night I just about 'ad enough of it, so out I goes ter get a drink. There was this place in the village an' when I walked in the door yer should 'ave seen the eyes. Everybody was starin' at me like I'd jus' crawled out o' the woodwork. Ter tell yer the truth, it was a poxy pint as well.'

'Your ole Dutch won't come back ter London then, Joe?'

'No fear! She said she's quite okay where she is. I'm glad really. She's a bundle o' nerves as it is, an' they ain't 'ad no bombin' yet. If she was back 'ere she'd die o' fright.'

The phone rang again and Horace picked up the receiver. His face looked serious as he turned to Ted. 'The fires are out o' control in the City! There's a great big crater near the Tower Bridge 'Otel, an' the flats in Dock'ead 'ave copped it!'

'Gawd 'elp us!' Ted gasped.

The door of the wardens' post suddenly burst open and a tall, lean figure rushed in, his face blackened and his steel helmet pushed to the back of his head. 'The water main's busted in Tower Bridge Road an' the bleedin' vinegar factory's alight!' he shouted. 'What's more, there's a bleedin' unexploded bomb in Conner Street!'

Ted looked over to Horace. 'You got that, son?'

The bespectacled warden grabbed the phone, 'Got it!' he shouted.

Joe stood up. 'I'll leave yer ter get on wiv it, Ted,' he said. 'Look after yerself. It's gonna get worse before the night's out.'

Joe kept his head low as he ran through the gates into the factory yard. Above the sky was blood-red, and the ground shook beneath his feet. Gun flashes lit the night and as he reached the shelter entrance a loud explosion made him clasp his hands to his ears. Down below in the stuffy refuge, Lizzie Conroy was leading a chorus of 'She's Only a Bird in a Gilded Cage', and Billy Richards was plucking away at his ukulele. Joe could see the Widow Pacey, impassive as ever, her arms folded and her eyes staring ahead. The Toomeys were singing and Ada Halliday was conducting the impromptu choir with her arms flailing. Mary Brown was busy at the tea urn, and some of the children were already curled up on the benches.

When Joe walked over Mary looked up. ''Ere, Joe. When they gonna put them bunks in 'ere?' she asked. 'Those kids look really uncomf'table on them 'ard benches.'

'Gawd knows,' Joe replied. 'They should 'ave bin put in long ago.'

Over in one corner a group of children were gathered together. Mary's son Jimmy was showing off his collection. 'I've got a bit wiv a number on it.'

'Let's 'ave a look,' Gordon Jackman said, peering into the cardboard box at the jagged chunks of metal.

'That's nufink,' Ronnie Bailey scoffed. 'My mate Arnie's got a great big 'cend'ry bomb in 'is 'ouse. It come in 'is roof an' didn't go orf. 'E's got stacks o' shrapnel as well.'

'That's stupid, Ron. 'Cend'ries can go orf any time. 'E could get burnt ter cinders.'

Ronnie Bailey blinked at the other young boy. 'It's all right. Me mate's dad keeps the bomb in a pail o' water.'

Gordon scratched the tip of his nose. 'I 'ad some newts and tadpoles once an' I kept 'em in a pail o' water. When they turned inter frogs an' fings they all jumped out an' 'opped up our passage. My mum wasn't 'alf scared.'

Jimmy lowered his head and called his friends together. ''Ere. See ole Muvver Adams over there?'

Six pairs of eyes glanced in the direction of the elderly lady who sat alone, her arms folded and her head resting against the wall. 'She's got loads o' cats an' when they 'ave kittens she drowns 'em all in a pail o' water.'

'That's 'orrible. She mus' be an' ole witch,' Ronnie said, pulling a face. 'Look at Muvver Pacey. She's a witch. When it's dark she turns inter a big black pijjin.'

Gordon pointed over to where the Toomeys were sitting, his eyes fixing on Lillian. 'I fink she looks like a witch.'

'No, she's a prosser.'

'What's a prosser?'

'I dunno. It's what me dad calls 'er.'

Just a mile away, another little backstreet was getting its first taste of bomb damage. Salter Street was littered with broken glass, roof slates and splintered wood from shattered front doors after a landmine had flattened a row of houses in Canning Street, the turning opposite. Down in the cellar of the Dolphin they heard the loud explosion and flakes of white plaster fell on to the beds.

Bill French had been lying awake and he jumped up quickly. 'Christ! That was a near one!' he gasped.

Dora and Jennie were huddled together, and Connie buried her head beneath the bedclothes as the landlord hurried up into the bar. The wooden shutters over the pub windows had held but broken glasses and bottles of beer were scattered across the floor. The large mirror behind the saloon bar counter was cracked, and chunks of plaster had fallen from the ceiling. Bill ran out into the street and looked along the turning. He could see the flaring gas main and the high jet of water bursting from a broken pipe. Men were already pulling at the rubble with their bare hands and there seemed to be people running everywhere. Fire bells were ringing out and Bill saw the local policeman cycling into the devastated little turning. The landlord scratched his head. There was nothing he could do. Too many people clambering over the rubble would be disastrous for anyone buried beneath it; help would be needed after the survivors were brought out. He went back into the pub and tried the gas. Luckily it lit, although the pressure was low. He filled the largest pot he could find with water and pulled out a couple of blankets from the bedroom cupboard. There was little else he could do for the moment, except busy himself clearing up the bars.

As dawn broke and the long, even wail of the all clear sounded, Bill and Dora opened up their pub. The dust-caked policeman stood at the end of the turning, directing the homeless into Salter Street. They filed past, grey-faced and shaking. Women were quietly sobbing and sleepy-eyed children looked around curiously as Dora poured tea into large mugs and passed them around along with sandwiches of cheese and breakfast sausage. Jennie and Connie came down into the public bar carrying more blankets which they wrapped around the elderly women.

The policeman cycled up and came into the bar. ''Ow we doin', Bill?' he asked, sitting himself down heavily beside the counter.

'Well, we got 'em settled fer a bit. What's the news?'

The constable took off his steel helmet and put it down on the counter. 'It was a bloody miracle. Everybody's accounted for. They was all over the shelter. We dug Mrs Harriman's dog out o' the rubble an' it shook itself an' trotted off large as life. It was a bloody miracle.'

As the winter sun climbed up into the sky, vans arrived to transport the homeless to the nearby rest centres. Dora and Bill began their task of getting the pub ready for the first customers and the girls left for work. They picked their way through the debris out into the Old Kent Road.

As they walked along to the Bricklayers Arms Jennie glanced at her friend. 'I was terrified last night, Con,' she said. 'I bet there wasn't 'alf some damage done.'

Connie shivered and pulled her coat up around her ears. 'When that loud bang went I ducked under the clothes. I thought the pub was goin' ter crash down on us.'

They could see the devastation of the air raid as they reached the corner of Tower Bridge Road. Streetlamps were down and there was glass and rubble everywhere. One or two of the shops had had their windows blown out and there was a large crater in the middle of the junction. Buses were being diverted and the trams were lined up waiting as emergency crews worked feverishly to lay new tracks.

Jennie slipped her arm through Connie's as they crossed the road. 'Well, it was quiet over Christmas, Con. I'm jus' sorry I talked yer inter that party,' she said, staring ahead. 'I thought it would do yer good.'

Connie smiled. 'The party was okay. It was jus' me. I wasn't really up to it.'

'You sure Sammy didn't try anyfing?' Jennie asked quickly.

'No, Jen. As I told yer, 'e got a bit 'andy, but 'e soon got the message.'

Jennie sighed. 'Me an' Steve are 'avin' it off, but yer guessed that, didn't yer?'

'Yeah, I guessed it.'

'Gawd knows what me folks are gonna say when they find out. Trouble is, Steve's older than me, an' 'e's got a bit of a reputation for runnin' aroun' wiv a dodgy crowd. Me dad don't like 'im very much. 'E finks Steve's too flash, but 'e ain't really.'

Connie shrugged her shoulders. 'It's never easy, is it? There's always problems when yer get serious wiv someone. I know 'ow it was when I started goin' wiv Robert. 'E was older, too, and not our sort. Poor Aunt 'Elen used ter worry 'erself sick about it. Fing is, yer gotta sort it out before yer get too close. Don't let anybody change yer mind for yer. Nobody could talk me out o' goin' wiv Robert an' I don't regret one minute of the time I spent wiv 'im. My only regret is that it was all too short. I miss 'im terrible.'

It was Monday morning and, as they reached the factory entrance Connie sighed deeply. There was another long day ahead, another long week of monotonous grind. It seemed as though everything was pressing down on her and squeezing the life juices from her protesting body. She felt old, dry and weary and she wished more than anything that she could walk on past the factory and just keep on walking. Connie realised she hadn't eaten any breakfast that morning. Her mouth was parched and her head felt heavy. She wanted a strong drink right at the moment and it made her feel anxious. She had been drinking too much; it was taking hold of her. She knew that if she didn't slow down she would make herself very ill. Would that be so bad, she thought? There seemed to be nothing for her to live for. Life without Robert was empty and meaningless. There was nothing to look forward to, nothing but dark days and darker nights. Only in the evenings, when she was serving behind the bar, could she begin to forget her misery a little, taking a drink or two and letting the burning spirit blunt her senses and promise a dream-free sleep. Alcohol had become like a friend to her, and she was afraid that it would betray her.

Jennie was looking at her strangely. 'C'mon, Con or we'll be late clockin' in,' she said with a frown.

Chapter Thirty-Five

Connie had hardly noticed him at first. He worked as a labourer at the factory and one of his tasks was to pull trolleys of treated leathers into the workroom. Jimmy Pope was tall and slim, with a pleasant smile and an open face that bespoke a cheerful nature. He was active and strong and when he was summoned to an army medical the girls at the factory got ready to say their goodbyes. Everyone was surprised, and no one more than he himself, when he was rejected for military service. They said it was a heart murmur and suggested that he consult his family doctor. When Jimmy followed the advice and contacted his ageing doctor he was told not to worry.

'The army people were probably coming down on the side of caution. Your father had the same condition, Mr Pope and, as I remember, he was nearing eighty-four when he passed away. It's hereditary and I shouldn't give it another thought. Just be thankful you've escaped the call-up.'

Jimmy was not sure he had escaped anything. Some of the call-up dodgers were getting a hard time and he knew he would have to carry his medical card around with him to satisfy the interfering busybodies. There was bound to be some malicious gossip too, but being a cheerful sort of person, Jimmy went back to work and decided he was lucky after all. He wrote a letter to his wife, who had been evacuated to Suffolk with the two children, telling her she could stop worrying about him going into the army. He had been rejected owing to a perforated eardrum. He thought a little white lie was needed to put Ruby's mind at rest. Knowing her, if he told her the truth she would be expecting him to drop dead at any minute.

Connie had been living with the sorrow of Robert's death for some time before she began to notice Jimmy. In some ways he reminded her of her lost lover. He was tall like Robert, and he seemed to have a similar devil-may-care attitude. In looks they were very different, however. Robert had been fair, with blue eyes which had made her weak with excitement. Jimmy was dark, with large brown eyes and he wasn't handsome. It was his mannerisms which reminded her most of Robert, and Connie found herself watching him whenever he came into the workroom. She felt no physical attraction towards the young man, only a curiosity, and Jimmy slowly became aware of it. He had heard about the tall, pretty girl with the long blond hair whose fiancé had been killed in action and when he noticed her watching him every time he came near her Jimmy began to get interested. He was missing Ruby and Connie Morgan was certainly very pretty. She must be feeling lonely, too, he reasoned. Maybe he should get talking to her and ask her out for a drink one evening. It wouldn't be for sexual reasons, he told himself without really believing it, but just a friendly relationship with someone who was also lonely.

He had started talking to Connie before Christmas and, after the holiday was over and he had said goodbye to Ruby and the kids once again, Jimmy decided it was time to try his luck. Her response to his suggestion that they go for a drink one evening surprised him.

'Okay,' she said without any hesitation. 'It'll make a change.'

Jimmy walked out of the workroom whistling to himself,

and Connie smiled at Jennie across the work bench. 'Well it will make a change, won't it?' she said.

Jennie raised her hands and grinned. 'I never said anyfing. Jus' be careful, yer know 'e's married.'

'Yeah I know,' Connie replied quickly. 'I'm goin' fer a drink wiv 'im, that's all.'

Jennie saw the look in her friend's eyes and she turned her attention to the leather strips she was stamping.

The January weather was particularly cold and the sky was heavy with gathering snow clouds. Inside the riverside pub the coke fire was banked high and the light from the flickering flames played on the low oak beams and grimy plastered ceiling. The landlord leaned on the bar counter, his chin resting on his cupped hand, his sleepy eyes struggling to stay focused on the old man facing him. They were discussing war, and the differences between trench warfare and tank battles. The old man was doing most of the talking and the landlord was striving to stay awake. The only other people in the bar were the young couple sitting near the warm fire, and they were beginning to feel the effects of the drink they had consumed that evening.

Jimmy was twirling his half-empty glass on the table. 'Do yer fink about meetin' somebody in the future an' gettin' married?' he asked her. 'I mean, yer young. In time yer might see fings differently.'

Connie shrugged. The whisky had started to take the coldness away and she felt strangely at ease. 'I dunno. I try not ter look too far inter the future. I 'ad a wonderful fella an' 'e's gone. No one could take 'is place.'

Jimmy looked into her icy blue eyes. 'I miss me wife an' kids,' he said without taking his eyes from her. 'Loneliness is a terrible fing, Con. We both know that.'

She returned his stare. He was attractive in a weak sort of way, she thought. He was somehow childlike and open, and his suggestive look did not anger her. She felt he was playing his hand without deceit, and she decided to go along with him for a while. 'Tell me, Jimmy,' she said, clasping her hands on the table top. 'Would yer cheat on yer wife?'

Jimmy was taken aback by the question. 'Yer mean would I make love wiv somebody else?'

'That's what I mean,' Connie said, a ghost of a smile touching her pale face.

'It's a difficult question. Ruby's away in the country an' I'm 'ere alone. I s'pose it could 'appen, if I met somebody who I was attracted to.'

Connie's smile broadened. 'Did yer fink about cheatin' on Ruby when yer asked me out fer a drink, Jimmy?'

The young man drained his glass and gritted his teeth as the spirit burned his throat. 'You're puttin' me in a corner, Con. I'd better get us anuvver drink.'

She watched him walk unsteadily to the counter and saw the landlord straighten up with a thankful look on his face. What had brought her with him to this quiet pub on a freezing cold night? she wondered. Was it just for company, and a chance to get pleasantly merry, or was it really her need for physical warmth? Would lovemaking help to take away the constant ache which tormented her every waking minute? She remembered how angry she had got when Jennie looked knowingly at her at the factory that morning, and she felt a little guilty.

Jimmy had sat down at the table with their drinks and he was looking at her. 'Yer was askin' me about what I was finkin' when I asked yer out. Well I tell yer, Connie, I've bin attracted ter yer fer a long time. I know it's wrong, but I can't 'elp meself. Yer a very pretty woman.'

Connie smiled and watched him as he dropped his eyes and ran his finger around the rim of his glass. 'Do yer want ter make love ter me?' she asked him suddenly, shocked at her own forthrightness.

'Yes, I do,' he said simply.

She took a sip from her glass and put it down on the table. 'I don't want ter get involved emotionally wiv anybody, Jimmy. I couldn't stand it. I like yer, an' I could easily go ter bed wiv yer, but yer married an' I'm not gonna get involved again. I couldn't.'

He looked at her closely, his eyes unblinking. 'Listen, Con. I fink the world of Ruby an' the kids, an' there's nufink I wouldn't do fer 'em, but right this minute I'd give anyfing ter make love ter yer. I've gotta be honest. Sometimes a man 'as physical needs, wivout gettin' serious or anyfing. I'm sorry, Con, but I can't lie ter yer.'

'Women 'ave needs, too, Jimmy.'

They left the quiet riverside pub and walked out into the black, cold night. She took his arm and their footsteps sounded loudly on the cobbled street. Connie felt warm inside and strangely elated. He was telling her about when he was a lad, and how he often used to play down at the water's edge. She could hear the excited lilt in his voice and felt his arm trembling a little. They entered Jamaica Road and soon they were standing outside his house. Jimmy glanced around nervously as he inserted the key and pushed on the front door. They walked into the dark, stale-smelling room and she was in his arms. His urgent kiss pressed down on her waiting lips and his hands groped about her body. The ceiling spun above her head as he eased her down on to the low divan and, as he slipped his trembling hands beneath her dress, she moved to help him. It was unreal, like a dream, and he was mute as his caresses became more intense. She was his secret adventure, his mistress for a night who he could not take to his marriage bed. She knew that it would be too much like betrayal for them to go to the bedroom. Here in the darkness, prone on the divan, the act of love would allow him some vestige of comfort. The sanctity of his marriage would not be profaned. She felt his loving and she closed her eyes. He was tender yet urgent. He was an experienced lover but he was inconsiderate, and it was over before she had become fully aroused. There was no fulfilment and no tenderness, only a sense of relief and thankfulness that she had been able to make peace with herself as a woman again. She held him as he lay exhausted against her body, and she dreamed that maybe sometime in the hazy future she would be able to give herself completely.

He left her a few doors away from the little public house in Salter Street. It was nearing midnight and when she let herself in the side door Connie saw that the kitchen light was on and Jennie was still up. Her small round face was creased in pain and anguish as she sat slumped in an upright chair beside the dying fire.

'Did yer enjoy yer evenin' out?' Jennie said wincing, her hands pressing down on the tops of her thighs.

Connie took off her coat and threw it over the back of a chair, ignoring the question. She searched Jennie's face as she stood over her. 'What's wrong?' she asked. 'Yer look white as a sheet.'

Jennie screwed up her face and tensed as another sharp spasm attacked the pit of her stomach. 'I'm in agony, Con. It's the pills I took. They're givin' me 'ell.'

'What pills? What yer talkin' about?'

The spasm passed and Jennie sagged in the chair. 'I'm a week overdue, and I'm always on the dot. Steve took me to a chemist 'e knows an' we got some pills. They're murderin' me. I'm in agony.'

Connie leaned forward in her chair. 'Yer silly cow. What yer let 'im talk yer inter takin' pills for?'

The white-faced young woman dabbed at her hot forehead with a creased-up handkerchief. 'I 'ad ter do somefink. They'd kill me if I was pregnant.' Another spasm knotted her insides and she got up quickly, holding her stomach and making for the yard. Connie followed her to the back door and stood biting her lip as her friend doubled up in pain.

'Leave me, Con. I'll be all right,' she groaned, running out through the open door.

Connie walked back into the kitchen and slumped down wearily in the armchair. For a while she stared into the white ashes, and then her eyes went to the sideboard. The bottle of whisky was still there as usual and Connie pursed her lips. Just a little one, she decided. It'll make me sleep. She walked over to the sideboard and as she uncorked the bottle she saw a note. 'Mr Preedy called to see Connie.' She poured herself a drink and swallowed it quickly. The name did not mean anything to her. She poured herself some more whisky. The sound of the back yard toilet being flushed made her gulp down the drink, and as she flopped back into the chair Jennie walked in.

Jennie grinned sheepishly and slumped down in the armchair facing Connie. 'I fink the pills are beginnin' ter work, Con. I feel sort o' funny,' she said.

Connie stood up wearily. 'Let's get yer up ter bed. Yer'll be all right. I'll stay wiv yer, Jen.'

Jennie waved her friend away. 'Don't fuss, Con. I wanna be on me own. Don't worry, I'll call yer if I need to.'

'Yer sure? I don't like leavin' yer like that.'

Another spasm made Jennie wince. 'I'm sure,' she grated.

Connie put her arm around her friend's shoulders. 'Yer'd better get ter bed, Jen. If yer mum sees yer like that she'll guess somefink's up.'

'Yer right. I'll get upstairs. By the way, there was an ole bloke called in ter see yer. 'E wouldn't leave a message. 'E said 'e'd come back termorrer night. 'E did tell me 'is name but I fergot it. Mum wrote it down somewhere.'

Connie got up and took her friend by the arm. 'Look, are yer goin' ter bed? I'll talk ter yer more in the mornin'. Don't worry, I'll make sure the fire's out an' I'll see ter the lights.'

Jennie sighed and clutched at her stomach. 'I'm on me way. Night, Con.'

'Night, Jen.'

The bad weather was settling in and the German air force had stayed away for another night. The morning had been bitterly cold with frost lying like powdered glass on the cobblestones. Jennie had told her mother she was feeling sick and was going to take the day off. Before Connie left for work her friend managed to give her a reassuring wink and a knowing smile passed between them.

At work it was some time before Jimmy Pope came into the workroom. He approached Connie's bench hesitantly and smiled at her, his face showing his embarrassment. She smiled briefly in return and carried on the conversation with her workmates. He had broken the ice and he felt better as he piled the leathers on to the work top. He had sat up until the early hours writing a long letter to Ruby. In it he had said how much he missed her and the kids and how much he loved them all. He had expressed his hope that soon, if the raids held off, she and the children might be able to return home. He felt a little better after he had finished the letter and he lay in his bed struggling with his feelings of guilt until sleep finally overtook him.

That evening the Dolphin was quiet. The bitter weather had kept all but the very hardy around their banked-up fires, but Billy Argrieves came in and stood at the counter. The collar of his navy-blue overcoat was pulled up around his ears and his cheeks glowed as he sipped his pint of ale. Connie noticed how nervous he still seemed. His hands shook as he held the glass and his eyes darted about like those of a stalked animal. He finished his drink and ordered a bottle of Guinness to take away, looking around quickly as Connie put the bottle down in front of him.

'Bloody 'ell,' one of the customers remarked as Billy left. 'Did yer see that? Billy Argrieves takin' 'is ole mum a drink. I don't believe it.'

Connie was about to say something but Bill French had walked over. He had noticed that the vociferous customer had been sitting in front of the fire for over an hour without buying another drink. At least Billy Argrieves was one up on him, he thought as he leaned over the counter.

''Ere, Sharkey. Don't yer fink it's about time yer left the lad alone?' he said. 'The poor bleeder's a bundle o' nerves as it is.'

Sharkey looked at his friend for support. 'Some people 'ave got short memories. I remember when Billy Argrieves was a bloody aggravator. If yer looked at 'im the wrong way yer was more than likely ter get a black eye. 'E ain't so cocky now, is 'e?'

The landlord stood up to his full height and frowned. 'Now listen 'ere, Sharkey. That lad spent more than two months on 'is back in the 'ospital, an' when 'e come 'ome 'e couldn't even wash 'imself. It took a lot o' guts fer 'im ter walk in 'ere on 'is own fer the first time. I'm not gonna stand around an' let the likes o' you take the piss out of 'im. Now, what I suggest yer do is shut yer trap, get yerself anuvver drink an' give somebody else a chance to 'ave a look at the fire, ovverwise yer can piss orf out an' find yerself anuvver pub ter drink in.'

Sharkey got up and walked over to the counter. 'Who upset you, Bill? Your ole woman bin gettin' on ter yer, 'as she?' he said in a familiar tone. ''Ere, give us anuvver pint fer Gawd's sake, an' 'ave one yerself. It might put yer in a better mood.'

Later a grey-haired old man came into the public bar. He walked up to the counter rubbing his hands together, his face glowing red above his bushy moustache. ''Ello, girl,' he said brightly. 'Give us a whisky. This bleedin' weavver's a perisher.'

Connie placed the drink in front of him and he took a quick sip. 'I was in 'ere last night but they told me yer was 'avin' a night off,' he said wiping his moustache.

'Are you Mr Preedy?' she asked, leaning on the counter facing him.

''S'right. Yer don't remember me, do yer?' he said smiling.

Connie stared at him, a puzzled frown on her face.

'It mus' be about eighteen months since I was in 'ere last,' he went on. 'It was wiv the darts team from the 'Orse an' Groom. It was the August before war broke out if I remember rightly. Anyway, I was tellin' yer 'ow me an' yer muvver worked tergevver once. Remember now?'

Connie nodded with a sudden smile. 'Yes, I remember,' she said with quickening interest.

The old man took another sip from his glass. 'I told yer I'd pop round if I 'eard anyfink o' that Norma Cantwell. It ain't good news I'm afraid.'

'What is it, Mr Preedy?'

'Well, I got talkin' to a pal o' mine,' he continued. 'I ain't seen 'im fer ages. We got chattin' about ole times an' it come up about when we worked tergevver at the tin bashers in your ole turnin'. Well Charlie, that's 'is monicker, 'e outs an' tells me about Norma Cantwell.'

'What about 'er?' Connie prompted.

'She copped it. Yeah that's right. Last November it was. Landmine be all accounts. It knocked a block o' flats down orf the Walworth Road. Bloody shame. Ole Norma was re-housed in there when they pulled Birdcage Lane down, so Charlie told me.'

Connie sighed. She had tried to resign herself to the fact that she would probably never locate Norma after visiting Birdcage Lane and discovering that everyone had moved away, but she had still clung to the faint hope that someone might know where she had gone. Now Norma Cantwell would never be able to help her. Connie straightened up and gave the old man a smile.

'Fanks fer rememberin' after all that time, Mr Preedy,' she said heavily. 'I appreciate it.'

'It was no trouble, luv,' he said with a wave of his hand. 'I was only too pleased ter let yer know. Sorry ter be the bearer of bad tidin's though. Still, it can't be 'elped. 'Ere, fill that up an' 'ave one yerself.'

Connie poured two drinks. 'Fanks very much,' she said, clinking glasses with him. ''Ere, by the way, Mr Preedy. Was there anybody by the name of Bonny workin' at the factory when you was there?'

The old man stroked his chin. 'The name don't ring a bell. It's a funny name. I reckon I would 'ave remembered a name like that. Why d'yer ask?'

'Oh nufink. I 'eard me mum mention it a few times,' she said.

The heavily built figure walked painfully through the dark, icy cold streets, keeping close to the sides of the buildings and wharves as he occasionally glanced behind him. There wasn't much time, he realised. They would soon come looking. They knew he would make for Bermondsey and his friends. It had been a long time since he had tasted the river air and smelled the soft grey mud. The area had been badly bombed but his friends would still be there. They wouldn't let him down. He heard slow plodding footsteps ahead and he darted into a doorway. A heavy padlock pressed against his back and he felt the sweat breaking out cold on his forehead. Christ! he muttered voicelessly. If it's the law he'll be trying all the doors! He held his breath as the footsteps got nearer and then suddenly they stopped. For a while he rested his aching head against the cold iron door, knowing he could soon be discovered. He heard the footsteps again. They were going away and he breathed easier. He knew that he had to press on. He was nearly there and if the street had survived someone would give him a meal and a place to sleep.

He stubbed his toe in the darkness and cursed. That old iron post had been there for years; he should have remembered it, he had played leapfrog over it enough times as a kid. He puffed heavily in the cold air. Prison had a way of making people forget. Everything seemed smaller than he had imagined it to be. As he looked around in the quiet darkness he could see that there were spaces and piles of rubble where his kind had lived, but at least the little turning was still there. It was scarred and the buildings had been badly damaged, but the little row of houses were still standing. He strained his eyes and saw the black silhouette of the ugly factory building standing out against the night sky. He reached the house he was looking for and he hesitated. The street was empty and no light filtered out on to the cobblestones. Maybe he had left, he thought with a sinking feeling. Maybe they had all gone. He knocked softly on the door and the iron knocker sounded like a hammer striking an anvil. He hunched his shoulders against the night chill and waited. Then he heard a door inside open and footsteps. The street door opened and he saw the familiar face staring at him in disbelief. He opened his mouth to speak and a wave of exhaustion and relief flowed over him. He staggered forward and gripped the door post.

'Can yer 'elp me, Joe?' the fugitive gasped.

Chapter Thirty-Six

Before he went to work Joe Cooper walked up to the corner of John Street and bought the morning paper. It was there inside the first page, with the headline: 'Dennis Foreman Escapes'. Joe hurried back home with the paper tucked under his arm. He was already aware that the long arm of the law would soon be reaching out to his neighbourhood. Dennis was well known in the area and it would be obvious to the police that he might well seek help there. He placed the open paper on the kitchen table and took his spectacles down from the mantelshelf.

> Dennis Foreman, who was serving ten years for his part in the 1935 Piccadilly jewel robbery, made a dramatic escape yesterday evening whilst being transferred from Pentonville to Dartmoor. The train carrying him to Plymouth was derailed outside Reading and Foreman made his escape by leaping out of the train during the confusion and disappearing into the darkness. The police spokesman said that Foreman was handcuffed to a police officer at the time but had been able to take the keys when the officer was rendered unconscious by the impact. Members of the public are asked not to approach this man but to inform their local police station or dial

Whitehall 1212. Our correspondent Jeremy Paine reports that the derailment was caused by a subsidence brought about by recent enemy bombing. Twelve people including the police officer were detained in Reading General Hospital with minor injuries.

Joe folded the paper and sat back in his chair. Denny had not said much about his escape. He had been exhausted when he knocked at the door and, after wolfing down a bowl of soup and a hunk of bread, he had collapsed on to the bed. When Joe got up that morning he had roused the fugitive with a cup of tea and some toast and told him to get dressed as quickly as possible. He knew the police would realise their quarry was making for London. It would not take them long to inform the local police, who knew of Denny's old haunts. Joe also realised that because of his own police record he could be visited by the police at any time. He would have to find a safe haven for Denny until he could be got out of the area. Joe wondered where he could go, and he decided there was only one thing to do for the moment. He would have to stay in the factory shelter, if he could be smuggled in without being noticed. Joe looked at the clock on the mantelshelf: it showed twenty minutes to eight. Very soon the workforce would be hurrying through the gates and it was then that Denny might make it inside without attracting attention.

At ten minutes to eight the two men stood just inside the front door. Joe felt apprehensive but there was no time to dwell on things. Denny looked pale and gaunt in the old overcoat Joe had found for him. He had washed and shaved and wrapped a woollen scarf around his neck. Fear showed in his eyes as he waited for the word from Joe, who had told him to slip out into the street at the last minute and trail in through the gates behind the latecomers. That way he might just make it. They had gone over the plan whilst they waited and, with a bit of luck, it seemed that it might just work. Joe could see the Barton sisters coming into the turning. They were invariably the last two to clock in each morning.

As they drew level with his house, Joe stepped out. 'C'mon you two. Late again?' he joked as he fell in step beside them.

They hurried through the gates, the two girls unaware that Dennis Foreman, the notorious jewel robber, was walking quietly a few yards behind them. Inside the yard, the fugitive veered off and darted safely down into the dark shelter.

The day went very slowly for Joe. He had managed to smuggle some sandwiches and a flask of tea to Dennis during the lunch hour but there was no time to stay for a chat. He always ate his lunch in the firm's canteen and to change his routine now would arouse suspicion. It was after dark when he got back to the shelter. He carried a broom and shovel with him in case anyone spotted him, but he need not have worried. The blacked-out street was deserted. Denny was lying on one of the bunks which had only recently been installed and he jerked up as the street warden came in.

'Did yer get the evenin' paper, Joe?' Denny asked, rubbing his eyes.

Joe pulled the *Star* from his pocket and tossed it on the bunk. 'There's nufink in there,' he said. 'I already looked. Yer yesterday's news!'

Dennis threw his legs over the edge of the bunk and sat forward, his elbows resting on his knees. 'The bloody time's dragged terrible. I was expectin' the law ter walk in 'ere any minute.'

Joe sat down on the bunk facing him. 'You'll be okay fer the time bein'. If there's an air raid ternight get inter that corner,' he said, indicating with his thumb. 'The crowd who sit there ain't very talkative. They won't start askin' questions.'

'I gotta get ter Norwich, Joe. I got a cousin there. 'E'll put me up till it cools orf a bit. Trouble is I can't jus' jump on a train. The stations are bound ter be watched.'

Joe nodded. 'The law's pullin' up civilians on stations. They're askin' fer identity cards. There's bin a flap over deserters and fifth columnists.'

Dennis scratched his head. 'I can't stop 'ere, Joe. I gotta do somefink. Don't yer know any local transport blokes yer can trust? I got me money stashed away up at me cousin's. I can send the money on. I'll pay well fer a ride out of 'ere.'

Joe thought for a while. 'I know somebody ter ask. I'll pop round there later ternight. In the meantime, take it easy. Yer safe 'ere, long as yer don't break inter song.'

Dennis grinned. 'I'm not likely ter do that. By the way. Fanks fer sortin' me out, Joe. I knew I could count on yer.'

The street warden looked hard at the heavy-set man facing him. 'Yer ain't said much about what 'appened, Denny. I got more out o' the mornin' paper.'

'I was knackered last night,' Dennis said as he lit a cigarette. 'I tell yer, when I jumped down orf that train I ran like the devil was after me. It was pitch-black an' I must 'ave fell over a dozen times. The last time I went straight in a ditch full o' water. Anyway I reached this main road an' I 'ad ter duck in the bushes every time a motor went by. Farther down I came across some road works. I ducked in the bushes an' waited till a lorry come along. When it slowed down ter get round the 'ole I jumped on the back. D'yer know, I didn't 'ave a clue where the bleedin' 'ell the lorry was bound for. All I was interested in was gettin' as far away from that train as possible. It seemed like I was on that lorry fer hours an', when it finally stopped at a transport caff, I 'opped orf and legged it. I finally found meself on Chelsea Embankment, would yer believe? Anyway, I jumped a bus, an' that's about it.'

Joe leaned back on the bunk. 'You 'ad some money fer the fare then. Where d'yer get it from?'

Dennis grinned. 'When I went frew the rozzer's pockets fer the keys I found some silver. I couldn't get ter the pound notes. If 'e 'ad any 'e must 'ave bin sittin' on 'em.'

'What made yer do a scoot, Denny? Yer done a lot o' yer sentence. Wiv time off yer'd be out in a year or two.'

Dennis laughed bitterly. 'Yer don't know the 'alf of it. Fer a start there ain't no time orf. I was involved in a scuffle wiv a screw an' bang went me remission. They reckoned I was gettin' ter be a trouble-maker, that's why I was on me way ter the Moor.'

Joe smiled and shook his head. 'Yer ain't changed a bit, 'ave yer? Yer always was a bit of a mad so an' so. Couldn't yer count ter ten before yer 'ammered that screw?'

'Yer done bird, Joe. I know 'cos sister Dolly wrote an' told me. Yer know what it's like. Yer banged away fer hours at a time an' yer get ter finkin'. I was broodin' about me missus. She sent me a letter sayin' she wanted a divorce. She told me she met this geezer who's got a respectable job an' she wanted nufink more ter do wiv me. I tell yer, Joe, it cracked me up. I was 'avin' a bad time wiv this screw an' when 'e started ter goad me I seen red an' clonked 'im. I busted the bastard's jaw.'

'When did yer get married, Den?'

'I met me missus when I got out o' the army in 1930 an' we got married the same year. I done seven years in the colours, Joe. Matter o' fact I signed up just after I left 'ere. I was posted ter India. I done almost four years out there.'

Joe changed his position on the bunk. 'It's bin a long time, Denny. Yer ain't changed all that much.'

'Nor 'ave you, Joe.'

'D'yer remember when we run the streets round 'ere? We 'ad some good times, didn't we?'

'We sure did, pal.'

Joe lowered his head and stared down at his shoes. 'I bumped inter yer sister Dolly just after Kate died,' he said quietly. 'She said she was goin' ter write an' tell yer.'

'Yeah, she did, Joe. Bloody shame the way she went. She was a diamond was Kate. I bet young Connie's all growed up now, ain't she? She was only two years old when I left.'

Joe looked up. 'Yeah, she's a real little beauty. Talk about a ringer fer 'er muvver.'

Dennis stood up and stretched. 'I'd love ter see 'er, Joe. Maybe I will when fings die down a bit.'

Joe lapsed into silence and stared down at the floor.

Dennis looked at him thoughtfully for a few moments, then he said, 'Look, Joe. There's a lot o' water gone under the bridge. I 'ad ter leave when I did. There ain't no grudges, is there?'

Joe shrugged. 'Like yer say, Den. It was a long time ago. We grew up since then. There's no grudges. We missed yer, an' Kate took it bad. We was all very close.' He paused. 'Anyway, I'd better get goin' if I'm gonna see this bloke,' he said, standing up and buttoning his coat. 'Take it easy. I'll be back soon as I can.'

PC Wilshaw stood on the corner of Ironmonger Street with his gloved hands clasped behind his back and watched the comings and goings. It was early evening and the Armitage workers were hurrying from the turning. The constable knew most of the workers by sight and his eyes darted from one to another as he chewed on his chinstrap and rocked back and forth on his size twelves. They had all been briefed at the station that morning and Dennis Foreman's photograph had been duly studied. PC Wilshaw was confident. I'll spot him if he shows his face around here, he told himself. It would be a nice arrest to make. There would be quite a bit of publicity and his photo would most certainly be in the daily newspapers. Could be sergeant's stripes in it, too, he thought.

The stragglers were coming out of the turning now and the constable decided to give it another few minutes then take a stroll along to Tower Bridge Road and back. Suddenly he spotted Toby Toomey hurrying along, an evening paper tucked under his arm. PC Wilshaw had been wondering what had become of the street totter.

''Ello, Toby,' he called over. 'Ain't yer out wiv the pram these days?'

Toby looked up from his thoughts at the towering policeman and grinned. 'No,' he said proudly. 'I got meself a respectable job.'

''Ave yer? What d'yer do now, Toby?'

Toby hooked his thumbs through his braces and puffed out his chest. 'I'm the 'ead barrel-washer at the pickle factory. It's a pretty important job, mate. Yer gotta be careful when yer dealin' wiv food. If I don't clean them barrels prop'ly people could get food poisonin'. Oh yes, it's a pretty important job.'

'I'm sure it is, Toby,' the constable said, hiding a smile. 'Not everybody could be an 'ead barrel-washer. 'Ow many yer got workin' under yer, then?'

Toby pursed his lips and drew in his breath sharply. ''Bout six or seven.'

The constable rocked back on his heels. 'I wanna ask yer somefink, Toby. You're a sharp character who keeps 'is eyes open. 'Ave yer seen any new faces in the area? Yer know what I'm talkin' about.'

The head barrel-washer stroked his chin. 'There's only one new face showed up round 'ere lately, mate.'

'Oh, an' what's this new face look like?'

Toby stroked his chin again. 'Well 'e's short an' stocky, an' 'e's got sort o' broad features. 'Is nose is flattish an' 'is ears are all screwed up like a boxer's. Yeah, an' 'e talks sort o' funny.'

'What d'yer mean, Toby?' the constable asked quickly.

'Well it's gibberish.'

'Gibberish?'

'Yeah, 'e talks foreign. 'E's Czechoslo-bleedin'-vakian.'

'Czecho what?'

'This fella my Lil's goin' wiv. 'E's a Czech. Sandor 'e calls 'imself. Mind you, I don't know if it's 'is real name or not, but our Lil . . .'

''Old up, 'old up,' the tall policeman said sternly. 'I'm not interested in your Lil's boyfriend. I'm interested in Dennis Foreman. Yer know who I mean, Toby.'

'Is that the dirty bastard who's bin exposin' 'imself in the market?'

PC Wilshaw groaned to himself and wished he had never bothered to start the conversation. Toby was getting worse, what with Czech boyfriends and marketplace perverts. 'Jus' keep yer eye open, Toby,' he growled. 'If yer see any strange faces who look a bit suspicious, come an' tell me, okay?'

Toby nodded and started off home. 'Come an' see me?' he repeated aloud. 'I should fink so. Nosy ole bastard. 'E's got more chance o' bein' struck by lightnin'.'

The weather had turned bitterly cold as Joe Cooper made his way to the Swan public house in Dockhead. Jack Rabin, the landlord, was friendly with many of the local villains. He might know of someone who could safely transport Dennis Foreman out of the area, Joe reasoned. It would have to be done very quickly. The police would be stepping up the search in the locality and they would certainly get around to checking all the public shelters. Joe was looking serious-faced as he pushed open the door of the saloon bar and walked in. The bar was quiet and Jack Rabin spotted him immediately.

'Well I never! If it ain't me ole mate Joe. 'Ow the bloody 'ell are yer? I ain't seen yer fer ages,' Jack said, thumping Joe on the back and holding out his hand.

Joe grinned as he took the landlord's outstretched hand in his. 'Nice ter see yer, Jack. I 'eard yer retired down ter Margate.'

'No such luck, Joe boy. Not wiv my ole dutch. She's keepin' me two steps away from the poor'ouse. Anyway, what yer 'avin'?'

'A nice pint o' bitter'll go down a treat, Jack.'

When Joe put down the money Jack waved it away. 'This one's on the 'ouse. Fer ole time's sake. Remember those get-tergevvers we 'ad wiv ole Solly Jacobs? We planned a few cracked 'eads in this bar, didn't we?'

Joe sipped his pint. ''Ere, Jack. Remember that Blackshirt march down the Ole Kent Road when we tore into 'em wiv those wooden clubs? I won't ferget it. That was when I got done fer assaultin' that copper. What a stitch-up job that was.'

'Yeah, bloody shame, Joe. 'Ere. I was down yer way a few weeks ago on a bit o' business. I passed yer turnin'. Those buildin's took a right pastin'.'

Joe nodded his head sadly. 'The Bartletts and the Rileys went in that. I s'pose it was lucky more didn't go. Nearly everybody was down in the factory shelter that night.'

Jack leaned forward on the counter. 'D'yer fink we've seen the last of the bastards? It's bin very quiet lately, ain't it?'

'I dunno, Jack. The Midlands 'ave bin gettin' it by all accounts, an' Glasgow an' Liverpool. They'll be back ter see us before long, yer can bet on it.'

The drinks had been flowing and a few familiar faces had joined the two. Names were being bandied about and various exploits were being recounted.

Joe decided the time was ripe and he beckoned the group together. 'Look lads, gavver round,' he said, glancing around the bar quickly. 'I don't wanna shout. I got a problem. A good friend o' mine wants ter get out o' the area on the quiet. 'E don't mind travellin' third class, if yer get me meanin', but it's gotta be done smartly. 'E can pay well, but the wages will 'ave ter come later.'

'What's 'e done, Joe, upset a few bookies?' one of the men joked.

Another one glared at him. 'Yer know better than to ask that,' he said. 'It's none of our business.'

There was now a marked seriousness amongst the group and Joe suspected that they knew who he was talking about.

Jack turned to one of the men. ''Ere, Don. What's the name o' that geezer what done yer bit o' business? 'E's pretty reliable, ain't 'e?'

Don Samuels nodded. 'Yeah, that was ole Bert Lucas. You should know 'im, Joe. 'E's related ter the Toomeys who live in your turnin'.'

'Christ! Not Toby Toomey?'

'That's 'im. I fink Bert's 'is wife's uncle. Somefink like that. Anyway, 'e's reliable, Joe. Why don't yer 'ave a word in 'er ear? She'll be able ter locate 'im on the quick.'

Joe thought for a while. 'I'd better pop in ter see 'er right away. I can't afford ter 'ang about too long. I'll see you lads later. Keep out o' trouble.'

Jack leaned forward on the counter. 'Give yer mate our best regards, Joe, an' tell 'im ter come round fer a drink when fings quieten down a bit.'

Joe grinned and walked out into the black.

426

* * *

It was turned eleven when Marie Toomey heard the knock on the front door. 'Well go on then, ain't yer gonna answer it?' she shouted at her husband.

Toby was dozing in the armchair and he jerked awake, his eyes opening wide. 'I wonder who that is, Marie?'

'What am I s'posed ter be, clair-bloody-voyant? Go an' find out.'

Toby opened the door a fraction. 'Who's there this time o' night?'

'Open the door prop'ly, yer silly git,' Marie screamed out from the end of the passage.

Toby did as she said and he saw Joe Cooper standing on the doorstep.

''Ello, Joe. Wassa matter, mate?'

'I'm sorry ter knock so late, but it's urgent. I wanna 'ave a word wiv yer missus, Toby.'

Marie walked down the passage. 'All right, get inside,' she barked at her husband. 'What can I do fer yer, Joe?'

'Is yer uncle still in the transport business, Marie?'

'Why, d'yer want 'im ter do a job for yer?' she asked, grinning.

Joe nodded.

'Yer better come in,' she said, showing him into the kitchen.

'Can yer get word to 'im, Marie? It's urgent.'

'Yeah it is, ain't it?' she smiled.

Joe looked at her and then at Toby with a puzzled frown. 'What is it, Marie?'

'D'you wanna tell 'im or shall I?' she said, looking at Toby.

'You tell 'im, girl.'

'Right. Now ter start wiv, I gotta tell yer I never like goin' out wivvout me earrin's in. 'E knows, don't yer, luv.'

Toby nodded quickly and Marie continued. 'I was gettin'

ready this evenin' ter go out wiv me friend from John Street an' when I come ter put me earrin's on they ain't there.'

Joe's puzzlement was increasing by the second and he stared at Marie, who seemed to be enjoying his bewilderment.

'I always keep 'em in me Oxo tin, along wiv me ovver bits an' pieces,' she went on. 'Anyway they ain't there, so I gets ter finkin'. The last time I could remember wearin' 'em was when I got back from seein' me mate an' the siren went. It was the Tuesday o' last week, wasn't it? Well, whenever it was, I can vaguely remember takin' me earrin's off in the shelter 'cos they was 'urtin' me ears. I fink I can remember wrappin' 'em up in me 'ankie an' puttin' 'em on the ledge be'ind where I always sit. I've searched this 'ouse 'igh an' low, an' they're not anywhere ter be seen. The only fing I could fink of was that I left 'em in the shelter. Well I sent Toby over ter see if they was there an' as 'e went in the shelter this great big bloke jumped out an' frightened the bleedin' life out of 'im. Well, Toby managed ter convince 'im that 'e was a good friend o' yers an' 'e could keep 'is mouth shut.'

'Bloody 'ell!' Joe groaned, clapping his hand to his head. 'Yer could 'ave got yerself mangled. That fella can be dangerous in a corner.'

''E's all right, Joe.' Toby cut in. 'We 'ad a nice chat – after 'e put me down. 'E told me 'e was out o' fags so I took 'im some back.'

Joe shook his head slowly. 'Toby, yer a gem.'

Chapter Thirty-Seven

Connie Morgan climbed down from the tram and walked slowly past the tall, imposing St Alfege's Church. Ahead she could see the river wall and smell the sour mud which belched its gases at low tide. A few people strolled past and noisy children hurried down on to the foreshore, eager to see what treasures the ebbing tide had washed and dumped. Above, the clouds were silver-edged as the late rising sun started its climb.

It was a mild Saturday morning in March 1941, and the early spring flowers were spreading their pale colours amidst the grey, austere surroundings. Connie had walked this way many times with Robert and the memories came flooding back to her as she reached the river wall. Together they had scanned the wide flowing Thames, made their plans and dreamed of peaceful times to come. Now she had returned alone. She had wanted to come to this place again, to think and to try to put her confused mind into some sort of order. The months had slipped by so slowly and she had become oppressed by the painful fixed pattern of her life. By day there was the inevitable factory grind and in the evenings the trial of always having to put on a happy face for the customers of the Dolphin. The ritual was harrowing and Connie felt she was being slowly swallowed up by the unbroken emptiness of her routine. Only the glowing feeling in her insides and the feathery lightness in her head made it all bearable, but that agreeable state was no longer easy to reach. It had been easy once, when her tolerance was very low and a couple of whiskies were enough. Now her search for comfort from the drink had started to become dangerous. It was more and more difficult to reach that numb state, and she had started to drink more and more.

The River Thames looked calm and still while overhead screaming, wheeling gulls swooped down and plucked at the bread thrown by noisy children. Connie walked slowly, her head still heavy and hung-over with the effects of the whisky she had consumed the night before. The events of the previous evening were hazy but she remembered the raucous crowd at the end of the counter. She recalled Billy coming into the bar and standing at the counter talking easily and looking relaxed, but after that it all became confused. She had a recollection of a dark-haired individual who was with the crowd and who had gone out of his way to impress her. He had bought her drinks and he had been very complimentary but she could not even remember his name. He was with a brassy woman, and when he had ignored his partner and turned his attentions toward her Connie remembered how angry the woman had become.

The gently turning tide was lapping against the massive wooden stanchions by the pier and it stirred the foreshore mud. For a while Connie rested by the wall, watching the children playing at the water's edge. Slowly her head began to clear. It was coming back now. She could see Billy's face and the murderous look in his eyes as he was hustled from the pub. Connie's head pounded as she breathed in the clear air and gradually her memory of last night's events became sharper. Billy had come in early and he had stood chatting to her for some time. She remembered how easy it had been to talk to him. He had taken pains with his appearance although his suit was fraying at the cuffs and showing signs of wear at the elbows. He was trying very hard, but it was easy to see that he was still struggling with his own personal demons. She could tell that the noise and the crowd were affecting him, and when the pub started to fill up he had become more and more edgy. There was a look in his eyes, she recalled, a strange, sorrowful look, and it touched her in a way she could not understand. It was when the crowd at the end of the counter became noisy that Billy started to become unsettled. She had been busy serving and she recalled hearing the sudden roar and seeing restraining hands pulling Billy away and pushing him out into the street. Bill French had raved at Billy and told him that unless he controlled his temper he would be barred from the pub in the future. Connie was saddened by the landlord's outburst. She had grown fond of Billy Argrieves. She liked his sharp sense of humour and his charming manner, and under normal circumstances it would have been quite easy for her to fall for someone like him. He was an attractive man, but she had promised herself that she would not get emotionally involved with anyone. Growing too fond of someone would only bring more heartache and despair. She had already lost everyone who had meant anything to her.

Connie turned her back on the river and strolled slowly towards Greenwich Park. It was there, too, that she had spent many happy hours with Robert and memories rose up swiftly in her mind as she walked into the tranquillity of the leafy avenue and took the path which led up to the observatory. At the top of the hill she turned towards the wide stone promontory and there she sat for a while looking down at the silver band of river and the resting dock cranes. The sun had slipped out from a cloudy sky and the early morning mist had cleared. Her heart was heavy as she stared down at the idle river. It would be so easy to go down to the river when the tide was full and the night was dark. She could slip from the pier and let the cold waters take her. There was no family, no one to grieve. Maybe her father was still living and he might read about her suicide in the papers. Maybe he would mourn for a while, but he would soon forget. After all, he had left Kate and his baby and had made no attempt to return. The realisation knotted Connie's insides. She experienced a cold fury which grew, and the thoughts of taking her own life disappeared. She stood up suddenly, her hands clenched. If her father was still living she would find him, somehow. She would talk to him and find out what sort of a man it was who would walk away from his responsibilities and just disappear. With burning anger rising in her chest Connie Morgan turned away from the hill and walked back down the steep path and out once more into the morning traffic.

The proprietors of the Dolphin were having a serious discussion and Bill French was adamant.

'I can't 'elp it, Dora. I've bin fair wiv the lad, but enough's enough. What 'appened last night could 'ave turned into a bloody riot. We've got the licence ter fink of. Once the law get called in it goes in the book, yer know that.'

'I know all about that, Bill, but I still say that crowd started takin' the piss. They're the ones you should bar. They're all Steve Barnett's cronies, an' I don't go a lot on 'im neivver. Our Jennie's besotted wiv 'im. I've tried talkin' ter the girl. I've tried ter warn 'er but it's like talkin' ter meself.'

Bill shrugged his shoulders. 'What can I do about it? That crowd ain't given me no cause ter bar 'em, except fer takin' the piss out of Billy Argrieves. Let's face it, Dora, 'alf the pub takes it out o' Billy.'

'Yeah, be'ind 'is back,' Dora reminded him. 'They wouldn't face 'im.'

'That's the 'ole trouble, Dora. Young Billy's always bin a bit wild. Since 'e's come 'ome the lad's got worse. I mean look at last night. Much more o' that an' we won't 'ave any regulars left. They'll all be too scared ter drink in the pub.'

Dora prodded the table top with her forefinger. 'I'm tellin' yer now, if yer bar young Billy I'm gonna tell that ovver mob they're no longer welcome in the pub, so there.'

Bill puffed hard and looked into his wife's determined face. 'All right, I'll leave it this time, but if 'e steps out o' line once more 'e's barred, an' I mean it.'

The landlady of the Dolphin felt somewhat satisfied by her husband's decision to give Billy Argrieves another chance, but she could see trouble ahead if the new crowd continued to drink in the pub. She was aware that Steve Barnett had invited them down to the Dolphin and, because Jennie served in the public bar, they all congregated there. Perhaps she should have a word with Bill about Jennie working in the saloon bar, she reflected. Although that wouldn't be a very good idea. The crowd would just change bars. They would then most likely upset the saloon-bar customers with their mouthings and nothing would be achieved. Maybe she should take it on herself to make it clear to the crowd that they were not welcome. She had heard a few nasty stories about them, and in particular the dark-haired one who had provoked young Billy. Some of the regulars had identified him as a devious character who owned a wholesale provision business and they had told her he was involved in a lot of black-market dealings. There were some nasty stories circulating about his wild parties, too, and Dora was worried about Connie. She seemed to have become the object of his attentions and it spelt trouble, she felt sure. Dora decided that she would have a word with Connie and put her on her guard, though she knew it wouldn't be easy. The girl had become even more withdrawn lately, and her drinking was giving the family cause for concern. She was now drinking heavily and she kept a bottle of whisky in her room, according to Jennie, who was more than a little worried about her friend's well-being. Dora sighed to herself. She shouldn't be saddled with all these problems at her time of life. Maybe it was about time she and Bill sold the business and moved into a little country pub.

Bill French was feeling very much the same as Dora. He was not very happy about the new clientele. Derek Angelo had been pressing him to take a batch of his under-the-counter cigarettes and tobacco which was marked up 'HM Forces Issue'. He had also been asked to handle a couple of cases of Scotch whisky, a deal he had declined, realising the problems it would pose with the brewers, as well as with Dora. Then there was the worry of Jennie, who had gotten herself attached to Steve Barnett and would not hear a word said against the man. Bill pondered his problems as he went over to the pub doors to open up for trade.

It was Saturday evening, and the first customer to walk through the door of the pub was Mrs Argrieves, who ordered a milk stout. 'You was a bit 'asty last night, wasn't yer?' she said quickly as the drink was placed in front of her.

'What d'yer mean, girl?'

'Bannin' our Billy, that's what I mean.'

Bill leaned forward on the counter, 'Look. I ain't barred the lad. What I did say was fer 'im ter watch 'imself. I can't afford ter keep a disorderly pub, now can I?'

'Well I wasn't in 'ere last night,' Florence began, 'but I 'eard all about what went on. Strikes me yer should be 'avin' a word or two wiv that flash load o' monkeys 'oo started it all. It's comin' ter somefink when yer can't 'ave a quiet drink in the pub any more.'

Bill looked the irate woman squarely in the eye. 'Your Billy threatened ter knock a customer's 'ead off 'is shoulders an' we 'ad ter get 'im outside quick, luv.'

Florence returned the stare, 'An' what started it? I'll tell yer what started it. This flash 'Arry took my Billy fer some ole plum, that's what. There was a bit o' piss-takin' an' then this bloke knocked my Billy's arm, on purpose I was told. There was beer all down 'is suit, an' when they all started laughin' at 'im 'e lost 'is temper. What's 'e s'posed ter do, walk away?'

The landlord opened another bottle of milk stout and put it beside the angry woman. ''Ere, Florrie. 'Ave this on me. Billy's welcome 'ere as far as I'm concerned an' I promise yer I'll keep me eye open fer trouble. I won't let that crowd get at 'im again, okay?'

Florence poured out the drink with a look of satisfaction. 'I ain't one ter complain, Bill, an' if my lad knew I was talkin' ter yer 'e'd go mad. Trouble is, yer see, 'e ain't prop'ly better yet. When 'e first come 'ome I couldn't get the bleeder ter wash or shave, yer know that. 'E slept in 'is clothes an' every night 'e'd scream out in 'is sleep. Gawd knows what 'e was goin' frew. It's bin 'ard, but the boy's beginnin' ter pull 'imself tergevver. Yer must 'ave seen the difference in 'im lately. I've got 'im ter wash an' shave, an' a lot of it is down ter young Connie. Our Billy's took a shine ter the girl. She's about the only one 'e feels comf'table wiv. 'E's always talkin' about 'er.'

Bill nodded. 'I know, Florrie. She's a good kid. It ain't bin easy fer 'er neivver, what wiv losin' 'er chap, an' all 'er family. I'll 'ave a word wiv Connie. She'll keep 'er eye on 'im.'

Customers had started to arrive and it was not long before Steve Barnett's friends began to congregate in their usual spot at the end of the counter.

Joe Cooper sat in his parlour deep in thought. Beside him on the table was the latest letter from Dennis Foreman, and it was causing him considerable anguish. Much had happened since the escapee had left Bermondsey concealed in the back of a lorry laden with a consignment of foodstuffs from the London docks. Dennis had been put down on the outskirts of Norwich, and soon he had been safely reunited with his cousin. Money had changed hands and a forged identity card had been provided. He now wore a moustache and parted his hair down the middle. A pair of thick spectacles completed the disguise and, as Joe studied the photograph sent with the letter, he had to admit that Dennis looked nothing like his former self.

There had been repeated visits from the police during the past few months. They had made it clear to him that he was known to be a friend of Dennis Foreman and any attempt to aid or to assist the escaped prisoner would render him liable to a long term of imprisonment, especially as he himself had previous convictions. For a time there had been a policeman lurking in the street. Strange faces in civilian clothes also seemed to be hanging around now and again and Joe began to spot the waiting detectives when he went for his morning paper or came out from the factory in the evenings. As time passed the watchers slowly seemed to disappear. There had been regular sightings of the escapee from as far north as Scotland and from various south-coast towns. One report in a Sunday newspaper suggested that Dennis Foreman had been killed in an air raid on Liverpool and another, more bizarre tale, told of his suicide by drowning. Credence was given to the story by the discovery of a torso which had been washed up on the beach at Skegness. The mangled remains had most likely fouled a ship's propeller and identification had been rendered impossible, the correspondent concluded.

Dennis had taken comfort from the varying stories of his demise and in his latest letter to Joe he indicated that it was about time he returned to his old haunts. Joe was not so confident. It had been quiet lately but any stranger in the area might well arouse curiosity. There was another part of the letter which caused Joe to worry. Dennis, now using the pseudonym William Smithers, had suggested that the Toomeys might like to take in a lodger. It would be a safe haven, Marie's Uncle Bert had told him, when the two had met to conclude their transaction. Joe thought otherwise. Marie was shrewd enough to keep Dennis's identity a secret and she would see to it that Toby kept his mouth shut, but Joe felt that Lillian was another proposition. It was common knowledge that she was very partial to members of the opposite sex, and the fact that she was at present seeing a lot of a certain foreign serviceman would not make the slightest difference to her roving appetites.

Joe leaned back in his chair and thought about how he would reply to the letter. Dennis had asked about Connie Morgan and said that he would like to meet her now that she was a grown woman. His desire to see her worried Joe. Connie had suffered enough as it was. One loose word might be enough to arouse her suspicions, for she was a smart kid. The shock of discovering the identity of her father after all this time could be too great. He would need to make this clear in his reply and would also need to remind Dennis of the promise he had made all those years ago: the promise the three of them had made together. Kate Morgan might not be alive, but her wishes should still be honoured, for Connie's sake if nothing else.

The crowd had gathered and the drinks were flowing fast. Bill French was helping Dora in the saloon bar but he frequently popped his head into the public bar as the evening wore on. There had been no air raids for the past two weeks and the Dolphin was becoming a very busy pub. Connie was disappointed that Billy had not put in an appearance, but Derek

Angelo had been eager to cultivate the pretty young barmaid and he was being particularly attentive. She had been plied with drinks and already her head was beginning to buzz and she could feel the familiar comfortable warm glow spreading around her insides. Connie studied the crowd and could not see the brassy woman who had been with Derek Angelo the previous evening. Derek had asked her to accompany him to a party after the pub shut and at first she had declined. But as the drink took hold her defences crumbled and the dark-haired young man had been very persuasive. So finally she agreed. What did it matter? she reasoned. He was friendly and generous, and there would surely be plenty to drink. What did it matter if she had to fight him off? She could drink herself into a sublime state and forget everything for a few hours. She could shut out the pain and sink finally into a dreamless sleep.

At closing time Dora voiced her worries about the assignation but Connie laughed them off.

'I'll be all right. The party's only a few streets away. Don't wait up, Dora. I've got me key.'

Across the road from the Dolphin Billy slouched in a doorway. He had been standing there for the past hour and the cold night air made him shiver. He had made several attempts to cross the street and enter the pub, but each time he had stopped at the kerb and then slipped back into the shadows. He wanted to see the pretty blond barmaid and talk to her again, but he felt ashamed. He had tried to ignore the taunts and the jests the previous evening. He had tried hard to remain cool and detached but the anger had welled up until he was looking down a dark, narrow tunnel. All he could see was the face of the man who was taunting him and his rage had exploded. She would think him crazy he thought, and tears rose into his eyes.

'Why can't they leave me alone?' he muttered through his gritted teeth. 'Why should they treat me like an idiot?'

He fought the anger and desperation which twisted up his stomach as he waited in the shadows, and then he saw her. She was leaving with the dark-haired man who had taunted him the night before. She was laughing and she tossed her long blond hair over her shoulder as the man slipped his arm around her waist.

Billy watched as they left the turning, then he stepped out from the shadows into the pale moonlight and walked slowly home.

Chapter Thirty-Eight

The first light of day filtered through the drawn curtains and Connie blinked as she slowly came to. She could see that the bedroom was well furnished and the ceiling was high, unlike her attic room at the pub. Her hands went down to the silk counterpane and suddenly she sat up with a start, pulling the bedclothes up around her nude body. Her head pounded and a feeling of nausea swept over her. The space beside her was dishevelled and she realised that someone had shared her bed. She glanced around the room as she fought her sickness and saw that her clothes were draped over a chair beside the bed. She slipped out of the sheets and felt the soft carpet beneath her bare feet as she stole a furtive glance at the door. She dressed quickly and then went to the window. The street was deserted except for a lone figure who walked by carrying the Sunday papers under his arm. Connie slumped down on the bed and put her hands to her head. It was still hazy but she remembered leaving the party with Derek Angelo and walking across the street. The rest was a blur.

The sound of a key in the lock startled her and she jumped up from the bed in alarm.

He came breezily into the bedroom, surprise showing on his dark features. 'Yer awake then,' Derek said, breaking into a grin. 'Phew! That was some party last night. 'Ow's yer 'ead?'

Connie sat down heavily on the chair. 'It's bangin',' she said. 'I can't remember much.' She looked towards the bed. 'Did yer stay 'ere last night?' she asked hesitantly.

He laughed aloud. 'Yer mean yer can't remember?'

'No,' she replied quickly.

'It's all right. Don't looked so shocked. Nufink 'appened,' he said sitting down on the edge of the bed. 'We didn't get very far, we was both too drunk.'

Connie stood up quickly and felt the nausea returning. She grabbed her handbag from the dressing table and put her hand to her forehead. 'I'd better get 'ome. They'll be worried. What time is it?'

Derek glanced at his wristwatch. 'It's ten past nine. What about some breakfast before yer go?'

The thought of food made her stomach turn over and she shook her head. 'No fanks, I mus' get 'ome.'

She hurried away from the terraced house in Dover Square and almost ran the short distance to Salter Street.

As she let herself in through the side door Connie heard Dora call out. 'That you, Con?'

The landlady of the Dolphin looked up as Connie walked into the kitchen. She was clad in a pink dressing gown and her hair was dotted with curlers. 'We was gettin' worried when yer never come in. You all right?'

Connie nodded and sat down in the easy chair with a sigh. 'It was late when the party ended so I slept on the settee. I'm okay, just a bit of an 'eadache.'

Dora took the teapot from the top of the kitchen range and poured out two cups of tea. She handed one to Connie and then sat down facing her. 'Bill an' me was a bit worried you goin' off wiv that Steve Barnett's crowd, Con. They're a no-good lot an', from what I've 'eard about their parties, a young girl ain't safe in their company.'

Connie gave Dora a wan smile. 'It's all right, I never got raped or anyfing. I just 'ad a lot ter drink, that's all.'

Dora sipped her tea. 'That's anuvver fing me an' Bill are worried about, Connie. Yer drink far too much fer a young girl. If yer not careful yer'll do yerself some damage.'

Connie did not reply. Instead she sipped her tea slowly, her eyes staring down over the cup.

'Billy Argrieves didn't come in last night, did 'e?' Dora asked after a lengthy pause. 'Bill told me 'is muvver came in earlier an' she was a bit upset.'

'What did she 'ave ter say, Dora?'

Dora put down her empty cup and studied her feet. 'Accordin' to 'er, my Bill was wrong ter say 'e was gonna bar young Billy. She reckons it was that Angelo who started it all. I fink she's right there. That crowd are a right flash lot. They fink they own the bloody pub.'

Connie sighed. 'I 'ope it don't stop Billy comin' in. 'E's got a lot better lately, an' 'e's chattin' more. 'E was tellin' me the ovver night 'e's finkin' o' goin' after a job. I 'ope 'e does. It'll be good fer 'im.'

Dora gathered up the teacups. 'You just be careful, Connie. Mind what I've said. We don't wanna see yer come ter grief. Gawd knows yer've 'ad yer share already.'

Connie went up to her room and threw herself down on the bed. The sickness had eased but her head was throbbing. She closed her eyes and tried to remember the party. She recalled dancing with Angelo in the crowded room. There had been a lot of drink and she vaguely remembered him encouraging her to try something different, which tasted bitter, like liquorice. She remembered getting hot and uncomfortable soon after. The only other thing she could recall was leaving the party and crossing the street and then climbing up a dark flight of stairs. Connie turned on her side and bit on her clenched fist. Derek said that nothing had happened, she thought to herself, but he hadn't sounded convincing. She wondered what had been in that funny-tasting drink and whether it had had anything to do with her ending up in his bed.

She thought hard about the man as she lay in the quiet room. He was attractive in a rugged sort of way and he had a sense of humour, but she could not understand why she had gone off with him to his flat. She did not feel physically attracted to the man. It must have been the drink, she concluded. Dora was right. She was drinking too much. On three occasions recently when she had been in men's company she had allowed them to take advantage of her. The drink was breaking down her self-control and making her an easy prey. She knew that she was behaving like her mother had and the thought was a painful one. She knew that people would soon start talking. They would call her a loose woman and say that it was only natural, that she was taking after Kate. The realisation made her feel suddenly frightened.

She sat up on the bed, her heart beating rapidly and looked around the room. Her eye caught sight of the little gold locket lying on the dressing table. For a while she stared at it, and then she went over and picked it up. Her eyes filled with tears of self-pity as she squeezed the trinket in her clenched hand. Helen seemed to be mocking her from beyond the grave and it made her angry that her aunt had waited until she was on her death bed before deciding to give her the locket. She must have known all along who Bonny was. Why else would she have concealed the whereabouts of the thing? Connie prised open the trinket and stared again at the tiny inscription. She wiped her tears away with the back of her hand and reaffirmed her vow that no matter what happened, no matter how long it took, she would find out about her father, and why he had walked out on his family all that time ago. It was a challenge she would never give up; it would be a quest which would sustain her, whatever lay ahead.

Billy Argrieves walked out into the Old Kent Road and made his way to the Bricklayers Arms. It was a fresh spring morning and the traffic was heavy as he reached the junction. He stood at the tram stop and waited in the queue for a number sixty-eight to arrive. His stomach was turning over at the thought of going to the labour exchange, but he knew that it was something he had to do. The alternative would be another medical to establish his amount of disability and what sort of pension the army would grant him. Billy was aware that his body wounds had healed completely and the assessment would be made solely on his emotional state. He could tell the doctors about the headaches and the nightmares which still plagued him, and the terror he felt just talking to other people. He could tell them how difficult it was to walk into a pub on his own, or even just go out of the house, and they might be sympathetic towards him. He would then be given a small pension and spend the rest of his life moping around the house and sinking further into depression. The local people would see him as some sort of idle layabout and take the rise out of him even more. They would not care that he was a war casualty, he would just be an idiot to them who they could mock and throw scorn at.

The noise of the tram interrupted Billy's thoughts as it drew up at the stop. He jumped aboard and climbed the steep flight of stairs to the upper deck. He realised that he had always ridden on the top deck of a tram. The rocking and swaying seemed more pronounced and he could see more from up there. He handed over his fare and watched as the miserable conductor clipped a ticket in the machine strapped around his middle. Billy was grateful for the man's silence. He knew that tram conductors were well known for their line of small talk and banter and he did not want to get involved in any sort of discussion. The tram shuddered as it progressed slowly past the stalls in Tower Bridge Road and Billy leaned back in his seat.

What sort of a job would they offer him? he wondered. It would probably be factory work, for he had no trade. Maybe they would offer him some sort of outdoor job. That would be better, he thought. Being cooped up inside did not appeal to him very much. In any case, he must get something. He would then be able to go into the pub and buy Connie a drink. She might even like to go out with him if she knew he had a job. The tram squealed to a stop outside the bomb-damaged vinegar factory and Billy felt the hurt and anger welling up inside of him as he thought of his last visit to the Dolphin. Connie must be thinking he was a trouble-maker who couldn't hold his drink. Even if he got a job and plucked up the courage to ask her out she would probably refuse. It was obvious she liked those smartly dressed people, like the crowd who started the trouble the other night. They were flash boys with money to burn and the dark-haired one must have impressed Connie for her to have left the pub with him like she did.

The tram swung around into Tooley Street and picked up speed. Billy closed his eyes and pictured her. Her hair was shining and she smiled at him. He saw her white even teeth and her pale-blue eyes which seemed to sparkle. He could see her clearly as she moved about the bar and he opened his eyes suddenly. He promised himself that if he got a job he'd get a suit and a new shirt. He could buy a pair of those shiny black shoes he used to wear and a new tie. He would have to try to ignore the taunts when he went into the pub though. Maybe if he smartened himself up the flash boys would leave him alone and Connie might be impressed enough to go out with him.

The thought of asking her out made him swallow hard. He would never be able to pluck up the courage. She would probably only laugh at him. As his thoughts raced Billy felt himself getting hot and uncomfortable. He fought to rid himself of the recurring vision and a cold sweat began to break out on his forehead. The plane was coming towards him, flying low, its wings spread out like a diving eagle reaching down for its prey. Gun flashes blinded him as bullets splattered into the sand and he clawed at the wet grit in an attempt to escape. He felt the bullet hit him and the burning pain in his back. Billy clenched his fists and breathed deeply as he tried to escape from the nightmarish images. He heard the conductor's voice coming from a long way off.

'Next stop the Tunnel.'

The tram shuddered to a stop and the white-faced young man jumped down. He walked briskly along Brunel Road, hoping his exertion would banish the dark thoughts that clouded his mind, and he was breathing heavily when he reached the labour exchange.

The week's work had started as usual for the head barrel-washer at Hayden's pickle factory. In the yard there was a line of empty, smelly hogsheads, and as he sat down on an upturned box and squeezed into his rubber boots Toby was feeling a little apprehensive. The sudden confrontation with the escaped prisoner in the shelter had been a shock to say the least, even if they had got on afterwards. But Marie had received a letter from the man, asking if she would consider taking him on as a lodger. It was that bloody interfering uncle of hers, Toby thought. Marie had told him about Dennis Foreman's new identity and said there was nothing to worry about, but what about that bleedin' copper? He was on the lookout for any new face in the area. Supposing he spotted

Dennis and saw through his disguise? It would mean prison for the whole family. Marie would be sorry. She wouldn't be able to nag those warders in Holloway. Then there was Lillian. She might take a shine to the lodger and find out who he really was. Lil was a good girl but she was apt to be talkative at times, Toby had to admit. Maybe he should put his foot down and firmly tell Marie he would not allow her to take in lodgers. That wouldn't do any good, he reflected. Marie never took any notice of what he said. He might just as well be the lodger himself, for all the respect they showed him. It wasn't as if he was still totting. He had a respectable steady job and he brought home his unopened wage packet every week. Some men wouldn't stand for it. Some men would have upped and left long ago.

The factory manager was staring down from his office window. 'What's he doing? Is he on strike or something?' he said aloud. 'The bloody clown's been sitting there with his hands under his chin for the last ten minutes.' He leaned out of the window and cupped a hand around his mouth. 'Oi you!' he called out.

'Who me?' Toby said, getting up from the box.

'Yes, you. Are you going to start work, or do you expect those barrels to get up and take a shower!?'

'I'm jus' gettin' started, sir. Right away, sir,' Toby replied, swearing under his breath.

The manager shut the window and Toby tied on his rubber apron which reached down to the floor. 'Bloody ole goat,' he mumbled aloud. 'I'd like ter nail 'im up in one of those dirty barrels an' roll the bleeder off Tower Bridge.'

By the time Iris Turner brought out his mug of tea at eleven o'clock Toby had made good progress. At least half of the barrels were cleaned and turned upside down to drain.

'There yer are, luv,' Iris said, giving him a beaming smile.

Toby grinned back and sat down on the box again. Iris stood over him and watched closely as he unwrapped his cheese sandwich, her large eyes unblinking and her full bottom lip hanging loose. Iris was a large middle-aged woman who had spent most of her adult life taking care of her ailing mother. When the old lady died Iris realised that she had left it a bit late to get married and, until Toby came on the scene, she was content to spend her time caring for her cats and going once a week to the women's meeting held at the local church. Things had suddenly changed for Iris. She felt sorry for the inoffensive little character and for the way he was spoken to by the yard manager. All Iris's mothering instincts came to the fore in the presence of Toby and it had become one of her little pleasures to take him his morning tea. Iris had realised with some surprise that strange feelings were manifesting themselves within her. She had even dreamed about Toby one night, and from then on she had decided to make a play for him. She soon found out by a tactful approach that he was married to a dominating woman who, according to the little man, frequently cracked the whip. Iris's womanly feelings blossomed whenever she saw him and at every opportunity she was on hand to give him comfort and to make him aware that she would be a good catch, should he decide to leave the virago.

While Toby munched on his sandwich Iris took out a small package from her apron pocket and unwrapped it.

'Would you care for a slice of Spanish onion, Toby? It's nice with cheese.'

Toby took the slice of onion and slipped it in his sandwich. He was not too fond of Spanish onions, and he knew that Marie would no doubt have something to say about his breath when he got home that night. Nevertheless, he did not want to upset Iris. She had been nice to him, and those large jars of pickles she smuggled out from the dispatch department were proving to be profitable. Toby was also aware of her interest in him and he felt flattered. He had started using brilliantine on his thinning hair each morning, to the disgust of Marie. 'It makes yer bonce look like a polished apple. Anybody'd fink yer was workin' in a bleedin' office,' she moaned.

Toby ignored the taunts and continued his efforts to improve his appearance for the benefit of Iris Turner, and it did not go unnoticed.

'Yer look smart this mornin', Toby,' she said. 'Is that lavender brilliantine you've got on yer 'air?'

Toby nodded with a sheepish grin. 'It 'elps ter keep the flies away, Iris. They swarm aroun' those dirty barrels.'

'Drink yer tea, Toby, it's gettin' cold,' she said, sitting down beside him on the upturned box.

The head barrel-washer had succeeded in removing the slice of onion from his sandwich and depositing it behind the box. He picked up his still-hot tea. 'It's okay Iris, I like it cool,' he smiled.

'I'll put more milk in it termorrer,' she said. Then she added quietly, ''Ow's yer wife?'

Toby wished he had kept his mouth shut. Milky tea made him feel sick, and so did the mention of his wife so early on a Monday morning. 'She's all right,' he answered without enthusiasm. 'She's 'ad a moan about the smell o' pickles on me clothes, but as I told 'er, I smelt a lot worse when I was tottin' fer a livin'.'

Iris shook her head. 'Yer ought ter get out more – on yer own, I mean. Yer should go fer a drink one night. There's a nice little pub called The Green Man in Bermon'sey Lane. It's near where I live. I go in there sometimes wiv me friend Audrey. I could meet yer outside there one night – if yer like?'

Toby wiped the back of his hand across his lips. The

thought of taking Iris for a drink seemed a pleasant enough arrangement, providing Marie didn't get to hear of it. The sudden vision of her chasing him around the house clutching a meat cleaver made him shiver. He glanced into Iris's large friendly eyes and he decided there and then to take the chance. 'It sounds a good idea. What about Friday evenin'? Marie goes out wiv 'er friend on Fridays.'

Iris rubbed her meaty shoulder against his bony arm. 'We can sit in the snug bar,' she said. 'It's quieter in there. They've got a nice pianer player in the pub an' 'e plays all the ole songs on Friday nights. I'll see yer outside about eight o'clock. Is that all right?'

Toby nodded. Marie usually left the house at seven o'clock. It should give him enough time, he thought.

The little meeting had been noted by the irritable yard manager from his office window. That barrel-washer is taking a bit of a liberty, he moaned to himself. It's that Iris Turner encouraging him. I'll have to get her transferred to another department. I can't have her chatting to him every morning, it's stopping him doing his work.

He opened his window and leaned out. 'Oi! You down there!' he shouted. 'Have you finished all those barrels? There's another dozen in the factory waiting to be cleaned.'

Chapter Thirty-Nine

As April showers washed the dockland streets clean and watered the budding flowers in the backstreet window boxes, the local folk were beginning to feel that the worst of the air raids might have passed. The Luftwaffe seemed to be changing their attacks to other large cities. The London air raids had become more sporadic, and many people began to sleep in their own beds instead of the uncomfortable shelter bunks. Clara Cosgrove loved her own bed, and she gave the shelter warden and his helpers due warning that if there should be an air raid they were not to disturb her. It seemed that Mrs Cosgrove had been bitten by something or the other and she put it down to shelter lice.

'It's them there bleedin' bunks, that's what done it,' she moaned. 'I mean ter say, yer can't expect anyfing else, can yer? Them bunks are made of bleedin' sackin'. They 'arbour fings like lice an' bugs.'

Joe Cooper tried to remonstrate with the irate old lady but she was adamant. 'Listen 'ere, Mister Know-all. I'm covered in bloody great bites an' it ain't me own 'ouse what's filfy dirty, an' I ain't bit meself. Them there bites are from lice. We all got bitten in the last war, when we was workin' in the rag sorters' yard in Bermon'sey Lane. Me an' ole Daisy Mooney got covered in 'em an' we 'ad ter be scrubbed all over wiv paraffin twice a day. Bleedin' uncomf'table, I can tell yer.'

'Now listen, Clara. I do them bunks out wiv insect spray twice a week an' nobody else is complainin',' Joe retorted.

'I can't 'elp that, Joe. I tell yer I'm covered. I've even got 'em on me . . .'

'All right, girl,' Joe butted in, not wishing to know the details. 'Yer do as yer see fit. But I tell yer, if there's anuvver bad raid don't moan at me if yer 'ouse falls down round yer ears, an' we 'ave ter dig yer out.'

Clara leaned on the door-post and crossed her arms in a gesture of defiance. 'Well I'm jus' tellin' yer, that's all.'

Joe wanted to tell her that she had probably been bitten by cat fleas. After all, she spent most of each day sitting with Mrs Adams in the cat woman's little front parlour. But the look on Clara's face stopped him saying anything further and he shrugged his shoulders as he walked away.

As the month slipped by the weather grew warmer and the days became longer. May started warm and sunny, and on the evening of the tenth the air-raid siren sounded early. Soon the guns were firing and explosions rocked the little backstreets. The raid developed into the worst one the dockland folk could remember. All night the roar went on as high explosives rained down all over London. Fires burned out of control. The docks and wharves were badly hit, and firemen were unable to pump water from the Thames due to a very low tide. The sky glowed dull red and black smoke hung in the air. All the London hospitals were crowded with casualties and queues of dazed victims waited at emergency dressing stations to be treated. Gas, water and electricity supplies were cut off and, as the shocked shelter-dwellers emerged at first light, the sight that greeted them was nightmarish. All around dockland the little streets which survived were strewn with glass and roof slates. High in the angry sky a huge cloud of smoke seemed to cover the whole of the capital and it reflected the flames of the many fires which were still burning out of control. The smell of cordite and burning timbers was stifling and fire bells sounded incessantly as the last reserves of fire fighters dashed to the raging blazes.

In Ironmonger Street, the raid had brought back painful memories of the night when the Dwellings had been destroyed, and the streetfolk felt a new sense of impending doom as they made their way home silently. Joe Cooper and his team of fire watchers had battled all night against the falling incendiary bombs, and they managed to save the little houses from burning down when they smothered a device which had fallen through Ada Halliday's bedroom ceiling.

At the height of the air raid Joe and his team had banged on Clara Cosgrove's front door but there had been no answer. They had been too hard pressed to return, but as soon as the raiders left they banged on Clara's door again. Still there was no answer and they decided to force entry in case something had happened to the determined old lady. Joe leaned heavily on the door and pushed it open. There was a scorching smell in the passage which seemed to be coming from the back of the house, and when the fire watchers stumbled into the little backyard they saw a pair of Clara's red flannel drawers smouldering on the clothes line. Beneath them was an incendiary bomb which had burnt itself out on the stone floor.

'Christ!' Joe gasped. 'She's a lucky ole cow. She could 'ave bin burnt alive.'

Clara was unrepentant. She woke with a start to see anxious eyes staring down at her. 'What the bloody 'ell d'you lot want!?' she blurted out, quickly drawing the bedclothes up around her neck.

'Yer drawers caught light, Clara,' Joe answered, grinning with relief. 'We jus' put 'em out.'

'Gawd 'elp us!' the old lady groaned. 'They was me clean ones. I only washed 'em out yesterday.'

Joe stared down at her. 'Yer sure yer all right, luv? It was a bad one last night.'

'I didn't 'ear a fing,' Clara said, scratching the back of her head and yawning, 'I must 'ave bin in a deep sleep. Well don't stand there gawkin'. I gotta get up an' sort out anuvver pair o' drawers.'

Like Ironmonger Street, little Salter Street had survived, although the turning was littered with broken glass and roof slates. The adjoining street had not been so lucky, however. A bomb had landed on a row of terraced houses and more than a dozen people had been killed. The nearby Old Kent Road had been badly hit, too. Shop fronts had been blown out by the blast of a high explosive landing in the middle of the road which created a deep crater that had rapidly filled with water. There was ugly devastation everywhere. Black smoke rose from many backstreets and the sickly smell of smouldering fires hung in the still air.

People appeared on the street and looked around in disbelief at the damage that had been inflicted. Road gangs were out pumping water from the crater and other men worked with oxy-acetylene torches to remove the twisted, mangled tramlines. Fire hoses criss-crossed the thoroughfare, and near the Bricklayers Arms junction a terrified, dust-streaked tom cat sat in a tree and watched the commotion. As evening set in, the beleaguered docklanders prepared for the worst. The shelters filled early and ears strained for the dreaded air-raid siren. But night fell and as the hours ticked slowly away it remained silent. Slowly the battered population drifted off to sleep, and when the new day dawned and the people roused themselves they rubbed their eyes incredulously. The morning was calm and the smoke had cleared.

* * *

The week following the terrible air raid was a quiet one and people began to hope that it may have been the last attempt of the German air force to bomb the capital into submission. Their spirits rose as the days passed and the pubs became busy once more. In the Dolphin, Connie and Jennie were struggling to cope with the trade on Saturday evening. The piano player was in good form and already the public bar chorus was giving an unrehearsed rendering of the latest tunes. The bar was noisy and filled with smoke and people were jostling for space as they shouted out their orders.

Connie was secretly pleased that Derek Angelo had not made an appearance. Ever since the night of the party he had been pressing her to go with him to a nightclub up West. Jennie had told her that Derek's business premises had been gutted by fire during the last air raid and he was probably pre-occupied with salvaging what was left. The crowd of smart young men was in its usual spot, however, but Jennie was taking care of that end of the bar and for that Connie was thankful. She was desperate not to become too involved with the crowd. The experience with Derek had made her cautious. She had become resigned to going straight to her room after the pub had closed and reading until she dropped off to sleep. Sometimes it was easy when the customers had been generous, but other times she needed to take the bottle out of its hiding place and fortify herself before going to bed. She had no strength to resist the bottle in her room or the tot which some kind soul bought her, but there were times when the drink hardly seemed to help her at all.

The evening wore on and Connie glanced at the door every time someone came in. It had been almost two months since Billy Argrieves had been forcibly ejected and she was giving up hope of his coming in again. She missed him and hoped he would make an appearance, although she tried not to dwell too much on him or to wonder why he had stayed away. Connie had told herself over and over again that no one would ever get beyond that self-imposed barrier she had created. Billy was a danger to her, she realised. If she was not careful he might weaken her defences, and she tried to put him out of her mind. He posed too much of a threat.

It had been more than six weeks since Billy Argrieves walked nervously into the local labour exchange and got himself a job. The official was feeling very charitable on that particular morning and he had listened while the hesitant young lad blurted out his requirements. Billy was duly dispatched to the premises of John Burton, Timber Merchants, where he spent some considerable time chewing on his green card before plucking up enough courage to enter the yard. The foreman was a kindly man who felt sorry for Billy's efforts to articulate himself and he signed his labour card.

Billy found the job to his liking, although at first his damaged back caused him pain. Working outside suited him and he soon became used to the physical nature of the job. The demand for timber was heavy and he was often able to earn a few extra shillings with overtime. The job helped to restore Billy's self-confidence and he began to make plans to get himself tidied up. On one thing he was decided: he would not enter the Dolphin until he was satisfied with the way he was dressed. There would be no cause for anyone to take the rise out of him and he would also be in a position to repay the blond barmaid for her kindness in buying him all those drinks.

Florence Argrieves had taken the tape measure to her son and when all of his details were entered on the form supplied by her next-door-neighbour she went to place the order.

'I've put the colour in the box, Edie,' she said. 'Now don't let the so an' so talk yer into 'avin' any ovver colour. Billy insists on it bein' grey. Oh, an' fer Gawd's sake don't let on it's fer 'im.'

Edie nodded. 'Don't yer worry yerself, Flo. If the nosy bastard starts askin' questions I'll say it's fer me nephew.'

'Fanks, Edie. Since my Billy clobbered 'im, the bleeder won't even look at me. I couldn't even get a pair o' shoe-laces orf 'is catalogue. Mind you though, Billy's payin' fer the suit, not me. Since 'e started work 'e's a changed lad. By the way, Edie. If that tallyman brings any o' those plain blue shirts round like you got your ole man, order us one, will yer? Put it on the book an' I'll settle up wiv yer. I'm buyin' it fer Billy.'

Two weeks later the young man stood appraising himself in front of the mirror. That afternoon he had got a haircut and he had paid a visit to the baths in Grange Road. He had to concede that the new grey suit fitted perfectly. His black brogues were well polished, his blue shirt looked very smart and a silver tie added the finishing touch. Florence had wanted him to wear a pocket handkerchief but he shook his head.

'I don't wanna look too flashy, Ma. This'll do.'

Ten minutes later his mother called up the stairs, 'Ain't yer goin' out? Yer bin standin' in front o' that mirror fer hours. If yer not careful yer'll 'ave the devil jumpin' out after yer.'

Billy looked down at his shaking hands and felt beads of sweat breaking out on his forehead. The thought of walking into the pub again terrified him. All eyes would be on him and people would be bound to notice he was wearing a new suit. Supposing the mickey-taking starts again, he thought to himself. Could I cope with it?

'C'mon, Billy. What yer doin' up there?' his mother bawled out.

With an effort he turned away from the mirror and hurried down the stairs to the front door. Florence watched through her lace curtains, a proud smile spreading over her face, as her son walked away along the darkening street.

People entered the Dolphin and the light faded until it was completely dark. Still Billy waited in the same spot where he had stood when he saw Connie leave with the dark-haired young man. He squeezed his clenched fists until it hurt and then rubbed his sweating palms down his trouser legs. It was the sight of the returning policeman which decided him to go in. He had given Billy a suspicious look as he strolled by earlier. With his heart beating rapidly the young man walked up to the door of the public bar and pushed it open. As he stepped through the heavy blackout curtain and looked around quickly he saw that the pub was packed. No one seemed to be taking any notice of him and slowly he edged his way towards the bar.

Connie saw him coming towards her and she let the drink she was pouring spill over. He looked so different. His dark wavy hair was combed back from his forehead and he was grinning nervously.

''Ello, Billy,' she said quickly, letting go of the pump handle as beer washed over her hands. 'Long time no see.'

He touched the knot of his tie with his thumb and forefinger. ''Ello, Connie,' he said. 'I've bin pretty busy. I . . . I got a job.'

'So I 'eard. Is it okay?'

He nodded as he reached his hand into his pocket. 'Yeah, I like it. It's out in the open an' there's a bit of overtime.'

The elderly customer beside Billy was waiting for his pint of ale and he tapped the money on the counter. 'I don't fink yer'll get any more beer in that glass, gel,' he remarked.

Connie winced. 'Sorry, Albert. There we are.'

Albert picked up his pint and backed away from the counter, glancing curiously at the young man next to him.

'What can I get yer, Billy?' Connie asked, resting her arms on the wooden surface and smiling broadly.

'I'll ... I'll 'ave a pint o' bitter, an' you 'ave one, too,' he said, grinning back at her.

'No, it's all right.'

The smile disappeared from his face and Connie straightened up. 'Oh, all right,' she said. 'Why not?'

''Ave a whisky.'

'A beer'll do.'

Billy's eyes opened wider. 'Go on, 'ave a whisky. I've seen yer drink whisky when I was in 'ere before.'

Connie returned his open look. 'Oh yer noticed me, did yer? Well jus' fer that I fink I will 'ave a whisky.'

They laughed together and suddenly she felt a pang of anxiety. She could see a certain look in his eyes. She had seen that look in Robert's eyes that day in the Armitage factory canteen. It seemed so long ago now but she had never forgotten it. It had been the start of something wonderful then and, as she remembered, Connie quickly lowered her eyes.

It was nearing closing time and Billy was finishing his third pint. He had been standing at the counter the whole time, watching her as she hurried to and fro with the many orders. The crowd in the corner had noticed him, but apart from a few wary glances they had ignored him. Billy watched the barmaids busying themselves behind the counter and occasionally he and Connie exchanged glances and he fingered his tie or pulled at his shirt cuffs. Connie could see the struggle going on inside him as he looked around nervously and smiled briefly as folk nudged their way to the bar. She became increasingly aware of her own conflict. Part of her wanted to stay and talk to him and part of her wished he had never come in that evening. Her resolution was being tested, and she gritted her teeth. It wasn't fair, she groaned to herself. It wasn't fair to him or to her. No one could replace her loss: no one could heal that aching she experienced every waking day which lasted through the long empty hours. Only the warm release she got from the burning spirit could help her forget. There was nothing she could offer to anyone; she had nothing left to give.

The bell had sounded and now Bill French was calling time. Billy had finished his drink and was watching her closely as she mopped the counter. 'Oh well. I'll be off then,' he said without moving.

Connie looked at him, a brief smile disguising her feelings. Go, Billy. For Christ's sake go, can't yer, she pleaded silently. 'Okay, Billy, see yer later,' she said to him.

He backed slowly away, his eyes never leaving her until he was near the door, and then he turned and was gone. Connie rubbed away furiously at the dry surface. She was being stupid, she told herself. Why was she allowing herself to become involved so easily? She had chosen her path, and now in a moment of weakness the way ahead had become uncertain. She looked around and noticed that Jennie was preoccupied. Quickly she poured herself a large drink and gulped it down. The spirit burned her throat and hit her stomach like a hammer. She blinked and saw Jennie looking at her. The publican's daughter came over and squeezed her arm. 'You all right?' she said with concern. 'Yer look terrible.'

Connie managed a weak smile. 'I'm okay, Jen. It's bin a busy night.'

'Yeah, it 'as,' Jennie replied, picking up the last of the dirty glasses. 'Look, Con. I don't wanna be a wet blanket or anyfing, but don't yer fink yer strongin' it a bit wiv the booze?'

Connie rounded angrily on her friend. 'It's all right. I was gonna put the money in the till anyway.'

Jennie shook her head. 'No, Con. Yer welcome to a drink

any time as far as I'm concerned. Trouble is I'm worried – fer you.'

'There's no need ter worry, Jennie. I'm okay. Really.'

Jennie touched Connie's arm. 'Go on, get up ter bed. I'll finish down 'ere. Jus' remember, I'm yer friend. If yer wanna 'ave a chat anytime, jus' say.'

Connie nodded. 'Fanks, Jen. I will,' she said with a sigh.

Billy walked slowly along the dark street, his footsteps sounding loudly on the flagstones. He was feeling slightly dizzy with the amount of drink he had consumed and more than a little pleased with the way the evening had gone. He had managed the first part. Connie had seemed glad to see him and she had found time to talk to him even though she was very busy. The next part was going to be harder. He had to bring himself to ask her out. Maybe she would come out with him, now that he was looking more presentable. He had reached his front door, and as he pulled on the door-string and let himself in he was whistling. Florence was sitting beside the empty grate listening to the wireless. She heard him climbing the stairs and her face broke into a satisfied smile. I must tell Edie how nice Billy looked in that suit, she thought. She heard his door shut and her eyes travelled over to the empty chair facing her.

'Yer should 'ave stayed around, yer no good bastard. Yer'd 'ave bin proud of 'im,' she said aloud.

461

Chapter Forty

It was a few days after the heavy air raid when Dennis Foreman, alias William Smithers, took up residence at number one, Ironmonger Street. He had arrived early on Monday morning carrying a small battered suitcase and a bunch of flowers which he had purchased from a stall outside Liverpool Street Railway Station. It seemed logical to Mr Smithers that a visiting relative might want to greet his kin with a small token of affection and it would also seem logical to any enquiring soul who might note his arrival.

Mr Smithers's ploy worked very well, for his arrival was noticed by PC Wilshaw, who had just left the Armitage factory after his usual morning cup of tea. He glanced at the short, stocky figure who rat-tatted on the Toomey's door and was rewarded with a wide grin. The PC noticed the heavily greased hair, the thick spectacles and the bushy moustache. He looked down at the man's trouser turn-ups and he could see they were exposing at least two inches of black socks and a pair of scruffy brown suede shoes. The police constable walked by grinning to himself. It figured, he mused. Anyone who looked as ridiculous as that would only be knocking at the Toomeys' door. He must be a relation, probably a brother or a cousin. Who else would take flowers to number one? Come to think of it, he might be a suitor calling on Lil Toomey. She had

had some very peculiar men friends in the past, he recalled.

The wanted man had passed the first test and he soon made himself at home. Lillian introduced him to her soldier sweetheart who mumbled an unintelligible greeting, and she fluttered her eyelashes at him when Marie showed her the flowers he had given her. Dennis was wary, for Joe had warned him about the man-mad Lillian in his letter, and from what he had learnt he decided not to lead the girl on in any way. He had no desire to become involved with anyone who attracted attention by outrageous carryings-on. His plan was quite simple, he reasoned. He would soon become accepted by the local folk and then he could slowly discard the disguise. It had worked for his old cell-mate, Nosher Warner, who had used the ruse to fool the police for quite a few years. Nosher had escaped from an outside working party when he was at Pentonville and he had eventually returned to his home in Hoxton disguised as a city gent. After a while the pinstriped suit and the rolled-up brolly were discarded in favour of a more becoming garb for the area. It was only when he became besotted with the wife of a local councillor and ran off with her, and the week's takings from the man's tobacco shop, that he was apprehended. Dennis did not intend to make the same mistake, and he vowed to give Lillian Toomey a wide berth.

The fugitive had made a point of warning Joe Cooper of his arrival, and they met in a quiet pub off the Old Kent Road. Joe arrived first and, halfway through his pint of ale, he saw the ridiculous figure enter the bar and blink owlishly as he approached the table. He held out his hand.

''Ello, Joe. Remember me? William Smithers from Dock'ead.'

Joe tried to hide his grin. 'Sit down yer soppy sod. Yer look like a refugee from Caine 'Ill.'

Dennis smiled. 'Gonna buy us a drink then?'

Joe got up and walked to the counter. It was early evening and the bar was quiet, much to Joe's relief. The landlord was studying the next day's racing in the *Evening News* and he looked up wearily as Joe put a ten-shilling note down on the counter. Dennis was busy polishing his spectacles on a large spotted handkerchief and when Joe put the pint down on the table the fugitive put them back on his nose.

'Christ! Yer must 'ave good eyesight ter see out o' them,' Joe quipped. 'It's a good job yer didn't bring yer white mackintosh wiv yer. Yer'd get run in fer impersonatin' a peepin' Tom or a fifth columnist.'

Dennis took off his glasses and put them in his coat pocket. 'We'll 'ave ter watch it, Joe. Don't start callin' me anyfink but William Smithers if there's anybody around. I've bin practisin' meself. I'm William Smithers from Barkin'. I'm over this side o' the water lookin' up Cousin Toby. I'm single, an' I've got a medical note which ses I'm unfit fer work owin' ter 'eart trouble. I've also got me identity card, an' a box o' pills ter make it look good.'

Joe shook his head slowly. 'Yer bin busy sortin' yerself out. Is that identity card all right? There's a few geezers bin nicked round 'ere fer carryin' forged cards.'

'Don't worry about that, Joe. My card is genuine,' Dennis said, grinning widely. 'The real William Smithers was killed in an air raid. It seems there's quite a racket in takin' cards off dead bodies. If nobody claims the corpse after a certain time they release the identity card. I tell yer, Joe, them cards fetch a lot o' money. My one cost a packet. So did the medical note.'

Joe sipped his beer thoughtfully. 'I thought yer was comin' back ter London a couple o' weeks ago. What kept yer?'

Dennis took a swig from his glass then leaned back in his chair. 'I 'ad ter sort me finances out, mate. There was all that money owin' an' I 'ad ter collect. It's all done now an' I'm set up fer a long spell.'

People were now coming into the pub and Joe began to feel uneasy. It did not go unnoticed by Dennis. He bought some more drinks and smiled at Joe as he sat down. 'Relax, pal. Yer look a bit bovvered.'

Joe sipped the froth from his filled glass. 'It's lookin' at you. I'm 'alf expectin' somebody ter come up an' put their 'and on yer collar.'

Dennis grinned and lifted his glass to his lips. Joe watched as his friend took a swig and smiled to himself when he saw the froth on Dennis's moustache. 'I gotta say it, Den. Yer do look stupid in that get-up.'

Dennis laughed aloud. 'What get-up? It's me own moustache, an' me own 'air. It's jus' combed different, that's all.'

Joe snorted. 'What about those glasses? Did they come orf the corpse, too?'

'As a matter o' fact, me cousin gave 'em ter me. 'E's got a new pair.'

'Well I fink yer attractin' attention ter yerself, Den.'

Dennis became serious and he leaned forward over the table. 'Look, Joe. I've gotta wear this get-up, as yer call it. Wivvout it I couldn't come back ter the manor. I tell yer, I couldn't stand livin' in the sticks. It'd drive me mad. Besides, people were beginnin' ter get nosy where I was. They don't ask so many questions in Bermon'sey. Anyway, let's change the subject. When am I gonna get ter see young Connie?'

Joe had been waiting for him to ask. 'I told yer in the letter, Den. She's left the street,' he said. 'An' I reckon yer should leave 'er fer the moment, she's got enough on 'er plate. An' I wouldn't like ter see 'er get 'urt.'

Dennis nodded. 'Yeah, yer right, Joe. It wouldn't do fer 'er

465

ter find out about 'er ole man, would it? Not after all these years. She should 'ave 'ad the chance ter get ter know 'im when she was a kid.'

'Yeah, well she didn't did she,' Joe replied, staring hard at his friend. 'There's too much water gone under the bridge now. I reckon it's better ter let fings stay as they are.'

Dennis took a gulp from his pint. 'Does she look that much like 'er muvver, Joe? Yer said she was a ringer fer 'er in yer letter.'

'Lookin' at that kid's like seein' Kate. She's the spittin' image.'

'C'mon, Joe, drink up,' Dennis said suddenly. 'This pub's beginnin' ter give me the creeps.'

On Sunday lunchtime Billy Argrieves came back into the Dolphin with his mother holding on to his arm. She was walking slowly and wincing with every step.

'What's the matter, Flo?' one of her neighbours asked.

'I tripped down the stairs,' Florence replied, holding her hip and grimacing with pain. 'Me bleedin' leg's gorn black an' blue. I should 'ave gorn ter the 'orspital wiv it really. It didn't seem too bad when I left the 'ouse, but the pain's terrible now.'

Billy led his mother to a seat and went to the counter.

Connie smiled at him. 'Is that a Guinness fer yer mum, Billy?'

'Yeah, an' a pint o' bitter fer me, Con,' he said, fumbling awkwardly with a handful of coins.

When Connie put the drinks down in front of him Billy gave her a shy smile and carried the filled glasses carefully to where his mother was sitting. The pub was packed and both Connie and Jennie were kept busy. The young man sat with his mother, his eyes constantly straying towards the bar counter. The crowd had gathered in their usual spot and Connie noticed that Derek Angelo was with them. Presently he caught her eye and beckoned her over. Without taking his eyes from hers he ordered a round of drinks and, when she placed the glasses on the counter and handed the change to him, he leaned across the counter. 'What yer doin' ternight, Connie?' he whispered in her ear.

'I'm servin' be'ind the bar,' Connie answered quickly.

'I mean after the pub closes,' he countered.

'I'm gonna get a good night's sleep.'

'Look, Con. I've bin workin' dead 'ard lately, gettin' me bomb damage sorted out, an' I reckon I need a break. When I leave 'ere ternight I'm gonna get a cab an' go up West ter that club I was tellin' yer about. Now why don't yer ferget yer early night an' come wiv me? I told yer, all work an' no play ain't good fer anybody. Now what about it?'

'No fanks, Derek. Like I said, I'm gonna get an early night.'

'Well I'll be back in 'ere this evenin' an' I'll ask yer again. Fink about it. You'll enjoy yerself, believe me.'

Connie turned away to serve another customer and her eyes met Billy's. He was staring at her with a sad look on his flushed face. She looked away and gripped the beer pump hard as she pulled it towards her. It felt as though she was being forced into a corner. Why can't they leave me alone? she asked herself. Why did it all have to be so complicated? Well, they were both going to be disappointed. They were not going to have the chance to get close to her. She was not going to let anyone get that close again – ever.

The lunchtime session was coming to an end and the customers were preparing to go home to their Sunday dinners. Billy and his mother had left suddenly and the crowd had become noisy. Occasionally Derek caught Connie's eye, pressing his question. He did not speak to her again until Bill called time. As he left he looked over to her.

'I'll see yer ternight, Connie. Fink about it,' he said, opening his eyes wide.

Connie watched him leave before going to help Jennie clear the glasses. The landlord had shot the bolts and was sweeping up while Dora went into the back kitchen and prepared to serve the Sunday lunch. When the usual chores were completed Connie joined the family around the table. She was quiet and thoughtful during the meal and later, when she and Jennie were washing the dishes, her friend turned to her.

'Yer looked a bit miserable this mornin', Con,' Jennie said. 'Was that Derek Angelo pesterin' yer?'

Connie shook her head. 'Not really. 'E wants me ter go up town wiv 'im ternight, to a nightclub.'

Jennie's eyes widened. 'Lucky you. Yer goin', ain't yer?'

'I don't fink so,' Connie replied as she picked up the clean plates and set them down on the dresser.

'Cor! Give me 'alf a chance,' Jennie sighed. 'It must be smashin' ter go to a real nightclub.'

'Get Steve ter take yer then. 'E promised to, didn't 'e?' Connie said sharply as she walked out of the kitchen.

It was cool and quiet in the attic room, and the partially drawn curtains kept out the sun. Connie spread out on top of the bed and closed her eyes. Maybe it was time to move on, she thought. The family were being nice to her and she was making things awkward for them with her black moods. Maybe she should try to get a room in Ironmonger Street. Ada Halliday had said she could rent her upstairs room any time she felt like it. There was a light tap on the door and Jennie called in.

'You awake, Con?'

'Yeah, c'mon in.'

Jennie walked into the room with her arms folded. 'Mum an' dad are snorin' in the armchairs an' I've read all the papers,' she said with a smile. 'Fancy a chat?'

Connie grinned and sat up on the bed. 'Sit 'ere,' she said, patting the counterpane.

Jennie sat down and crossed her legs. 'Me an' you are friends, Con. We should be able ter talk about fings, shouldn't we?'

Connie touched her friend's arm. 'Of course.'

'Well, I've bin worried lately.'

'About what, Jen?'

'You.'

'Me? Why should yer be worried about me?'

Jennie traced a line on the counterpane and pursed her lips. 'Well, yer drinkin' a lot lately, an' yer bin like a bear wiv a sore 'ead. Are yer gettin' fed up 'ere, Connie?'

Connie leaned back against the propped-up pillow and closed her eyes for a few seconds. 'I s'pose I 'ave bin goin' it a bit wiv the drink lately, but it's the only fing that seems to 'elp. When I get tipsy I can sleep well. I blot everyfing out. There's no grief, no nufink.'

Jennie looked hard at her friend. 'P'raps you should go out wiv Derek ternight. P'raps you should try an' let go. Nufink's gonna bring yer fella back, Con. Maybe I'm soundin' 'ard but it's true, yer know it is.'

'I know that, Jen. I've gotta live wiv it, but it's 'ard, it's very 'ard. It might be easier if I could cry over 'im, but I can't. There's no more tears left, just an empty space. I can't fill that space. I can't get near a fella wivvout makin' comparisons. I 'ad everyfing once. No one can take Robert's place.'

'P'raps that's where yer goin' wrong.'

Connie looked up from the bed. 'What d'yer mean?'

'Well, yer got a future ter fink about, Con. People our age can't dry up an' live alone. That's fer older people. Let go o' yerself. Yer no different from me. Yer need a fella jus' like I do, even if yer don't want ter get too serious. Jus' grab any opportunities that's goin'. Let a fella take yer out, an' if 'e gets too fresh, tell 'im yer got an' 'eadache, or yer comin' on. I've faked the curse a few times.'

Connie laughed. 'What, you an' Steve?'

'No, 'course not. Steve's different. 'E's older, an' 'e can always get me goin'. Well, most times.'

Connie turned on to her side and rested on her elbow. 'Are you two serious?'

'We're serious, Con, but I don't wanna fink too far inter the future. I'm livin' fer terday. Me an' Steve's got a good fing goin', an' I'm not lookin' ter get married or anyfink like that. It suits me the way fings are. Besides, can yer imagine what me mum an' dad would say if I suddenly told 'em me an' Steve wanted ter get spliced?'

'I can imagine what they would 'ave said if they'd found out about those pills yer took, Jen.'

Jennie grimaced. 'I've learned me lesson. We're very careful now. I told Steve straight. "Yer slipped yer braces over yer shoulder an' I got pregnant. Yer better start wearin' somefink from now on."'

The gathering clouds hid the lowering sun and a breeze rustled the curtains. Connie suddenly swung her legs over the bed and went to the dressing table. 'See this, Jen,' she said, taking the little gold locket in the palm of her hand. 'It was me mum's. She always wore it. In fact I never see 'er wivvout it, unless it was in pawn. I always thought it was buried wiv 'er, but when me aunt died she give it ter me. Well the pawn ticket anyway. See the inscription inside?'

Jennie looked closely at the tiny etching. 'Bonny? Was that yer dad?'

'I never knew me dad, Jennie. Me mum would never speak about 'im. I thought that one day she would tell me all about 'im but she never did. She took the secret to 'er grave.'

''E must 'ave 'urt 'er bad, Con. It seems strange she never told yer about 'im. D'yer fink this Bonny is yer dad?'

'I'm sure of it. Trouble is, I've come to a full stop wiv me search. Yer remember that ole man who come ter see me that night? Well, 'e used ter work wiv me mum at the sheet-metal firm in Ironmonger Street. 'E was tryin' ter get some information fer me. I asked 'im if 'e ever 'eard o' somebody called Bonny an' 'e said 'e 'adn't. I'm gonna tell yer somefink, Jennie. Not so long ago I was finkin' of endin' it all, but then I got ter finkin' about me farvver. I got so mad when I thought about 'im leavin' us. I knew then that I 'ad ter find 'im, somehow. I wanna face 'im, Jen.'

Jennie was staring down at the locket. ''Ave yer thought that 'e might 'ave bin killed in the bombin'?'

'Yeah 'e could 'ave bin, but somefink tells me 'e's alive. I don't know what it is, but I've just got this feelin'. One day I'll meet up wiv 'im, I know I will.'

Jennie reached out her hand and touched her friend's arm. 'Yer'll find 'im one day, Con. I'm sure yer will.'

Connie smiled. 'Fanks, Jen. You're a good friend. I don't know what I would 'ave done wivvout yer.'

'Shut up, yer makin' me blush,' Jennie said, getting up and going to the door. 'I've gotta do some ironin'. I'm goin' out wiv Steve ternight. Look, Con. If yer do decide ter go out wiv Derek there's a couple o' decent dresses in me wardrobe. You can borrer one if yer like.'

'Fanks, Jen. I'll fink about it.'

The light was fading and a few spots of rain fell against the window panes. For a while Connie stared at the tiny locket, and then she lay back on the bed with her hands clasped behind her head. Maybe Jennie was right, she thought. Maybe she should think about going out. Billy seemed to be about to ask her, but that would be out of the question. He was too nice a lad. He would only end up getting hurt. Derek Angelo was different. He posed no problems, except for his desire to get her into bed. She felt she could handle him, but with Billy it was different. She had felt from the first a natural sympathy for him, and it seemed that somehow their suffering had made them familiar to each other. There could be no pretence with Billy. She was afraid that he would touch her heart and she would be unable to give him her love. She knew she must not weaken now. She must be strong, for both of them.

Chapter Forty-One

The Sunday evening session at the Dolphin was as hectic as usual and Connie noticed that Billy had not made an appearance. It was around nine-thirty when one of Florence Argrieves' neighbours came in to say that the old lady had been taken to hospital after collapsing when she got home from the pub that lunchtime.

'Billy was really upset,' the neighbour said. ''E came running inter me an' we got Doctor White in. 'E didn't argue. 'E sent fer an ambulance straight away. The poor cow was shakin' all over an' she was grey wiv the pain. If yer ask me I'd say she's cracked 'er 'ip. I felt really sorry fer young Billy. 'E went in the ambulance wiv 'er an' 'e's goin' back ter see 'er ternight.'

Dora went back into the saloon bar to tell her husband and then popped her head back into the public bar. 'Jennie, don't yer get chattin' too much ter that mob an' leave Connie short-'anded. I can't 'elp out in 'ere. We're busy in the saloon ternight.'

The drinks were flowing fast on that warm evening. The customers had been generous and Connie was beginning to feel a bit light-headed. Smoke hung like a drifting blanket in the airless bar. The piano was playing and one or two elderly ladies were singing loudly. Connie had already served the crowd on two occasions and now Derek beckoned her over yet again. When she had completed the order and passed over his change he gripped her wrist firmly.

'Well, Con, yer comin' ternight, ain't yer,' he said. 'I'm not takin' no fer an answer. Yer'll enjoy it, I promise.'

She smiled wanly and shrugged her shoulders without answering as she moved away to the other end of the counter. The drink was weakening her strength of will and her resolve was slowly crumbling. Jennie's words rang in her ears and she chewed on her lip. It wouldn't hurt any, she thought. It would be a new experience going to a nightclub, and Derek wouldn't be too much of a problem.

Bill was calling for people to finish their drinks and Derek leaned over the counter, his face flushed. 'I'll be back wiv a cab in 'alf an hour, okay?'

Connie looked at him sharply. 'I've gotta get cleared away an' then get changed. I might not be ready by then.'

He grinned. 'Okay, three quarters of an hour, 'ow's that?'

Jennie was mopping up the spilled beer from the counter and she nudged her friend. 'Good fer you. Get up an' sort yerself out somefink ter wear. I'll finish off down 'ere.'

Connie hurried up the stairs and went to Jennie's room. She could feel her head buzzing and, as she opened the wardrobe and looked at the dresses, something told her she was making a mistake. She removed a blue dress and held it up against her as she looked into the long mirror. Her features seemed blurred as she studied herself. Connie laid the dress on the bed and selected another from the wardrobe. The red dress looks better, she thought, and she hurried with it to her room. As she was putting the finishing touches to her make-up Jennie came in without knocking. She was carrying an oatmeal-coloured jacket.

''Ere, Con. Try this on,' Jennie said. 'I usually wear this wiv that dress. It's a three-quarter.'

Connie slipped the jacket on and swung round. 'What d'yer fink, Jen?' she asked.

'Yer look real nice. Yer'll 'ave ter fight 'im off ternight.'

Connie picked up her small clutch bag from the dressing table. 'I don't know if I'm doin' the right fing, Jennie. Maybe I shouldn't go.'

Jennie raised her eyes and gently pushed her friend towards the door. 'It's a bit late fer that now,' she said. 'C'mon, on yer way or 'e'll be finkin' yer ain't goin'.'

Connie reached the top of the stairs and Jennie called out. 'Con.'

'Yeah?'

''Ave a good time, but be careful, okay?'

Connie smiled and hurried down the stairs. Derek was waiting outside as he had promised. He leaned out of the cab and gave her a wolf whistle as she climbed in.

'Yer look very nice – an' on time, too.'

The cab drove slowly over Blackfriar's Bridge and turned left along the Embankment. Derek broke the strained silence. 'I asked yer out 'cos I was a bit concerned about yer, Connie,' he said.

'Oh, an' why's that?' she asked, looking at him.

'Well, I was worryin' in case yer thought I took a liberty wiv yer at the party.'

'I didn't fink that at all,' she replied, looking away from him. 'I jus' 'ad too much ter drink. I shouldn't 'ave gone up ter yer flat anyway.'

'We're still friends then?'

'O' course.'

In the gathering darkness the tall buildings loomed up against the night sky. Soon they had skirted Trafalgar Square and had driven up into Charing Cross Road. Everywhere sandbags fronted the buildings and people in service uniforms strolled by. The cab made a detour around a huge pile of rubble and turned into Shaftesbury Avenue.

Derek sat smoking a cigarette, his eyes occasionally glancing at her. 'We're almost there,' he said, throwing the cigarette stub from the cab.

Soon the taxi swung into Dean Street and pulled up. He helped her from the car and paid the driver. She looked around at the passing crowds, a strange feeling stirring inside her. The last time she had been up West was with Robert. She recalled those evenings she had spent with him in the little restaurant, and the night he had taken her back to the hotel. It seemed so long ago now and she sighed deeply.

They had gone down a flight of stairs and entered a foyer. The air was heavy with strong perfume and there seemed to be tinted mirrors everywhere. A pretty girl stood behind the cloakroom counter and a tall thin man in an evening suit approached them.

'Good evening, Mr Angelo,' the man said formally. 'Your party's arrived. I'll show you to the table, if you'll follow me.'

Connie was puzzled as she fell into step beside her escort. Derek had not mentioned that they were meeting other people. They walked into a large room and as they weaved their way between the tables Connie felt that everyone's eyes were staring at her. The ceiling was low and velvet curtains were draped around the walls. A band was playing on a dais and in front of her she could see couples dancing. They had reached the table and immediately a tall distinguished-looking character in evening dress got up and shook hands with Angelo.

'Hello, dear boy. Glad you could make it.'

Derek introduced Connie and the tall man shook her hand

with a limp grasp. As she sat down Connie studied the group. There were five other people sitting at the large round table. Next to the tall character, who had been introduced as Francis Hammond, there was a slim young man who toyed nervously with a silver cigarette case. On Francis Hammond's left an elderly couple was seated. The woman had her hair piled up on top of her head and the man was bald and wore gold-rimmed spectacles. Another, younger couple completed the party. The man had sandy-coloured hair and was smartly dressed in a grey suit, and the woman with him was striking in a low-cut black dress which made her tanned shoulders look even more golden. Her raven hair shone in the subdued lighting and her dark eyes flashed. Connie was taken by her looks and she stole admiring glances in her direction as the conversation began.

The woman smiled at her, showing large white teeth as she parted her glossy lips. 'You look very pretty, Connie,' she gushed, glancing briefly at Derek. 'We've been hearing about you, haven't we, Arnold?'

Her partner grinned and gave Connie a searching look. 'Derek wasn't exaggerating. You are pretty,' he said smiling at her.

Connie felt herself blushing and she was glad when Francis Hammond took up the conversation. 'Well, have you sorted out the damage, Derek? I'm sure Bernie here can work out the details. What do you say, Bernie?'

The elderly man nodded quickly as he snipped the top of his large cigar with a pair of silver clippers. 'No problem, Francis. I'll get the claim forms ready and send them off first thing tomorrow morning. I'll need to go over those books, too, Derek.'

The waiter had been hovering in the background and, when Francis beckoned to him, the man hurried over. 'I think we're ready to eat, Jules. Oh yes, and you can serve the wine now.'

For the next two hours Connie felt as though she had been

transported to the other side of the celluloid screen. It seemed to her just like an evening out in some exotic city from one of the films they showed at the Trocette. When the food was served from silver trays the elderly woman at her side began to notice her disorientation. She pointed to the various dishes and suggested certain items on the menu which Connie found to be quite delicious. The bottles of wine were soon empty and more were ordered. The band was playing a waltz and the elderly couple took the floor. Connie watched as they danced around. Bernie had a serious expression on his bloated face and his wife almost looked glamorous as she turned around stiffly in her long sequinned dress, her heavily powdered face set in a fixed smile. Connie noticed that Derek was constantly talking to the dark-haired woman, and that her partner appeared not to be in any way bothered by the attention being paid to her. He was ignoring them and seemed much more concerned with encouraging Connie to talk about herself. Connie felt a little embarrassed by the good-looking man's attentions but his wide smile was disarming. Derek's behaviour was making her uncomfortable, however. He seemed to have totally forgotten her, and she noticed the eye movements and the exchanged smiles between him and the dark-haired woman. Francis Hammond was talking to the slim young man who listened intently, his chin resting on his cupped hand, and Connie gazed thoughtfully around the room.

Suddenly the young man in the grey suit got up and came round the table. 'Would you like to dance?' he asked her.

She shook her head vigorously. 'No fanks, I'm . . .'

'Come on,' he said, reaching down and taking her hand. 'It's a slow one. We can just shuffle around.'

They were playing a dreamy tune and the floor was crowded with dancers. Connie began nervously but he moved easily and she found it quite simple to follow his movements.

He held her firmly and she could smell the after-shave he wore. 'There, you see. We're doing well,' he whispered into her ear.

Connie smiled and tried to relax as he glided her slowly around the floor.

'I suppose Derek's told you all about us, hasn't he?' her dance partner said, his face close to hers.

'No. I was surprised when we got 'ere, Derek didn't tell me there'd be anyone else,' she said quickly.

'That's typical of Derek. Would you like me to put you in the picture?'

'If yer like.'

'Well, the woman Derek is so engrossed with is Beth Knowles. She's my cousin and she owns a beauty salon in Bond Street. All very posh too. Francis is an associate of Derek's. They do quite a lot of business together, as you've no doubt gathered by their conversation. The slim young man is called Trixey by his close friends.'

'Trixey?' Connie laughed.

'That's right. Tommy Crossley is his real name. He and Francis are very good friends, if you know what I mean. Young Tommy's got loads of money. His father's got some sort of fancy title. The other couple, Freda and Bernie Grossman, are old friends of Francis. Bernie's an accountant. He keeps the books for the organisation Derek's involved with. His wife Freda is a lovely lady. She spends most of her time organising various functions to raise money for the war effort. That's about it, I think.'

Connie looked up at him as they danced around the middle of the floor.

'What about you? You 'aven't told me about yerself.'

'Well that's another story,' he laughed.

'Well?'

'You really want to know?'

'I've found out about everybody else. I might as well know about you,' she said smiling.

'My name is Arnold Jerrold. I'm thirty-five, single and unattached. I live in Stepney and I ran a clothing factory once.'

'Oh, an' what d'yer do now?' Connie asked.

'I work for the government, for the duration of the war, that is. It's all very hush-hush, but it's really very boring. Anyway, that's enough of the war. Let's talk about you.'

The music ended and the dancers applauded as they left the floor. Connie felt his hand on her back as he led her to the table, and when they were seated he poured her some wine. There was no sign of Derek nor Beth Knowles. Freda and Bernie Grossman had returned to the table and Freda was gently chiding her perspiring husband. 'You were moving too fast. That was a waltz not a foxtrot.'

He laughed as he dabbed his forehead and turned to Connie. 'We've been dancing together now for more years than I care to remember, young lady. And she still tells me I can't dance. What should I do with her, eh?'

Freda tapped her husband's wrist playfully. 'I'm off to powder my nose. Will you come with me, young Connie?' she asked.

They crossed the large floor together and made their way to the ladies room.

'Where exactly do you come from, my dear?' Freda asked as she dabbed at her face with the sponge from her compact.

'I live in Bermon'sey.'

'And are you a good friend of Derek's, may I ask?'

Connie leaned against the pink wash basin. 'Derek comes in the pub where I work in the evenings. 'E asked me out ternight. I don't know 'im all that well though.'

Freda clicked her compact shut and turned to Connie. 'Let

me give you a bit of advice, young lady. You seem to be a nice girl and you're very pretty. You should be very careful in your dealings with some of these older men. They're inclined to be devious, and I might as well tell you, Derek Angelo isn't exactly a knight in shining armour. People like him are taken by pretty faces, especially if they belong to younger women. I've been watching you at the table. I thought you were looking a little angry with Derek. I see he's disappeared, and that's made me angry too. He shouldn't have left you like that.'

Connie shrugged her shoulders and ran a hand down the back of her long fair hair. 'It's okay, Freda. Arnold's bin takin' care of me.'

The elderly lady's face became serious and she opened her mouth to say something but changed her mind. When they left the powder room and were walking back to the table, she turned and said, 'You just be careful, dear. You could quite easily get hurt.'

The Grossmans had said goodnight and left, Freda giving Connie a meaningful wink. Francis Hammond had become embroiled with his companion over the merits of Italian art and there was still no sign of Derek and Beth Knowles. Connie had begun to feel quite tipsy. The wine and spirits had combined with the opulent atmosphere and they had taken their toll. A waiter came to the table and handed Arnold a note and, as he read it, a slight smile came to his face.

'I'm sorry, Con. My cousin Beth got a phone call from home. It seems there's been some trouble. Derek's taking her back and he asked me to look after you. I hope you don't mind?'

Even in her befuddled state Connie became suspicious. She realised that it was all too contrived. Right from the start Derek had made a play for the Knowles woman. How convenient that Arnold should be with his cousin that evening. No wonder

Derek hadn't said anything about meeting other people at the club! Connie felt angry. Derek must have taken her there only to introduce her to his friend. Well, it wouldn't make any difference, she told herself. Derek Angelo or Arnold Jerrold, they would both get the same answer. The band had returned and were playing again though only a few couples were dancing.

Arnold was standing with Francis Hammond who was waving his hands. 'No trouble, dear boy. Leave it with me. We can sort out the bill later. Tommy and I will be staying here for a while.'

Connie and Arnold left the club together and he hailed a taxi. Connie heard him mention River Street, Stepney, to the driver and she bit on her bottom lip. Freda's words ran through her bleary and confused mind.

'I mus' get 'ome. It's very late. They'll all be worried,' she said weakly.

'Sure,' he replied. 'We'll stop off at my place first. Derek might well have gone there to wait for us.'

They travelled through the blacked-out city streets in silence. Soon they were passing along Commercial Road and when the driver swung into a little side street and pulled up Arnold seemed to come to life again. He paid the driver and steered her to a grimy-looking door between two shuttered shops. She felt herself being almost pushed into the house and up a dark flight of creaky stairs. She tripped at the top and Arnold laughed. 'Stay where you are while I light the gas,' he said.

Connie could feel waves of nausea coming up from the pit of her stomach and she drew deep breaths. With the flare of the match and the growing light from the gas mantle she saw that the landing had no floor covering whatsoever. Seeing the dirty floorboards and peeling wallpaper made her want to run into the street but Arnold was still holding her arm. He opened a door and steered her into the dark interior. There was a strange smell, like mothballs or disinfectant she thought, and when he lit the gas jet over the mantelshelf and pulled the dusty curtains quickly Connie knew that she had been stupid to come back with him to this place. There was no sign of anyone living in the flat. The grate was empty, not made up with paper and sticks of wood like fireplaces would normally be. The small table had an old newspaper spread over it, and ancient dust-covered pictures hung around the walls. When Connie poked her head into the tiny scullery she winced: pots and pans littered the draining board and the iron gas stove. Arnold had opened another door which led into the bedroom. He came over to her.

'I'm sorry about the state of the place,' he said, studying her closely. 'I'm only staying here until I get my bomb-damaged flat repaired. Look, why don't you put the kettle on and make us some tea while I move those things from the settee.'

Connie went out into the scullery and filled the kettle. While it was heating up over the tiny gas jet she found the tea-pot and caddy. 'Where's the milk?' she called out.

'It's on the window sill. I put it out there this morning to keep it cool.'

Connie lifted the window frame and saw the shattered bottle lying on the rusted iron fire escape below. She threw down the sash and turned out the gas. 'It's been spilt,' she said flatly as she came back into the room.

Arnold cursed. 'I'll kill that moggie.'

Connie looked down at him as he sat on the torn settee. 'Look, I'd better get goin',' she said. 'Derek's not gonna show up, is 'e? I'll get a taxi.'

He got up slowly, a grin breaking out on his face. 'C'mon,

what's the rush? We can amuse ourselves for a while. He'll probably show up later.'

She shook her head. 'No, Arnold. I'm goin'.'

He reached for her and she swayed backwards away from his outstretched arms.

'No, Arnold!'

He was grinning widely now, as he gripped her firmly by her shoulders. 'You've had too much to drink to think of going home now,' he said, his eyes darkening. 'Besides, there won't be any cabs around this area. It's a dangerous place for a young girl to be wandering around in.'

'Yer could 'elp me get a taxi,' she said with a desperate tone in her voice.

'I've got a better idea. Let's go in there,' he leered, nodding towards the open door.

'No!' she groaned as she felt his hot breath on her cheek. He pulled her to him and he was propelling her along, half carrying her until she found herself beside the bed. His head was buried in her hair, his wet mouth against her neck and ears. She tried to fight him off but her strength was failing and her head spun. She pounded his chest with her fists. 'Yer lied ter me!' she shrieked. 'Derek's not comin'! Let me go!'

Then she was lying beneath him and his hands were pulling at her clothes. His full weight was pressing down on her as he reached beneath her dress. Connie's mind was racing as she remembered how it had happened before. She brought her hands up to his face but he gripped her wrists and pinned them to her sides. She was helpless beneath his writhing body. She felt the sharp pain as he forced himself upon her and then she ceased struggling. Tears of anger and disgust fell silently as his animal passion mounted. It soon was over, and he slumped down on her, his sagging body pressing heavily on her chest.

When he had recovered his breath he placed his hands

beside her and lifted himself up. 'Why did you fight me, you little whore?' he asked her with a sneer. 'You know you wanted it.'

Connie choked back her tears and stared at him with hate in her eyes as he moved away from the bed. She was numb and unable to answer. The physical disgust at the way he had humiliated her caused waves of nausea to rise up from her stomach. Icy fingers seemed to squeeze her head and she began to tremble. The sight of his sneering face made her want to throw herself at him and tear at his eyes but instead she clenched her fists and felt her fingernails bite into the palms of her hands. She felt dirty, ashamed and disgusted, and a deep anger rose up inside her.

She was cold sober now as she pulled herself round and sat with her head in her hands on the edge of the bed. The stark realisation that she was a victim of their plotting made her head pound and she felt her face redden.

'You two worked this all out, didn't yer?' she said, her voice shaking.

He laughed aloud. 'Derek told me all about you and him. I know you two have been under the blankets together.'

'Nufink 'appened that night,' she sobbed.

'Don't give me that. It's not what he told me. Anyway, here's your money. I don't expect you to do it for nothing,' he sneered, throwing some notes down beside her on the bed.

'You dirty animal!' she cried out, standing up and rushing at him, her fists pummelling his chest.

He gripped her wrists and laughed loudly. 'Proper little demon aren't you?'

Connie sagged and he pushed her roughly away. 'Take the money. It'll pay for a cab.'

'Keep yer money, yer no-good bastard! Is that the only way yer can 'ave a woman – by rapin' 'er?'

'It's much better when you put up a fight,' he sneered. 'It makes it more exciting. Anyway, you wasn't raped. You got paid for it.'

Connie bit her lip until it bled and she fought back her tears. She picked up the money and looked at it. 'Yer couldn't buy me. I wouldn't go wiv yer willin'ly if yer offered me a fortune,' she snarled, throwing the money in his face as she ran out of the room.

Chapter Forty-Two

'William Smithers' paced up and down in his little room, occasionally drawing the curtains back and glancing down into the street below. The workers had passed through on their way to the factory and now it had become quiet. He could see the rag-and-bone man leaning on his barrow beside the ruins of the buildings opposite, and he noticed Widow Pacey walking towards him, carrying a large bundle. He adjusted the curtains and continued to pace back and forth. Time was dragging slowly and he looked down at the alarm clock beside his unmade bed. It was just after nine and already it seemed as if he had been up for hours. It was quiet in the house since Marie had gone to get her shopping and Lillian had left for her new-found job at the clothing factory in Tower Bridge Road. Toby had been gone since seven-thirty and it had been he and Marie arguing before he left which had first awakened Dennis. He had heard Marie screaming something about Toby spending too much time in front of the mirror and Toby replying that he had to keep up appearances, and then the front door had been slammed shut. Dennis had tried unsuccessfully to get back to sleep and, as he paced to and fro, he was deep in thought. Had he known of the plot hatching inside Lillian's head he would not have tarried so long in his room.

The Toomeys' scheming daughter grinned to herself as she

clocked in and joined the rest of the girls at the workbench. She was very familiar with the house routine, especially on Monday mornings. Her mother always went to the Tower Bridge Road for her shopping, then she called in to her friend Patience for a cup of tea and a chat. She never ever got home until after midday, and today her mother had lots to tell her trusted friend. It seemed ridiculous to Lillian that her father should be playing around with someone else, but her mother had said that she was positively convinced of it. What the eye did not see the heart could not grieve over, Lillian reasoned and, as far as she was concerned, her Sandor was not going to see anything. It had to look good, she told herself as she put a hand to her brow and swayed against the bench.

'Are you all right, Lil?' the girl next to her asked.

'I'm all right. It's just that fright I 'ad.'

'What fright?'

'Oh it was nufink really. It was just that a man jumped out on me last night as I was goin' 'ome from the pictures.'

'Did 'e? I bet it scared yer. 'E didn't touch yer, did 'e?'

Lillian shook her head. ''E made a grab fer me but I run all the way 'ome. I fink it's the shock comin' out on me.'

The machines had started up and the girls decided to wait until tea break to hear more about Lillian's traumatic experience.

Suddenly she swayed again and staggered into the girl next to her. 'I'm sorry, Bet. I seem to be all wobbly.'

Betty got down from her stool purposefully. 'Yer should be 'ome in bed,' she said quickly.

Lillian hoped she would be, very soon. 'Don't make a fuss, Bet. I can manage,' she said weakly. 'Yer a girl short as it is.'

'Never you mind about that,' said Bet. 'I'm goin' fer the forelady.'

The old hands exchanged glances and carried on at the

machines while Lillian tried her hardest to look ill. Meanwhile Bet had found the forelady.

'Miss Brownin'. Lillian Toomey's 'avin' a wobbly,' she said.

Nora Browning knew Lillian Toomey very well and she was aware that the girl had had many different things in her time, but a wobbly was something else. 'A wobbly?' she repeated.

'She does look ill, Miss Brownin'. She's gonna faint soon, I'm sure she is.'

'All right, Betty. You go back to your machine. I'll be along in a minute.'

When the matronly-looking woman approached the workbench the final scene was already being enacted. Lillian had been propped up against the leg of the bench and someone was holding a cup of water to her quivering lips.

'Now what's the matter here?' Nora asked, standing with her hands on her hips.

'She jus' fainted, Miss Brownin'. I turned round an' there she was fainted,' Betty told her. 'She was stretched out on the floor.'

Nora bent down and looked closely at the Toomey girl. Well, the silly cow looks okay, she thought. She doesn't seem to have lost any of her colour.

'C'mon, Lillian. Let's get you on your feet,' she said sternly.

Lillian staggered up and sagged into her helpers' arms. 'I'll be okay. Let me go back ter work.'

It was the only time Nora had ever heard Lillian Toomey volunteering to go back to work. The girl must be ill, she thought. 'Okay Lillian. You come with me. You can sit in the sick bay. When you're feeling able you'd better go home for the day.'

It was not long before Lillian was walking quickly home, a satisfied grin on her face. The church clock showed five minutes after nine and she crossed her fingers. Her mother had said William never left the house until after the pubs opened at eleven. There would be plenty of time, she told herself. Soon she had reached the market and with a quick glance at the stalls she took a side turning. It wouldn't do for mother to see me, she thought as she hurried along to Ironmonger Street. As she walked into the turning and took the key from her handbag Lillian saw Widow Pacey looking up the street, clicking a few coins together.

''Ello, Lil,' Widow Pacey called out from her street door. 'No work?'

Lillian made a face and touched her forehead as she let herself in.

'There's bin somefink wrong wiv that fer years,' Widow Pacey mumbled aloud.

Dennis Foreman heard the front door open and shut and a puzzled frown creased his forehead. Marie must be back early from the market, he thought. The knock on his door made him jump and he realised how nervous he was.

'Who's there?' Dennis asked quickly.

'It's me, Lillian. Can I come in?'

Dennis cursed as he opened the door. Lillian was smiling sweetly at him, her eyelashes fluttering. He stood back and she walked in.

'I thought yer might be a bit lonely an' wanted ter talk a bit,' she said, staring around the room.

'I'm okay. I was goin' out soon,' he said with purpose.

'Oh dear, yer bed's not made. Let me do it.'

Before he could refuse Lillian had pulled up the bed-clothes and was shaking his pillow. 'There we are. That's better,' she said, sitting down on the bed and hoisting her skirt before crossing her long legs.

He mumbled his thanks and put his hands into his trouser pockets. 'No work then?' he asked.

'They gave me the day off. Said I looked a bit peaky. I feel fine – now.'

Dennis looked away from her dark, liquid eyes and walked around behind the table, trying not to stare at her half revealed thigh. ''Ow's yer young man?' he asked, his voice sounding croaky.

'Oh 'e's all right, but don't let's talk about Sandor. Let's talk about you,' she purred, swinging her leg suggestively. 'Yer much more interestin'.'

He backed away towards the window and glanced out quickly. 'I'm expectin' somebody soon. I thought it was 'im,' he said weakly.

Lillian leaned back on the bed. 'Yer not dad's cousin, are yer?' she asked with a searching look.

'Well, I'm sort of 'is distant cousin, if yer see what I mean.'

Lillian did not, and she did not really wish to know either. Her mind was centring around something much more simple. 'Are yer frightened of women, William?' she asked him with a grin.

''Course not.'

'I fink yer are. Come over 'ere.'

Dennis felt that his play-acting was convincing but it was leading him into a fix. He had to think fast. 'It's not that I'm frightened o' women, Lil. I just don't get excited that way, if yer know what I mean.'

The Toomey girl sat forward on the bed, a puzzled frown on her face. 'Yer mean women don't excite yer?'

Dennis felt he had her measure now and he sat down next to her. 'Look, Lil. I fink yer very pretty. In fact I'd go furvver than that. I'd say yer was beautiful.'

She was smiling now, her eyes widening. 'Do yer really fink I'm beautiful?'

'I do,' he answered. 'But yer see, Lil. Men like me like to

491

'ave a pretty girl fer a good friend. Yer know, one they can confide in an' tell their secrets to.'

'What d'yer mean, men like you?'

'I'm queer,' Dennis said, holding his head in his hand and trying not to laugh. He did not dare to look at her for too long in case he gave himself away.

There was a shocked look on her face and slowly it changed into an expression of pity. She reached out and touched his shoulder lightly. 'Yer can't 'elp the way yer are, William,' she said gently. 'Jus' you remember, I'm yer friend. Yer can tell me fings an' I won't tell a livin' soul. Not even Sandor.'

'Yer mustn't tell Sandor,' Dennis said dramatically. ''E might not understand.'

She patted his knee. 'I won't tell a livin' soul. Yer secret's safe wiv me, William.'

Marie Toomey had finished her shopping and she walked slowly along to John Street. Patience O'Brian was a good friend. She always listened carefully to what she had to say, and usually had some sound advice to offer. Patience was made that way, she thought. Not like those interfering busybodies in the street. If she let on to one of them it would be all round the turning in five minutes. Patience wasn't like that. Shame about her old man. All those years at the gas works, then he had to go and get himself killed six months after he retired. Still, walking down the middle of the Old Kent Road blind drunk wasn't a very sensible thing to do, she mused. Something must have turned his brain. Maybe it was the shock of retirement? It did that to a lot of people. There was old Mr Copperstone, she recalled. He was only retired for six months and he drank a bottle of rat poison. Nasty one that was. Some people whispered that it had been administered. People had never stopped talking about it. Mrs Copperstone went stark raving mad a few months later. Pity that old git of mine didn't think of taking rat poison, she thought, or maybe getting himself knocked up in the air by a tram. Trouble with Toby is, two pints of beer and he falls over before 'e's even left the pub.

Chewing on her thoughts, Marie arrived at Patience's house and her knock was answered by the lady herself. Patience O'Brian was a petite, smart-looking woman in her late fifties. Her deep-set blue eyes looked out of a tiny, well-moulded face and her hair was raven without a trace of grey. She beckoned her friend in.

'I've got the kettle on, Marie,' she said. 'Put yer bag down in the passage, it looks 'eavy.'

They had sat together sipping tea for some time before Marie brought up the subject. 'Patience. I'm worried about my Toby.'

'What's wrong, Marie. Is 'e ill?' her friend asked.

'No, 'e's as fit as a fiddle,' Marie replied, dabbing at her eyes.

'Whatever's wrong, girl?'

'I fink 'e's got anuvver woman.'

'I don't believe it. Not your Toby.'

Marie nodded. ''E 'as, Patience. I'm sure of it.'

'What makes yer fink 'e's playin' around then?'

'Look, luv. My Toby was never one ter wear out me block o' Sunlight soap, an' I used ter get on to 'im every week ter change 'is socks. It was the same wiv 'is underclothes, but since 'e's 'ad this job e's a changed man. 'E goes out every mornin' smellin' like a Lisle Street whore, an' 'e smacks brilliantine on 'is 'air an' stands in front o' that mirror lookin' at 'imself until I feel like crownin' 'im.'

'Well maybe 'e likes ter look smart when 'e goes ter work, Marie. Lookin' smart goes a long way, girl.'

'Patience, 'e's a bloody barrel-washer, not a bleedin' pen-pusher. Barrel-washers don't wear collars an' ties.'

Patience smiled. 'Well, I fink yer makin' too much out of it. Lots o' men start ter smarten themselves up as they get older. My Frankie did, Gawd rest 'is soul.'

Marie screwed a handkerchief up around her fingers. 'There's somefink else.'

'Oh, an' what's that?'

''E's got more darin' lately.'

'Darin'?'

'Well, we 'ad a row the ovver mornin' an' 'e told me straight 'e's bin goin' up the pub on Friday nights when I'm out. When I asked 'im what pub 'e uses 'e told me ter mind me own business.'

'Why don't yer say yer'll go out wiv 'im, Marie? P'raps 'e'd like yer to?'

'I already did.'

'What did 'e say?'

''E told me 'e wants ter be on 'is own ter fink. That ain't like my Toby.'

'Well, I did warn yer, Marie. I told yer not ter be too 'ard on 'im.'

'I've bin a good wife,' Marie sobbed. 'I might 'ave got on to 'im at times, but it was fer 'is own good.'

'C'mon, yer do go a bit strong. What about when Toby lost the pram. Yer took the poker to 'im, yer told me yerself.'

Marie did not answer but continued to twist the handkerchief around her fingers.

'Then there was the time 'e brought that dirty ole carpet 'ome. What did yer do then?'

'I made 'im take it out in the yard an' scrub it,' Marie sobbed, feeling suddenly very sorry for her wayward husband.

'There yer are then. That's what I mean. Listen, Marie. A

man'll work 'ard an' give up all 'is wages, an' e'll go wivout 'is pint o' beer, just as long as yer give 'im yer respect. Do that an' yer 'ome an dry. Trouble wiv you is, yer ain't give 'im no respect. All yer do is ruck 'im. No man's gonna stan' fer that. It don't matter 'ow meek an' mild they are, sooner or later they're gonna turn, an' when they do, watch out.'

'What am I gonna do, Patience?'

'I'll tell yer what yer gonna do. Now listen ter me.'

Toby Toomey walked home on Friday evening feeling rather low. Friday evening was normally his night out with Iris, but tonight she was taking Monty to the vet to get him neutered. She had said that poor Monty would want a bit of nursing after all that pulling about and she ought to stop in with him until he perked up a bit. They had arranged to change their evening to Monday and Toby did not feel like having to wait until then. As he walked home he wondered what neutering was. Maybe it was something to do with worms, he thought. Mrs Adams bought dozens of worming powders for her cats. He'd seen her buy them at the cats' meat stall in the market. Perhaps Iris didn't know about worming powders. He would have to remember to tell her on Monday.

When Toby put his key in the door he could smell steak and kidney pudding. It was years since Marie had cooked steak and kidney pudding. He was licking his lips as he walked into the parlour and his eyes opened wide. A clean tablecloth had been spread over the rickety old table and Marie was standing in front of the freshly laid grate. She wore a new apron and her hair was out of curlers.

'Sit down, luv. Yer mus' be fair worn out,' she said sweetly.

Toby looked behind him, and then back to Marie. 'That smells nice. Is it . . .'

'Yes it is, Toby. I know it's yer favourite. I thought it was about time I did a nice steak an' kidney pudden.'

Toby sat down at the table. Something was wrong, he thought. Maybe Marie was going a bit funny in the head. No it wasn't that. He stroked his chin thoughtfully. It must be something else. Maybe she intended to poison him. Christ! She's poisoned the dinner, he decided. No, he was being silly. Marie would be more likely to throw him out if she wanted to get rid of him or even just smash him over the head. It must be something else. That was it! She was going to ask for a rise. Well she was going to be unlucky. The pocket money she gave him just about stretched to a couple of pints and a sherry for Iris and now that old misery-guts had got Iris transferred from the packing department the supply of illicit jars of pickles had dried up. It was going to be a tight squeeze as it was.

Toby finished his meal and Marie brought in a large chunk of suet pudding smeared with golden syrup. Finally he leaned back in his chair and rubbed his middle contentedly. 'That was really 'andsome, girl,' he said stretching. 'I fink I could just about manage anuvver cuppa.'

Marie tripped out into the scullery and fetched the tea. She sat opposite him, a smile forming on her lips, and when he drained the cup she motioned to the easy chair. 'Yer look tired. Why don't yer put yer 'ead back fer 'alf an 'our? By the way, I've got the evenin' paper. It's down by the chair.'

Toby looked at her closely, expecting the worst, but she remained quiet. He went over to the chair and settled himself down for a snooze.

'D'yer want me ter wake yer up later, Toby?' Marie asked. 'I know yer go out on Fridays.'

'No, dear. I fink I'll stay in ternight.'

She sat sewing in the chair opposite him, occasionally looking over. Toby was snoring lightly, his mouth opening and shutting at regular intervals. The wireless was playing softly and Marie hummed to herself contentedly. Patience was a wise old owl, she thought.

When Toby climbed into bed and made himself comfortable he was still puzzling over Marie's sudden change of mood and, when she slipped in beside him and laid her arm on his stomach, Toby really began to worry.

The weekend was free of arguments. The meals were on time, and Marie remained very attentive. On Monday morning Toby got ready for work quickly. He felt he should not spend too much time in front of the mirror. He didn't want Marie to get upset and slip back into her old ways. When it was time for him to leave for work Marie kissed him on the cheek and he walked towards the pickle factory deep in thought. Iris wouldn't like to hear about Marie's change of mood, he mused. Better if he kept quiet about it. He spent the day worrying and, when he got home that evening, Marie was more than usually attentive. Toby had eaten his fill and was settling down for a quick nap when she sprang it on him. 'I was wonderin' if yer'd like an' early night, luv?'

'Sorry, Marie. I'm goin' out ternight.'

When he had left Marie kicked the cat and threw two of her best plates against the scullery wall. 'I'll be 'avin a few words wiv Patience termorrer,' she grumbled aloud.

Chapter Forty-Three

Jennie was feeling as though she had not slept a wink. She cut two thick slices of bread and put them under the gas-stove grill. It had been well after midnight when she got in, and then the sound of a taxi drawing up in the early hours and the door slamming had awakened her. She poured herself a mug of tea and dropped three spoonfuls of sugar into it, then walked back into the parlour and sat down wearily at the table. She had had a few heated words with Steve the night before and as she slowly stirred her tea and went over the argument in her mind the smell of charred bread drifted in. She got up quickly and swore violently as she stubbed her toe hurrying out to the scullery. She cut two more slices and slipped them under the grill and this time she stood over the gas stove, yawning widely. Monday was always a bad day for Jennie and this Monday was going to be a bad one, she knew. It was always the same when she and Steve rowed. It upset her for the whole day and, as she buttered the toast, she vehemently cursed Monday mornings.

She had finished her breakfast and was pouring her second mug of tea when Connie walked in, still clad in her dressing gown. Her eyes were swollen and her face ashen.

Jennie filled another mug. 'Yer late, Con,' she said. 'I thought yer'd be dressed by now.'

Connie sat down heavily in a chair and sipped her tea. 'Tell 'em I'm sick, Jen,' she said in little more than a whisper. 'I can't face it this mornin'.'

Jennie grinned. 'Late night was it? I 'eard the taxi draw up.'

Connie made no reply and Jennie's face suddenly became serious. 'Yer really do look sick, Con.' she said, standing over her friend.

Connie looked up quickly, a hard glint in her eye. 'I'm sick of work, sick of men and I'm sick of workin' be'ind that bar every night,' she said bitterly.

Jennie's face dropped and Connie sagged in the chair. 'I'm sorry, luv. I didn't mean it ter sound like that. You an' yer family 'ave bin really good ter me, but I've gotta get away. I can't face anuvver night be'ind that bar.'

'I take it last night 'ad somefink ter do wiv yer decision, Con. Did Derek give yer a bad time?'

Connie laughed bitterly. 'I got dumped, Jen. Yeah, 'e went off wiv one o' the women at the party, an' I got lumbered wiv a no-good bloke who kept tryin' it on.'

'Party, yer say? I thought you an' 'im was goin' on yer own?'

'That's what I thought, but it was all planned. I ended up gettin' a taxi 'ome from Stepney.'

'From where!?'

'That's right, Stepney. That's why I was late 'ome.'

''Ere, this bloke didn't 'urt yer, did 'e?'

'No, 'e didn't 'urt me,' Connie lied. ''E was just persistent, that's all.'

'Did this bloke take yer ter Stepney, Con?'

Connie nodded and stared down at her tea.

'Why did yer go wiv 'im?'

'It's a long story, Jen. I'll tell yer later. In the meantime, can yer make excuses fer us? Tell the forelady I'll be in termorrer.'

'Okay, but are yer really serious about not workin' be'ind the bar any more, Con?'

Connie pulled her dressing gown tightly around her slim figure and folded her arms. 'I'm goin' back ter where I used ter live. One o' the women in the street said I could always lodge wiv 'er. She's got a spare room, or she did 'ave. I'm goin' ter see 'er this mornin'.'

'I'll miss yer, Con. Mum an' dad will too. They fink a lot of yer an' they reckon yer the best barmaid they've ever 'ad. Me dad even reckons yer faster than me wiv the addin' up.'

Connie gave her friend a wan smile. 'I can still come round an' see yer mum an' dad, an' we'll still see each ovver at work, won't we? It's just that I mus' get away. You understand, Jennie, don't yer?'

'Yeah, I understand. I s'pose I'd 'ave ter do the same if I was in your shoes. Anyway, I mus' get ter work or I'll be late. We'll talk ternight, okay?'

Connie got up and walked to the door. 'Ternight, Jen.'

Back in her room Connie got dressed quickly and slipped out through the side door into the street. She wanted to get out before Dora and Bill went down for breakfast. It would be too difficult to talk to them so early in the morning, she thought. She walked slowly into the Old Kent Road and saw that the large clock over the hatters-shop doorway showed a quarter to nine. She ambled along idly, looking in shop windows and gazing at the passing traffic. Last night's events had shocked and terrified her. She could still remember vividly how frightened she felt when she had found herself in that grimy flat and how disgusted she had been when Arnold had offered her money. The realisation that she had been treated like a prostitute made her feel physically sick. Derek Angelo was as much to blame, she decided. It was he who had told Arnold about her in the first place. She was sure that if she saw him again she would fly at him and tear at his face. Dora and Bill would become involved if she stayed at the pub, and it wouldn't be fair to them.

She had reached the Bricklayers Arms junction. The sun was climbing and starlings chattered loudly in the tall plane trees which stretched along the New Kent Road. It was still too early to knock on Ada's door, she thought, and she looked around her. A young woman was pushing a pram through the gates of the memorial gardens which lay back from the main road. Connie followed the woman into the gardens and found an empty wooden bench beneath a tall sycamore. It was peaceful there, the traffic noise deadened somewhat by the high, vine-covered fencing. The woman had walked on along the gravel path and left at the far gate without stopping, and the only other person in the gardens was an old man who sat reading the morning paper.

Connie leaned back on the bench and attempted to get her thoughts together. It had been inevitable that things would go the way they had, she was forced to admit, and there was no one to blame but herself. She had drunk herself almost into a stupor whenever she could and then allowed herself to be manipulated and violated. She had been warned. Jennie and her mother had both tried to spell out the dangers. Then there was Freda Grossman. She had seen the danger at the nightclub and had tried to warn her. Connie realised that she had been stupid and naive. She had thrown caution to the wind and gone like a lamb to the slaughter. The men had seen her as an easy conquest and had exploited her cruelly. She had been called a whore, raped, assaulted and treated like dirt. She felt she had sunk as low as it was possible to get, and she only had herself to blame. She remembered how people had said that she was very much like her mother in looks, and she shivered as she realised how the likeness had become so much deeper. Her mother had been raped and deserted, and she had ended her days in loneliness and misery. Maybe that was to be her own destiny.

Connie sat up straight on the bench as she felt her breath coming faster. Panic knotted her insides and she licked her dry lips. She felt the desperate need for a drink and the desire made her angry. She knew that it was drink which had led her into this situation. She had used it so that she would not have to face the misery of her life, and now it was destroying her. She clenched her fists and gritted her teeth. She knew that she would have to fight it or it would be too late. She had become lost in a swirling storm of delirium and she felt it pulling her down, down into the blackness from which there was no escape. Her palms were sweating and her stomach was turning over. Pains wracked her body and she closed her eyes in desperation.

'Please God! Don't let me sink! Don't let it swallow me up!' she said aloud.

People had come into the gardens. An old man was leaning heavily on his walking stick and humming to himself as he passed. Two young women strolled by, pushing prams and giggling at a joke they were sharing, and a workman was coming closer, sweeping the path with a wide broom.

Connie got up quickly and walked out through the gate, glancing around furtively as if they might be looking at her. The pain in her insides was easing as she walked along the Tower Bridge Road. A market trader whistled after her and another eyed her up and down as she passed his stall. Connie turned off the thoroughfare into the little maze of backstreets. She could see the ruins of the Horseshoe as she walked through John Street, and in a couple of minutes she was standing at the top of her own little street. To her left was the burnt-out oilshop and barrow sheds, and Connie found herself wondering if old Misery Martin was still alive. Opposite, the rag shop that had always been closed was now a wardens' post. She saw the row of tumbledown houses which led right up to the factory gates, and she looked up at the ruined dwellings facing them. Connie remembered with sadness the countless times she and Molly had climbed those creaky stairs and how her cousin had had to stop on each landing to catch her breath. She thought of Helen and the intimate chats they used to have, and she remembered Matthew. Poor Matt, she thought. He had been kind and understanding, and now he was dead. They were all dead. She could see the factory looming as large and ugly as ever at the end of the turning. Its iron gates were pulled back, and beyond them was the cobbled yard which she had crossed every morning. It seemed such a long time ago now.

Widow Pacey was whitening her front doorstep. She looked up enquiringly as Connie passed, and then went back to her task, humming softly to herself. At number twelve Connie stopped and lifted the old iron knocker. When Ada Halliday opened the front door and saw Connie standing there her eyes lit up and she stood to one side.

'Come in, girl. I was wonderin' when yer was gonna pay me a visit,' she said happily.

Connie walked into the parlour and looked up at the old clock on the mantelshelf. She noticed that the two hands were still locked together at twelve o'clock. Ada was standing behind her. 'Well sit yerself down then. Would yer like a nice cuppa?'

Connie smiled and nodded and, unable to contain her impatience, she called out into the scullery, 'Is yer room still goin', Ada?'

She laughed as she heard Ada's joking reply. 'No, I've got a young man livin' wiv me.'

'If yer'll 'ave me, Ada, I'd like ter take it.'

'I told yer, girl. It's yours whenever yer ready. This street's where yer belong, Connie luv. I used ter remember when yer was just a toddler. This little turnin' might not be much, but it's yer 'ome. It's where yer grew up.'

They sat in the parlour, cups of tea on their laps and Ada talked at length about the street folk.

'It's not altered much since yer left, Con. The Toomeys are as scatty as ever. Young Lillian is goin' strong wiv a foreign soldier. Marie told me 'e's a Czech. 'E seems all right but the trouble is, yer can't understand a word 'e ses. Oh, an' the Toomeys 'ave got a lodger. 'E looks a funny bloke. Relation o' Toby's, be all accounts. I was only sayin' ter Mrs Richards the ovver day, 'e looks sort o' familiar. I've seen 'im somewhere before. I've bin puzzlin' me brains but fer the life o' me I can't fink where I've seen 'im. Mind you though, 'e keeps 'imself to 'imself. More than I can say fer some of 'em round 'ere. You take ole Mrs Adams. She knows everybody's business. You mark my words, before long she'll know all there is ter know about 'im.'

Connie was content to sip her tea and let Ada chat away. Although the ruined buildings opposite were a dark reminder of all the tragedy in her life, she was glad that she had come back to the street again. It seemed to Connie that if there was going to be any chance for her to pull herself together and make some sense of her life she had to get back to her roots, here in this little street, where she was born, where she had grown up. It was here that the long, strange path of her life had begun, and she had to retrace that path to its beginning. She had to go back to the people she knew, like the idiotic Toomeys, the Widow Pacey and her trusted old bag-wash pram, the dependable Joe Cooper, the Richards, Lizzie Conroy, old Mrs Cosgrove and the Browns and George Baker, Mrs Adams the cat lady, and kind Ada Halliday. There were others, too. Perhaps one of the vaguely familiar folk who walked in and out of the turning and just passed the time of day held a clue to the secret parts of her past.

Ada had refilled the teacups and was sitting back in her easy chair. She had been studying the pale-faced girl and saw a trace of desperation in her blue eyes. Whatever had happened to her since she left the street would no doubt be revealed in the girl's own good time, she told herself. For the present she would make her welcome, feed her up and keep an eye on her. It would be nice to have her company, too. The house had been a dreary place ever since Jack passed away.

'Is that okay then, Ada?'

'What's that?'

'I said, is it all right fer me ter move in ternight?'

''Course it is, luv. Sooner the better.'

Connie put her cup down on the table. 'Yer looked miles away then, Ada.'

The buxom woman smiled and her face relaxed. 'Oh I was jus' finkin'. Now yer movin' in I'm gonna get that bloody clock fixed.'

Joe Cooper walked along the street that evening and, as he neared the wardens' post, Dennis Foreman came out of Number One. 'Fancy a pint, Joe?' he asked. 'I need ter talk ter yer.'

Joe grinned. 'Gettin' yer down, is it?'

'What, lodgin' wiv the Toomeys?' Dennis said, a look of mock horror showing on his face.

'Well they ain't exactly yer ideal family, are they?'

'They're all right – now I've got Lil sorted out,' Dennis grinned.

They had crossed over into John Street. 'Yer ain't bin playin' around wiv 'er, 'ave yer?' Joe asked, a shocked look on his wide face.

Dennis laughed aloud. 'No fear. Matter o' fact I put 'er straight. I told 'er I was queer, so if I start winkin' at yer, take no notice.'

'Gawd, Den! Yer gettin' worse. We'll 'ave ter stop goin' out tergevver, people are gonna start talkin'.'

'Well I 'ad ter do somefink, didn't I? She come up ter me room this mornin'.'

'Oh?'

'Too true, Joe. I 'ad ter fink quick. I don't want that bloody Sandor what's 'is name on me back, I've got enough troubles as it is.'

They had reached the Jolly Compasses and when they had settled themselves in a corner Dennis took out a folded sheet of newspaper from his coat pocket.

'See this, Joe? It's a page of the *Daily Mail*. I was passin' the time in the public library this afternoon an' I saw it.'

'What is it?' Joe asked, taking the paper and unfolding it.

'Look, there. It's an article by this geezer who's bin researchin' criminal be'aviour. 'E's mentioned the Piccadilly jewel raid, among ovvers, an' the bastard ses there that I'm still at large.'

'Well you are, ain't yer?' Joe grinned.

Dennis stroked his forehead. 'Bloody 'ell. Articles like that stir up people's interest. I was beginnin' ter feel more relaxed lately, an' now this.'

'I wouldn't worry too much Den,' Joe laughed. 'Not many people round 'ere buy the *Daily Mail*.'

'Yeah, but they go ter the public library, don't they? I read it, didn't I?'

'Look Den, people in the street 'ave got used ter yer now an' I see yer've already left those stupid glasses orf. Nobody's passed any remarks about it, 'ave they?'

'Well, no.'

'There yer are then. Just take it easy.'

Dennis chuckled. 'I was sayin' that ter yer not so long ago. Mind you, I get nervous sometimes. I imagine somebody's gonna feel me collar. I couldn't go back now. They'd 'ave ter kill me first.'

Joe looked up quickly. 'That sounds a bit drastic. If they catch yer yer'll 'ave ter face the music. The way you're talkin's like somefink out of a James Cagney picture.'

Dennis leaned forward over the table. 'I mean it, Joe. I've got a gun stashed away in the 'ouse an' I'll use it if I 'ave to.'

'Christ!' Joe exclaimed. 'S'posin' Marie comes across it an' shows it ter Toby? The silly bleeder might shoot 'er wiv it.'

'Don't worry, mate. She won't find it. I've got it well 'idden. Anyway, let's change the subject. Talkin' about guns an' gettin' caught is givin' me the creeps.'

Joe took a sip from his glass. ''Ere, by the way. I bumped inter Ada 'Alliday on me way 'ome from work. She told me Connie's bin round ter see about lodgin' wiv 'er. Ada said she's gonna 'ave 'er spare room.'

'That'll be nice, Joe. I was wonderin' when I was gonna get the chance ter see young Connie.'

'Yeah, well I'd be careful what yer say ter the girl when yer do bump into 'er if I was you.'

Dennis grinned. 'I'll be careful, don't yer worry. I tell yer, seein' Connie is gonna bring back a lot o' memories, espesh'ly if she looks as much like Kate as yer said she does.'

Joe nodded slowly. 'Yer wait till yer see 'er.'

Dennis took a gulp of beer and leaned back in his chair.

''Ere, d'yer remember when me an' you an' Kate used ter bump in the Trocette when we was kids? I don't fink we ever paid, did we?'

Joe smiled. ''Ere, what about that time we all got caught smokin' them fags in the buildin's an' they told yer ole man. 'E

507

was standin' at the door wiv the belt in 'is 'and an', if I remember rightly, it was Fran Collins who talked 'im out o' wackin' yer.'

'Yeah, I remember, Joe. Ole Fran could do no wrong in my eyes after that. Smashin' lady, wasn't she?'

The little pub had become crowded. The piano player was idly tinkling on the keys with one hand, the other clasped around a pint glass. Suddenly Dennis looked up at Joe, a thoughtful expression on his face.

'That's "Pasadena",' he said. 'D'yer remember that tune? I wrote the words down once, on me ole man's time sheet I found be'ind the clock. Gawd knows what it was doin' there. Blimey, did I get a pastin' fer that.'

Joe was watching the piano player. 'D'yer remember Kate singin' it? She 'ad the words off pat,' he said quietly.

Dennis nodded. 'Funny 'ow it all turned out. We was a good team, wasn't we?'

'We sure was, Den. Kate was really upset when she read about yer little escapade, an' she took it bad when she 'eard yer got nabbed.'

They had lapsed into silence for a while, and Dennis drained his glass quickly. 'C'mon, Joe. Let's find ourselves anuvver pub,' he said. 'I'm beginnin' ter feel morbid sittin' 'ere.'

Chapter Forty-Four

Connie Morgan had found it easier to settle back into Ironmonger Street than she had first imagined. People she had known were soon chatting to her once more and after two weeks it seemed to her as though she had never been away. Ada Halliday had made her really welcome and the little upstairs back room which had been made available was comfortably furnished and spotlessly clean. Ada insisted that Connie ate with her in the evenings for, as the jolly woman had said, 'It's just as easy ter cook fer two as fer one, an' besides, there's two of us ter do the washin' up, girl.'

Living away from the Dolphin seemed strange to start with, but there were no difficult customers to pacify, and no drinks on offer. For the first two days Connie knew that she was experiencing the symptoms of coming off the drink. She felt edgy and her body became prone to cold sweats. Her head ached and her mouth became dry and furred. It was noticeable in her appearance, too. As she looked in the mirror the young woman could see quite clearly that her hair had lost its sheen and her face had become rather puffy, with reddish patches beneath her eyes. Sleep was easier now, however, and the feverish dreams had passed.

It was early June. The warm weather was settling in and the morning skies were clear and sunny. Each day Connie walked to her job at the leather factory feeling a little less depressed and a little more able to face the monotonous grind. Jennie was keeping her informed about life at the pub, and each evening Connie walked back through the bustling streets and sat down with Ada after their tea, talking about everyday things. Ada was a good person to talk to, and she occasionally brought a smile to the young woman's face with her little anecdotes of life in the old days. Sometimes the two would listen to the wireless or take an evening stroll through the backstreets, stopping on the way to chat with one of Ada's multitude of acquaintances. It was a simple, uncomplicated existence, and it had brought her peace of mind. Connie felt that at last she was beginning to pull the threads of her life together. The desire for a drink had eventually vanished, and she felt better able to cope with her own sense of loss and sadness whenever she stepped out of the front door and saw the ruined buildings facing her.

It was on a Monday morning when Jennie told her friend the news. ''Ere, Con. Poor ole Mrs Argrieves died yesterday. Billy popped in the pub an' told me mum. 'E said she got pneumonia from that fall she 'ad. Poor Billy looked really upset. I did feel sorry fer 'im. The funeral's on Friday. By the way, 'e asked 'ow you was gettin' on. 'E said ter remember 'im ter yer.'

Connie was saddened at the news. She knew Billy's mother had worked hard at getting him through his dark periods. He was going to take his loss badly, Connie felt sure. Billy had fought his personal battle and it looked as though he had won it, but how would his mother's death affect him? Connie's concern was made worse by Jennie's observation.

'Yer know, that Billy finks a lot of you, Con,' she said. ''E's asked me a few times where yer livin'. I reckon if 'e knew 'e'd be round ter see yer. That's why I made out I didn't know yer address. I did right, didn't I?'

Connie's face looked pained. 'It's awkward at the moment, Jen. I'm jus' settlin' in at Ada's, an' I'm tryin' ter get meself sorted out. If Billy showed up now fings could get complicated, y'know what I mean.'

'I understand, Con. Billy knows we work tergevver, so I'll jus' say yer send 'im yer best regards an' that yer stayin' wiv friends fer the time bein'. 'Ow's that?'

'That's fine, Jen. Maybe I'll come round an' see yer folks soon. I'll prob'ly see Billy then.'

It was during her first week back in the street that Connie was stopped by Dennis Foreman. He had introduced himself by saying that he was a friend of Joe Cooper and used to live in the street years ago. He also said that he knew her mother and was very sorry to hear of her passing. Connie was puzzled by the man. He had a piercing stare that made her feel uncomfortable and she could not exactly understand why. As the days went by and she passed him on the street Connie became increasingly aware of his interest. She could feel his eyes on her and she began to wonder about him.

She decided to tackle Ada about the stranger and was surprised by the woman's response. 'There is somefink funny about that bloke, Con,' she agreed, a puzzled frown on her face. 'I remember seein' 'im the first day 'e come inter the street. Funny-lookin' sod 'e was. 'E was wearin' these 'eavy glasses. Milk-bottle glasses, I calls 'em. 'E don't wear 'em now. Anuvver fing is, the bloke's smartened 'imself up since 'e's bin 'ere. That's a nice suit 'e wears now, an' those shoes 'e 'as on are pretty tidy, too. When I first saw 'im 'e looked like somefink out o' the music 'all. Joe Cooper told me 'e's a cousin o' Toby's. There's somefink perculiar about the man. I can't put me finger on it, but there's definitely somefink strange about 'im. I've never seen 'im wiv a woman, an' the only bloke 'e seems ter knock around wiv is Joe Cooper.'

'P'raps 'e only likes men,' Connie said, smiling.

'What, yer mean 'e might be one o' them there nancy boys?' Ada queried.

''E could be.'

'No, I don't fink so, Con. There's a couple o' them sort get down the market on Saturdays. They talk funny, an' they always seem ter be carryin' a shoppin' basket. One of 'em's called Francine. 'E always carries an 'andbag around wiv 'im an' 'e's always stoppin' me fer a chat about somefink or the ovver.'

Connie grinned. 'Well if I see Mr Smivvers wiv a shoppin' basket or an 'andbag I'll let yer know, Ada.'

A few miles downriver from Ironmonger Street another Mr Smithers walked into the town hall offices in Barking with a macabre request. He had been sent there by the local police who had informed him that it was where the records were kept of the blitz victims who had not been officially identified, and who had been buried with just a number to note their passing. Lance Corporal Percival Smithers of the Royal Artillery had recently been posted to Shoeburyness, and passing through Barking had given him the opportunity to look up the elder brother he had not seen for a number of years. When he called into the local police station for directions he was informed that the address he sought was no more. The street had been destroyed by a landmine and many of the people living there had been killed. Lance Corporal Smithers found himself being led through a maze of dark, reinforced corridors until he was shown into a small stale-smelling room below ground level. The short-sighted clerk looked over his metal-framed glasses at the intruder and motioned him to a seat while he thumbed through a huge pile of documents. Finally he looked up with a painful expression on his thin face. 'Whom exactly do you seek information on?' he asked.

Percival Smithers gave the clerk a hostile look. He folded his arms and said, 'Mr William Smithers.'

'And what exactly is your relationship to Mr William Smithers?' the clerk asked turning back to the pile of documents in front of him.

The soldier was getting irritated by the clerk's off-hand attitude. ''E's exactly me elder bruvver,' he said without blinking.

'Address?' asked the clerk in a tired voice.

'Mine or me bruvver's?'

'Your brother's address please.'

'Twenty-seven, Stonely Street, Barkin'.'

The clerk thumbed through a sheaf of papers and then said, 'Stonely Street was destroyed by a landmine on the fifteenth of October last year.'

Percival Smithers was finding it exceedingly difficult to hold his temper. 'I know that,' he said. 'The police told me. I wanna know if yer've got any news about me bruvver, that's all.'

The tired-looking clerk sighed and clasped his hands over the sheaf of papers, moving his thumbs together. 'Well, most of the Stonely Street victims were identified by relatives or by their identity cards. There were other victims who carried no identity on their person. Some bodies were dismembered, or totally unidentifiable. We may have a few points to go on, however. Now Mr Smithers, were you aware of any birthmark or tattoo mark that would make a positive identification of your brother possible?'

'Yeah, as a matter o' fact there is. Me bruvver 'ad a tattoo mark on 'is left arm. It was entwined 'earts wiv an arrer frew 'em.'

'Upper or lower arm?'

'Lower.'

The clerk thumbed through the papers once more, then suddenly his face brightened up. 'Ah. Here we are,' he said. 'Victim number 245. Yes, I think we've found your brother, Mr Smithers.'

When the sad-faced soldier finally walked out of the town hall the clerk made certain enquiries and had the National Register of Citizens checked. He then picked up the telephone and dialled the local police station. His required duties finished, he sat back and sipped his lukewarm tea. It had been quite a productive day, he thought. Another paper could now be moved into the file marked 'Identified'. The police sergeant who had taken his call checked the records at the station, and finally the number of the missing identity card which once belonged to the late William Smithers went into a special list.

The balmy days of early June passed peacefully in the little backstreet. People were now sleeping in their own beds at night, although the occasional air-raid siren sent most folk scurrying into the factory shelter. Others slept through the raid, including the frail Mrs Cosgrove who was now almost totally deaf. Connie roused herself on hearing the siren and sat in the downstairs room with Ada until the all clear sounded. It seemed to most people that the last terrible raid in late May had been a desperate gamble. Two of the locals had very strong opinions about the way the war was developing and as usual they were eager to make their views known. The venue for their discussions had changed, however, since the Horseshoe had taken a direct hit. Terry and Bill had now become nomads and their evening travels took them to a pub in the Old Kent Road. With filled glasses in front of them the two felt able to assess the situation.

'Yer gotta understand, Bill, the air raids are bound ter die out now,' Terry said. 'They can't keep it goin', wiv all those planes what's gettin' shot down.'

'Well I don't fink they're shootin' many down, Tel. Them guns jus' blast away ter frighten 'em.'

'I don't know about frightenin' the bleedin' Germans, Bill, they frighten the bleedin' life outta me, what wiv the noise they make.'

'Well, I don't fink we're shootin' many down wiv our guns. I mean ter say, 'ow can yer be expected ter shoot planes down in the pitch-dark?'

'We've got searchlights, Bill. It's in the papers every mornin' 'ow many's bin shot down.'

'Yer can't believe all yer read, Tel. I remember readin' that the war was gonna be over by 1940. We're inter 'forty-one now an' it looks like it's gonna go on fer a long time yet. Ole Churchill said it was gonna be a long 'ard struggle.'

'Well we ain't gettin' so many raids now, are we?'

'Granted, but I'm willin' ter bet there's somefink afoot. I fink they're gettin' ready ter use a secret weapon on us. They've got somefink up their sleeve, mark my words.'

Terry laughed aloud. 'Don't talk tripe. The reason they've cut down on the raids is because they made a bloody mistake. Ole Goerin' fought we was all gonna panic an' sue fer peace. Well we ain't gonna, an' I reckon that there Field Marshal Bleedin' Hermann Goerin's tearin' 'is 'air out right this minute.'

Bill sipped his drink. ''Ere, Tel. Talkin' o' tripe reminds me. My ole woman ses she 'eard that ole Catchpole's sellin' black-market meat.'

'Well 'e'll 'ave ter be careful, Bill. There's a bit in yesterday's paper about this geezer what's bin sellin' corn beef under the counter an' e' got six months.'

Bill nodded. 'Seems ter me they're all at it now. If yer pay over the odds yer can get a Scotch whisky in most pubs. I wonder if they do the business in 'ere?'

Terry looked around the bar. 'No, I don't fink so. By the look of 'im be'ind the counter 'e's never even 'eard of it.'

The mystery of the lessening air raids was solved for Terry and Bill on the twenty-second of June when Germany invaded Russia. The bulk of the German air force had been sent to the Eastern Front, according to the daily newspapers, and for once Bill and Terry did not query the validity of the report.

The news of the invasion was greeted with shock and sadness by the Bermondsey folk, especially those who lived in the Rotherhithe area. There had been many friendships made with the Russian sailors who drank in the local pubs when their timber ships put into the Surrey Docks.

For Terry and Bill there was now another topic to discuss, and they tackled it with their usual aplomb.

It was a warm Friday evening towards the end of June and Connie left the factory at five o'clock and walked leisurely along the traffic-filled thoroughfare, her thoughts centring around what Jennie had told her during the day. They had been working side by side on a batch of leather cuttings and the publican's daughter had been full of her torrid romance with Steve. She had also said that his crowd was congregating at the pub in larger numbers, much to the chagrin of her parents, who saw their increasing presence as a threat to their regular trade. The usual customers had nothing in common with the noisy gang, and Jennie had said that her father was showing concern over her developing romance. She had also mentioned that Arnold Jerrold had made a few brief appearances lately. Hearing his name sent a spasm of anger through Connie and she comforted herself with the thought that she would not have to face him again. She was feeling happy now that she was back in the street with her bad experiences behind her. Ada Halliday had made her feel at home and was always fussing over her welfare. She knew now that the street was where she belonged and for the first time in a long while Connie knew the feeling of contentment.

She had just reached the market when she almost collided with Billy Argrieves. He had turned away from the vegetable stall with a carrier bag in his hand and suddenly his eyes lit up.

''Ello, Con. 'Ow yer doin'?' he greeted her brightly.

Connie's cheeks flushed with surprise and she smiled. 'I'm okay. What about you?'

'Oh I'm all right. Jus' gettin' the spuds fer me tea. Where're yer livin' now? I've missed seein' yer in the pub.'

Connie noticed that the stutter seemed to have left him and he looked more relaxed. His fresh face glowed with good health and he seemed to have put on weight. He smiled at her and Connie saw the pleasure in his dark eyes.

'I'm back in Ironmonger Street. It's where I used ter live,' she said without hesitation.

'I know it,' he said. 'C'mon, I'll walk yer 'ome – if yer don't mind?'

She laughed at the concern showing on his face. ''Course I don't. C'mon, this way.'

They strolled by the stalls and turned into a backstreet. 'I was sorry to 'ear about yer mum,' she said after a while. 'Jennie told me.'

His face became serious. 'Yeah, it was sudden, although she was ill fer a time. I miss 'er, Con.'

Anxious to change the subject, Connie asked, 'Yer still workin' at the wood place?'

The smile returned to his face. 'No, I got a better job. I'm workin' at a buildin' firm. It suits me fine. I'm learnin' all about bricklayin', carpentry an' plumbin', an' I'm still workin' out in the open most times. I couldn't stand bein' shut inside a factory all day.'

'Yeah, I know what yer mean,' Connie replied.

They had reached Ironmonger Street and Connie stopped. 'Well, 'ere we are. It's bin nice meetin' yer again, Billy,' she said. 'Yer still goin' in the pub then?' she added, suddenly feeling she wanted to prolong the conversation.

'Yeah, I still go in there. That noisy mob still gets in the corner but I ignore 'em. After all I don't want ole Bill French chuckin' me out again, do I?' he said grinning widely.

Connie was pleasantly surprised at the change in him. She could see that he had won his hard-fought battle. He had a new-found air of confidence about him, and his whole manner seemed different. She smiled at him. 'Nobody's gonna chuck you out any more, are they,' she laughed.

'What about you, Connie?' he asked, a look of concern showing on his face. 'Yer okay now? Yer 'ad a bad time, didn't yer?'

'We've both bin through a lot, Billy. I fink I'm sortin' meself out, an' it looks like you 'ave, too.'

He nodded. 'A lot was down ter you, Connie. Yer was very good ter me. It 'elped me more than yer know.'

She waved his thanks away with a sweep of her hand. 'Yer did it yerself, Billy.'

He looked down at his feet. 'I felt I was sortin' meself out an' then me muvver died. I knew then that I was at the crossroads. I realised I could easily slip back wivvout 'er be'ind me. That's when I really started, Con. I found this ovver job an' got meself a new suit. Now I'm lookin' ter learn as much as I can about the buildin' trade an' maybe start up meself when the war's all over. There'll be plenty o' business fer good builders.'

'Well I fink that's great, Billy. I'm really pleased for yer.'

He looked at her closely and she saw that certain light in his large dark eyes. It stirred and excited her, and for a brief moment she wanted to turn and flee. She had met him by chance and suddenly her emotions were quickening inside her. Connie felt a stirring in her heart, and she realised it was the first time a man had had that effect on her since Robert had been killed. She knew that her feelings for Billy were more than just physical and she became afraid and anxious, for she was still determined never to become involved with anyone again and there was a deep anger which would stop her giving her love to anyone now: an anger at the way men had used her body selfishly with no tenderness or consideration for her. She knew it was not fair expecting Billy to understand the sordid details of her life. Connie lowered her eyes.

Billy picked up the shopping bag from between his feet. 'Well, I'd better get orf,' he sighed.

Connie smiled and moved a loose strand of hair from her face. 'Yeah, me landlady will be wonderin' where I've got to.'

Billy looked awkward as he stepped back a pace. 'Look, Connie. If yer fancy a night out I'd be 'appy ter take yer somewhere,' he said nervously. 'It's nice talkin' ter yer an' that an' I'd like ter do it again.'

She looked into his dark, smouldering eyes and knew that she would have to say no, but the words froze on her lips. He looked so childlike and vulnerable. He seemed to be peering into her soul and she felt her heart melting.

'I'd like that, too,' she said at last.

Chapter Forty-Five

Toby Toomey had spent quite some time thinking about his problem and he was no nearer solving it as he walked home on Friday evening. For a few days Marie had been acting like she had when they first got married. His tea had been ready when he arrived home last Friday evening and she had gone out of her way to make him feel comfortable. There had been no nagging during the weekend, and the only comments she passed on his appearance were complimentary. His favourite meals had been served up, and afters, too. She had even suggested an early night, and that had not happened for years. It was a pity he had had to go out that evening, he thought. Toby had to admit that at first he had thought she was up to no good, but his favourite meal of steak and kidney pie had not been poisoned, and she had not asked him for an increase in housekeeping money. He had put her change of attitude down to genuine remorse for the way she had been treating him and, just as he had been getting used to her fussing over him, she had changed back to her old self again. He considered the possibility that Marie had found out about his little jaunts with Iris but he dismissed it. If Marie had found out she would definitely have poisoned his steak and kidney pie. No, it must be her change of life, he told himself, or perhaps she was going off her head. Whatever it was, it was certainly puzzling. Maybe he ought to have it out with her when he got home.

Toby had almost reached the corner of Ironmonger Street when he was hailed by PC Wilshaw. ''Ello, Toby. Yer still washin' barrels out, then?'

Toby nodded and made to walk on when he saw that the policeman was coming over to him. The chief barrel-washer cursed to himself. He had too much on his mind to feel like standing around chatting, and besides it didn't look good being seen talking to the police. People might take him for a copper's nark.

The local bobby came up to Toby and stood facing him, his hands clasped behind his back. 'Remember that little chat we 'ad a little while ago, Toby?' he asked, his eyebrows beetling.

'No, what was that about then?'

'Don't yer remember me askin' yer ter keep yer peepers open fer any strange characters yer might see in the manor?'

'Oh yeah, I remember,' Toby answered. 'Well I ain't seen anybody who looks strange, except my ole woman. She's gorn strange lately.'

PC Wilshaw laughed to himself. Being married to you is enough to make any woman become strange, he thought. He gave Toby an enquiring look. ''Ow yer gettin' on wiv that lodger o' yours?'

Toby realised he had to be careful what he said. Marie had drilled into him what he should say if anyone did ask him about Dennis Foreman. 'That's Will Smithers,' he replied as casually as possible. ''E's me cousin an' 'e's stayin' wiv us fer a while.'

'I see,' said the policeman, rocking back on his heels. 'Well if yer do see any strangers 'angin' about round 'ere, don't ferget ter give me the nod, okay?'

Toby walked away mumbling. 'Bloody nosy bastard. Somebody in the street must 'ave told 'im we've got a lodger.'

PC Wilshaw had gone back to take up his position outside the baker's shop once more. He knew that he had to stay alert. There had been a shake-up at the station after that article in one of the daily newspapers about unsolved crimes and the chief had been taking some flack, word had it. Bloody politicians, he moaned to himself. Why do they have to keep interfering? The guv'nor's a tyrant at the best of times, and now the politicians are on his back he's a sight worse. It had not helped matters when the rumour was spread around that Dennis Foreman might try to creep back into the neighbourhood now that the fuss had died down. The old man had passed the word down for every constable to be on his guard. He had sifted through the rogues' gallery and new prints of the Piccadilly jewel robber were now stuck up in the station.

PC Wilshaw grinned to himself. Well the villain won't get by me, he vowed. If he dares to show his face around here I'll nab him.

Ada Halliday was doing her front doorstep on Saturday morning when Joe Cooper walked by. She looked up, her face red with the exertion, and she wiped the perspiration from her brow with the back of a grubby hand.

''Ello, Joe,' she said. 'It's all bloody go, ain't it?'

He grinned. 'I'd 'ave done yer step fer a couple o' bob.'

'Gertcha, yer saucy git. Yer wouldn't know where ter start,' she laughed, leaning over the step once more.

'Don't yer believe it, Ada. I used ter do me mum's step years ago an' I ain't fergot 'ow it's done.'

Ada put the block of hearthstone back into a tin box and leaned back on her haunches. ''Ere, 'ow's yer wife, Joe? 'Ave yer 'eard from 'er lately?'

'I got a letter day before yesterday. She said she's quite

'appy where she is an' don't wanna come back till she's sure the air raids are finished.'

Ada was not one to mince her words. 'Well I fink she's bein' selfish, if yer ask me. A woman's place is wiv 'er ole man at times like this. I wouldn't be parted from my ole man if 'e was alive, Gawd rest 'is soul.'

Joe smiled weakly. 'It takes all sorts, girl. 'Ere, 'ow's young Connie settlin' in?'

Ada stood up and puffed with the effort. 'She's gettin' on fine, Joe. Settled in a treat. I was a bit dubious at first, I must admit.'

'Why's that, Ada?'

'Well, there's a lot o' bad memories fer the kid in this street, ain't there? Every time she looks at that ruin it mus' bring it all back, stan's ter reason.'

'There's a lot o' good memories too, Ada. Connie grew up in the street. It mus' stand fer somefink.'

'Yeah, true enough. I fink she's come ter terms wiv fings. She's a real nice girl. Seems such a shame what she's 'ad ter go frew. Me an' 'er 'ave some nice chats after we've finished our tea every evenin'. She's told me a few fings about that pub she used ter work in but there's a lot she ain't told me, I'll be bound. Apparently there's a right crowd gets in there, be all accounts. Seems ter me she's better orf away from the place.'

'The Dolphin, wasn't it, Ada?'

'That's right. D'yer know it?'

'I know where it is, but I ain't never used it.'

Ada pressed a grubby hand to her side and winced. 'Connie said the family treated 'er well. She's a friend o' their daughter apparently. They work tergevver at the leather factory in Tower Bridge Road. That's 'ow young Connie got the job at the pub. What's puzzlin' me is, why she should suddenly leave there? If the family treated 'er decent it mus' be somefink else. P'raps one o' the customers upset 'er? Yer can bet a pound to a pinch o' shit somefink 'appened ter make 'er leave. It couldn't 'ave bin the work. Connie ain't frightened of a bit o' collar.'

Joe took his cap off and scratched the back of his head. 'I might go round the Dolphin fer a drink wiv ole Will Smithers. They won't know who we are an' we might 'ear somefink. Anyway, Ada, I'm off. I've got a bet ter put on.'

Connie took her time getting ready on that Saturday evening. She had arranged to meet Billy Argrieves at the Bricklayers Arms at seven o'clock and she wanted to look her best. As she sat at the dressing table and studied herself in the mirror a familiar feeling of anxiety returned to her, but she shrugged it off. Billy was like her, she told herself. They were two of a kind. He had struggled to pluck up the courage to ask her out: he had hesitated, flushed up and had finally managed to come out with it. Connie smiled to herself as she remembered. There was no need to worry about Billy. He would probably be more nervous than she was. As she brushed her long blond hair, she was aware that she had at first felt pity for Billy. Connie remembered how sad it had made her feel to see him sitting alone in the corner and her heart had gone out to him. But then Billy had done something about the situation he found himself in. He had been courageous and determined, and her pity had turned to admiration. She knew now that watching him fight had helped her in no small way, and for that Connie was grateful. Billy's transformation had awakened something in her that she had thought was gone for ever. She had slowly come to think of him in a different way. Billy had revealed himself to be an attractive young man with a disarming, gentle way about him. He had quickened her empty heart.

* * *

Joe Cooper and Dennis Foreman strolled leisurely along the Old Kent Road. It was a warm Saturday evening. The shops were already shuttered and the quietness was occasionally interrupted by the passing of a noisy tram. The fugitive had now discarded his eccentric garb in favour of a well-cut navy-blue suit and he looked markedly different from the character who had knocked on the Toomeys' front door not so very long ago. Gone were the thick-lensed spectacles, the brilliantine-layered hair and the witless look. He had kept his bushy moustache, however, and it had the effect of making him look somewhat older. The two were chatting lightheartedly.

'I tell yer, Joe. Those Toomeys are a real scream,' Dennis was saying. 'I walked inter a right ole argument last night. Marie was accusin' Toby o' playin' around wiv anuvver woman. Can yer credit it?'

Joe grinned. 'Don't yer be so sure. 'E's a dark 'orse, that Toby. 'E ain't so daft. It wouldn't surprise me if 'e's got a bit on the side.'

The two men turned off the main road into a backstreet, their hands in their pockets and their checked caps worn at a jaunty angle. 'The Dolphin's jus' round the corner,' Joe said, indicating that they should cross the street.

Dennis glanced at his friend. 'D'yer reckon there's anyfink gone on there then, Joe?' he asked.

'I dunno,' Joe replied. 'Ada seemed ter fink there 'ad. She's a knowin' ole bird is Ada. We'll jus' keep our ears open an' see what transpires.'

'I only 'ope there's nobody in the pub who used ter know me,' Dennis said, grimacing at the thought.

'Yer should 'ave kept those stupid glasses on,' Joe laughed. 'Mind you, wiv them on yer looked like Sharkey the bomb-thrower.'

Dennis's grin left his face as they reached the pub and pushed open the door of the public bar. Inside the air smelled stale with tobacco smoke and a blue haze hung over the drinkers. The two made for the counter and Joe ordered the first drink. Bill French was serving and he gave the newcomers a mild glance of curiosity as he filled two glasses with ale. Joe and Dennis found a seat and sat back, casually taking in the atmosphere. At the far end of the counter a crowd of well-dressed men had congregated and soon they were joined by two young women who wore fur coats and had heavy make-up on their bloated faces. The crowd laughed loudly when one of the men said something and one character banged his fist down hard on the counter.

Dennis looked at Joe and then his eyes travelled around the bar. He noticed a few looks of distaste among the customers and he glanced back at his companion. 'They look a right flash lot, don't they,' he said quietly.

Joe nodded. 'I fink that's the crowd Ada was talkin' about. They're all strangers ter me.'

Dennis sipped his pint and studied the crowd for a few seconds before saying anything. 'I don't know any of 'em,' he said presently. 'They seem like the local mob. They do like flashin' their money about.'

Joe's alert eyes glanced in the direction of the landlord. ''E looks a bit brassed off wiv 'em, too, if yer ask me, Den. Jus' clock 'is face.'

An old man with a blood-red complexion and watery eyes was sitting at the table next to them. He was watching the antics of the crowd with a look of disgust. Presently he picked up a tobacco pouch from the table and proceeded to fill his stained clay pipe. High-pitched laughter came from the end of the bar and the old man looked over at Joe and Dennis. His eyes met Joe's and he grimaced. 'Bloody noisy bastards,' he said, packing the pipe with a vengeance. 'I don't know why ole Bill allows 'em in the place.'

Joe leaned over. 'D'yer know that crowd, Pop?'

'Know 'em? Yeah I know 'em. See the one standin' next ter the big tart? That's Steve Barnett. 'E's got a business. I fink 'e's cartin' the guv'nor's daughter out. That's 'er be'ind the bar,' he said, indicating with his eyes.

'That ovver bloke next ter 'im is Derek Angelo. 'E's in ter just about everyfing around 'ere, an' a right loud-mouth git in the bargain. Those two tarts wiv 'em are a couple o' prossers. I've seen 'em wiv loads o' different blokes.'

Dennis leaned his elbow on the back of his chair. 'I'm just about ter get me an' me mate a drink,' he said. 'D'yer fancy one?'

'Gawd bless yer, son. I'll 'ave a nice drop o' bitter if yer don't mind.'

Dennis grinned. 'I'm Will, an' this is me mate Joe.'

The old character rested his gnarled hands on his walking stick. 'I'm Albert,' he said. 'Albert Swan.'

Dennis brought back the glasses and they continued talking.

'This yer regular pub, Albert?' Joe asked.

'Bin comin' in 'ere fer donkey's years I 'ave. Mind you though, I won't be fer much longer if that load o' rubbish keeps comin' in. They fink they own the bleedin' pub.'

Joe gave Dennis a sideways glance and said, 'They seem run off their feet be'ind the counter, Albert.'

Albert Swan rose to the bait. 'Yeah, they miss young Connie. She was a good 'un she was.'

'Was she?'

'Yeah. I liked young Connie. Quick as a flash she was. Yer didn't 'ave ter wait fer a pint when she was around.'

'What 'appened to 'er, Pop?'

'I dunno. She left sort o' sudden-like. I don't fink she liked that flash mob. They was always chattin' 'er up, espesh'ly that Angelo bloke.'

Dennis waited until the old man had rekindled his pipe then said, 'I s'pose them barmaids 'ave ter put up wiv a lot, one way an' anuvver.'

'I grant yer that,' Albert said, puffing on his pipe. 'Trouble is, some people don't know when ter draw the line. Yer take young Connie. I used ter 'ave a laugh wiv 'er, but I always knew where ter draw the line. I used ter buy 'er a drink sometimes. I was on whisky at the time, but I can't drink it now. Me doctor told me ter lay off of it 'cos o' me blood pressure. Anyway, I used ter buy 'er a whisky an' she downed it like a good 'un. She could 'old 'er drink could Connie. Never turned an 'air, she didn't. Yeah, there was a lot in 'ere that was sorry ter see 'er go. Young Billy Argrieves was right upset. I fink 'e took a shine to 'er. Can't say as I blame 'im.'

Another person had joined the crowd and his entry had not gone unnoticed by Albert Swan. 'See 'im jus' come in?' he said. ''E's a new bloke. I don't know 'is name but 'e's right flash wiv 'is money. Always got a roll of it. 'E pulls off pound notes like 'e's unrollin' wallpaper. Got a big mouf as well.'

Joe and Dennis laughed at Albert's description. What he had said was quite telling, but he seemed to be suddenly distracted by two elderly ladies who came over and sat at his table. Albert had now switched his attention to the women and he began enjoying a bawdy repartee with them.

Dennis had a twinkle in his eye as he finished his drink. 'What say we stand at the counter fer awhile, Joe?' he said. 'Old Albert looks like 'e's preoccupied.'

Joe felt apprehensive. His long association with Dennis had taught him that the man could be a nasty character at times, and never more so than when he had a few pints inside him.

From what Albert Swan had told them it was possible that Connie had fallen foul of the crowd and Dennis seemed determined to learn more.

'Okay,' Joe answered reluctantly. 'But mind 'ow yer go, Den. Yer can't afford ter put yerself on offer.'

As the evening wore on the noisy crowd became more raucous. The two brassy women were giggling at the antics of the men and there was a noticeable gap between the crowd and the rest of the people at the bar. It seemed to Joe as though the regular customers wanted to avoid becoming involved in any form of conversation with them. He realised that he and Dennis were standing much closer to the mob than anyone else but his friend seemed perfectly relaxed, and he occasionally glanced across to the crowd as laughter erupted. Joe saw that Dennis was watching the latest character to join the group. The man was doing most of the talking and the two brassy women seemed to be hanging on to his every word. The newcomer had noticed Dennis's interest and he was glancing over more and more. Joe became increasingly worried. His intuition told him that no good was going to come of the evening and he attempted to defuse what looked to him like a dangerous situation by engaging his friend in conversation. Dennis almost ignored him as he continued to watch the neighbouring crowd.

Suddenly the vociferous Arnold Jerrold looked pointedly at Dennis. 'What do you think, friend?' he asked loudly.

Dennis returned his stare. 'I'm sorry. I didn't quite catch what yer was talkin' about,' he said calmly.

Arnold grinned. 'I was just saying that you've got to be careful in what you say these days, especially in pubs. Pubs are a haven for fifth columnists.'

'I make yer right, friend,' Dennis replied, with just a slight intonation on the last word.

Arnold dusted an imaginary piece of fluff from his immaculate blue suit. 'There you are, Steve. Our friend agrees with me.'

Steve Barnett was feeling slightly uneasy. There was something about the stranger that worried him. The man seemed too casual, and the ghost of a grin that was playing around the side of his mouth seemed threatening. The women, too, had realised that Arnold Jerrold might be overstretching himself and they had retired to powder their noses.

'I was in the merchant service, friend,' Arnold went on. 'Wireless. I was a wireless officer actually. I got torpedoed twice, and I was subsequently made medically unfit for service. The point I'm trying to make is, less careless talk, less convoys getting attacked.'

Steve winced. He had heard it all before. Arnold had masqueraded as a pilot, a commando, a naval officer, and now as a merchant marine officer. He knew that Arnold carried a dubious medical certificate which pronounced him unfit for military service, but he could see that the man who was now the object of his attention had not fallen for the patter. His eyes were calm and almost wicked-looking.

'C'mon, Arnie. Let's make a move,' Steve said.

Arnold was enjoying himself. 'There's plenty of time, Steve. Our friend here knows the score. In fact I'm going to buy him a drink. What's your pleasure, friend?'

Dennis waved his hand in reply but Arnold ignored him. 'Bill, give our friend and his partner a drink.'

The crowd had become somewhat subdued and the two women, knowing Arnold Jerrold of old, decided to keep their own company at the far end of the bar.

The drinks had arrived and Arnold sidled over to stand beside Dennis. 'I've not seen you in here before,' he said.

'Yer wouldn't 'ave done,' Dennis replied. 'I've never bin in 'ere before.'

'I don't know why we bother to patronise the place. They seem a miserable lot,' Arnold sneered.

'P'raps they don't like the noise you lot make,' Dennis said, sipping his drink.

'Do you think we make a lot of noise, friend?'

'Put it this way, friend,' Dennis said in little more than a whisper, 'if this was my regular pub I'd be a little bit put out, ter say the least.'

Joe winced as he waited for the response, but when it came it was unexpected. Arnold suddenly burst into laughter. 'I like you, friend,' he said loudly.

'Well I'm pleased,' Dennis said, a slow grin breaking out on his pale face.

Arnold looked along the counter then leaned towards Dennis. 'I'll tell you something, friend. This might not be the greatest pub, but they do have some very pretty barmaids here. You see young Jennie there? Well my friend Steve here is taking her out. Then there was Connie.'

'Connie?'

'Yeah. She used to serve behind the bar. What a figure! She was hot stuff. We got on very well I might add. Seems she had a thing about sailors. In fact . . .' Arnold whispered the rest of his words into Dennis's ear.

Joe watched as the grin disappeared from his friend's face. Dennis reached for his half-filled glass and slowly poured the ale down Arnold's front. With measured accuracy he drew his fist back and threw a punch which landed hard in the middle of Arnold's shocked face. The man fell back and collapsed in a heap, blood pouring from his busted nose.

Bill French vaulted the counter and spread himself between Dennis and the rest of the crowd. 'C'mon, I don't allow fisticuffs in my pub,' he said, glaring from one side to the other.

Dennis looked over the landlord's outstretched arms. 'Any o' you lot wanna make anyfing of it? You're welcome ter try yer luck.'

Steve shook his head. 'I don't know what was said, pal, but I expect 'e asked fer it.'

Bill glared at Dennis. 'Right mate, yer'll 'ave ter leave. I can't afford ter lose me licence.'

Joe grabbed his friend's arm. 'C'mon, let's get out of 'ere.'

As they walked quickly along Salter Street Joe turned to Dennis. 'I knew there'd be trouble. I jus' knew it,' he said. 'What did 'e say ter make yer belt 'im, fer Chrissakes?'

'It's better yer don't know, mate. Jus' leave it at that, will yer?'

Chapter Forty-Six

It was a hot, dry July, and the smell of drains was permeating the back streets. The council water carts came out in force to wash the dry dust away and flush the stinking sewers, and the children found a new game to play. They sat in little groups and focused the hot sun's rays through pieces of eyeglass on to scraps of newspaper and watched with pleasure as yesterday's news smouldered into flame. It was too hot for rattling door knockers or for strenuous games like tin-can copper. Instead the kids sat in the shade and bet their treasured cigarette cards against the turn of a dog-eared playing card. When they grew tired of gambling they roamed amongst the rubble and built their Indian camps on the ruined houses and tenement blocks. The more daring balanced precariously on high rafters and atop swaying brick walls. One little girl in Ironmonger Street was very proud of her find which she pushed around in a doll's pram, hidden beneath a piece of sacking: the nest of rats was quickly removed when discovered and the little girl was scrubbed vigorously with carbolic soap by her horrified mother. The council sent men to deal with the infested ruins and damaged sewers, and complaints poured into the council offices about the dangerous state of the bomb sites.

Another feature of wartime which troubled the authorities was the black market, which was flourishing in Bermondsey as much as elsewhere in London. People who were registered with a devious grocer or butcher could surreptitiously buy extra rations, but those whose tradesmen did not oblige had to obtain their extras by other means. There was always someone who could supply foodstuffs at outrageous prices, and occasionally the purveyor found himself in front of the magistrate, informed on by an angry customer. Daily newspapers reported on the growing scandal of the black market and articles graphically highlighted the terrible cost of bringing supplies in by sea.

For Connie, the summer days were idyllic. She had kept her appointment with Billy and she remembered their first night out together with pleasure. They had walked along the riverside and visited a quiet pub, talking easily as they sat on a cool veranda overlooking the Thames. They laughed and joked happily, relaxed in each other's company, and the hours had seemed to fly past. When it was time to go home he had escorted her to the front door and said goodnight with a hesitant peck on her cheek.

They were meeting regularly now, and Connie felt as though a new spirit of life was coursing through her body. She was happy in Billy's company. He made no demands on her, and he did not try to intrude on her secret thoughts. He seemed happy just to be with her, and Connie recalled with a smile how she had returned his hesitant kiss on their first date. The promise of her new relationship thrilled her, and suddenly the days ahead did not seem so dark and empty. She was captivated by the way he smiled and at times his dark eyes seemed to engulf her, but he never tried to prove himself. The way he treated her was strangely gracious for a man, and she was grateful for the space it allowed her. Time would pass, she knew, and when her wounds were properly healed she would be able to give herself completely. For the moment Connie felt content simply to enjoy each day as it came, and at last she had stopped worrying about the future.

Chief Inspector Coggins had, in his own words, 'rung the changes at Dockhead nick'. During his short reign he had made quite a few unpopular decisions and upset more than a few of his officers with his methods. The duty rosters had been revised and the filing system reorganised to his satisfaction, and there had been a buzz of activity when a certain article appeared in one daily newspaper highlighting the amount of unsolved crimes in the London area. Inspector Coggins decided to respond to the politicians' criticisms by showing them that at least his station was 'on the ball', as he put it.

When PC Wilshaw walked into Dockhead police station at midday on Saturday, ready to get on with his daily written report, he saw that a major tidying-up was under way. Papers were strewn about the desks and the station sergeant was in a foul mood.

'You can see the problem, Wilshaw,' he said with a red face. 'The guv'nor wants the rubbish sorted out, so you'll 'ave ter do yer report somewhere else.'

PC Wilshaw sat down to ease his aching feet and glanced idly at the pile of papers lying on the desk in front of him. One of the constables came in carrying another bundle and threw it down on a table.

'There's another lot for the bonfire, Sarge,' he said, to the chagrin of Sergeant Carter.

Another constable scanned through the bundle and suddenly he laughed aloud. 'Bloody hell, there's some evil-looking characters here.'

Wanted posters were being passed around and comments were made which brought gales of laughter from the officers. ''Ere, get a load o' this one,' someone said. 'William Smithers.

Last known address Barking. Wanted fer bigamy. Look at that dial. Who'd wanna marry that?'

'Well two did,' the sergeant growled.

PC Wilshaw was on his feet in a flash and he snatched the wanted poster from the constable's hand.

'Let's 'ave a dekko at that,' he said excitedly.

Two lines had been drawn through the poster and the word 'Deceased' was printed on it in red ink. As PC Wilshaw studied the photo his brow creased in a frown.

'I knew that name rung a bell,' he said at last. 'I've bin puzzlin' over that name an' it was stuck up in 'ere all the time.'

'We took it down when we got the update through,' the sergeant butted in. 'That was the instructions. We're on a clean-up campaign, Wilshaw, didn't yer know? Anyway, what yer gawkin' at it for? The case is closed, and the geezer lived at Barkin'. Nufink ter do wiv us.'

'What I'm sayin' is, William Smithers lives in Ironmonger Street.'

The sergeant raised his eyes to the ceiling. 'What, 'im?'

'No, not 'im. William Smithers.'

'Well I s'pose there's more than one William Smithers. After all, it's a common enough name.'

Consternation was showing on PC Wilshaw's face. 'Yeah, but the William Smithers in Ironmonger Street is only stayin' there. 'E comes from Barkin', accordin' ter Toby Toomey.'

'Who's Toby Toomey, Wilshaw?' the sergeant asked with a sigh.

'The bloke 'e's lodgin' wiv.'

The station sergeant sat down heavily and cleared the papers from his desk with a sweep of his arm. 'Right. Now what we gotta establish is, whether or not your Mr Smithers is a pucka Mr Smithers, or is 'e usin' the deceased's identity card.'

'Right,' grinned PC Wilshaw.

The station sergeant picked up the phone. 'Joan? Get me Barkin' nick, will yer?'

Chief Inspector Coggins stared up from his desk at the two men in front of him. 'Barking said that the deceased was identified by his brother and the identity card was not recovered, that right?'

The sergeant nodded. 'Yes, sir. They gave us the ID number from the register.'

The inspector rubbed his stubbled chin. 'There's the possibility of a mistaken identification of the body. You sure your Mr Smithers is not the one in the photo, Wilshaw?'

'Two different people, sir.'

'Right, sergeant. I'll get someone round to Ironmonger Street right away. You get back to the beat, Wilshaw, and stay in the vicinity. You might be needed.'

A bright sun shone down in the little backstreet as Dennis Foreman walked slowly along towards Joe Cooper's house. The turning was busy as women came and went with their Saturday shopping and people stood chatting together on their front doorsteps. Children played in the gutter, and at the far end of the turning the knife grinder was bent over his spinning stone, working the treadle with his foot. Dennis knocked on number sixteen and Joe came out carrying his coat. 'It's a nice day fer a pint, Will,' he grinned.

'Where we goin'? Fancy the Compasses?' Dennis asked.

'If yer like. I've gotta stop off in John Street though. I wanna put a bet on.'

The two left the street just two minutes before PC Wilshaw arrived and, as he took up his position opposite Ironmonger Street, the beat bobby was feeling rather pleased with himself. His observations had been productive, and it would certainly stand him in good stead with the guv' nor, he felt sure. The constable rocked back and forth, his eyes searching the length of the turning opposite. Everything looks in order, he thought. There's old Mrs Adams nattering away as usual, and there's that peculiar-looking bagwash woman standing by her front door, arms folded as always. Don't get many strangers in that bloody turning. Even the locals give it a wide berth. Can't say as I blame them. Hold tight, who's that? Oh, it's only the tallyman. Poor sod. Where's the plain-clothes brigade got to? Taking their time, as usual. PC Wilshaw took out his silver pocket watch and studied it, squinting his eyes. Ten minutes past twelve. I hope they don't leave it too long, he thought. I'm off at four.

At five minutes before one o'clock the two detectives walked into the turning, glancing briefly across to where the constable was standing. They rat-tatted on the Toomeys' front door then looked up at the upstairs window. Inside the house there was panic.

Lillian came hurrying down the stairs, her eyes open wide and her mouth hanging open. 'Quick! It's the police!' she said breathlessly.

'The police! Oh my Gawd! They're after 'im,' Marie gasped, peeping through her clean net curtains.

Lillian stood transfixed in the parlour doorway. 'What can we do?' she said helplessly.

Marie stepped back from the window. 'I dunno if they're coppers or not,' she said. 'They're in plain clothes.'

Lillian started to shuffle around in her anxiety. 'They're tecs all right. I see 'em come up ter the door from the bedroom winder. I reco'nise the big ugly one. 'E was the one who nicked me that time.'

'What, the one who said yer was whorin'? I'll 'ave somefink ter say ter that monkey's uncle.'

There was a second rat-tat and Marie winced. 'Go on then. Yer better let 'em in,' she said to her daughter.

Lillian crept down the passage and gingerly opened the front door.

'We're police officers,' the taller of the two detectives said. 'We'd like to talk to a Mr William Smithers. We understand he rents a room here.'

Lillian put on her most innocent look. 'Yes, that's correct. Mr Smithers lives upstairs, but 'e's not in. I fink 'e's gone shoppin'.'

Marie had come into the passage and stood staring over Lillian's shoulder. 'What yer want 'im for?' she asked sharply.

'It's just routine enquiries. I don't think there's anything to worry about. Can we come in? We'd like to look at Mr Smithers's room.'

Marie bit on her lip. 'I don't know about that. Mr Smithers might be upset about people lookin' in 'is private room.'

The ugly detective sighed. 'We can get a search warrant, lady. Now can we take a look?'

'Well, if yer must. It's the first door top o' the stairs,' she said crossly, omitting to tell them about the low ceiling.

When the two detectives went up the stairs Marie put her finger to her lips. 'Where's Dennis gorn? We'll 'ave ter try an' warn 'im,' she said in a whisper.

'I dunno, Mum. 'E could be anywhere.'

Marie and her daughter sat listening to the creaking ceiling with serious expressions on their faces.

Marie put her hand to her cheek. 'I only 'ope Toby don't come in wiv the shoppin' yet.'

They heard footsteps on the stairs and the two officers came into the parlour, the taller one rubbing his head. 'Well everything seems in order,' he said. 'Would you mind if we waited for a while? Mr Smithers might be back shortly. It would save us another journey.'

Marie nodded. 'Sit yerselves down. I'll put the kettle on.'

The detective raised his hand and glanced quickly at his silent partner. 'No thanks. We've just had ours.'

The other policeman could not remember having had a cup of tea recently but he guessed his senior must have a reason for refusing. He stared around the room and his eyes rested on Lillian Toomey's crossed legs. She gave him a smile and licked her top lip suggestively. The silent detective coughed into his closed hand and transferred his gaze to the ceiling. Occasionally his ugly partner glanced at his wristwatch and consulted the clock on the mantleshelf. Marie stayed out in the scullery, watching the kettle and trying desperately to think of some way to warn Dennis Foreman.

Saturday lunchtime was not the best time to drink in the Compasses, Dennis was beginning to realise. Women came in with their shopping bags and moaned about the food shortages, and market traders rushed in and elbowed their way to the counter, aware that for every minute they were away from their stalls customers were most likely being undercharged by the minders. The place was too small, Dennis decided, and he looked at Joe. His friend was listening to an elderly lady who had just in come from the market.

'No bleedin' oranges, no bleedin' bananas, an' no bleedin' pomegranates,' she was saying. 'It looks bleedin' bare on them stalls. I can't remember when I last see a banana, or a bleedin' pomegranate. The poxy apples look maggotty as well. I dunno, I'll be glad when this bleedin' war is over.'

'What yer got fer the ole man's tea, Jane?' the woman next to her asked.

'A scrag o' mutton, an' if 'e gives me any ole cheek about it, I'll aim it at 'im.'

Dennis finished his pint and looked at Joe. His friend seemed eager to get away from the two women and when Dennis caught his eye he drained his glass and nodded with a wry smile.

The two walked slowly through the market, hands in their pockets and caps askew. 'That beer tasted a bit watery, Joe,' Dennis remarked. 'It's gettin' 'arder than ever ter get a decent pint o' beer.'

'The Dolphin sells a good pint,' Joe said, a grin breaking out on his face.

'Yeah that's true, but the company ain't all that clever though, is it?'

They had reached the corner of Ironmonger Street. A few yards away, standing in a shop doorway, the beat bobby tried to look unconcerned. He had his orders to observe only, unless Mr Smithers tried to leave the turning in a hurry. He watched as the two men stopped outside the wardens' post and he noticed that the bagwash woman had her pram parked outside the Toomeys' front door and appeared to be leaning against the wall. What's going on there? PC Wilshaw asked himself as he saw William Smithers take the woman's arm and help her along the street, followed behind by Joe Cooper who pushed the pram. The three of them disappeared into Widow Pacey's house and the constable stroked his chin thoughtfully.

Had the beat constable been able to see inside the front door he would have witnessed a remarkable recovery.

Widow Pacey had straightened up and shrugged Dennis off. 'There's nufink wrong wiv me bleedin' leg,' she said with a bright flash of her deep eyes. 'I wanted ter keep yer from goin' in the Toomeys.'

Joe had parked the pram at the bottom of the passage and

as he ambled into the small parlour he started. 'What's all this about, girl?' he asked, scratching his head.

Widow Pacey looked at Dennis Foreman, a knowing look on her large red face. 'Yer might 'ave fooled most of 'em down the turnin', Dennis Foreman, but yer didn't fool me,' she said with a wizened smile. 'Which was just as well, 'cos there's a couple o' rozzers in the Toomeys. Two plain-clothes blokes they was. They've bin there since one o'clock. I see'd 'em when I got me last load o' bagwash. Anyway, while yer decidin' what yer gonna do about it I'll put the kettle on. I s'pose yer wanna cup o' tea, or 'ave yer bin on the piss?'

'We'd love a cuppa, girl,' Joe butted in.

Widow Pacey sat at the table with her arms folded facing the two men. 'I twigged yer the moment I first see'd yer,' she said. 'Me an' my ole man used ter kick yer arse when yer got lippy as a kid. Those scatty glasses an' that smarmed-down barnet didn't fool me fer a minute, Den. I watched yer grow up round 'ere. Funny, my ole man said yer was 'eadin' fer no good. 'E could see it.'

Dennis grinned sheepishly. 'Well fanks fer what yer did, luv. Yer saved me bacon, an' I'm really grateful.'

'Don't yer be so sure. Yer ain't out o' the woods yet,' the bagwash lady warned him, scratching her arm. 'Anyway, drink yer tea, it's gettin' cold.'

Dennis looked at Joe. 'Me stuff! I got that stuff stashed away there!' he exclaimed suddenly. 'I've gotta get it some'ow.'

'What stuff, Dennis?' Joe asked.

His friend gave the Widow Pacey a sideways glance before answering. 'You know, and the rest o' me money. It's all wrapped up tergevver.'

Joe grimaced. 'They've prob'ly searched the place. They must 'ave found it.'

Dennis laughed. 'I don't fink so. Toby showed me where ter

stash it. There's a tin bath 'angin' up in the back yard. There's a brick under it that pulls out. Toby's bin 'idin' a few bob there fer years, an' Marie's never found it.'

''Ow're yer gonna get it wiv the law sittin' in there?'

'I dunno. I'll 'ave ter fink o' somefink.'

'It's gonna be tricky, Den. Yer gonna 'ave ter ask Toby ter get it, ain't yer?'

The small parlour had become quiet as the three sat thinking. Suddenly the sound of police bells and screeching brakes shattered the silence. The two men jumped up and Joe looked through the net curtains. He could see three police cars in the turning. One was blocking the entrance to the street, and the other two had parked outside the Toomeys' house. Uniformed and plain-clothes policemen were spilling from the cars and entering the front door.

'They're on to yer, Den!' Joe said loudly. 'There's dozens of 'em!'

'Christ! I can't stay 'ere. They'll be searchin' the 'ole street!' Dennis said, holding the top of his head.

'Yer can't get out o' the street, that's a dead cert.'

'What about the shelter?' Widow Pacey asked suddenly.

'They'll check that,' Dennis said heavily.

Joe glanced at Widow Pacey. 'What about the roof?'

''E might be able ter get up there, long as 'e don't break 'is neck in the process.'

Dennis ran out into the backyard and looked up at the sloping roof. 'I'll be able ter make it from that upstairs winder. What about me stuff though?'

'Leave it ter me. I'll fink o' someway ter get it to yer,' Joe said, pushing Dennis along the passage.

A short while before Chief Inspector Coggins had sent two of his men down to Ironmonger Street and he had sat thoughtfully staring up at the ceiling. Suddenly he had got up and opened the office door. 'Sergeant!'

Sergeant Carter hurried into the office. 'Yes, sir.'

'Sergeant, my ulcer's playing me up.'

'Sir?'

'When my ulcer starts I know things are not right. What was the name of that family Wilshaw said Smithers was lodging with?'

'The Toomeys, sir.'

'Are they known to us?'

'Toby used ter be a totter. 'E got done fer drunkenness, an' the daughter Lillian's bin done twice fer solicitin'. Nufink else though, far as I know.'

'Remember the watch we kept on that area, sergeant?'

'Fer Dennis Foreman?'

'That's right. He came from Ironmonger Street originally. It wouldn't be the first time we've gone fishing for tiddlers and caught a salmon.'

'Yer mean?'

'Yes, Sergeant, Dennis Foreman. He could be our Mr Smithers. It might be the reason the man is still at large. He could be living right under our noses. I'm going to take notice of my ulcer, Sergeant. What's our immediate strength?'

Sergeant Carter grinned. 'Quite a few eating in the canteen. Then there's a few constables we could pick up on the way.'

'Let's get things moving, Sergeant. I want to be in on this one myself. We might put this station on the map at last.'

PC Wilshaw looked at his pocket watch once more and stroked his jaw. What are they doing in there? he wondered. They've been in with the old girl for over half an hour. Maybe it would be better to go over and let the plain-clothes boys know the whereabouts of Smithers. Trouble is, it might upset the applecart. If Mr Smithers happens to be watching from the window and sees a policeman knocking on the Toomeys' door he might do a runner. No, it would be better just to observe. After all, orders are orders, he told himself.

The sudden arrival of half the establishment of Dockhead police made the beat bobbie think that it was time to act. Couldn't they trust two burly officers to sort it out without sending down most of the station? he asked himself. Well it was about time he pointed the lads in the right direction, he decided as he crossed the road. In the turning everyone had come to their front doors. People had begun to congregate in small groups and they made fun of the serious-looking policemen.

'Oi, what's our Lil done now?' someone shouted out.

Someone else said, ''As Toby done ole Marie in then?'

Another wag yelled out, 'Yer got the wrong turnin', it's Sidney Street yer want. That's where Peter the Painter lives.'

PC Wilshaw was trying to get someone to take notice of him but the police were already swiftly engaging in a house-to-house search, led by Chief Inspector Coggins. Widow Pacey's house was not left out, and the police looked into her parlour and paid no attention to the three empty teacups which stood on the table. By now Dennis Foreman had managed to spreadeagle himself in a roof gulley that ran back from the street between the ramshackle houses. He could not be seen from the ground or from any of the windows, and for the moment he felt safe.

Chapter Forty-Seven

Toby Toomey walked back from the Tower Bridge Road market feeling hard done by. The shopping bag was heavy and he hoped he had bought everything on the list that Marie had given him. It was bad enough having to do a bit of overtime on Saturday morning, he thought to himself, without coming home and having Marie moaning at him about her aching back and groaning that she could not manage a heavy bag. Lillian, too, seemed to have suddenly developed a bad back and like a fool he had volunteered to get the weekly shopping. Well, if I've left anything out it's just too bad, he thought. I'm not running back down that market. Marie'll have to lump it.

As he walked out of John Street, Toby saw the commotion. Police seemed to be everywhere, and his heart sank as he slowly realised that the activity was centred around his own house. With a feeling of dread he quickly walked up to his front door and the two constables standing guard gave him a suspicious look.

'It's all right, I live 'ere,' Toby scowled as he walked in through the open doorway.

Inside Chief Inspector Coggins was talking to Marie and, as Toby stepped into the parlour, he got a warning look from his frightened wife.

The inspector eyed the diminutive character and nodded.

'You're Mr Toomey I take it?' he asked formally.

'Yes, sir. I'm 'im,' Toby replied, looking rather bothered.

'You know why we're here I take it, Mr Toomey?'

'No.'

'Well we're waiting to talk to a Mr Smithers, your lodger.'

'Oh, an' why's that then?'

The inspector ignored the question. He turned to one of the plain-clothes officers. 'Will you get that idiot Wilshaw in here quick as you can,' he said irritably.

The officers hurried out and Coggins turned back to Toby. 'I understand Mr Smithers is your cousin. Is that so?'

'No, not really, sir.'

'But you said he was,' Coggins said, looking at Marie.

Marie stuttered as she tried to speak and the inspector sighed. 'Look, I think you should be aware that harbouring an escaped criminal warrants a long prison sentence. I hope I'm making myself clear.'

Toby took off his cap and scratched his head. 'Well, sir. It's like this yer see. I've bin on to 'er fer months now ter take in a lodger. Yer see, I don't earn enough wages ter get a night out even, an' I told 'er if she took in a lodger it would 'elp me out a bit.'

Coggins sighed heavily. 'Get on with it, man.'

'Well yer see,' Toby went on, 'we get lots o' callers askin' if there's any rooms goin' an', when Mr Smithers knocked at me door, I 'appened ter be in. Well, I took the bull by the 'orns an' told 'im 'e could 'ave the room. Now when she come in,' Toby continued, jerking his thumb in Marie's direction, 'she raised the bleedin' roof. I couldn't understand what all the fuss was about at first, but when she explained fings I see a bit clearer.'

'I wish I did,' the confounded inspector mumbled.

'Well, yer see, our Lil's got a bit of a reputation wiv the blokes. Nufink bad, yer understand, but me ole woman – I mean

Marie – reckoned the neighbours would talk. They'd most likely say she 'ad 'er fancy man livin' 'ere. Now Marie an' me 'ave always bin respectable. We don't want people finkin' ovver-wise, so I said ter tell everybody Mr Smivvers is me cousin. That way it stops the tongues waggin', if yer see what I mean.'

Chief Inspector Coggins ran his fingers through his receding hair. It would do no good to implicate this family in harbouring a criminal, he told himself. He would never get a conviction after a judge heard that story. The man even looked like he was telling the truth, although Coggins suspected otherwise.

The detective had returned with PC Wilshaw who was looking a little agitated. 'I told 'em Smithers 'ad gone in the bagwash woman's 'ouse, sir,' he said, puffing out his chest.

Coggins waved the explanation away with a sweep of his hand. He took out a pencil and a folded sheet of paper from his coat pocket and sat down at the table with a deep sigh. He unfolded the paper and spread it out in front of him.

'Come here, Wilshaw,' he beckoned. 'Now describe Smithers.'

The constable rubbed his chin. ''E's about five seven, dark complexion an' 'e wears thick glasses. 'E goes about twelve stone, an e's got brown eyes an' a bushy moustache. Also e's got smarmed down 'air, parted in the middle.'

'Right, let's see what we can make of this,' Coggins said, setting to work with the pencil.

When he had finished with the wanted poster he turned it around and pushed it towards Wilshaw. 'Well?'

The constable's eyes were popping. 'It's 'im! It's William Smithers!'

Chief Inspector Coggins stood up. 'You've had an escaped criminal as a lodger Mrs Toomey,' he pronounced sternly.

'We could 'ave bin killed in our beds!' she moaned, and then fainted away.

Toby looked down at the prostrate figure of his wife and

stifled a grin. Marie had never fainted before in her life, but he had to admit it looked real. They helped Marie back into her chair and put some smelling-salts under her nose.

Coggins gathered up his briefcase and turned to Toby. 'We'll be taking Smithers's belongings with us,' he said. 'There will be uniformed officers in the street, so don't worry about him coming back. It won't be long now before we get our Mr Smithers.'

Out in the street Coggins held a briefing. 'Now listen. We've established that Mr Smithers is Dennis Foreman. Our man's bottled up somewhere in the street. He can't get out through the rear of these houses because the backyards look out on to a high wall. It's too high, even for Foreman. I'll take a guess our man's in that factory. There's a public shelter in the yard, that's why the gates are kept open. Foreman could have slipped in there without being seen, what with all the sightseers that were standing around earlier. Now, the factory is surrounded by a twelve-foot wall and it's topped with barbed wire. He could be inside that factory somewhere and there's no way out for him except through those gates. We're going to do a thorough search and we're going to pay particular attention to that shelter. Now for Christ's sake be careful. We don't know yet if he's armed.'

As soon as the police had left number one carrying the lodger's belongings, Marie made a full recovery. For the first time in years she wanted to hug Toby. He had handled the situation perfectly. For a few horrible moments she had seen the doors of Holloway prison closing behind her. Even Lil was still shaking and Marie marvelled at how calm her husband seemed.

In fact Toby was secretly worrying about the parcel Dennis Foreman had secreted in the backyard wall. He decided that at the first opportunity he would get it to Joe Cooper. If anyone knew where Dennis was right now, it would be him. Toby went to the window and could see the police milling around outside. The two burly constables were still on guard at the front door and Toby swore under his breath. He would not feel safe until that package was out of the house. He had taken it from the hiding place on one occasion when Dennis was out of the house and had opened it furtively. The revolver had frightened him and he had carefully replaced the parcel in the wall, half expecting the gun to go off. If the police found that gun and the money they would all be in trouble.

Connie Morgan had been doing her washing in the backyard when Ada called out. 'There's somefink goin' on at the Toomeys', Con. There's police everywhere.'

Connie stood with Ada at the front door watching the commotion, and it was not long before Mrs Adams walked up to them, cuddling one of her cats.

'What's goin' on?' Ada asked.

Mrs Adams shrugged her shoulders. 'Somebody said Toby's done 'is ole woman in. Mrs Richards 'eard it's that Mr Smivvers they're lookin' for. I always reckoned 'e was a bit shifty.'

Connie had to admit to herself that she felt sorry for the man. He had always seemed pleasant and polite, although his piercing eyes had made her feel uncomfortable. Joe Cooper had told her that he was an old friend and he had got into some trouble years ago, but to keep the knowledge to herself. He must have done something bad, Connie thought as she watched the police going in and out of the Toomeys' house. She stood at the door talking to Ada for some time and then went back to get on with her washing. The water had become cold and she went into the scullery and scooped a pail of boiling water from the stone copper to pour into the tin bath out in the yard. As she scuffed the washing up and down on the scrubbing board

Connie heard a noise which seemed to come from the direction of the roof. She looked up just in time to see a leg disappearing over the guttering above Widow Pacey's house. A few minutes later Joe came out into his yard and looked over the high wooden fence.

'Busy, Con?' he called over.

Connie nodded, brushing a strand of hair from her face. 'Is it Mr Smivvers they're looking for, Joe?' she asked.

He nodded. 'There's police everywhere. They're searchin' the factory yard.'

Connie raised her eyes to the roof. 'I 'ope they didn't bring ladders,' she said quietly.

He looked hard at her. 'Yer know where 'e is then?'

'I just seen a leg goin' over the roof. I knew it 'ad ter be 'im. What they want 'im for, Joe?'

'It's a long story, Con. I'll tell yer later.'

The sun had dropped below the rooftops and the evening sky turned red. The police had finished their search of the factory yard and they started to clamber over the ruins of the buildings. They checked the shored-up block entrances and stood together, debating their next move.

Insepector Coggins scratched his head.

'Well he's still in the street somewhere,' he said. 'It'll be dark in a few hours and then we've got problems.'

One of the detectives came up, brushing dust from his trousers. 'He might have slipped away by now,' he grumbled.

Coggins turned to the man with an expression that forbade criticism. 'My ulcer tells me different. We'll get him, don't worry.'

'Where can he be, sir? We've turned the place inside out. He ain't a bird. He can't fly away.'

Coggins suddenly slapped the man on the back. 'Roberts,

you've given me an idea!' he exclaimed, his eyes narrowing. 'I want ladders. At least two, and long enough to reach up to that roof. I bet our man's nesting up there somewhere. Go on then! Hurry, man!'

Above the street Dennis Foreman rested his head against the cool slates and thought about his next move. It would be useless to climb down into Widow Pacey's house, he realised. The police could make another search at any time and it would look bad on the old lady if he was found there. There was only one thing to do, he decided. Quickly he unlaced his shoes, tied them together and hung them around his neck. Next he took off his socks and stuffed them into his trouser pockets. Slowly and carefully Dennis eased his way up the attic roof on to the slate-covered slope. His bare feet allowed him a grip and, breathing heavily with the strain, the fugitive inched his way along the side away from the street, a few inches below the topmost ridge. Dennis realised that he could not be seen from down in the turning nor from the backyards, but he moved very slowly and carefully. If a slate became dislodged and tumbled into one of the yards it could alert the police and the game would be up. His breath came short and he repeatedly stopped to rest. Finally, aching and sweating he reached a position directly above the Toomeys' house. For a while he rested, then slowly he eased his way down the slope until he reached the guttering. Gritting his teeth Dennis slid his legs over the edge and felt the drainpipe. Clamping it with his knees he steadied himself, and then gradually he shinned down into the yard. By the time he reached the ground his feet were bleeding and his trousers had ripped against the brick. He crept over to the tin bath and gently took it down from the wall. Quickly he opened the package and took out a revolver, which he tucked into his belt. Breathing heavily, he put his hand back into the bundle and brought out a large wad of notes. Suddenly the yard door opened and Lillian walked out with a bundle of washing in her arms. As she saw the shadowy figure looming in front of her Lillian screamed in terror and fell over the tin bath.

The sudden din alerted the policemen standing on guard at the front and they shouldered the door open and rushed along the passageway. Lillian tried to push past the policemen as she ran hysterically from the yard and obstructed them long enough for Dennis to clamber up over the rickety fencing. As he climbed down into the yard of the wardens' post the other side, he dropped the money. But there was no time to go back for it, and he quickly ran to the heavy iron door and turned the handle. It creaked open and Dennis dashed into the dark interior and slammed the door shut behind him.

A black maria with two ladders strapped to the roof screeched to a halt at the end of the turning.

Inspector Coggins rushed up. 'Forget the ladders, Roberts! We've got him cornered! He's not going anywhere.'

'Where is he?'

'We've got him trapped in the wardens' post. It's sealed off. Get your lads over here and we'll plan our next move.'

The shouting and the sounds of heavy boots on the cobbles carried into the dark, quiet interior. Dennis fell over objects and barked his shins as he looked for the light switch and, when he finally managed to turn on the light, he could see that there was no lock on the back door. He drew the gun from his belt and hurried over to the front door. Gingerly he turned the heavy handle and pushed. The door would not give. It was locked from the outside. The air was stale, and Dennis felt beads of sweat breaking out on his forehead as he went back to the rear door. He could hear noises a little way along and he realised they would be coming over into the yard very soon. He looked around in desperation and saw the shelving in a corner. With a frantic strength he yanked the shelving down and grabbed two large pieces of wood. He wedged the shorter piece under the iron handle of the back door and fixed the larger piece between the ceiling and the top of the handle. When he was satisfied the handle could not be moved either way Dennis Foreman rushed across to the front door. He knew that they would soon be coming for him, but it would take them time to get the key. There was no way they could knock down the heavy iron door. The whole place had been reinforced to protect the wardens from blast. He reckoned that he had a few minutes to spare before all hell broke loose. The cupboard would do, he decided, and quickly he dragged it up against the front door. When they rush me I'll have a chance, he told himself.

It had gone quiet outside. Dennis eased his aching back against the stone wall and placed the revolver on the floor beside him. He laughed bitterly to himself as he realised he had just five rounds in the cylinder. He knew that he could not let himself be taken without a fight. The clock on the wall had stopped and Dennis guessed that it would be dark in another hour. It was strange, he thought. Only a few hours ago he had been having a quiet drink with Joe, and now he was cornered like a rat in a trap. He stared down at the revolver. This street was where he had grown up and, despite all his wanderings, it looked as though he was going to end his days in the shabby little turning.

The news had travelled fast and everyone in the street was either at their door or crowded into the little parlours. Old George Baker was huddled up in his favourite chair with a sad look on his face and his eyes were watering. 'Who'd 'ave thought it,' he was saying. 'I knew 'im when 'e was just a lad. Many a time I've seen 'is ole man clout 'im fer somefink or the ovver. Bloody shame.'

Mary and Frank sat with the old man. 'What'll 'appen to 'im, Pop?' Mary asked.

George looked at his daughter. 'When they do get 'im they'll lock the poor bleeder up an' throw away the key.'

Frank was not so sympathetic. 'Let's face it, Mary. 'E did rob a jewellers.'

George gave his son-in-law a blinding look and Mary shrugged. 'I know 'e did wrong, Frank, but yer gotta feel sorry fer the bloke. 'E never 'armed anybody.'

Billy Argrieves had arrived at Ada's house and he was standing with Connie and Ada at the front door. 'I 'ad a job ter get in the turnin', what wiv all them ropes they've got round the place,' he said. 'What's goin' on?'

Just as Connie finished explaining to Billy they saw Widow Pacey appear at her front door. She walked up to them, her face set firmly. ''E was in my place earlier,' she said, nodding her head towards the end of the turning.

''E got out on the roof. It's where 'e was 'idin'. I knew it was gonna end up like this. I saw it on 'is face. 'E 'ad the mark on 'im.'

Ada glanced at Connie, and Billy looked uncomfortable. They could see the police standing behind their vehicle and groups of the street dwellers standing in small groups staring towards the wardens' post. The light was beginning to fade and a chill breeze started to blow down the turning.

'I can't stand watchin',' Ada said, hunching her shoulders. 'C'mon in, I'll put the kettle on.'

They were sitting in the small parlour, drinking tea. Ada and Widow Pacey were facing each other in the armchairs and Connie and Billy were sitting together at the table.

''E was surprised when I told 'im I reco'nised 'im,' Widow Pacey was saying, 'but I 'ad 'im taped right from the start. I bin in this street more than forty years. I seen 'im grow up. The three of 'em was always tergevver as kids. 'Im, Joe an' yer muvver, Con. They was always tergevver. Like peas in a pod. Matter o' fact I got some ole photos of 'em indoors. I jus' bin lookin' at 'em.'

'Yer say yer got some o' me mum, Mrs Pacey?' Connie asked.

'Yeah. I'll pop back an' get 'em. It'll pass the time away.'

When Widow Pacey left Ada turned to Connie. 'She's a strange woman. I've lived down this street enough years an' I've never 'ad much ter say to 'er until lately. Some o' the fings she says frightens me. Did yer 'ear what she said about Dennis Foreman 'avin' the mark on 'im?'

Billy grinned. 'That's the sort o' fing my ole mum used ter come out wiv.'

'Well it scares me, that sort o' talk,' Ada said with a shiver.

Widow Pacey came back with a large tattered album under her arm and laid it down on the table. 'There we are,' she said as she began to turn the pages. 'There's the three of 'em. They couldn't 'ave bin more than seven or eight at the time. There's anuvver one of 'em. That's much later. See yer mum there, Connie? Yer can see the likeness, can't yer. My ole man took most o' these. 'E was always messin' around wiv that box camera of 'is. There's anuvver one o' yer mum an' Dennis. They must o' bin about twenty at the time.'

Connie studied the photo and saw that Dennis had his arm around her mother. The widow pointed at the two young people in the picture. 'They were goin' out tergevver at the time,' she said. 'There's one of Joe Cooper an' Sadie.'

'Yer say me mum an' Dennis Foreman used ter go out tergevver, Mrs Pacey?'

'Yeah, about the same time Joe started goin' out wiv Sadie. I remember it well 'cos it was the talk o' the street. We all thought Joe an' yer mum would end up tergevver, but instead 'e latched on ter Sadie Armond an' yer mum got tergevver wiv Dennis. Funny turn out that was.'

'Why was that, Mrs Pacey?' Connie asked, looking intensely at the old woman.

'Well 'e suddenly left. Dennis Foreman I mean. Just seemed ter vanish. There was a lot o' talk about 'im joinin' the army or runnin' off ter sea. Nobody really knew what 'appened to 'im, until it was in the papers about 'im doin' that jewellers raid. Nobody round 'ere clapped eyes on 'im again until a few months ago. Although nobody knew who 'e was – 'cept me.'

Billy had been watching Connie's face and he saw the colour drain away. She was still looking closely at the photo of Dennis and her mother. Suddenly she looked up at the old widow. 'Mrs Pacey, did yer ever 'ear the name "Bonny" used?' she asked quickly.

The old woman looked at Connie strangely. 'I've not 'eard that name fer years,' she said, creasing up her eyes. 'Funny yer should ask me that. Yeah, I remember the name. It was a nickname they used when they was kids. I've 'eard 'em shoutin' it out when the three of 'em used ter stand under me winder. As a matter o' fact, I . . .'

Her words were interrupted by a loud bang and Billy jumped up. 'That's a gunshot!' he gasped.

They all hurried to the door and looked along the turning. They could see the police crouching down behind the vehicle and people peeping out from their doorways.

Mrs Richards hurried along to Ada's open front door. ''E's got a gun!' she said breathlessly, her hand held to her cheek. ''E's fired at the coppers!'

Connie had pushed her way past Ada and Billy and suddenly she was running along the street. Ada yelled out for her to stop but Connie ran faster.

'Quick, Billy! Stop 'er!' Ada screamed.

Chapter Forty-Eight

Dennis Foreman sat hunched against the cold wall and listened to the voices outside. It wouldn't be long now, he thought. They'd be looking to get it over before it got dark. Would they try to rush the place, or would they play the cat and mouse game? He heard mumbling close by and the sudden noise of a key grating in the lock of the iron door. He sat up straight and picked up his revolver.

Slowly the door creaked open a few inches and a voice shouted, 'Dennis Foreman. This is the police. We're asking you to come out with your hands above your head. Did you hear?'

'Get stuffed!' Dennis shouted.

The door opened another few inches and the voice called out, 'Foreman. If you're carrying a gun throw it out.'

The fugitive stood up and pointed the revolver at the gap between door and framework. Slowly he squeezed the trigger and the deafening bang reverberated around the room. Running feet sounded on the cobbles and he heard shouting, then it became deathly quiet. Dennis leant heavily against the wall and slid back down on to the floor. Well they know the score now, he told himself. They'll think twice before they rush the place.

Outside, the police crouched behind the car. Inspector Coggins was frantically signalling the two constables away from the iron door.

Suddenly one of the policemen behind him shouted out, 'Grab 'er!'

Coggins turned to see a young woman running towards them, her long hair blowing out behind her. She dodged the first policeman and as she reached the car Coggins pounced up at her and pulled her down beside him.

'What the bloody hell do you think you're doing, young lady?' he shouted at her.

'Don't shoot 'im! Please!' she moaned, tears streaming down her white face.

'Listen, Miss. We're not going to shoot him. At the moment he's trying to shoot us.'

'Let me talk to 'im. Yer must let me talk to 'im,' she pleaded, wringing her hands.

Chief Inspector Coggins put his hand on Connie's shoulder and gently pulled her down out of the line of fire. Another shout went up and Coggins saw one of the constables struggling with a young man.

'Bring him up here,' he called out.

Billy shrugged the constable off and slumped down beside Connie. She looked at him for a second and then fell against his body, burying her head in his chest. 'Oh Billy! It's me dad in there!' she cried. 'They'll kill 'im!'

Coggins moved closer. 'You say it's your old man in there? Dennis Foreman is your father?'

'Yes! Yes!' she shouted.

'What's your name, young lady?'

'Connie. Connie Morgan.'

Coggins gently patted her on the back. 'Take it easy, lass. We won't harm him, unless he does something silly.'

'Let me talk to 'im,' Connie pleaded, raising her tear-filled eyes to the inspector's face.

'No, it's too dangerous. I can't take that chance.'

'D'yer wanna get people killed!?' Connie screamed. 'I've gotta talk to 'im. 'E'll take notice o' me.'

Coggins gritted his teeth and looked across the street at the iron door. It was still ajar. 'All right,' he said with a sigh. 'But only if you do exactly as you're told, okay?'

She nodded, blinking back her tears.

'Right, now listen. We'll cross over there, away from the door, and then we'll inch along that wall until we're close. You'll let me do the talking and don't say anything until I ask you to speak. Is that understood?'

'Yes,' she whispered.

'C'mon then,' the inspector said quietly, taking her arm.

It had grown very quiet as the two neared the door. 'Dennis Foreman,' the policeman called out. 'This is Inspector Coggins. I've got a young lady with me. Connie Morgan. She says she's your daughter. She wants to talk to you.'

The silence seemed to grow deeper. Inspector Coggins could hear himself breathing. The young woman beside him said nothing as she continued to stare at the door.

'Let 'er speak,' Dennis suddenly called out.

Coggins nodded to Connie and she swallowed hard. ''Ello,' she said, her voice shaking. 'This is me, Connie. I wanna talk ter yer. Can I come in?'

Coggins pulled Connie back against the wall to prevent her going any closer. 'She can talk outside, Dennis.'

Connie tried to pull her arm away from the officer's grasp. 'I wanna come in,' she called out. 'I wanna talk ter yer. I know about Bonny. Can yer 'ear me? I know about Bonny.'

There was a scraping noise from within, and then she heard Dennis's voice. 'Okay. Yer can come in, Connie,' he said. 'But I warn yer, Coggins. Try anyfink an' I'm gonna use this gun, understand?'

'All right, Foreman. No one's going to try anything. You've got ten minutes.'

Connie moved up to the door and slowly eased her way through the gap. Dennis Foreman stood facing her, his eyes staring at her, his lips pressed into a thin line. She walked slowly towards him, tears starting up in her eyes again.

'I knew I'd find yer one day,' she said, fighting to control her voice. 'I never give up 'ope. "Bonny" led me to yer. The name in the locket. The locket yer gave me mum. It wasn't buried wiv 'er. I've got it. It was all I ever 'ad of yer. Why? Why did yer leave us? Why did yer walk out on me mum all those years ago?'

Dennis lowered the gun and reached for her. He held her arm gently and slowly shook his head. 'Sit down, Con,' he said quietly. 'There's so much yer don't know. Let me try ter explain.'

Darkness was falling down over the ramshackle houses and, along the street, folk stood silently at their front doors like shadowy statues, their silhouettes dark against the grey walls. Coggins crouched down beside the car, his fingers drumming on the metal. The minutes ticked slowly away and only the occasional nervous cough or a shuffling of feet broke the silence. The inspector began to get fidgety and he wondered whether or not he had made the right decision.

Suddenly Connie Morgan appeared in the doorway and walked slowly towards the police car. She was not crying any more and her face looked impassive. As she rounded the car Billy stood up and took her arm.

She looked at the inspector without showing any emotion. 'Dennis Foreman said 'e needs five more minutes, then 'e'll give 'imself up,' she said simply.

Detective Sergeant Roberts looked enquiringly at the

inspector who nodded. 'I think we can give him another five minutes, Roberts.'

Connie walked slowly away from the wardens' post, her head lying against Billy's shoulder, his arm around her waist. They reached Ada's house and Connie straightened up. Ada was at the door beside Widow Pacey and Joe Cooper.

'Yer shouldn't 'ave done it, Con. Yer could 'ave got yerself killed,' Ada said, resting her hand on Connie's forearm.

'It's all right, Ada. I wasn't in any danger.'

Ada was about to speak when the shot rang out.

'Christ!' Billy gasped, swinging around. ''E's shot 'imself!'

Connie dropped her eyes to the pavement. 'I knew 'e was gonna do it. I asked 'im ter give 'imself up. I pleaded wiv 'im, but I knew it was useless. It was in 'is eyes, Billy. I could see it in 'is eyes.'

Ada looked at the young man. 'Take 'er upstairs, Billy. Don't leave 'er.'

Billy Argrieves nodded. 'I won't leave 'er, Ada. She'll be all right.'

The sun had risen over the little street and already the children were out. The rag-and-bone man had arrived with his creaking barrow, his unintelligible cry for old lumber echoing through the turning. The wardens' post was securely locked and a sad-faced policeman stood on guard at a discreet distance. Children jumped in and out of a skipping rope and rolled their marbles along the gutters just like on any other Sunday morning, but today they did not stray to the top of the turning. Folk returned with the morning papers and glanced furtively across to the sand-bagged entrance as they passed by. A few people stood at their front doors, talking quietly and shaking their heads as they recalled the events of the previous day. Some of the street folk turned their heads and lowered their voices when they saw the young woman walk up to number sixteen and knock on the door.

Joe Cooper looked surprised as he opened the door. 'C'mon in, Con,' he said with a tired smile. 'Yer'll 'ave ter excuse the place, I ain't cleared up yet. Bin sittin' in the chair all night.'

Connie walked into the parlour and sat down beside the hearth. Joe threw a paper off the chair facing her and slumped down heavily, his eyes searching her face enquiringly. She drew a deep breath.

'Joe, I need ter talk ter yer,' she said with a sigh. 'An' I need some answers.'

'I'll 'elp yer if I can, girl,' he said, a concerned look showing on his face.

Connie leaned forward. 'Yer know they let me talk ter Dennis Foreman before 'e killed 'imself?'

Joe nodded, 'I know, Con. But what made yer do it?'

'I 'ad to, Joe. Last night Widow Pacey showed me an' Ada some photos. They was photos of you an' Dennis an' me mum. She told me about 'ow you three was always tergevver when yer was kids. There was one photo of me mum wiv Dennis. 'E 'ad 'is arm round 'er. Mrs Pacey said they used ter go out tergevver fer a time.'

Joe nodded. 'That's right, Con. They did, fer a time.'

'Yer see, Joe, it suddenly all fitted tergevver. I was convinced that Dennis Foreman was me farvver an' I knew that if I got a chance ter talk wiv 'im, I'd find out fer sure. I knew 'e wouldn't lie ter me.'

Joe looked closely at the young woman. 'Did 'e tell yer? Did yer get ter the truth?'

In answer Connie reached into her blouse pocket and Joe's eyes widened as he saw the locket lying in the palm of her hand.

'Yer reco'nise this, don't yer, Joe.'

He nodded slowly.

'This little locket kept me goin'. It gave me somefink ter 'old on to when the grief was so bad I thought about endin' it all. Yer see, I was sure that one day this would lead me ter the truth about me farvver. 'Elen Bartlett gave it ter me jus' before she died. I thought this locket was buried wiv me mum, but it never was. I fink it was me aunt's dyin' wish that I should 'ave the chance ter find out who me farvver was. Yes, I did get ter the truth. Dennis Foreman told me everyfing, Joe.'

''E told yer?' he said, looking down at the little trinket in Connie's hand.

'Yeah. 'E told me about the inscription inside. 'E told me you was Bonny. This locket is the one yer gave ter me mum. It's the one she always wore around her neck, until the day she died.'

Joe lowered his head for a few moments and when he looked up Connie saw tears in his eyes.

'Why, Joe? Why wouldn't me mum tell me about yer? Why did she shut me up every time I asked questions?'

The ticking of the clock sounded strangely loud as Connie Morgan and Joe Cooper sat facing each other. She was leaning forward in her chair, waiting for the answers she so desperately needed. He looked into her eyes, almost pleading with her as he sought awkwardly for the right words. He wondered if she would ever understand.

'Yes, Connie. Yer me daughter,' he told her. 'I've watched yer grow up from a leggy little mite into a beautiful woman, an' all those years I've 'ad ter love yer from a distance. I've seen yer suffer 'eartbreaks wivvout bein' able ter 'old yer close an' let yer spill yer tears over me an' it tore me 'eart out, Connie.'

'But why, Joe? Why?'

He sighed deeply. 'Yer mum, Dennis an' me grew up tergevver in this little backstreet. We was inseparable as kids an', as we got older your mum grew ter love me – in a grown-up way I mean. I loved 'er, too, but Kate was impatient. It was 'er way. I wasn't ready ter settle down an' she began ter play Dennis off against me. They started goin' out tergevver an' I can still remember 'ow upset I got. I know now that Kate was only tryin' ter make me jealous, but I was too stupid ter see it at the time. I thought she'd lost 'er feelin' fer me. Anyway, I met Sadie a few months later an' we got married inside a year. Like I said, I wasn't ready ter settle down, but I must o' felt I was gettin' me own back in a way.

'Me marriage soon started ter go wrong. Sadie found out she couldn't 'ave children an' she took it bad. The followin' year she caught polio. Yer mum an' me seemed to be drawn back tergevver some'ow. We'd never stopped lovin' each ovver, Con. We managed ter meet away from the street an' nobody suspected anyfing, except Dennis. 'E knew all along that it was me Kate really wanted. There was a big bust-up at first, an' me an' Dennis 'ad a set-to, but we sorted our differences out an' we got back ter bein' friends again. When you come along fings were bad between me an' Sadie. She suspected I was seein' somebody else an' she told me then she would never divorce me. Sadie's a Catholic, yer see. Kate 'ad wanted us ter get married one day so I could be a proper farvver ter yer an', when I told 'er Sadie wouldn't give me a divorce, she got very moody. Fings were really strained between us and it all came ter the boil at the time of the factory outin'. Everybody was gettin' sossled an' me an' yer mum 'ad a big row. She said then that me an' 'er was finished. I got completely blotto an' a lot o' bad fings was said.

'A few days later Kate said she wanted ter talk ter me. She 'ad it all worked out. She said yer mus' never know who yer farvver was. She didn't want people ter point yer out in the street an' make life bad fer yer. She was only finkin' o' you,

Con. Kate made me swear on yer life that I'd never breathe a word about bein' yer farvver. She made Dennis promise, too. Yer see, 'e was the only ovver person who knew I was yer farvver. I was there at the time. I remember Dennis gettin' angry. 'E said it was wicked ter make 'im swear on a child's life. What 'e said was 'e'd swear on 'is own life. It's the fing that I can't get over. I've bin sittin' up all night dwellin' on it. Dennis broke 'is promise an' then killed 'imself a few minutes later. Jus' finkin' about it makes me go cold. I still can't believe 'e's dead.'

Connie had been listening intently, her eyes never leaving his face. Joe paused and she stared down into the empty grate, trying to take in everything he had said. When she looked back into Joe's eyes she saw the deep, lonely pain that had haunted him for so long.

'I fink I understand a bit better now, Joe,' Connie said quietly. 'I know me mum never stopped lovin' yer.'

'I've never stopped lovin' 'er, Con,' he said, his eyes filling with tears.

Connie looked down at her hands. The room was very quiet and in the silence between them the ticking of the clock seemed to echo.

Joe looked up at her. 'Yer muvver was some woman, Connie,' he said quietly. 'I 'ope yer can understand why she made me swear not ter let on ter yer. It was the way she was. I couldn't make 'er change 'er mind. In fact I went ter see 'er the day before she died. I asked 'er ter tell yer, or let me tell yer, but she was still determined you shouldn't know. Kate said she'd 'ad ter bear the pain o' me bein' out o' reach an' she didn't want yer ter go frew the same torment every time yer see me in the street. 'Er words were, "no farvver is better than 'alf a farvver". That's the way she was, Con.'

Connie was looking down at the locket she held in her hand,

and Joe followed her eyes. 'The day I went ter see Kate she said she wanted that locket ter be buried wiv 'er. I'm glad 'Elen Bartlett kept it. Maybe Kate 'ad whispered somefing in 'er sister's ear.'

Although the morning was warm Connie shivered. She stood up suddenly and looked down at Joe. 'I feel as though I'm floatin',' she said, trying hard to smile. 'It seems 'ard ter realise I won't 'ave ter spend any more time finkin' an' wonderin'. Now I'm gonna 'ave ter get used ter callin' yer "Dad".'

He was on his feet and he held his arms out to her. She rushed forward and hugged him tightly, squeezing him to her. He could feel her body shuddering as she sobbed uncontrollably.

'There, there. Let yer tears spill over me, darlin',' he said softly as he cuddled her. 'It's what dads are for.'

She laughed through her tears and took the handkerchief from his hand. When she had wiped her face Connie looked up into his eyes. 'Let's keep the secret, Dad – fer the time bein',' she said, her eyes shining.

Joe grinned happily. 'Yeah. Just the two of us.'

She blew her nose and dabbed at her eyes. 'It'll 'ave ter be three, Dad. I must tell Billy. I can't keep it from 'im.'

Joe put his arm around her shoulder. 'Is that the young lad who was wiv yer last night?'

Connie nodded. 'We're goin' steady. I'm gonna marry 'im next year.'

'Oh, 'e's proposed, then?'

Connie laughed. 'No. 'E doesn't know yet.'

Joe shook his head, the grin spreading. 'Jus' like yer mum. The poor lad won't 'ave a chance. Anyway luv, when you two do get married I 'ope yer gonna let me give yer away.'

She laughed happily. 'Who else? After all, you are me dad.'

Epilogue

Bright summer sunlight shone in Connie's eyes as she stepped into the street. Children were gathering around Tony Armeda's ice-cream cart and along the turning Widow Pacey was whitening her front doorstep. Connie looked over to the ruined buildings and her mind went back to the first faltering steps she had taken on her first date. It seemed a lifetime away to her now. At last she knew the path that she had been following so fatefully. It had led her to her first love. It had led her to happiness, and then had cast her down to the depths of despair and degradation. But she knew that she had never really been alone. Someone had walked the path before her and from the shadows she had been led out into the light. Now she had been brought home again, to her father.

And there was Billy. She saw him now, coming towards her along the street and without hesitation she ran to him and threw her arms around him. She looked up into his dark, startled eyes and said, 'I've so much ter tell yer, Billy.'